PRAISE FOR
THE PRIVATE LIFE OF JANE MAXWELL

"Gott aims true in this action-packed, emotionally resonant series opener about hope and heroism in the face of overwhelming loss."

—*Publishers Weekly* (starred review)

"This is a fast, fun book. ... [A] queer homage to superhero television."

—*Tor.com*

"*The Private Life of Jane Maxwell* did a great job of drawing a line between the comic book reality and the reality of good fiction."

—*The Lesbian Review*

By Jenn Gott

The Beacon Campaigns
The Lady of Souls
Fixing Fate
Heart's Blood
Whispers of the Ice

Hopefuls
The Private Life of Jane Maxwell
Who's Afraid of Amy Sinclair?
Janie One More Time

JANIE
ONE MORE TIME

JENN GOTT

HOPEFULS
#3

JANIE ONE MORE TIME

Copyright © 2022 by Jennifer Gott

Cover design by Jenn and Graeme Gott
Cover images: girl © Ekaterina Bagautdinova/Shutterstock;
hall © vipman/Shutterstock;
hands © Clara Lilley/Unsplash;
houses © Avi Waxman/Unsplash;
bike © Paolo Chiabrando/Unsplash;
dad © Juliane Liebermann/Unsplash

ISBN 978-1-959129-01-1 (hardcover)
ISBN 978-1-959129-00-4 (paperback)
ISBN 978-0-9908914-9-9 (ebook)

JANIE
ONE MORE TIME

THE FIRST PAGE IS NOTHING BUT DARKNESS.

Almost. A single sound bubble, jagged and jarring, interrupts the lower right corner. Pale yellow, it matches the wood of the ruler that lines its bottom, the *CRACK!* erupting from a safe march of numbers and tick lines.

Flip the page, and Jane Maxwell's head has jerked upright, the issue already in full swing. A paper is stuck to her forehead, the edge of her glasses sticking crookedly out one side. In the next panel the paper flutters down and she catches it. Next: framed from her perspective as she takes in the lined binder paper, the bubbly letters written in leaky ballpoint pen.

Jane stared at it for a moment, nonplussed. Her mind and emotions were oddly blank, an empty sheet waiting to be filled.

"Nice of you to join us again."

Ink and paint pooled out as Jane lifted her head, filling in the scene around her. Loose, sketchy lines spread out and snaked up a forest of desks and baggy, wide-legged jeans. A base layer of watercolors washed in next: faded blue denim, white shirts, a checkerboard pattern of sickly green and speckled gray linoleum spreading across the floor like mold. Jane straightened her glasses, and the final detailing snapped across the page. Teenage faces staring at her with alternating fascination, loathing, and mirth. A chalkboard, covered in sloppy, towering letters, reminding students of an upcoming test. A thickset man with a military buzzcut hunched over her, his meaty fist around a ruler splayed flat against Jane's desk. Jane jolted back in her seat. "What the . . . ?"

She glanced down. The paper in one hand, her other laid on the desk. The back of her left hand was covered in blue doodles, and her wedding ring . . . her wedding ring was gone.

"Shit!" Panic seized hold, obliterating the many other questions she should be having. Jane clutched her finger, as if somehow her ring would magically reappear. Several more giggles broke through the room as she furiously patted down her pockets. It had to be here, it had to be here, it had to be—

"Hey! Watch your tongue, girl," boomed the buzzcut above her.

Jane barely heard him. She slid from her desk and ducked, running her hands across the grubby floor. Too many chairs and desks surrounded her, too many to count, too many shoes to check beneath. Jane jumped back to her feet. "Okay, nobody move—" she started, but then she glanced to the side, and all speech abandoned her.

A teenage girl sat in the next desk over. With a pretty, heart-shaped face and a row of zits on her chin bumping up beneath a layer of carefully applied makeup. Dark brown hair that fell to her shoulders, tendrils framing her face. Wide eyes, staring up at Jane in concern; a soft beauty mark rested beneath the right one. It was a face Jane knew in an instant, knew better than she knew her own. It was a face she hadn't seen in decades.

Not like this, anyway.

"Clair?"

It couldn't be Clair, but it had to be. The question came out breathy, soft as a prayer. Clair's impossibly young face blinked at her, confusion drawing her brow together. "Um . . . yeah?"

A heavy, exasperated sigh broke the moment. "Is there a *problem*, Miss Maxwell?"

Jane spun around. The buzzcut ogre of a man who'd been towering over her was glowering in her direction. Arms crossed, neck muscles bulging. He looked vaguely familiar, though damned if Jane could figure out from where.

"A problem," Jane repeated. "Yes. Yes, there's a problem. I . . ."

Though what could she say? What *was* the problem? Clearly, something was deeply, fundamentally wrong here, that much was obvious, and yet . . . how was she supposed to even begin to identify the many, many problems with this situation?

It didn't matter that she couldn't explain it. Mr. Ogre was clearly not interested in hearing it.

Jane turned away from him. She focused on Clair instead. Even in this younger state, Jane's wife was a stable point to ground herself on.

"It's too real to be a dream," Jane said softly. She reached out, combing her fingers through the length of Clair's hair. Silk strands slid effortlessly between her fingers. Clair had always had the softest hair of anyone Jane had ever met—soft as a baby's. This was perfect, too real for any illusion.

Clair blushed, her attention sliding from Jane to the open textbook in front of her. She shifted uncomfortably in her seat, and Jane pulled her hand away.

"Jane!" Mr. Ogre raised his voice again. "Take your *seat!*"

Jane waved him off. She raced over to the window. The view looked out over a parking lot. A slab of beige bricks to one side, a looming, sickly oak tree to the other. Recognition prickled up Jane's spine.

She had faced plenty of dangerous situations in her time as a superhero, of course, so she was no stranger to fear and dread. She'd battled people who could spray acid and stop time and turn the world to ice around them. She'd been in high-speed pursuits, leaped onto a moving train, and caught lasers in the palm of her hand. Once, she was even lashed to a table while her evil parallel self threatened to kill her and steal her superpowers. But *this* . . . this was something else entirely. A far darker kind of evil.

This was high school.

"Fuck," Jane muttered, while Mr. Ogre shouted, "All right, that's enough! Detention, missy. You can drag your backside to the principal's office right now."

Jane turned back. Mr. Ogre had gone bright red, a vein popping on the side of his buzzed head.

Except it wasn't "Ogre." Now that Jane recognized the situation, bits of ancient, dusty memories began to claw their way to the surface. This room—the podium in the corner instead of a desk, like he was someone so important—belonged to her sophomore history teacher. Mr. . . . Santorum? Santini? Something starting with "S," at any rate.

Mr. Ogre—Mr. S—pointed one sausage finger toward the door. "Now!"

A laugh burst out of Jane, as sharp as an end-of-period bell. Mr. S's face flushed even deeper crimson.

"You want to make that a week's detention?" he asked, his voice suddenly low and deadly.

Jane's laughter cut itself off. "Oh, wait. You're serious."

"Nooo," Mr. S said, dripping with sarcasm. "I always joke about giving detention to insolent little snots."

"Wow." Jane blinked. She knew he'd always been kind of a dick—she'd hated history for years after that—but seeing it again for the first time in, what, two decades or so? That was something else entirely. The disdain he was regarding her with now, the superiority . . . The whole class was frozen, some in terror, others in smug rapture at the spectacle, all of them waiting to see what would happen next.

Jane looked around the room, all those faces staring back at her. Clair's had gone white with concern, gripping her pencil so hard it might snap. Cal, by contrast, had a shit-eating grin. He surreptitiously raised his thumb, egging Jane on. The only other member of the Heroes of Hope present, the group of superheroes and friends that had been together since middle school, was

Marie, but she wasn't even looking up now, instead was studying the textbook in front of her as if she could escape into it.

Options floated in front of Jane, a Choose-Your-Own-Adventure comic of nothing but bad outcomes. Submitting to his authority went against every grain of Jane's being, but standing and fighting didn't feel like the smart move either.

A glance down confirmed what Jane already suspected: that whatever the situation was, she looked as if she belonged in it. Gone were her normal clothes, her grown-up body. In their place was a baggy black T-shirt for *Star Trek: The Magazine*, a green striped button-down hanging open like a jacket over it. Wide-legged cargo jeans rounded out the ensemble, absolutely covered in pen doodles. A curtain of dry hair blocked the classroom from view. Jane ran her hands over her twiggy arms, not a trace of muscle definition to be found.

She gritted her teeth. She started toward the door, but Mr. S's voice crashed over the classroom once again. "Forgetting something?"

When she looked back over her shoulder, he was pointing at a stack of textbooks tucked beneath the chair she'd been sitting in.

Jane bit down her frustration as she doubled back to collect them. She had been in middle school when the Columbine shootings happened, and she'd gone into high school with the building transformed in its wake: metal detectors at key entrances and exits, rent-a-cops patrolling the corridors, and a list of rules about a mile long, including one banning the use of backpacks between classes. Jane straightened up, grunting beneath the weight of her books. She'd forgotten what a pain in the ass it was to haul them around everywhere.

Mr. S was already marching to the classroom's phone, calling ahead to the principal's office, as Jane let herself out into the hall. At least here she had a moment to think. If she could avoid the security patrols, she'd actually have some peace and quiet, until the next bell anyway.

Jane glanced both directions down the hall. It stretched out, only vaguely familiar. Arbitrarily, she set off to the right. At the first corner, she found a water fountain, and Jane paused and dropped her books to the floor, shoving them beneath with the side of her shoe. Already a plan was unfolding in her mind. It wasn't a *great* plan, mind you, but action always gave Jane a sense of composure, even in the face of the greatest evil.

So, step one: get the hell out of this place.

And then . . . Okay, so, that was it, really. She'd worry about figuring out steps two and beyond later.

She splashed her cheeks with some water from the fountain and set off with a confident stride, her earlier sense of panic feeling silly. She was a *superhero*, for god's sake. She could handle this.

That confidence buoyed her forward until, in the distance, a figure stepped into view from around the next corner. Cheap white shirt blaring in the afternoon sun, polyester black pants, gold badge strapped to his hip. Fascist flattop, blond hair blending into his washed-out skin.

Jane darted to the side, but not fast enough.

"Hey!" the rent-a-cop shouted. He started jogging toward her, belt jangling with his overwrought accessories.

Jane veered. She grabbed the door of the nearest classroom, but it was locked, the lights inside shut down. Not that she was afraid of the rent-a-cop—really, he didn't stand a chance if it came down to it—but she'd been hoping to escape the building without causing more of a scene than she already had.

"Hey! You there! What are you doing out of class?"

Jane drew a breath, squaring her shoulders.

Too late, she realized she should have used her superpowers to pull the light around her, bending it across her skin until she appeared invisible to the outside world. She hadn't thought fast enough, though, thrown off by her situation. But fine. If it was going to come down to this, then let it come down to this. She half turned her head, making sure to keep her features obscured by the curtain of her hair, the fall of the shadows across her face. "You really don't want to do this."

She made sure to hold her voice steady, authoritative. Just a hint of warning around its edges. It was a tone Jane had practiced a lot, in the days since becoming Captain Lumen, and usually it worked. Of course, usually she was wearing her iconic red suit when she used it. And had some muscle on her bones.

"Are you threatening me?" The rent-a-cop's hand went to the radio on his shoulder. Outside, a real officer—one with a proper badge, handcuffs, a gun—patrolled the parking lot. Always just one call away.

"Not at all. I just wanted to give you fair warning."

She turned around.

A full page spread stood at her back, Captain Lumen in all her glory. Shoulders tall, head high, light streaming out from her to capture the full silhouette of her hero pose. Jane stood smaller in the foreground, her gangly teenage body doing the best it could. She held her hands by her sides, ready to conjure the light within her.

Only nothing happened.

Jane looked down at her upturned palms. A smudge of blue ink streaked her hand. Nothing else. No glow, not even a spark, and worse, no feeling of power flooding to her fingertips.

Her powers were gone.

"Are you fucking kidding me?" she said as the rent-a-cop slammed a heavy hand on her shoulder and squeezed tight.

"All right, missy. You're coming with me."

TWO HOURS EARLIER . . .

"Look, I'm not saying it's a bad choice, I just don't see why we need that much of it," Jane said. "We're only hosting, what, twenty people? Twenty-five, max? How many pigs in a blanket do you really think they'll go through?"

A messy huff came over the comm in Jane's ear, along with the solid *thud* of a punch. "It's your company's first movie deal, Jane," Clair's voice said. "I think we can spring for it."

Jane ducked. She fired off a quick laser bolt from the palm of her hand. "I'm not *saying* don't spring for it! I'm just saying there's a level where it becomes excess, and we don't—"

"Hey!" Granite Girl's voice cut in. "Do you two think maybe you could settle this some other time? We're kind of in the middle of something here!"

As if to illustrate her point, a car went flying across the street in front of Jane. It crashed into the corner of a real estate office, slamming against the concrete with the scream of twisted metal.

"Oh please," Jane said. "Like we can't handle a few stray Shadow Raptors." She drew up a fresh laser bolt, blasting near the lizard feet of the one racing down the opposite sidewalk.

The irony of this statement was not lost on Jane. She'd been terrified of the things when she'd first come to this world, this parallel version of the Earth she knew—one so similar, except that superheroes and lab-created monsters were real.

Then again, that was a long time ago. Back when Jane didn't even realize she had powers, and the Shadow Raptors they were fighting were the original stock. That batch had died out long ago, either through defeat or the ravages of their tragically short lifespan. The ones they faced these days were knockoffs, cooked up from fragmented recipes that floated around the dark web. Hardly an effort for Grand City's most elite superhero team, but who else was going to clean up the mess?

"That's not the point!" Granite Girl said. "These comms are supposed to be for official use, not for you two to work out domestic logistics!"

A colorful starburst bloomed in front of Jane, Pixie Beats returning to her full size. She was already midpirouette, her pointed toe connecting sharply with the Shadow Raptor's jaw. She landed lightly beside them, bedazzled sneakers touching down as softly as slippers.

"Cut them some slack, G," Pixie Beats said as she leaped up again, shrinking to the size of a coffee cup. Her voice still carried clear as a bell over the comms in their ears. "I think it's kind of cute."

"*Cute?* You think it's cute that they're hogging comm traffic in the middle of a mission to plan a *party*?"

A flutter of color flitted by, just fast enough to feel like a shrug. "You're just mad because we're not invited."

"Wait," came a third voice, deeper and tinged with a Hispanic accent. A gust of wind kicked at the ground as Windforce said, "We're not?"

Jane tapped her earpiece. "We talked about this, remember? The last thing we need is people seeing us as a group outside of uniform. It's too easy to put the clues together."

"Yeah, but you wouldn't even *be* here if it wasn't for us,"

Windforce said. He landed in front of her, the flaps of his vibrant blue-and-white skydiving wingsuit fluttering beside him as the wind dissipated. Jane could feel the disapproval of his frown, even with his face hidden behind a full spandex mask.

The trouble is, it was hard to argue his point. Jane had gotten her start in comics by writing about *them*, after all.

True, she'd been on her original Earth at the time, rather than the parallel version she was living on now. And while her first inclination might be to dismiss the role Windforce and the others had played—she hadn't even technically met them when she wrote these characters, after all—it turns out that Clair's mental powers had been allowing her glimpses into their lives, which she'd then shared with Jane during brainstorming sessions. The whole of Jane's initial success was built upon the team's real-life antics, and it was this experience that had given Jane the confidence in her craft she'd needed to start up her own comics publishing company after she'd arrived here.

So yes, in some respects, every achievement in her career was in part thanks to them. But at what point do you stop thanking your muse and start taking credit for your own success? It's not as if the team drew the comics for Jane, or provided specific dialogue, or told her the angles to use in her framing, or the color scheme that would best convey the meaning she was going for. Hell, they hadn't even known they were inspiring her, until they'd kidnapped her from her own world to playact as their Captain Lumen during a crisis. It was only then that Jane learned where her stories had come from, and the team learned they'd been turned into comics somewhere else in the multiverse. She hadn't even published any of their stories here.

Before Jane could form a counterargument, a chunk of rubble came flying toward them. "Duck!" Jane shouted, but Windforce was already on it—a flick of his wrist, and a gust lifted the debris up and away without concern.

"But wait, wait," someone else said over the earpieces. Delta-man, his voice booming with confidence. "We're still going to the premier, right?"

"If and when it actually happens," Jane said, because she knew better than most that a film deal did *not* necessarily mean a movie in the end, "then yes. Absolutely, we'll figure something out. In the meantime, it's better if we keep our friendship as low-profile as possible. Just like we've always done."

She threw her arms wide, an unspoken *"Okay?"* tossed in Windforce's direction.

He waved his hand in dismissal, a gust sending him skyward.

"We really should talk about the premier, though," Clair said a moment later as she raced past Jane's position. The comment was tossed like a volley through the open air, Jane's wife twisting her head to be heard over the commotion.

"We will!" Jane shouted across the street as Clair dodged another piece of incoming debris. *"If* it happens!"

It didn't take them much longer to wrap up their business with the Shadow Raptors, the last stragglers bound and lined up on the edge of the sidewalk like disobedient children. They'd managed to snare one of the masterminds as well—one of two brothers, as identified by facial recognition once they'd ripped off his rubbery rottweiler mask. The other, sadly, had gotten away, but the Heroes would track him down eventually. In the meantime, the diamond they'd been after was safe. Now Grand City police were on the scene, already stealing the credit as the Heroes scattered to various corners of the city.

Jane and Clair piled into a low-slung red sports car. A jagged *SLAM* of car doors filled the space, orange lettering underscored only by the soft *clicks* of their seatbelts in the lower corners. There was a time, before they'd taken over the roles of Captain Lumen and Mindsight, when this world's version of them used to come and go separately. On motorcycles, no less, each of them with a signature bike and flashy moves. It was hard for Jane to picture, even though she'd drawn it plenty of times in her comics.

But that was when they weren't themselves: Jane's doppelgänger, soon to be a hero turned villain; Clair's, ignored and barely acknowledged. These days they were a package deal, in and out of uniform. Some of the team had expressed concerns about that at first, comments Jane had swiftly ignored.

"Ready?" Clair asked now. They had parked in a discreet back alley, out of sight from the media. Still, it wasn't smart to linger once a mission was done.

Jane retrieved her phone from the pocket of her suit. "Yeah, just let me check in first."

Normally, she'd wait until she was back at headquarters, but the cofounder of her comics publishing company was on vacation this week, Blue's first since they'd started the business, and Jane was flying solo running the place. Accommodations had to be made.

Jane double tapped her phone, the screen springing to life. "Goddamn."

Clair glanced over. "That bad?"

The screen was so flooded with notifications that Jane couldn't even form an answer.

"This is what no one ever tells you about being a superhero," Jane said as she scrolled through a flurry of Slack messages, trying to make sense of it all. "I swear, these people are worse than having a kid sometimes."

"I keep telling you, you can skip a few missions. The team and I can handle things until Blue gets back."

"No. I've *got* this."

Clair turned back to the window, unconvinced. "Do you want me to drive, at least?"

Jane didn't answer. She didn't need to. They both knew what the answer would be. The question had been asked mainly so Clair could later say she had. Jane locked her phone, slipping it back into her pocket, then punched a button on the steering wheel as she shifted the car into drive. "Call Sara."

"*Calling Sara,*" the car's buttery-smooth computer voice mirrored.

Even on handsfree, Jane didn't love driving while talking on the phone, but she needed to check in with Dream Sequence and it was better than relinquishing control of the vehicle to Clair. Not that Clair couldn't drive. It's just that she hadn't, in the time since she'd . . . come back.

Jane tried not to think about that, but once the memory had slipped into her mind it was nearly impossible to dismiss. She did her best. She grabbed the mental sheet even as it slid across the desk of her mind. Concept art only, the most she ever allowed herself to picture. Yet even those loose cartoons, loops and lines in blue pencil, were enough to seize her heart. Headlights riding up the side of an arched tunnel. A headstone in a cemetery, seen from behind—but Jane didn't need to read the face of it to know it had made her a widow.

She flipped the paper over, reminding herself that this wasn't the end of the story. That if she kept going, through all the pain and heartbreak, beyond the darkened pages where nothing had mattered, past the dreamy images that used to invade her mind every time she'd see a city bus, a sharp knife, a high bridge— somewhere on the other side of all that, there were pages of rebirth and reunion. Of riotous joy, exploding across the back of her eyelids so often that in the early days of Clair's return it was hard to remember that this was a natural high.

A deep breath, in through Jane's painted, superhero-red lips. *One, two, three,* as the phone rang through the car's sound system. That was all a long time ago, she reminded herself, breathing out. This was here, this was now. This was Clair in the car beside her, taking off her mask and running a hand through her bobbed hair after another job done.

The ringing cut off. "Jane, thank god." Sara's voice filled the car, chasing the last of Jane's ghosts away.

"Yeah, sorry, I got held up," Jane said. "Talk to me."

Sara took a breath, then filled Jane in from the beginning. It was, thankfully, not the worst emergency, merely the sort of minor disaster that often raced through Dream Sequence Comics like a gust of cold air slipping past someone's ankles. They were still small and scrappy, after all, and prone to things like printing companies screwing up orders, vendors cancelling last minute, their website going down after a server hack. This was a fight with a distributor, their office claiming one thing, Jane's records showing another. It was the sort of situation Blue normally took care of, not even bothering Jane with it. Dammit, of all the weeks for her to finally take that long-awaited camping trip . . .

"Okay," Jane said once Sara had finished laying out the problem. "I'll swing by the office and log in to Blue's email, see what she told these people last time. It shouldn't take long."

This last comment she said more to Clair than to Sara, turning her attention just long enough to see her wife toss a shrug as Clair gave in to the inevitable. *I love you,* Jane mouthed, her attention already sliding back to the street as the traffic started moving again. They'd have to park at a distance, find somewhere quick to change, but it was still faster than going back to headquarters and then driving all the way across town again.

Jane glanced at the clock on the dashboard. "Give me ten minutes. I should be able to—"

"Look out!"

It happened so fast. A blur of color streaking in from somewhere high above them, like a boot stomping down on their car. Jane reacted on instinct, her world narrowing and turning sharp with colors and cleanly defined lines. The blur becomes a woman, hovering for a single panel in midair just before she makes impact. Jane's red boot slams against the brake. The frame of the panel curls forward around her foot, as if it, too, is lurching under the force of the sudden stop.

"What was *that*?" Sara asked. "Jane, were you just in an accident? Are you okay?"

"I'm fine," Jane cut in. "But I've got to call you back."

She punched the button on the steering wheel, ending the call over Sara's sputters.

Dammit, their attacker had done a superhero landing on the hood of Jane's car. One knee tucked as if absorbing the impact, the other pointed forward, ready to draw her back to her feet.

She straightens up, frame by frame, unfurling before them. A shimmering jumpsuit of swirling blues and pinks, glittering like a star field.

When she was done, she pointed dramatically at Jane in the driver's seat. A spray of five-pointed stars ran up her forearm toward her elbow. There was something familiar in the pattern, but Jane did not have time to place it.

"Captain Lumen," the woman boomed, "you are found wanting."

"Great," Jane said. "This one's personal."

"What'd you do to piss her off?"

"What makes you think it was me?" Jane glanced beside her, checking that Clair's seatbelt was still firmly latched in place. "Maybe it was my worse half."

It felt plausible enough to Jane—certainly more likely than *her* doing something to draw a villain's ire.

Clair was less convinced. "It's been years since you took over UltraViolet's life, Jane," she said. "At a certain point, you have to stop blaming her for all your problems."

Jane ignored this comment. On the hood, the woman raised her other arm and opened both palms toward them. Jane ducked to the side, already anticipating a blast of superpowered energy to come crashing through the windshield.

But then a beat passed, and nothing happened. Jane tentatively sat back up.

The effects hit her as a wave of nausea. The world warped like a bad trip, her head floating detached in the middle of a sixties technicolor swirl. For a second, Jane's consciousness seemed to exist in a bubble of its own making, unmoored from the trivial concerns of where she was or what was happening around her. Under other circumstances, it might have been nice to forget about the world for a moment, but the cold grip of anxiety was already creeping into Jane's otherwise empty buzz.

She found herself back in the car a second later. Her head spun and her vision fishbowled around her, points of focus ballooning cartoonishly huge, the rest of the world squished out around the periphery. Jane tried to blink, tried to speak, but every motion dragged the same as trying to run in a dream. She pitched her head slowly in Clair's direction, her thoughts sloshing around in her skull.

"What's the point?" a voice said. Her own voice, an action-figure-sized version of herself sitting on the dashboard in full Captain Lumen regalia: red suit, red mask, hair up in a high ponytail. Jane paused, temporarily distracted by the sight of it—of her. Some part of her knew she must be hallucinating, that there was something important she needed to be focusing on instead, but that knowledge was fuzzy with distance, hovering high above her. Jane's cartoony hand reached out, her finger huge as she poked at the tiny figure on the dash.

Doll-Jane pushed the finger away. She got to her feet, plastic knee joints clicking, and began to pace just above the car's air vents.

"You're in trouble now, Jane," the tiny doll said. "This is some next-level shit. They'll need a real hero to save them from this one."

Jane bristled. "I am a real hero."

Doll-Jane's laugh was sharp, a slap across Jane's cheek. *"You?"* She cackled. "Oh, Jane. How can you hope to protect a city when you can't even protect the ones you love?"

"What do you—?" Jane started, but Doll-Jane motioned to the seat beside her. Jane turned, and a scream ripped itself from her throat.

She snapped her eyes shut against the image: Clair, cold and dead in the seat beside her. The same slack face Jane had seen as the doctors rushed in during the final moments; Jane had realized, even before they did, that it was over.

"No." Jane tore up the image, in half and then half again. No, it had to be another delusion, just like the doll-sized version of herself. *"No,"* Jane repeated, louder this time. No, she would not accept that fate—not again. She'd already lived through that once, in dark issues best not revisited. Jane took a breath, grounding herself on the slim touches she still had on reality. Her hand on the steering wheel, the stitching perfect beneath her fingers. Her other resting on the gearshift. She did not hesitate. Her hand tightened around the gearshift, throwing the transmission into reverse.

Jane slammed the gas pedal.

Acceleration hit, ripping the hallucination from the sketchbook of Jane's mind. The car screamed as it raced backward. Metal dragged against pavement, something jostled loose from the weight of the woman's landing. By some miracle the engine was still running, so Jane wasn't going to complain. She let up on the clutch and threw the wheel hard to the side, popping her eyes open. The visions were gone. The car's nose spun away, and Jane shifted gears. Before they'd even come to a stop, Jane hit the pedal again, peeling down the street.

"Are you okay?" Jane was nearly breathless, her heart racing as if she'd just escaped on foot rather than in the car.

Clair, pale and queasy but very much *alive*, waved off Jane's concern. "Yeah. Yeah, I'm . . . I'm fine."

Jane nodded. The roar of an engine drew Jane's attention to her rearview mirror—the woman had stolen a car and was tight on their tail. Jane downshifted, pushing her car faster as she wove between the tangle of city traffic. She dug their earpieces out of the charging unit in the center console, passing one to Clair before tucking her own into place.

"Guys!" Jane shouted, even though she knew her voice would carry across the comm without effort. "Get your asses back here, Mindsight and I have another baddie after us."

Deltaman's voice was the first one to click back into the system. "Are you kidding me? We just *stopped* an attack."

"Yeah, well, it's not like supervillains sync their Google Calendars," Jane said. "I'm leading her out of the city, but we'll need backup. Deltaman, Granite Girl, meet me at Ostertag Plaza, I'll do my best to lure her there. In the meantime, I need Pixie, Rip, and Windforce to lock onto my position. These powers are next level, I'm not sure I can hold her off all the way to the meetup."

"What kind of powers are we talking?" Rip-Shift asked.

Jane darted a look at Clair. Her hands tightened on the steering wheel as they veered around a corner. "Hard to say," she said after a second. "Hallucinations of some sort."

"Anything like Dreadscape's?" Granite Girl asked.

Jane hit the button on her comm, silencing her mic. "That was real?"

While Jane's comics had been inadvertently lifted from real life, there were times the details Clair provided were fuzzier than others. She and Jane had filled in a lot of blanks over the years, ideas sprawling across the floor of their cramped apartment as Jane sketched everything down as fast as they could think of it. She remembered Dreadscape, kind of, though he'd only appeared in a few issues in the middle of a much larger plot arc.

But Clair had a greater insight into the actual world they'd found themselves in, thanks to the memories tucked away in the brain she'd taken over from her doppelgänger. Everything wasn't perfectly accessible all the time, but it was a lot more than Jane would ever have. So it didn't surprise Jane that Clair was able to answer Granite Girl, her voice cool and collected as she said,

"No, his made you feel like you were dreaming while awake. This was more like you were staring into a mirror reflecting the ugliest part of your soul."

A cold chill settled over Jane. Shit, what had Clair seen in her own visions?

"Poetic as that is, it doesn't help me," Granite Girl grumbled over the comm. "We can't fight what we can't understand."

"Yeah, well, as soon as I know, you'll know."

Jane opened her mouth to respond, hoping to jump in front of whatever sharp reply Granite Girl would inevitably offer, when a flash of blue caught the edge of the rearview mirror like a lens flare. Jane spotted it, too late. She hit the brakes, threw the wheel hard to the left. Not fast enough.

Each panel is a full two-page spread. Intricately painted, not a single detail obscured or overlooked. Turn the pages slowly, luxuriating in the nuance, the artistry. They're Renaissance paintings, and they may as well be framed and hung on huge white walls. Take your time. Marvel at the way the light of the explosion throws a blue wash across the normally blood-red sports car. The underside of the black tires look almost wet as they face the open sky for the first time in their lives. A glimpse through the window shows the passengers, strapped inside. Their hair is hanging up from their heads—if you turn the comic upside down it would be easy to image them as a pair of astronauts, floating weightless in a capsule. An outstretched hand runs between them, and if Jane just keeps drawing this moment out, an endless series of spreads that change only a fraction from page to page to page, then she can hold this instant in her mind forever. The ultimate slow-motion sequence.

Until someone realizes they can turn back to the beginning, flick each page like a flip book. And then it's over, the image crumpling like the hood of the car as they strike pavement.

Later, one of her friends will probably tell Jane that they were lucky: the car landed on its nose first, collapsing sideways and then, finally, somewhat gently, onto its back like a defeated beetle. But in the moment that it took her to blink, to feel her bones knock together in the final slump of the car coming to its end, it did not feel lucky. A scream filled the car, Clair's name rubbing Jane's vocal cords raw as Jane fumbled with seatbelts and scrambled across the gap between them, and she probably did not even hear the call-and-response of "Jane, Jane, it's okay, I'm okay!"

Jane did not remember clambering free of the twisted wreckage. It was like a set of pages were stuck together, and she skipped straight from the one where she was reaching wildly for Clair, to the one where they were huddled in a lump together on the pavement, Jane's arms wrapped fiercely around Clair as she cried into her hair.

"Shh, it's all right, it's all right, we're safe," Clair was whispering to her by the time Jane started to come back to herself. A sense of calm seeped from the tips of Clair's fingers, sinking into Jane's exposed wrist.

Jane sat up sharply, suddenly embarrassed that Clair had to use her powers like that. She brushed her hair out of her face, the loose strands that had slipped from her tight ponytail. "You're sure you're okay?" she asked, but Clair was already standing up, her attention moved on.

"Jane?" Clair asked as she turned in place. "Where the hell are we?"

A GOOD QUESTION. JANE ROSE UNSTEADILY TO HER feet. Gone were the high-rises and crosswalks at the heart of Grand City—in their place, stretches of strip-mall parking lots sprawled in a tangle of suburban commerce. They were standing in the middle of one, the crumpled wreck of their car smashed against a pale blue minivan and a squat red hatchback. A giant Braddock's grocery sign loomed on the horizon, a mess of smaller retailers and fast-food logos scattered in the slots beneath the anchor store.

"We should go," Clair said, tugging Jane's sleeve. "Right now."

Jane wasn't about to argue. The parking lot wasn't exactly a hot spot of pedestrian activity, but already a handful of people had stopped to gawk, and a bubbly gray sedan so rounded it resembled a jelly bean was inching down the nearest aisle to get a better look. Something about the whole thing tugged at

Jane's mind, but she shook it off as she and Clair raced for the back corner of the lot. A place like this offered so much less opportunity to get out of sight than the urban jungle they were used to.

She followed Clair's lead, the two of them snaking between cars to avoid curious eyes. A convenience store with a little gas station out front took up the farthest edge of the parking lot; behind it, a concrete wall rose sharply, holding back the hillside and the spread of cramped houses jammed along the crest. It would provide as good of cover as they were likely to find.

They ducked around the convenience store, squeezing between overflowing dumpsters. A tiny patch of broken asphalt provided them with a pocket of space to pause and catch their breath. A single folding chair was set up near the back door to the shop, a battered metal TV tray listing toward it. Jane sat heavily, burying her face in her hands while Clair paced the perimeter of their tiny courtyard. The chair creaked ominously beneath her weight, but Jane didn't care if it collapsed.

"Did you notice how no one had their phones out?" Clair asked.

Jane gave a strangled laugh as she raised her head. "*That's* what you're worried about?"

"Oh, come on. All those people, and not a single one takes so much as a photo?"

"What difference does it make? We still don't know where we are and our comms are dead, which means we've lost contact with the team. I think we have bigger problems than whether or not someone snapped a pic for social media."

"I don't know," Clair said, her voice slow. "Something is very wrong here."

"I'll tell you what's wrong. Where did the woman who was attacking us go? I find it hard to believe she just gave up."

Clair went silent for a minute, considering. "Give me your phone."

"What, why?"

"Just do it."

Jane grumbled but dug into her pocket, passing her phone over. A flutter near the base of the closest dumpster caught her eye: a page from a sales flyer, bright colors splashed across the paper. She got up from the rickety chair, stepping closer.

Meanwhile, Clair gave a messy, frustrated sigh behind her. "There's no signal," Clair said. "I don't understand—we're not exactly in the middle of nowhere. We should at least have a few bars."

"Yeah, I think I can explain that one." Jane reached down, shaking out the rumpled flyer as she picked it up. The paper was new, no weathering or faded colors, yet an array of boxy old TVs lay before them. Beneath that, an ad for a Nintendo 64—Jane recognized it from long afternoons in Keisha's living room, the group of them sprawled on their stomachs as they battled with rude squirrels or high-pitched Pikachus.

Clair leaned over to see around Jane's shoulder and sucked in a breath. She pinched the edge of the flyer, using her empathic powers to absorb whatever faint emotional impressions she could. "What the hell? *Time* travel?"

"I don't think so." Jane flipped the flyer over. "You're right, though—something is very wrong here."

"Oh, *bra*-vo," came a sarcastic voice from above. "Ten points to Captain Lumen."

They jumped back. Jane shoved herself in front of Clair, a protective stance to block her from the reappearance of the villain who'd gotten them into this mess. It was ingrained behavior by this point, something Jane couldn't stop herself from doing even if she'd wanted to.

The woman who'd chased them here—wherever "here" was—was back, sitting on the edge of the wall, one leg crossed casually over the other. She clapped slowly.

Clair touched Jane's wrist, a free finger slipping against Jane's skin. The idea of running away entered Jane's mind, half-formed like a question she hadn't quite settled. It did not come from her own mind, though it was so natural it may as well have, and only Jane's experience with Clair's empathic powers allowed her to tell the difference. Jane wrapped the feeling up, stuffing it down with a decisive *No* that she knew would carry back to Clair. A feeling of resolve slid back to her, a silent agreement: they'd stay and fight this one out.

All this passed in a split second, wedged into the gutter between the panels of their attacker's claps. Jane straightened her spine. Clair released Jane, her fingers twitching and ready to go for her gun.

The woman stopped clapping. She shifted, jumping from her perch on the wall—landing first on a dumpster, then the broken pavement. As she straightened up, a glint of sunlight caught a piece of tech at her wrist. A very *familiar* piece of tech, although admittedly this one was definitely slimmed down and refined from the devices that let the Heroes hop from one version of Earth to another.

They were on a parallel world. With none of the tech they needed in order to get back.

Jane cursed silently. If their own world-hopping devices were as slim as the one this woman wore, maybe they would be a standard-issue part of the uniform, just in case—but what were the odds they'd be zapped to another Earth while on a mission? As far as Jane knew, the Heroes were the only ones with access to that technology.

"Where did you get that?" Jane asked, pointing.

The woman glanced at her wrist, almost as if she'd forgotten it was there. A wicked grin split her face. "Ah, Captain. I don't give the answers away. I can only help you see what's always been in front of you."

Jane huffed. Such a useless answer, coached in metaphor and self-importance. True, she didn't actually expect an enemy to up and *tell* her something like that—the question had slipped free, more a wish than a realistic query. Still, the disappointment stung. But Jane supposed that question would be something to sort out another day, once they were back where they belonged.

"Enough with the schoolyard riddles," Jane said. She raised her hands, palms out. She could feel the light of the world, constantly surrounding her, waiting for her command. "Hand it over, and I promise we'll be merciful."

The woman laughed. One loud crack that split the back lot. "Yeah, gonna have to decline that offer, sweetie. It *is* funny that you mention schoolyards, though. Now that you bring it up . . . I think perhaps that's exactly what you need."

"What do you—?" Jane started, but then three things happened in such rapid succession they may as well have been all at once.

The first, innocent enough: the woman snapped her fingers.

The second: Jane's eyes rolled back as she started to collapse.

The third: the woman raised her arm, pointed her own world hopper at Jane and Clair, and fired.

Jane!

Panic, not her own, hit Jane's mind as a flash of blue enveloped them. She and Clair stumbled back, through the swirling fog, Clair collecting Jane's falling form as they reappeared in the middle of the same bustling street they'd disappeared from while Jane had been driving.

"Captain! Mindsight!"

The rest of the team swept in around Jane and Clair.

"Where were you? What happened?"

Clair didn't have time to answer, though, because Jane had lost consciousness, limp in Clair's arms, and who knows what that woman had done with the snap of her fingers. Clair cradled her there on the street, letting the rest of the Heroes swirl around her.

"Jane? Jane, can you hear me? Are you all right?" She brushed her fingers over Jane's face just as Jane's eyes popped open wide.

Jane screamed.

She scrambled out of Clair's arms, leaping back and whirling as she took in her surroundings. "What the heck?" she shouted. "Where am I? What's going on? Oh my god, my mom's gonna *kill* me."

"Your *mom*?"

But Jane didn't respond, didn't even seem to hear Clair. Instead, she stared down at herself, her red suit, pawing at it as if she didn't recognize it. Her breath was racing in her chest as she paced around, freaking out. "Oh my god, oh my god, what's happening, this isn't real, it can't be real, right?"

"*Jane.*" Clair's voice was firm, and only now did Jane's head whip around.

Jane raised her arms defensively. "Stay back," she said, her voice wavering.

"Jane, it's okay. It's okay. Just give me your hand. I can help you, I promise."

A sliver of hesitation. Clair forced herself to take a breath, to not get destroyed by the gesture. She tugged her fingerless gloves off as she held her hand out to Jane.

"Let me help you," she reiterated.

Cautiously, Jane stretched her hand out. Clair wasn't going to miss her opportunity—before Jane could change her mind, Clair darted forward and seized her wife's hand, palm to palm. Their eyes widened: Jane's, apparently in shock at the sensation of Clair's powers; Clair's, at what she found.

She dropped Jane's hand. Took her own step back. Slowly, she turned to look at the rest of the team.

"Guys?" Clair said cautiously. "This isn't our Jane."

THE MEMORIES CAME BACK TO JANE ALL AT ONCE. THE
mission, the chase—a parallel world, a snap like a rubber band
yanking her out of herself. A weightless fall and then the slam
of a ruler against the desk. They flooded Jane as she sat outside
the principal's office, beneath the glare of the school secretary
and the whirring of a stale heater. Jane leaped to her feet as the
office door swung open. "That bastard!"

Her mother's voice crowded in, a bold speech bubble slapped
rudely across the page. "Janie!"

Jane whirled. Mrs. Maxwell, as she used to be: high-waisted
jeans, dyed black, shaded on the page with India ink; a baggy cotton top with a row of embroidered flowers sketched loosely near
the *V* of the neckline; brown leather clogs; teased hair cheaply
bleached. An enormous purse sags against her hip, her hands
gripped tightly around the strap over her chest. She's framed by
the open doorway, the shot angled up and slightly tilted as if
she's a superhero towering over the city.

This was the Olivia Maxwell of her forties—well past her early, lean years, long before she'd found either the diet and exercise regimen that Jane's mom had embraced in the wake of Mr. Maxwell's departure, or the dietitians and fitness coaches that Senator Maxwell had hired for his wife back when he was still mayor of Grand City. The Mrs. Maxwell of this era filled Jane's memories as soft and warm and embarrassing, an outdated real estate agent working part-time so she'd still be home when Jane got out of school. She stood there now, glaring at Jane, and all Jane could think was how *young* she looked.

"Mom?" Jane's voice was pinched, squeaking out as a nervous mouse scuttling in the corner of the room. Instinctively, Jane tucked her hair behind her ears so she wouldn't look so "sloppy," as her mother always put it. "What are you doing here?"

Olivia adjusted the strap of her oversized purse as she marched forward. "That's what I'd like to know. What were you *thinking*, just walking out of class! You know they called me at work? Dragged me down here in the middle of the day? I had a showing this afternoon, but *no*, I had to toss it to *Debbie*, and I swear to god if she gets commission, I will—"

"Mrs. Maxwell?" the secretary asked, breaking the tirade.

"What?" Olivia snapped. She took a fast breath, shutting her eyes just long enough to compose herself. "I'm sorry, yes. I'm Mrs. Maxwell. Can I help you?"

But if the secretary was offended, or had even noticed Olivia's rudeness, she didn't show it. She blinked, her eyes magnified behind glasses that would have been more appropriate in the eighties, giant plastic frames in pink so pale it was almost ivory. "Principal Gray will see you now." She turned back to her computer, her keyboard *clacking* loudly beneath her acrylic nails.

Olivia took another steadying breath. "Right. Time to see how bad the damage is."

"Mom, I didn't—"

"Not another word." Olivia raised a finger. "I don't want to hear it from you, not right now, do you understand? We'll talk later."

A dry burn settled in Jane's stomach. She looked at the floor, stuffing her hands into her pockets. "Yeah. Sure. Later." Her fingers wrapped around an open pack of gum, warm and soft from being in her jeans all day.

She followed her "mother" through the door.

Principal Gray.

He sat at his desk, a giant poster of a tropical beach set behind him like the backdrop of a fish tank. With his puffy cheeks and eyes nearly as wide as a cartoon character, it was hard for Jane not to see him as a goldfish, *glup-glupping* as he watched them enter.

Olivia rushed forward, rounding one of the chairs across from him and settling in before being invited. "Mr. Gray, thank you so much for your time, I'm *so* sorry for my daughter's behavior. I assure you, it won't happen again."

"Hang on," Jane said, her glasses slipping down her nose. "Don't I get a say in this?"

Olivia's response brokered no argument. "No." Olivia laid her hands on the edge of the principal's desk. "How can I make up for this?"

"Please, call me Bob," Mr. Gray said. He stole a glance at Jane, who shoved her glasses back in place and then crossed her arms, leaning against the brick wall of his office. "As for your daughter, it's really not a matter of *apology*, Mrs. Maxwell. You see, here at Central Oak High, we take our student body very seriously. If Janie's having a problem, we prefer to get to the bottom of it, rather than worry about strictly disciplinary measures."

"Of course." Mrs. Maxwell nodded vigorously. "Of course. That's so admirable. But I can assure you, there's nothing going on at *home* that would have caused such behavior."

"That's reassuring to hear—but unfortunately, kids don't just act out like this without motivating factors. Much as we like to tell ourselves otherwise. Now, Janie's a good kid. Mr. Santori wants to give her a detention, but I'm more inclined to write this off as a one-time incident."

"That's very generous of you."

Mr. Gray lifted his hand, palm out. "However. We will want to make sure this doesn't happen again, so I would like some reassurance. A gesture on Janie's part."

Jane raised an eyebrow. It sounded disturbingly like he was

asking for a blowjob, as far as she was concerned. Not that she had any reason to think he was that kind of twisted asshole, but—well, you never really knew. Especially not with men in positions of power.

"As I'm sure you're aware, we're well in the middle of preparations for Homecoming," Mr. Gray continued. "And I think it would be a wonderful show of her commitment to this school if Janie lent a hand to the student planning committee."

The laugh escaped Jane before she could stop it. A single sharp burst, a pin to the balloon of Mr. Gray's enthusiasm. She hadn't exactly been the queen of afterschool activities in her real past, and she sure as shit had no intention of spending any more time in these halls than necessary while she was stuck in her current situation.

Whatever that was.

Jane, it seemed, was the only one to find the suggestion absurd. She looked between Olivia and Mr. Gray, one staring at her with open irritation, the other smoothly neutral.

"Oh, shit," Jane said. "You're serious."

"Language!" Olivia barked, but it would take a lot more than a swear to rattle a high school principal. Mr. Gray leveled her with a heavy look, his previous veneer of patience at its limits.

Jane drew her lips into a placating smile. She'd been a hero long enough to know when she'd been defeated, and this was clearly one fight she was not going to win. Choking down her words, she added, "I mean, uh, 'That sounds amazing, Mr. Gray. When do I start?'"

"My secretary will give you the schedule." Mr. Gray stood up, holding out his hand for Olivia to shake, the two of them already dismissed. His we're-all-friends smile was firmly back in place. "Lovely to meet you, Mrs. Maxwell. We can't wait to see what sort of potential Janie has in store for us."

"Yeah," Jane muttered to herself. "You and me both."

JANIE LEANED IN, EYES WIDE, AS SHE PICKED UP A GIZMO from the tray beside her. "I can't believe I'm gonna grow up to be a *superhero*! This is wicked cool."

They were back in the labs by now. Actual *labs*, in an actual *superhero hideout*. They'd brought her here after Janie had calmed down. As if there was something wrong with her, like she needed a trip to the doctor. Which, okay, what had happened was bad, it's not like Janie was trying to argue that. And she *had* flipped out, pretty hardcore, when she'd first arrived. But she felt *fine* now. So that was something, right? Like, it could have been way worse. She could have grown an extra ear, or something, in the . . . process. Probably.

There'd been a *lot* of arguing, at first. Like, a *lot*. Way more than Janie felt was normal for a group of superheroes—even if they were all just grown-up versions of Cal and Keisha and Tony and Marie and Devin beneath their masks. Janie had done her best to follow it all, but so much of it was just *Blah blah, parallel worlds, blah blah, body-swap, blah blah*, and honestly if Janie wanted to listen to a bunch of nerds geek out over sci-fi concepts she could have just stayed home.

She supposed she should be more freaked out than she was. That would have probably been normal.

Never mind. What mattered is that the one thing she *did* manage to follow is that no one had the faintest idea how to *un*-body-swap her, so as far as Janie was concerned, she might as well enjoy it. It sure as heck beat going to school.

Now Janie prodded the end of the gizmo she'd found, the end of it *zapping* against her finger.

The grown-up version of Marie turned. Her eyes narrowed into a scowl. "Put that down!"

"I was just—!"

"I don't care." Marie marched over, snatching the gizmo from Janie's hands. She waved it in Janie's face. "This is a highly advanced piece of medical technology, not a *toy*. Besides, do you see me coming into *your* room and touching *your* stuff without permission?"

Janie rolled her eyes. She leaned back, palms crinkling the paper on the padded exam table. "I mean, you *did* basically kidnap me, drag me to the future, and age me into an adult without my permission, but whatever, I guess you can yell at me for touching your toy."

Marie opened her mouth to argue, but Clair stepped forward, wedging herself between them.

"Jane—*Janie*," Clair corrected herself. At least Janie had managed to get that straightened out. God, she couldn't imagine why this other version of herself was okay with being boring old "Jane." But whatever. Clair reached out, rubbing a hand over Janie's shoulder. "That wasn't us, okay? And I promise, we're going to do everything in our power to get you back where you belong. Trust me."

Janie swallowed, her mouth gone dry. She slid out from under Clair's touch, adjusting her glasses to cover for the motion. "Yeah. No, I know. I get it."

"Besides," Marie said. "This isn't your future. It's a parallel world. Imagine for a minute that there's another Earth, except that instead of—"

"I've seen Star Trek. I *know* what a parallel world is." Janie glanced around, suddenly nervous. "Oh, crap. This isn't like the mirror universe, is it? Like, you're not all evil versions of yourselves, right?"

"No evil twins." Clair's soft smile settled over Janie. "It's more like that episode of *The Next Generation* where Worf kept bouncing from *Enterprise* to *Enterprise*, and everything was a little different each time."

Janie nodded. "Gotcha."

"Except that in reality, there's a time distortion between all the different worlds," Devin said. "And ours is running about twenty years ahead of yours."

"Which means nothing that happened here is guaranteed to happen to you," Clair said. She spoke with a level voice, steady and reassuring. "Do you understand that?"

Another eye roll. "Yeah, whatever. It's still the closest to seeing the future I'm ever going to get, so don't ruin it for me, okay?"

And really, all things considered, it wasn't a terrible future as far as Janie could tell—the name issue aside. She glanced down, flexing her fingers. A warm light began to glow at the tips, brighter than a flashlight. With a sigh, Janie let it go, the embers burning out. She smiled to herself, pleased at how quickly she seemed to be getting the hang of this.

Clair's mouth pinched. She turned away, as if the sight of Janie's new-found superpowers was somehow distasteful to her. "There's got to be something we can do."

Janie edged a little to the side, the paper crinkling beneath her. The others drifted toward a set of screens along the wall, going over theories, strategies—a lot of weird superhero science, nothing Janie could follow. That was just as well, as far as she was concerned.

It was still so *weird*, seeing them like this.

Not even the superhero part, though that was obviously a trip to learn about. But the team were so unbelievably badass, Janie couldn't look at them and *not* see superheroes. Devin was pointing grandly at a digital board full of complicated equations, the wing flap of his blue-and-white suit stretching with his motions. He'd grown his hair out, then flattened his curls and bound them together near the top of his head, and though it was weird to see a man with his hair in a bun, Janie couldn't deny that he made it look, somehow, *cool*. Marie kept cutting in front of him, reaching up to correct his math. She was so tiny, still, and Janie held back a private laugh, because the Marie she knew hadn't grown since sixth grade, but kept insisting that her next spurt would hit any day now. Her arms were toned as heck, though, and somehow even her tininess did not diminish the feeling that she could kick your ass. Tony and Keisha leaned side by side against a nearby wall, listening to the techno jumble like they understood it, him in Matrix-leather and her in some sort of vibrant punk-rock-ballerina style, a denim jacket paired with eighties-ish neon leggings and a fluffy tulle skirt. Cal stood tall in the middle of the room, arms crossed, black body armor sculpted over him like some sort of action hero. And Clair . . .

Janie's breath caught when she looked at Clair. She had shed the trench coat she'd been wearing, dropped the fedora. She stood there now in a blue button-down blouse, gray pants, white suspenders. An empty holster hung from her hip like a 1920s gangster. Janie had never been particularly into older women, but she found herself warming to the idea now.

"—already used the scans on Janie to isolate the signature of her universe," Marie was saying as Janie slid off the exam table. They were still huddled off to the side, their backs to Janie, their voices thrown low the way that grownups think makes it harder to hear. "We can run a search algorithm, but Clair . . . there's no way to know how long it could take. You said yourself, her world-hopping tech looked way more advanced than ours. We've got no idea which sector of the multiverse she took you to. It's not quite the nightmare scenario, but—"

"Yeah, I get it." Clair's voice was prickly, the same way it was when they were little and Clair tried to cover up how nervous she got during a thunderstorm. Janie could practically see an outline of that younger version, sketched over this grown-up woman—like someone had tried to erase the lines, but the impressions carved into the paper still remained.

Clair's younger ghost straightened her shoulders, trying to be brave, and the adult puppet followed suit. "Then that just gives us time to sort out how to reverse the effects. Where are we on analyzing the powers of the woman who attacked us?"

The rest of the team exchanged a glance. All save for Marie, who was studying Clair as if trying to see something that wasn't quite present.

Devin stepped forward, tapping a giant pane of glass sitting near one of the laboratory's counters. Janie sucked in a breath as the glass shimmered, the plain transparency replaced by a series of intricate charts and graphs, overlaid with equations in sloppy handwriting.

"Our best lead is a set of tetricore readings. We picked them up during the attack, and there were traces of it left behind on Janie when you brought her back."

"So we think this is the source of the woman's powers?" Cal asked, stepping in seamlessly when Devin had paused for breath.

Marie shrugged. "I mean, there's no way to know until we run more tests. But sure. It seems likely."

"The good news," Devin continued, "is that we've already dealt with an Enhanced who drew his strength from tetricore energy. Remember Psy Mask?"

"How could we forget?" Keisha said. "Still got the scar from that damn kid." She stretched out her arm, pulling her sleeve up to show the back of her elbow. A jagged ridge cut through the deep brown of her skin.

Devin cleared his throat. "Right. Well. His powers meant that he could manipulate the surface properties of whatever he touched—essentially, make people think they were looking at something else, without actually altering what the thing fundamentally *was* or how it worked. We think this new baddie does essentially the same thing."

"But her powers are nothing like Psy Mask's," Tony said.

"On the surface, no." Marie cut forward, her tiny body hip-checking Devin aside as she wedged herself in front of the screen full of equations. "But if you think about it, she body-swapped Jane with a version of *herself*. Was that a coincidence? Or was that a clue, that maybe she only *can* body-swap the same person? The hallucinations were a reflection of your own insecurities. There's a theme here, I'm just . . . not sure exactly how all the science ties together."

Tony raised a hand. "But what good are body-swapping powers if you'd need a parallel self to make it work? Doesn't that seem . . . I don't know, kinda limited?"

"Yeah, that's exactly my point," Marie said. "I don't think the powers are *about* body-swapping—I think body-swapping is more like a weird side effect of her ability to manipulate . . . I don't know, perception or identity or something."

"Is that even possible?" Tony asked.

Marie cut him a look. "Asks the guy who can cut a hole in the world and step from one spot to another in an instant. *Yes*, it's possible. Try to keep up."

Tony's face soured. "I was just *asking*."

"But asking a stupid question," Marie said. "Do I look like I have time for those?"

"See, you're asking me that, but you clearly think the answer is obvious, so doesn't that make *it* a stupid question?"

"Okay, enough," Cal said. "Bottom line, how does this help us undo Jane's swap?"

Marie and Devin exchanged a glance. "We're . . . not really sure yet," Devin said. "We'll need to run some tests on Janie, see if we can detect the swap on a physiological level. That's the first step. Hopefully, after that we'll have a better sense of what to do next."

Janie raised an eyebrow. It didn't sound like much of a plan to her, but what did she know?

"Okay." Keisha glanced over at Janie. "In the meantime, Clair, you're going to need to put Janie up somewhere. Take her to a hotel room or something."

Clair jerked back as if she'd seen a spider. "I'm not taking her to a *hotel*! She's, like, *twelve*—I could be her *mom*."

"She doesn't *look* twelve."

"Gross, Cal."

Keisha ignored him. "Look, I'm not saying you should sleep—"

Janie loudly cleared her throat. "Um, ex*cuse* me," she said as the group *finally* turned to notice her. "I'm not *twelve*. I'm *fifteen*."

Clair whipped her head around. Her eyes had popped wide, a look of utter terror etched onto her face. "You're what?"

Janie squirmed. "I'm fifteen?" She didn't know why she was phrasing it as a question. Something about the look on Clair's face, the feeling like Janie was missing something important.

"Fifteen." Clair's voice was so tight it was nearly breathless. "So you're a sophomore?"

"Yeah . . ."

"Shit," Clair whispered. She turned away, just for a moment, just long enough to run her hands through her hair. "The date—what's the exact date, from your perspective?"

"Um . . . I don't know, end of August? Thirtieth, thirty-first?" she said, and Clair's face turned white, her eyes closing as if in prayer. Janie's stomach jumped. "Why, what's . . . what's important about the date?"

But Clair wasn't paying attention to her anymore, probably didn't even hear her. Instead, she'd turned back to the rest of the Heroes, who were studying her with almost as much confusion as Janie.

Clair took a deep breath. "I'm afraid our problem just got a whole lot bigger."

* * *

THREE PANELS, STACKED ON TOP OF EACH OTHER.

The first: a battered locker, painted a deep salmon pink. Flecks of buttery yellow, army green, and tan stick out where the paint has chipped away, the previous color schemes hidden like some kind of archeological dig into the school's garish past. The combination dial looms large in the middle, an all-seeing eye.

The second: Jane's teenage face. A subtle hint of the dial reflects in her glasses. She's got her head turned, just a little, with uncertainty, and her lip is scrunched out as she catches the side of it with her teeth.

The third: the locker again, only this time Jane's hand hovers, warily, beneath the dial. Across all three panels, the dial, Jane's eye, and the dial again are stacked in perfect alignment down the center of the page, caught in a staring contest. Jane could swear the locker was mocking her. Such a simple test, and yet—one she knows she will fail.

The soft slam of a body landing against the locker beside her drew Jane's attention.

"Hey," Clair said. "You okay?"

Jane startled. God, Clair was so young. Not that Jane expected anything different, not here, but still: seeing her in person like she'd stepped out of Jane's old photo albums . . . Clair's hair was longer in the past, shoulder-length, the top clipped back into a half ponytail. Two tendrils had been kept loose, to frame either side of her face. Star-shaped earrings dotted her lobes. Up close, she smelled like bubble gum and peach body spray, a sweet summertime smell that tugged at the pit of Jane's stomach with deep-set nostalgia.

"Yeah," Jane said as she turned back toward the puzzle of her locker. "Yeah, I'm good. Why wouldn't I be?"

"Um, because you lost your frickin' mind earlier? Because you got sent to the principal's office?" She studied Jane in silence for a moment while Jane idly spun the locker dial. "Because apparently you've forgotten your locker combination already?"

"Can you open it for me?"

A request, more than a question. Jane and Clair always exchanged locker combinations immediately, each of them memorizing both. They had a whole litany of each other's numbers memorized: phone numbers, locker combos, birthdays, heights; later, as they grew and their lives became more entangled, that trust would branch into social security numbers, bank accounts, PINs, passwords. Jane and Clair shared everything, hid nothing. But it had started here, these simple secrets held fast between them.

Clair eyed Jane warily as she bumped her out of the way. Her youthful fingers spun the dial. Clair's nails were painted sky blue, with tiny green shoots budding up from the base. Jane had probably done the detail work—her Jane, anyway, though Jane could see the memory of it as clearly as if she'd done it herself. The two of them sitting across from each other on Jane's bed, a tray spread with various bottles of nail polish between them. Jane used to love doing Clair's makeup. The excuse to hold Clair's hands in hers, the skin so warm between them. The chance to lean in close to her face.

The locker popped open. Clair stepped aside, motioning for Jane to go ahead.

Jane scowled, shoving the memories aside as she grabbed some textbooks at random, stuffing them into her backpack.

"You sure you're okay?" Clair asked. This time her voice was softer, her head dipped so that no one in the hall could overhear them. She reached forward, laying a hand on Jane's shoulder.

Jane flinched from the touch before she could stop herself. Half instinctive, not wanting her emotions to be read right now—not that there was any indication this version of Clair could do that—and half because, well . . . this wasn't *Clair*. Not really. Not yet.

Jane slammed the locker door shut. "I'm fine." She turned away, starting off down the hall.

"Where are you going?" Clair called.

Jane stopped. She turned back around. "Home . . . ?"

"Janie, come on. I know you don't want a lecture, but do you think it's going to get better if you ditch her for the bus?"

"Ditch who?"

Clair didn't answer. She was already walking the other direction, glancing once over her shoulder.

Jane's sneakers slapped against the linoleum as she dashed

to catch up. Clair navigated the halls with surety, but almost nothing was familiar to Jane. A handful of memories drifted past her, hazy comic pages of stolen moments. Nothing solid.

A familiar laugh bounced down the hall.

Jane drew to a stop. "*Allison's* here?"

Clair shot Jane a sidelong look as she adjusted her backpack on her shoulder. "I mean, I would hope so? She's never left without you before." She shook her head. "Honestly, what's gotten *into* you today?"

"You wouldn't believe me if I tried," Jane said, but Clair had already started bounding forward, buoyed by the end of the school day.

The crowd parted, a pack moving off, and there was Allison by a bank of lockers.

"All right, I'll catch you guys later," Allison said to a group of her friends. She turned away, throwing just one strap of her backpack over her shoulder. Her attention landed on Clair, and then Jane, her eyes narrowing slightly. "You two ready?"

Clair nodded for both of them—just as well, because Jane sure as shit wasn't able to move or communicate on her own.

All she could do was stare at this would-be sister.

Jane had seen photos of Allison as a child and a teenager, of course. There were a few still hung in private corners of the Maxwells' house, and occasionally Mrs. Maxwell posted "throwback" photos on Facebook for the girls' birthdays. Allison had never existed in Jane's original world, only the adopted one she'd moved to as an adult, so these photos and a handful of stories were all Jane had to go on to imagine what their childhood might have been like, if things were just a little different.

But it was one thing to have an academic understanding of how Allison used to be, and another to see her in the flesh, a real-life teenager moving off without a backward glance at her kid sister.

She strode forward with the same surety that she would as an adult. The same purpose. As if the world belonged to her, as if there was never any question that she was on the right path. Wide bootcut jeans pooled so far across her feet that her shoes disappeared. Two separate camis layered over a snug white

T-shirt. Allison's hair was dyed a cheap bottle-blond, brown roots caught up in a variety of mini braids vaguely attempting to be white-girl dreads. Clumps of these were held back with a series of vivid butterfly-shaped hair clips. As she walked, she pulled an old Nokia phone from her pocket, a wedge of pale blue plastic.

Though it probably wasn't old here, Jane reminded herself.

Outside, Allison led them to a modest car, an old green Toyota Jane recognized as having once belonged to her father. Allison's keys jangled as she opened the doors. Clair moved breezily to the backseat, letting herself in without hesitation. She slid her backpack into the well by her feet and then glanced through the window, up at Jane. Jane yanked open the front passenger door and let herself inside.

She realized her mistake as soon as she clicked her seatbelt into place. Allison was already glancing back and forth between Jane and Clair—and Clair, seen only in the rearview mirror, was staring at Jane like a kicked puppy. Of *course* Jane would have made a habit of sitting in the back with Clair. Of course she wouldn't dare pass up the opportunity to be near her, to let their knees knock together, their fingers brush on the seat between them.

Allison's brow crinkled in scrutiny. "Did you two have a fight or something?"

"No," Jane said quickly before Clair could say anything. "I'm just . . . not feeling great. I'd rather be able to look out the front windows."

As a lie, it wasn't terrible. Jane, at least in her own world, had been prone to car sickness when she was little, growing out of it only in her teens. Even by this point, it still wasn't uncommon for her to need the extra view, the breath of fresh air from the vents.

Allison's mouth compressed with something unspoken. She reached across Jane, cranking the top of Jane's window down. "Just don't puke in my car," she said as she dropped the Nokia into her cupholder.

Jane had never had a cellphone as a teenager. Too expensive, too unnecessary as far as her parents were concerned. *What, you're too good for a pay phone?* her dad used to say, whenever Jane asked him for one. As an adult, Jane had to grudgingly admit that her parents had been right. In that era, there really was no reason for it. Jane would call from a friend's house or a payphone if she was going to be late, leaving a message on the house's answering machine. At night, she'd squirrel the cordless handset away, calling Clair as they did their homework together or watched *Wheel of Fortune* in their own separate living rooms, trying to guess the answers over the empty stretch of phone line between them.

But now, here . . . who knows what other kind of differences there might have been? Jane pulled her backpack into her lap as Allison backed out of the parking space, her hand across the headrest of Jane's seat. One by one, Jane opened the pockets and compartments of her bag.

"How come I don't have a phone?"

"What do *you* need a cell for?" Allison said.

"What do *you*?"

Allison didn't answer. She shot Jane a look as she approached a stop sign, rolling through the intersection.

Jane's hand shot out, gripping the dashboard. "Jesus, Allison! You want to try actually *stopping* at one of those?"

"What's your problem today?" Allison said.

"Nothing," Jane managed to creak out.

Clair leaned forward, lowering her voice. "Hey. It was just a stop sign."

Jane forced herself to swallow down the lump of panic in her throat. Forced a nod, forced her fingers to let go of the dash. *Just a stop sign.* She supposed that was true, for someone who'd never been in a fatal car crash like her own Clair had been. Jane would never be able to see it that way. Every missed stop, every ran light, every illegal U-turn, every tailgater, became a trap waiting to spring. Waiting to steal everything away from Jane in a heartbeat. Again. This time, there would be no coming back from it.

"—but if you're really pissed about it," Allison was saying as Jane snapped back to reality, "maybe you shouldn't go around cutting class in the middle of the day. Honestly, Janie. What was *that* about?"

"What other time is there to cut class, except the middle of the day?" Jane said. "It's not like I can cut *after* school."

"Okay, Smarty Pants. Not the point, and you know it."

"Can I make a call?" Jane asked, ignoring this. She picked up Allison's phone from the cupholder before she got an answer, tapping a button to bring the tiny screen to life. She doubted any of the Heroes' numbers would actually work in this world—assuming she could even remember them—but she figured it couldn't hurt to try.

Pixelly text glowed from the display. The time and date, staring back at her.

Jane sucked in a breath. "Oh, *shit*—Ow!" She rubbed the side of her head, where Allison had just flicked hard above her ear.

"Language," Allison said, but Jane barely heard her, couldn't care. Because she knew now they had much bigger problems than Jane's potty mouth.

She stared down at Allison's Nokia, the screen glowing blue-green, blocky text spelling out the date. August 31, 2000. Just over two weeks before the night that, on her Earth anyway, she and Clair had confessed their feelings and shared their first kiss. Two weeks before things between them changed forever, the course of their lives entwining.

Two weeks for Jane to figure out how the hell to set things back to normal.

THE KNOCK ON HER DOOR WAS *SHAVE AND A HAIRCUT*.

Jane sat up fast, the journal she was reading sliding off the bed. She scrambled to retrieve it as the final *two bits* tapped on her door. "Come in!"

The door cracked open, and a much-younger version of her dad's face poked inside. "Hey, hey," Paul said. One hand still on the doorknob, he hovered on the edge of Janie's bedroom. "Just wanted to see how you were doing. I heard there was a little trouble at school today."

His eyes swept over the room as Jane set her journal back on the bed. Papers and mementos spread over the blankets, to the point where there was barely room for Jane herself. She had retreated to her bedroom as soon as Allison had driven them home. Olivia was still at work, thankfully, and Allison hadn't even so much as grunted in acknowledgment as Jane hightailed it up the stairs.

Thus had begun a careful analysis of every difference Jane could find between her own life and this version she'd found herself flung into.

Like everything else, her room was familiar . . . and also not. The walls were covered in her drawings, but not always the same ones Jane remembered. The dresser contained the mess she was known for at that age, both strewn over the top and stuffed into the drawers, though it was impossible to tell if any of it was the same junk she'd thrown there in her own past. In the closet, clothes she remembered mingled with those she didn't. Next came the desk. A dusty computer was nestled into the corner, given to Jane after it had served its time in the dining room as the family PC. Jane hadn't used it much by this point in her own life, but she booted it up anyway because who knows what she might find? She rifled through the desk as she waited, then dug into the back of the closet where she used to keep a box of stuff she didn't want her parents finding. Looking at it now, Jane couldn't understand why the things inside had been considered "private," but she deeply remembered the need to keep it hidden. This is around when she'd settled on the bed, digging out more and more items, more and more memories rising like flotsam to the surface.

By the time Paul had knocked on her door, Jane still didn't have any answers. But she did at least feel a bit more grounded in this time and place, old memories settling around her shoulders like heavy blankets.

Jane looked up now, from the mess to Paul's face. He'd wiped his expression clean, though Jane could see the hidden curiosity about what the hell his daughter was doing tearing her room apart. Jane bristled. The fact that he *didn't* ask was, in some ways, more invasive than if he had.

"It's fine," she said, trying to address both his unspoken question, as well as the one that had apparently drawn him home early—her trouble at school.

"It's not fine, honey. It's not like you to get sent to the principal's office."

Jane scoffed as she studied this version of her dad. "It's not a big deal. Mom's handling it. You didn't have to come home early just for that."

Paul chuckled as he checked his watch. "What are you talking about? It's 6:30."

As if this was normal. As if, at this point in his career, he wasn't staying out until at least nine each night. As if he wasn't using his hours as an excuse to cheat on Jane's mom. As if he actually showed up, put in the time, cared about his family instead.

It was a good effort, she would grant him that. He certainly looked the part of the concerned dad. But Jane would not be so easily fooled. This was Paul Maxwell—always was, always would be.

"Was there anything else?"

A frown crinkled Paul's brow. Now, at least, he looked familiar. He took a breath as if he was going to say something, then seemed to think better of it. He patted the doorframe instead. "Dinner's nearly ready. Why don't you come on down?"

"I'll be there in a minute," Jane said.

Paul tipped his head, not quite sure what to make of that. "Okay," he said finally. "Don't be late, though."

"I won't."

He shut the door behind him. Jane shuddered, as if she needed to shake the whole experience from her system.

A few minutes later Jane left her bedroom. From downstairs, the sounds of Fleetwood Mac drifted up to greet her, familiar notes and lyrics that were woven into her DNA. This was the music of Jane's early childhood, when her parents had still been fairly happy together, when they took long car rides to visit family or go hiking at their favorite park, and Jane would fall asleep in the backseat of the car while this music echoed out from the tape player. Jane couldn't say exactly when it had stopped—the car rides, the music, the happiness—just that it grew more and more infrequent as she'd reached adolescence, until one day it was gone altogether.

Now it reached up to seize her once more, but something about it was wrong. Fleetwood Mac had long since disappeared by the time Jane had been a teenager in her own world. She crept down the stairs, holding her breath. The stereo in the formal living room was playing, Stevie Nicks's voice spilling through the house. Jane toed around the corner toward the kitchen as another voice rose up to greet it. Her dad's, bursting with enthusiasm. He belted out the lyrics, deeper and slightly offkey.

Jane edged closer.

The kitchen doorway frames Paul and Olivia, standing in front of the stove. Paul's hands at Olivia's hips as he encourages her to sway. Musical notes swirl through the kitchen around them, mingling seamlessly with the aroma lines wafting up as Olivia opens the oven. In the next panel, she swats Paul away with an oven mitt. "It's going to burn, dumbass!" she says, the letters soft gray, playful, and the whole page is covered in a haze of loose watercolor as if lifted from a dream. Paul takes the mitts from her and lifts the casserole dish out of the oven, the image centered on the moment he raised it over Olivia's head. His mouth is still open, his eyes nearly closed, as he continues to croon Fleetwood Mac lyrics in his wife's direction. The lyrics follow him over the next panel as he shimmies toward the kitchen table.

Olivia turned, her face flushed. "Oh! Janie!" she said, raising her hands to her heated cheeks. "Good, you're here. Grab the glasses, will you? We're just about ready."

Jane nodded numbly. She crossed through the kitchen, reaching for the cabinet where they'd always kept the glasses—only to be met with a shelf of bowls. Jane shut the cabinet door, hoping no one noticed. Paul was still fussing with the pan, and Olivia had moved toward the hallway.

"Allison!" Olivia hollered. "Get your butt down here if you don't want to starve! I'm not calling you again!"

A sharp reply, too muffled for Jane to make out, barreled down from upstairs. Olivia waved her hand in dismissal, turning away.

Jane pulled another cabinet open at random, relief flooding her as she spotted rows of familiar glasses. She grabbed three, then realized her error when she turned and spotted the table. She snatched another.

Paul smiled across the table at her as Jane laid them out at each of the four place settings.

The rest of them were already seated when Allison burst in a minute later. Moving so fast that her braids flared behind her, papers on the fridge fluttering in her wake. She grabbed herself a Coke and slammed into her chair, popping the top of the can with a snap and a hiss. Allison slurped up the beginning of the soda, ignoring the glass Jane had laid out for her. A portable CD player was strapped to her hip, early earbuds snaking up to both sides of her head. She bobbed and bounced to her own tune, drowning out the seventies folk-rock still pouring in from the living room. Tinny notes seeped out, something fast and angry.

"Allison," Olivia said, "how many times have we asked you not to listen to that at the table? Allison!"

"What?" Allison dragged one of her earbuds out, leveling her mom with a heavy look.

Jane bit her lip to keep from laughing. Oh, but she would enjoy using this against the Allison she knew, once she finally got back.

A soft knot formed in Jane's stomach, the laughter souring in a pit. *If* she got back.

Olivia took a breath and paused a second as if counting to five in her head. "We don't ask much, honey, but dinnertime is family time. Can you please listen to that when we're done?"

Allison rolled her eyes. But she did hit stop on her CD player, and she did pop the other earbud out, even though she made a big show of unplugging them from the player and dropping the cords onto the table. "Happy?"

"Yes, thank you."

"So!" Paul said brightly. He scooped up a sloppy enchilada from the pan on the table, cheese trailing as he laid it gently onto Olivia's outstretched plate. "Who's gonna go first?"

His glance cut sideways toward Jane. Expectant, as if waiting for her to chime in.

Jane sat there, pinned. Was she forgetting some old family ritual? Her mind scrambled, picking through images of old family dinners—what few of them actually materialized, anyway.

Family mealtime had fallen away long before her teenage years, a dusty past Jane had tried not to think about when she was this age, as she'd nuke a TV dinner or eat takeout pizza on the couch by herself. Jane stared at the meal in front of her now, blood rushing in her ears.

"All right, then," Paul said eventually. He turned away. The saucy spatula made circling motions as he shifted his attention across to his wife and then, finally, to his other daughter. "Allison. You're up."

Allison heaved a sigh. "Seriously?"

"Seriously. You know the drill." He stole a fast glance at Jane, before refocusing on his oldest daughter. "One thing from your day. Go."

"Well, there was the time my dad annoyed the crap out of me at the dinner table."

"A *real* thing." Paul slid an enchilada onto her plate.

"That is a real thing."

"Nope," Paul said. "Roll again."

Allison rubbed her forehead, as if this whole exercise was enough to cause her a migraine. "I got an A-minus on my math test," she said finally.

"Oh, honey!" Olivia chimed in. "That's great!"

"An A-*minus*?" Jane said, looking up. The question was out before she could stop herself. "You're happy with that?"

Olivia reached over, folding her hand across Jane's. "Janie, don't be rude. Not everyone is naturally gifted in math like you are."

"I'm *what*?"

Olivia didn't answer, though, her attention still fixed on Allison. "See, I told you that extra studying would help," she said, and Allison snorted.

Jane looked at her sister. True, Jane didn't grow up with a version of Allison in her original life, but she'd learned more than enough in her time since coming to the world of the Heroes— and Allison, the version she was coming to think of as "her" Allison, never accepted standards that were less than perfect in anything.

It was too much.

"Excuse me," Jane said as she stood up from the table. She knew that walking out probably wasn't the best idea, but the kitchen was stuffed with too many implications to consider and puzzles to navigate. The air felt hot all of a sudden, stifling Jane as she made her way toward the door.

"Hold up, young lady," Olivia called after her, and Jane's feet stopped involuntarily. "Where do you think you're going?"

"Um . . . to Clair's?"

"After the stunt you pulled at school? Dream on, missy. Now, if you really don't want dinner right now, fine, you can go to your room and finish your homework. But don't you dare try to sneak any pizza rolls later."

Jane blinked. "Pizza rolls."

"Yes, pizza rolls." Olivia raised her fork, pointing. "Don't think I don't know how many you go through—who do you think restocks the freezer all the damn time?"

Jane shook her head. "Okay. I promise, no pizza rolls."

"Good," Olivia said. "All right, then. You're excused."

"Thanks," Jane mumbled. She took one last look at the room. At Allison, already ignoring her as she snuck the earbuds back in place. At her mom, turning away to resume eating. At her dad— at Paul—as he watched her. The look on his face could almost be called wary, if he'd ever given a damn about her.

Which he didn't.

BY THE TIME THEY CHECKED IN TO THE HOTEL, IT WAS nearly midnight. It had taken Devin and Marie hours to get all the scans of Janie they wanted, and once it was done Janie felt like her whole body had been cataloged—all except for her raging stomach, because they hadn't stopped to feed her.

The hotel was a few blocks away from the high-rise the Heroes operated out of. Janie and Clair walked, a heavy bag slung over Clair's shoulder, Janie hidden behind a giant, floppy hat and a pair of eighties-ugly sunglasses with lenses that hid half of Janie's face. "How am I supposed to see in these things in the dark?" she'd asked when Clair first handed them over, but Clair just smirked, told Janie that wouldn't be a problem.

Janie raised her eyebrow but dutifully switched to them, passing her regular glasses over to Clair to tuck away into a hard-shell case.

To her shock, she could see perfectly. The glasses, ugly as they were, must have been prescription—and the light-based powers in the body she was borrowing apparently did more than just create little flashlight bursts from her fingertips. Janie found she had no difficulty navigating even the darkest street. She spent the whole walk peering into shadowy corners, asking if Clair could see what Janie was pointing to and then nodding in satisfaction when Clair confirmed that no, she could not.

In the lobby, Clair checked them in. "Yeah, I've got an app reservation," she told the receptionist, whatever that meant. She held out a slim black screen she'd said was a phone, though Janie still wasn't sure if that was a joke or not. The receptionist just nodded, scanning the barcode it displayed.

A wide mirror ran along the wall behind the reception desk. Janie studied herself in it as the receptionist tapped away at her computer. She was fitter than she expected to be at this age, old but not *old* old. She turned her head, trying to tell herself that the hat and glasses gave her a vaguely Audrey Hepburn glamour, not really quite believing it.

"Okay, you're all set," the receptionist said. She glanced up, first at Clair and then at her own reflection off Janie's sunglasses. "Maxwell, huh? Any relation to—?"

"No." Clair held her hand out, her palm encased in a navy-blue fingerless glove. The receptionist passed over a set of credit-card-style keys.

"Who did she think I was related to?" Janie asked a moment later, once they were safely tucked into the elevator. "Is there, like, a famous actor named Maxwell now?"

Clair adjusted the weight of the bag on her shoulder. "Something like that."

Janie tried not to be too annoyed at Clair's vague answer. The whole team was being weirdly tight-lipped about details with her. Something about "spoilers," which was a load of crap as far as Janie was concerned. What was the point in getting pulled into essentially the future if you didn't get any hints of what would happen? Besides, it's not like knowing the names of a few celebrities would hurt anyone. Certainly, she'd already learned the biggest secret just by knowing about everyone's superpowers, right? So where was the harm?

But Janie was too tired to fight it. She started to pull her sunglasses off, but Clair's hand found her sleeve, stilling her. "Not yet," Clair said, not even looking at Janie. "Not until we're in the room."

At the eighth floor, they stopped. Clair led the way. When she reached the room, she held one of the cards against the handle until a ring above it turned green, then pushed the door open and motioned for Janie to go through.

"Whoa," Janie said. "This place is *sick*."

The room was basically a studio apartment, cool enough to be something straight out of a movie. Two floor-to-ceiling windows ate up the far wall, a giant flat-screen TV sitting above a fireplace between them. A small but completely functional kitchen sat at the end of the entry hall, all crisp white, natural wood tones, and steel accents. Twin beds were tucked into the far side of the room, overlooking the city. Janie turned in place, gawping as Clair moved past her and set the bag on one of them.

"So, are you loaded or something?" Janie asked. She raced over and threw herself on the other bed, the mattress bouncing delightfully beneath her. A mint tumbled off the pillow; Janie scooped it up and popped it into her mouth. She looked around for a trash can.

Clair took the wrapper from her. "I do all right," she said vaguely, which was a definite *Yes* as far as Janie was concerned. "But honestly, the TV isn't that impressive. Technology has come a long way since your era."

Janie went still, propped up on her elbows. "I didn't . . . I didn't say anything about the TV?"

Clair pinched her nose. Janie could swear a soft "fuck" escaped Clair's lips, barely a whisper. "I'm sorry. My powers . . ." Clair motioned vaguely, trailing lazy circles between them.

Janie's eyes popped. Panic cut a fast track to her heart. "You can *read my mind*?"

"No," Clair said quickly, but then she winced. "I mean . . . yes?

Sort of? It's transferred through physical touch—or touching something you've touched." She raised the mint wrapper, turning her back on Janie as she went to throw it away. "I'm sorry. I don't intentionally spy on people I know."

Slowly, Janie let out her breath. *She didn't mean to,* she told herself. The mint had turned chalky on her tongue, pocked from sitting still, but there was nowhere for Janie to spit it out. She bit down, hoping to break it into small enough pieces to swallow. It was fine. Everything was fine.

Besides, it's not like Janie had been thinking anything she shouldn't be. Admiring the room, the TV. There were a lot worse things Janie's mind could have been circling. She glanced over.

She missed Clair.

Which was stupid, because, like, Clair was *right there*, sitting on a couch across from the TV. All grown up and poised, stunning with her fancy retro haircut and silk blouses and flowing vintage skirts. Even now, in the middle of this weird, mixed-up crisis, even though Janie knew she was stressed, she still looked flawless, not so much as a smudge in her makeup. She was so mature. So *capable.* The way she was handling everything, tapping away on her so-called cellphone, the screen so thin it may as well have been made of glass. Janie always knew Clair had the potential to become someone truly powerful, but to see the way time and maturity would shape her like this . . .

It was awe-inspiring, when you got right down to it.

But it still wasn't *Clair*. Not really. Not the one Janie knew, anyway—the Clair who always smelled of peach body spray, who'd sit on the phone with her for hours as Janie struggled over an essay, who had a fear of bridges and thunderstorms and small, dark spaces.

Janie couldn't imagine this new Clair being afraid of anything.

Janie sighed. All the technological magic of the future couldn't give her what she really wanted, and in its absence, the wonders at her fingertips felt more like distractions. Something put in front of a puppy to keep it from chewing up the sofa.

"I'm hungry."

"Hmm?" Clair didn't look up from the cellphone screen, but she did turn one ear toward Janie.

"Look, I don't know how often you people eat in the future, but you pulled me out of class just before lunch. I haven't eaten all day."

Of course, who knew how recently this body had eaten, though it sure as heck hadn't been since she'd gotten here. In truth, Janie wasn't anywhere near as famished as she expected to be after so many hours, but food still sounded good right now.

"Oh god, Janie—of course, I'm so sorry." Clair fished around in an end table beside the couch, finding the TV remote. This made no immediate sense to Janie, but she got up and joined Clair on the couch anyway, slumping over the armrest so that she landed on her back across the cushion. Clair turned on the TV.

Rather than a channel switching on midprogram, a grid of icons, more like a computer than a TV, filled the screen. Janie watched, fascinated, as Clair navigated across the icons like it was nothing.

"*Parental* controls?" Janie said, incredulous. "I'm not a *kid*."

"You are to me," Clair said as the screen spun while it saved its new settings. "Besides, we don't want you getting exposed to too much of the outside world, remember?"

Janie rolled her eyes. "Yeah, because that would be a disaster."

The screen came back to life. Half the icons were grayed out, a lock symbol blocking access. "It's not up for debate. But here." Clair selected an icon with the same symbol as the hotel chain they were staying at, and passed the remote to Janie as it loaded. "This will let you order room service. Help yourself."

Janie scrambled to sit up. She boggled at the screen, the "room service" icon already lit up. "Wicked," she said with a laugh.

"Yeah, I thought you'd like that one." Clair turned back to her cellphone, already absorbed in what she was doing.

Janie fiddled with the buttons of the remote. "You're not ordering?"

"Not hungry," Clair said. "Besides, I've got way too much to do."

"Like what?" Janie leaned over, but Clair snapped the cellphone against her chest. Janie threw her hands up. "Oh, come on. How much harm can there be in telling me? It's not like anything in the future can be more surprising than superpowers."

Clair's face twitched. She paused, just for a moment, running her finger along the edge of her cellphone as if weighing her next words. "I'm just trying to hold things together at Jane's job. She's . . . important at her company, and she left things kind of abruptly."

Janie sat back in the couch, trying not to puff up with pride. Important. She liked the sound of that, even if it didn't actually tell her anything.

"That's cool," she said, trying to sound casual. The odds of her getting anything more out of Clair right now were pretty low, she knew, and she didn't want to push her luck too badly. She turned her attention to the TV, a seemingly endless menu glowing down at her. Janie grinned, assessing the selection of pizza toppings, the wide array of desserts. *Help yourself,* Clair had said, and so, with the repeated click of a button, Janie did.

EXHAUSTION SMOTHERED JANE AS SHE STUMBLED
down the stairs the next morning.

It would have been nice if sleep had given her a respite from her circumstances, but alas, her dreams had been filled with high school corridors, a desperate race to find Clair, a constant inability to move. All the while, a chilling laugh bounced between the cinder-block walls, crawling over Jane's skin and nuzzling against her ears. There was something haunting about it, almost familiar, as if Jane could rip the mask off their attacker if she could just grab hold. The harsh beeping of her bedside alarm clock was almost a blessing.

The smell of coffee lured her into the kitchen. Jane lurched zombie-style across the linoleum. The world snapped into focus as she blearily slid her glasses onto her face. Paul and Olivia were already there, Paul reading a newspaper at the table, Olivia rinsing out a bowl in the sink. Because of course Jane couldn't have gotten lucky enough to avoid them.

"Janie!" Paul said. He folded the corner of his paper down. "You're up."

Olivia turned, eyebrows shot toward her hairline. "Well! Someone's on her game today."

Jane grunted, the best response she could manage. She took a mug from the tree on the counter and grabbed the coffee pot.

"Excuse me, young lady," Olivia said, her arm shooting out. She snatched the coffee pot from Jane's grasp, so quick that Jane barely had time to process what was happening.

Jane yelped something incoherent, grabbing toward the pot.

"No caffeine until senior year," Olivia said. "It'll stunt your growth."

"But—!"

"*No.*" Olivia raised a sudsy spoon in warning. "You're in enough trouble after yesterday. Don't push your luck."

Jane sneered. "Fine." She shuffled to the back door, grabbing a pair of grubby sneakers off the mat. Exercise wasn't her first choice, but it would do in a pinch. A pair of balled-up socks were stuffed inside the shoes, and Jane tried not to think about how gray they were as she unrolled them, choosing to be grateful that she didn't need to make a trip back upstairs instead. She pulled out a kitchen chair, sitting and sliding the socks onto her feet before she could change her mind.

Paul set down his newspaper, draped over his empty breakfast dishes. He watched as Jane tugged the laces loose in her shoes. "Going somewhere?"

"Just a run."

A cackle burst out of Olivia, snapping through the kitchen like an electric charge. "Oh," she said a second later, when Jane glared at her. "Sorry. Were you serious?"

"Thanks, Mom." Jane turned back to her shoes. "Real supportive."

Olivia didn't bother answering, just tossed an indifferent shrug in Jane's direction. Jane leaned over to finish putting her shoes on.

She was just straightening back up, laces tight, when a familiar sight caught Jane's eye. A photo in one of the sections of the newspaper Paul was already finished with, folded and tucked beneath Paul's coffee mug. Even upside down and rendered on newsprint, the bright red of Captain Lumen's sports car was unmistakable. The twisted wreck she and Clair had left behind was blocked off with police tape. Jane's stomach lurched—she'd forgotten all about the car. Somehow, she'd have to find time to steal away and try to recover it, or at least the most damning of the superhero tech it contained. True, this version of the past wasn't fully *her* past, but that didn't mean she wanted cutting-edge technology working its way into the hands of curious engineers in the year 2000, regardless of which 2000 this was.

"Can I see that?" Jane asked, holding her hand out for the paper. Hopefully, the article would give her some clue as to how much they'd already examined the wreckage, and who might have access to it now.

Paul raised his eyebrow. He followed Jane's gaze down to the photo. "Pretty nasty crash, huh?" he said, drumming his fingers over the picture. "Still want to get your learner's permit?"

Jane rolled her eyes. "Can you just pass me the paper?"

"It's nothing you need to worry about." Paul slid it out from underneath his coffee.

For a second, Jane actually thought he was going to listen to her, but no, of course not. This was *Paul Maxwell* she was dealing with, after all, and since when did he ever care what Jane wanted? Instead of doing the decent thing and handing it across the table to her, he reached down and tucked the newspaper into a leather briefcase by his feet.

"I should get to the office," he said, rising from the table. He walked around to the sink, giving Olivia a quick kiss, and Jane turned away. His hand landed on Jane's head as he passed, tousling her sleep-tumbled hair. "Is your homework all done?"

Jane hesitated. In truth, she hadn't even thought about homework—and why should she? She was a grown woman, as far as she was concerned, and hadn't needed to turn in schoolwork in years. "Yeah, of course," she said hurriedly as she slipped from beneath Paul's hand and his gaze, racing for the back door.

"*Janie*," Olivia said warningly.

"Don't worry, Mom, I've got this," Jane said, letting herself through the door. "Well, gotta go, bye!" She let the door slam shut behind her before anyone else could lecture her. The morning air bit at her cheeks and the back of her exposed knees as she set off across the back porch. Jane moved quickly, ignoring Paul and Olivia's concern for her grades. Even with a quick run, she'd still have time to go through her homework before first period. How hard could it be?

"THAT'S WHAT YOU GET FOR EATING AN ENTIRE PIZZA AND half a chocolate cake by yourself," Clair said. She was leaning against the bathroom doorframe as Janie flushed the toilet and staggered to the sink to wash her face.

"Don't be stupid," Janie moaned. "I've eaten way more than that before."

"Yeah—when you were a *kid*. I tried to tell you last night: you're not that girl anymore. You may still have your own thoughts and personality, but you're living in a mid-thirties body now. The rules are different."

Janie scowled. She didn't entirely believe Clair, though frustratingly, she couldn't think of a good counterargument. Janie had, after all, spent most of the night battling a stomachache.

Clair clapped her hands together, the sound *cracking* through the room and making Janie flinch. "Okay, come on. Get dressed." She turned away, walking back into the main room of their hotel suite.

"Where are we going?" Janie asked, peering around the doorway after her.

"The gym."

A snort of laughter escaped Janie. "No, seriously. Where are we going?"

"The gym," Clair repeated. "You're going to work off all that garbage you ate."

Janie's eyes widened. Crap, she was *serious*? "Oh no. No way."

"Janie."

"Not happening."

"Trust me. I know the rules of this age a lot better than you do. You'll feel better if you get up and work some of that off."

"That is, like, literally the *last* thing I want to do right now. That sounds like torture."

"I know. Welcome to your thirties, kid. Torture is just how it goes."

Janie heaved a sigh, a quiet "ugh" slipping out under her breath.

Could she have protested harder? Probably. Blame her exhaustion, or just her normal habit of listening to Clair when she put on her firm voice. But while Janie continued to grumble, she did pull some clothes from the bag Clair handed her, as instructed, and she did retreat to the bathroom to change, as instructed, and she did put the hat and sunglasses back on, as instructed, and she did stuff her feet into Jane's Converse sneakers, as instructed.

Outside, the first thing that struck Janie was how *loud* the future Grand City was.

Granted, it's not like she often visited the heart of the city on her own world. Most of her life was spent in the tidy suburbs surrounding it, but there were still the usual school trips to the natural history museum and the capitol building. And there was one time when the whole Maxwell family had accompanied her dad downtown while he attended some banquet in a hotel ballroom. Janie had been ten and had felt like someone straight out of a storybook, imagining herself as a poor orphan living with her elderly aunt on the upper floors of the hotel. She was always doing this sort of thing at that age—inventing other lives for herself, full of all the drama and heartache she read about but never understood. They were private games, played out only in her mind, the world seeming to color and illustrate the situation around her as it populated with all sorts of imaginary people and circumstances. That evening, in her best velvet dress left over from the previous Christmas and brand-new polka-dot stockings, she was sneaking down from her apartment to infiltrate a ball being thrown by the crown princess of a remote country tucked into some snowy European mountains, and it was up to Janie, junior detective, to suss out who among them was responsible for a string of murders in the building the week before.

As she trailed behind Clair now, Janie wished she had some sort of game to lose herself in. She wasn't *scared*, she told herself—she was fifteen, after all, hardly a child anymore. And no matter how weird and improbable this whole situation was, she was determined to handle it with all the maturity she could muster. Still, it would have been nice if she had something familiar to ground herself to.

That something should have been Clair. By rights, if anything was going to be recognizable in this upside-down world that wouldn't exist for another twenty years, it would be her. Time difference or no, Janie and Clair had been best friends for as long as either of them could remember.

Instead, she'd been acting . . . just *off*.

Clair always enjoyed walking with Janie. To and from school when the weather was nice and they had time to kill; wandering aimlessly around the mall on weekends; to a quiet little diner for study sessions when they had a big project or test coming up. They didn't need to talk, though they did plenty of talking, too. But even in silence, there was a companionable air between them, an unspoken ease.

Not today. The adult version of Clair moved through the city with a purpose that Janie could barely keep up with. She wanted to reach out, grab Clair's hand. She even started to, but just before Janie's fingers could twine with Clair's, Clair had stepped wide, avoiding something on the sidewalk, and Janie pulled back, heat burning her cheeks. She couldn't prove that Clair had done it on purpose. But the rebuke stung just as sharply as if she had.

Finally, on the subway, they were able to pause for a moment.

They sat beside each other, close but not too close, the only two people in their half of the subway car. Janie took a moment to catch her breath, though honestly, she was surprised she wasn't more winded. Instead, her muscles felt . . . stretched, in a warm, good sort of way. Which was weird, because Janie hated exercise, and she was loath to think Clair might actually have been right about "working off" some of the cake Janie had eaten the night before. But her stomach *did* feel better, darn it.

Not that Janie was going to admit that. Instead, she cleared her throat.

"So, um. What's the nightmare scenario?"

Clair blinked in confusion as she turned to Janie. "I'm sorry?"

"The nightmare scenario," Janie repeated. "Yesterday, when we were in the lab? Marie said since you had the signature to track down my world, this wasn't the nightmare scenario, but that—"

"Okay, yes," Clair snapped. She fidgeted in her seat. "I remember now."

"Well? What is it?"

Clair turned her head away, staring out the subway windows. She didn't say anything for a while. Long enough that Janie worried she'd said the wrong thing. Again. Janie had only been trying to make conversation, to understand her situation a little better. It was a question that had risen within her somewhere in the middle of the night, while her stomach had been roiling. Yet somehow, without even realizing it, Janie had messed things up. It was like she barely even knew her best friend anymore. Or, no, it was more than that. If Clair had simply changed, Janie felt sure she could navigate the differences better. It was more like Clair was reacting to Janie herself, rather than anything Janie was saying.

Her stomach tightened. What had *happened* to the two of them, in the long years between when this Clair was her Clair and now?

"Traveling between parallel worlds . . . it's not exactly the same as hopping on a plane to London," Clair said finally, drawing Janie from her thoughts. "I mean, even back before the world was fully mapped and explored, there were still only so many places you could be, you know? The planet's huge, and good luck finding one tiny individual if you don't know where to start, but theoretically, given enough time and assuming the person you're looking for stayed put . . . someone could *eventually* find them, right? Like, they've got to be somewhere, and there's technically only so many places that somewhere could be."

"Sure."

"Okay . . ." Clair still wasn't looking at Janie, talking instead to the pole between their seats. "So the difference here, is that parallel worlds are literally infinite. Which means if you get lost . . . even if your team had millions of years to spend on it, and they were super methodical and checked off every parallel world they came across one by one, there's still no guarantee they'd ever end up on the world you got lost on. Or they could find you on the first try. There's really no way to know."

Janie sat back, absorbing this.

Nothing Clair said was *news* to Janie, no. Not technically. Janie was familiar enough with both science fiction and pop-culture science to understand the concept of parallel worlds. Devin had spent a winter obsessed with them, in fact, digging around the internet and the library and correcting the group on common misconceptions, none of which Janie remembered anymore. So she knew the spread of parallel worlds was, technically, *infinite*, but now, rocked by the sway of the subway car, she was starting to understand what it meant.

"That's not really what I'd consider the nightmare, though," Clair said, more to herself than to Janie. She paused, closing her eyes for a moment as if she was wondering if she should even continue. Even once she did, her words were measured, doled out with a spoon.

"For me . . . the real nightmare would be how long do you keep searching? Because what if you decide it wasn't worth it, that you'd realistically never find her, only it turns out you gave up just one world too soon? How do you *ever* decide when to quit?" Clair's brow tightened, and her voice caught as she added in a whisper, "I don't think I ever could."

She turned away again, but not before Janie caught the beginning of a blush creeping into Clair's cheeks.

"But you have my signature," Janie said. "Or . . . the one from my world. So you can find it."

Who was she reassuring here? She wasn't sure she knew.

Clair paused. Just for a second, like a hitch in her breath. "That narrows it down, yes."

Before Janie could say anything else, an announcement chimed overhead, a voice too polished to be real telling the passengers the next stop. Clair didn't even wait for the subway car to slow down before she was back on her feet, one hand gripping the overhead rung for support. Like she couldn't get away from the conversation fast enough. For once, Janie didn't blame her.

A brisk walk up the stairs, and now they emerged into a wide city plaza. Basically a park made of brick, from the stone benches to the fountain to the handful of sculptures. A few small triangles of dying grass gave a feeble attempt at nature, along with a couple of trees confined to huge planter boxes. Clair was already several feet ahead, striding through the city with ease.

A scream split the noise of the city just as Janie started after her.

Janie staggered back as a literal, honest-to-god monster leaped across the plaza. She craned her neck, staring at its underbelly. Scales and talons and muscle—the torso of a man, the legs and tail of a T. rex. It was there and gone again in a flash, and before she could even begin to process what was happening, Clair's fingers snared tightly around Janie's wrist. A blistering sense of urgency raced into her. "This way. Now!"

Janie didn't argue. She clutched her hat, the brim flapping. They ran back down the stairs, ducking into the subway platform.

"In here." Clair dragged Janie through a door, into a wall of odor so foul it reeled Janie back onto the main platform.

"Oh god! You can't be serious."

But she was, as serious as the funk coming out of the restroom behind her. Clair yanked Janie in.

Janie's shoes stuck to the tile floors with each step. She tried to take shallow breaths, and when that wasn't enough, she grabbed the top of her shirt and stuffed her face behind the collar.

"What the heck was that thing?"

Clair did a quick check of the stalls. "Doesn't matter. You'll be safe here until I get back."

"What, you're going back out there?" As much as she hated the prospect of being trapped in a disgusting public bathroom, the thought of being trapped in a disgusting public bathroom *all by herself* was somehow ten times worse. "Did you see that thing? It was . . . it was . . . ."

"My job," Clair said. Already she was digging into the pockets of her coat and drawing out a black mask to ring her eyes. "And nothing I haven't dealt with before, believe me."

Try as Janie might, she couldn't think of a reasonable argument. It didn't matter anyway, because Clair didn't give her the chance. The door slammed shut with a resounding thud. Panic prickled from the tips of Janie's fingers to the base of her feet.

Under ordinary circumstances, Janie would take a couple of deep breaths to try to calm down. It's what her mother always told her to do, and darn if it didn't work. That wasn't exactly an option here, and suddenly she was enraged that this was the only trick she knew. Furious, she turned to the mirrors—and nearly screamed at what she saw.

Her reflection was disappearing, bit by bit like she was being erased. For a second, all Janie could do was stand there, fear and awe seizing her in equal measure. It was done in an instant, so fast she could barely react. Here one second, gone the next.

Sort of. She was still *here*, she reassured herself, at least in some capacity, otherwise how would she be able to see her lack of reflection? Unless that, too, was a trick? Quickly, before she could doubt herself too much, she pushed down on the top of the faucet. Water spurted out, the metal cold and vaguely slimy under her touch. So, not a ghost or whatever. That was good to know. But if she was still *here*, just somehow strangely invisible, then that must mean . . .

A smile crept up Janie's face, known only from the pull of her muscles.

Now *this* was a superpower she could get behind.

TURNS OUT, HOMEWORK WAS HARDER THAN JANE WANTED to admit.

"Goddammit," she mumbled. She was hunched over her desk. Homeroom, before first period. She stared down at the worksheet in front of her, her mind blanking. Beside that was a half-finished essay that, according to her planner, was also due today. The start of it was great—Janie had clearly put a lot of thought into it—but Jane sure as shit had no idea where it should go from there. Jane drummed her pen against the desk, her frustration brewing hot just beneath the surface.

"Brainy Janie!"

A body slammed into the desk behind her, the force hitting the back of her chair.

Jane gritted her teeth as she turned around. Cal, as she remembered him from her youth, grinned back at her. Zitted face made to look wider than it really was by the buzzed haircuts his mother gave him once a month. Baggy, stonewashed jeans from Goodwill. A washed-out T-shirt, black faded to gray, from when Foo Fighters went on tour in 1997. The braided cord of a necklace poked out from the neckline, once off-white but long since darkened to muddy tan—god, Jane had forgotten he used to wear that thing, refusing to ever take it off. A pair of cheap sunglasses was propped on his head, as if he was ready to sprint down to the beach. As usual, he was chewing gum for breakfast, ready to spit it out as soon as the teacher yelled at him for it.

Cal motioned at Janie's planner. "Whatcha drawing?"

Jane glanced down, startled. In the stress of figuring out her schoolwork, she'd started sketching on the corner of the page without realizing it. Now a shaky rendition of Clair's face—her grown-up face—stared back at her. Jane covered it with her fingers. "Nothing. Just a doodle."

Cal snapped his gum. "She's hot."

"Don't you have homework to do or something?"

He barked a sharp laugh. "Yeah, okay, Mom. I'll get right on that." Cal turned, digging a pen out of his backpack. With a grin, he leaned forward, trying to scribble along Jane's shoulder.

Jane jerked away. "What the hell, Cal?"

"Oh, come on, lighten up." He got up and settled instead in the chair beside her, his legs spread wide in the aisle, his arm thrown casually over the backrest.

Jane returned to her homework. She breathed in deep, counting to ten. It wasn't his fault, really, she told herself—Cal was obnoxious in any reality, and here he hadn't yet grown up enough to know he was doing it.

A pen tapped her on the arm. "So," Cal said. "My mom wanted me to find out if your rates are gonna be the same."

A careful stillness settled over Jane, her superhero training kicking in. When sparring with villains, it was important not to tip your hand, especially if you didn't know something. Not that Cal was a villain—he'd gotten that phase out of his system a few years ago, reset by a careful memory wipe from Clair. And this wasn't even the same Cal, years too young to be remotely tempted down a dark path.

Still. With Cal, any Cal, sometimes the impulse was hard to shake. "I . . . haven't quite decided yet."

"Oh. That's cool." Cal flipped his pen back and forth between his fingers, the ends tapping madly against the desk as he see-sawed it. "It's just, you know. She wants to get a jump on things. You saved my ass last year for Algebra, and I guess she assumes I'll need it again."

Jane blinked, the pieces clicking together. "I tutored you. In math."

Cal laughed. "Yeah." He leaned forward, his breath souring Jane's mood as he flashed a grin. "Though if there's anything *else* you want to add to your curriculum this year, you know, I wouldn't complain."

Jane opened her mouth, a sharp retort on her tongue, but Cal was literally saved by the bell. The door banged open, and a group of students poured into the room. Cal slid from his seat, sauntering to the front corner, where the alphabet had fated him a place by the teacher's desk. He spat his gum into the trash can as he went, the glob *thunking* against the metal base.

The next few hours passed in a blur, remembered only in fragments. Jane's hand, cramped tightly around her pencil as she scribbled furious notes. A close-up of the sweat on her forehead, her brows scrunched tight beneath it. Her eyes glancing anxiously at the clock, and then again a few panels later, to see it had somehow only moved an inch. The *briiiiiing* of the bell ran like an intermittent banner across her life, slices that were broken up by packs of gray students and dense shots of legs shuffling between classes.

Finally, *finally*, her lunch hour arrived.

She made her way toward the cafeteria, her stomach clawing up toward her ribs. God, she'd forgotten how *hungry* she'd been as a teenager. Ordinarily, she'd be able to go until almost two before she even started thinking about food, but now? Jane had stuffed two full-sized candy bars from the vending machine down her gullet between second and third period, and she was still ravenous.

Clair was waiting for her by the door. They only had one class together before lunch, a fact that used to throw a pall over Jane's whole morning. Clair wasn't looking as Jane approached, but then she turned, spotted Jane, and her whole body lit up. Jane bit her lip. God, how did it honestly take a young Jane as long as it did to realize they were mad for each other? It was so *obvious* now, looking at it from the other side.

"Hey," Clair said as they got in line. "How was your morning?"

Jane picked up her tray, and Keisha and Marie got in line behind them. They greeted each other without ceremony.

"It was fine," Jane said. She regarded the spread in front of her. When she was a teenager, she thought the *one* good thing about her high school was that at least they had a pretty cool cafeteria, especially compared to some other districts. There was a standard Hot Lunch line, sure, but only the poor kids lined up there. For everyone else, a buffet of options lay before them, a collection of base foods available every day, with a rotating entrée on a set schedule. Jane moved past trays of chicken nuggets, buckets of fries, a rolling rack of shriveled hot dogs.

Clair reached out, shoveling some of the chicken nuggets onto her tray. She started to pass the tongs over to Jane. "What about Mrs. Fenton?"

Jane raised her hand. "Oh, no, thank you."

Clair raised her eyebrow, but set the tongs down as Jane racked her brain for what Clair could have been talking about. Mrs. Fenton was Janie's German teacher. In her own world, Jane and Clair had taken French together, four years straight through, just so Jane could listen to Clair as she twisted her tongue around all those vowels. She still didn't understand what this world's Jane had done so wrong to get stuck in German, but *c'est la vie*.

They inched down the line. The fried food gave way to a basket of the largest muffins Jane had ever seen, and then, wedged between that and the entrée almost as an afterthought, a scant collection of salads in clear clamshell plastic.

Jane grabbed one.

"Um, what are you doing?"

Jane looked up. Behind her, Keisha was staring at Jane as if she'd grown three heads, and Marie was laughing openly.

"What?" Jane asked.

Clair nudged her elbow. "Jane, it's pizza day," she said softly.

Jane turned. Ahead of them, trays of square pizza slabs oozed grease beneath a set of heat lamps. Jane remembered loving them as a teenager, attempting to pile them just so that the cashier wouldn't notice if she'd snuck two, but now . . .

"Yeah, I think I'm good," Jane said. She stole a vanilla yogurt from the nearby cold case.

"Girl, don't tell me your skinny butt is going on a diet," Keisha said.

"Yeah," Marie said, "you're not suddenly anorexic, are you?"

"Marie!" Clair gasped.

"What? It's a fair question."

"Sure," Keisha said, "but that is *not* how you go about asking someone a thing like that."

"I'm not *anorexic*," Jane said. "And I'm not going on a diet. I just . . . I wanted a salad, okay? Why's this such a big deal?"

"Um, because you hate salads?" Marie said. "You call them rabbit food?"

"Oh my god," Jane said, exasperation staining her breath. She grabbed a bag of cheese Doritos and threw it onto her tray. "Are you happy now?"

"I never *said* you couldn't eat salads," Marie said. "God."

"Can we please just pay?" Clair asked. "We're holding up the line."

Jane lifted her tray. "Yes, *please*."

They went to the registers, Jane attempting to juggle her tray as she slipped a few rumpled bills from the pocket of her jeans. "I've got it," she said when Clair was given her total, because this at least she remembered: Jane covered Clair's lunches more often than not.

And then it was just a matter of following the tide. Like a school of fish, the group of them navigated the choppy waters—dodging flung trash and tossed insults. Halfway down the cafeteria, where their favorite table lay, they met up with the others, and the seven of them settled into their familiar places.

All but Clair—as Jane looked up, the chair across from her sat empty.

Jane whipped her head around. Clair was a few feet away, standing near a trash can in the center of the cafeteria traffic. She craned her neck as if looking for something, and then her face lit up as she spotted it.

"Hey!" Clair called, waving. "Over here!"

As if on cue, the crowds parted, and a *girl* stepped forward. She grinned, hurrying across the cafeteria to Clair's side.

Clair brought the girl over to the table, her cheeks tinted the slightest pink. She motioned at her friends.

"Guys, this is Hailey. She's new in my homeroom. Hailey, you've already met some of them, but this is Keisha and Devin and Janie."

Hailey turned, a dazzling smile washing over the table. Jane's mind froze, the image of her instantly filling in with inked outlines and vibrant markers. A slanted text bubble, *HAILEY,* slid into the corner, before the whole thing filtered instantly back to the real world as Hailey took her seat.

She was the poster girl for a young lesbian's vision of themselves. An Ellen DeGeneres pixie cut, dyed Tori Amos red. Maroon lipstick. The stud of a nose ring twinkling like a playful wink. She wore pinstripe pants and shoes with spats, and a neat little waistcoat over a dark purple silk shirt. A metal necklace hung down to her navel, and chunky rings adorned her fingers. It was a style far more polished than any real person had the right to look, especially a teenager—she may as well have just stepped from the pages of *Out* magazine.

And she sat down right beside Clair.

Jane's hand tightened around her plastic fork.

"So what's the deal with starting just *after* the school year?" Tony asked as everybody began to dig into their grease-topped stacks of pizza.

"Oh," Hailey said. "My dad's job. They transferred him, but there were, like, *so many* delays with the move, it's not even funny. We just got into town yesterday."

Clair brightened. "Hailey's from *California.*"

"Wow, really?" Keisha asked.

Hailey waved this off. "San Francisco, yeah. It's no big deal."

Tony snorted. "Tell that to someone who grew up *here.*"

"Seriously," Devin said. "I'd love to go someplace like California."

Cal raised a fry in Hailey's direction. "Yeah, but isn't everybody, like, gay in California?"

Jane glanced up, Clair glanced down. Hailey glanced at Jane. Nobody else seemed to notice.

"Cal!" Keisha chided.

"What?" Cal said around a mouthful of fry. "I'm just saying, I think there's a lotta gay out there, and I mean I'm not exactly up for being hit on by a bunch of guys all the time."

"Yeah, because you're so attractive to gay men," Devin said, rolling his eyes.

"You don't know! You don't know! I mean, I'm a good-looking guy."

"Wait, let me get this straight," Marie said. She raised a hand, trying to hold off Cal's objections. "You *really* think they're just going to see you, they're going to take one look at you, and they're going to get *so* horny they swarm you?"

"What?"

"Is that what you're saying?"

"No!" Cal scowled. "I didn't say that."

"It kinda sounded like that's what you said," Keisha said.

Cal scoffed. He tossed a fry across the table, but Keisha ducked at the last second, and it flew, unceremoniously, over her shoulder. Clair watched it land.

"I did *not* say that. I just don't want a dude hitting on me. Is that so wrong?"

"Statistically, they're like ten percent of the population, bro," Devin said. He ran his hands over his tight curls as he thought for a second, just long enough for Jane to wonder if this was the year he'd become obsessed with statistics. "Which means there's gotta be at least, what, fifteen or so gay guys in this cafeteria right now? Are you worried about getting hit on here?"

"That can't be right," Tony said.

Devin shrugged. "Do the math."

"*Pfft.* There are no gays in Central Oak," Cal said.

Hailey smirked. Clair continued to study the congealing cheese of her pizza.

Marie pointed across the cafeteria. "What about Gavin?"

"Yeah, *other* than Gavin, obviously. I mean, like, everyone else. You know. Normal people."

"*Normal* people?" Jane said. It came out before she could stop herself, a reflex from years spent in the open. Only now did Clair look up, though she still kept her head ducked, staring at Jane through the loose tendrils around her face. Their eyes locked, mirrored panels stacked on top of each other as the rest of the cafeteria fell away.

Hailey cleared her throat. "I'm bi."

Silence screeched over the table like a record scratch. And just like that, the page between them was ripped out. One by one, all the friends turned toward the new girl.

Cal slapped Devin's shoulder. "You see! California!"

"Ow," Devin muttered. "Dude, not cool."

"Okay, but when you say you're bi," Marie said, leaning over the table so that her voice wouldn't carry, "like, you'd do a guy . . . or a girl?"

"*That's* hot," Cal said, and now it was Devin's turn to hit him. "Ow!"

Hailey shrugged. "Yeah. Or whoever."

"What else is left?" Marie asked, laughing under her breath.

"Have you actually done it, though?" Clair asked before Hailey could answer. "Kissed a . . . a girl?"

The whole table turned back to Hailey, holding their breath. All except for Jane, who was watching Clair and grinding her teeth at the way Clair was trying desperately not to watch Hailey for an answer.

Hailey grinned. "Yeah."

"Ugh," Marie said, turning away.

"So hot," Cal repeated.

Devin hit him again. "Dude, didn't you *just say* you didn't like gays?"

"I said I didn't want to get hit on by a guy. This," he said, pointing at Hailey, "is very different." He licked his lips.

Jane turned away, her face twisted into an open gag. As she was shifting her attention back to her food, though, her eyes were drawn up.

Clair was staring at her, a weird little pinch on her lips.

Jane froze. She glanced at Hailey, then back at Clair. "No, that wasn't about the idea of a girl—"

The screech of a bullhorn cut her off. Jane winced, and the table turned around until they spotted a group of student council prep-types, standing at the end of the cafeteria, trying to get everyone's attention.

Hailey leaned over, whispering something to Clair.

"Okay, just a couple of quick announcements," the head of the student-council types was saying. "As you all know, Homecoming is coming up in three weeks. I'd like to remind you all that the sooner you buy your tickets, the sooner we'll know how much we've raised for our annual field trip, so please, let's get the spirit out there. Second . . ."

Clair and Hailey stood up, trays in hand. "I'll catch you after English," Clair whispered across to Jane.

Jane's mouth dropped open. "Wait, but—!"

But Clair was already gone, swallowed up by the disinterested crowd. And all Jane could do was sit there and watch the place where she'd disappeared.

With her.

THE POWERS MUST HAVE KICKED IN DURING THE PANIC OF the situation, some survival instinct in Janie's borrowed muscles that remembered how to do this even if Janie didn't consciously have control over it.

For a moment, Janie forgot all about the chaos raging outside. She stood there distracted by her empty reflection, laughing at the weird rush of vertigo that washed over her when she looked down and saw absolutely nothing. What a totally weird delight. She raised her arms, and a subtle tickle brushed against her, the light hugging tight like a second skin.

The beginning of an idea crept up Janie's spine. If she was invisible . . . then surely it had to be safe for her to go outside. Or at least get out of this foul-smelling bathroom.

She rushed through the door without any further internal debate, but the stench was so entrenched that it simply up and walked out of the bathroom with her. If she truly wanted it gone she'd probably need a shower and a change of clothes, but at the very least getting outside would air the situation out.

It was a poor excuse, and Janie knew it. She just wanted to get out there and see what was going on for herself. Probably, an adult would tell her that she was being irresponsible and reckless —they might even call her a child. Whatever. There were no adults here, not even the one staring at her in the mirror anymore.

Besides, how was she going to get in trouble if no one could see her? Really, it was safer to be out there, invisible and able to know what was going on, than trapped in a windowless bathroom with only one way in or out. What if one of the monsters came down into the subway?

That was a good justification anyway, at least good enough to propel her back to street level.

Outside was like the scene of a disaster movie. One of those summer blockbusters where aliens were invading and the world needed some ragtag group of heroes to pull off a ridiculous space stunt in order to save humanity. Trees were ripped from their planters, benches and trash cans overturned. People were running everywhere, screaming. Janie expected billows of newspapers to tumbleweed across the open plaza, abandoned, though that particular detail was weirdly missing. Instead, a tangle of empty cardboard coffee cups rolled away from a trash can like rats escaping the Titanic.

Janie kept close to the buildings, trying to stick to the outskirts. True, no one could see her, but that didn't mean she should be careless. She had no delusions about being able to actually fight off such a freakish creature. Really, she just wanted another look at the thing.

As if summoned, a monster roared and went flying over one of the few trees still standing. A little larger than a person, its heavy lizard tail whipped past as it landed. Cement cracked beneath its back feet, talons chipping away bits of sidewalk as it took off again. The whole thing was covered in shimmery green scales, from its lizard head to its burly, man-like arms, to its clawed feet.

Janie darted to the side. She ducked behind a stone planter, instinct making her seek cover even though she was invisible. The monster roared again as it landed hard, then swung its head toward a group of pedestrians cowering nearby. The taste of vomit hit the back of Janie's throat. She peered around the planter, her mind already dishing up images of gore and devastation.

But that didn't happen. Because just then a shimmering beam of light ran down the middle of the plaza, like a tear splitting the skin of the world, and the Heroes poured through.

Clair, of course, must have been there from the beginning, was probably even the one to alert the others of the danger. She cut across the spill of the new arrivals, drawing the monster's attention away from the pedestrians. Even in costume, Janie recognized her easily—well, it helped that she was wearing the same coat. Janie watched in awe as she dipped into a side sweep, a vintage-looking gun leading the way. She fired off two quick shots, bullets sinking deep into the thigh of one of the monsters, who roared as it crashed to its side.

She was joined by Marie, and now Janie understood why she'd heard them call her Granite Girl. Stony arms led the way as she crashed onto the scene like a bowling ball.

The next one she spotted came swooping in from the sky. Devin, in his Windforce bodysuit, blue-and-white flaps of fabric running from wrists to ankles like a flying squirrel. Even his face was covered, a full spandex mask slightly puffed in the back from the bun he'd stuffed his hair into. Hot on his heels, a whirl of color leaped onto the scene, expanding to full size as she somersaulted in. Keisha's Pixie Beats's style was easy enough to recognize, a whirling mix of neon and denim fluttering through the air. The two of them ushered the pedestrians away from the scene.

The rest of the Heroes poured in as a group and now, before she knew it, they were all here. Or at least, Janie was pretty sure that was all of them, since Tony, or Rip-Shift, in his Matrix coat zipped up the shimmering tear of light behind him. Still, it was hard to keep track in the middle of the action. No sooner would she spot one racing by on the heel of the monster than she'd lose sight of them when another swept in to land their own dizzying attack.

Because the Heroes weren't the only ones to arrive. As Janie watched, a strange roar filled the air—not quite a scream, not quite a whistle, something high-pitched and almost on the edge of hearing, a piercing *SKREEEE* that split the plaza. The Heroes turned, as five more monsters leaped down from the roofs of nearby buildings.

One of the lizard men landed in front of her, the sidewalk cracking beneath him. Janie gasped.

Its head swung in her direction. Yellow eyes swept over and past Janie, sideways lids snapping as it tried to locate the source of the noise. It huffed in a breath, its nose lifting as it sniffed for its prey. A thin tongue flicked from its mouth, tasting the air.

To heck with playing possum. Janie turned and ran. She didn't know if it was smart, didn't care. Fear had propelled her, her legs bounding forward with surprising ease down the sidewalk. Wind snatched her hat, but what difference did that make? She ran in the direction of the subway. Suddenly, the stinky bathroom didn't sound so bad.

If she was looking where she was going, maybe she would have made it. Instead, she made the mistake of glancing back, and in that moment she collided with someone—a random passerby, gawking at the chaos. They bounced off each other with an *oof* and a loud grunt, the man merely setting his foot back to catch his balance, Janie falling to her butt on the cold sidewalk. Her sunglasses clattered to the pavement beside her.

"The fuck?" the man shouted—an understandable reaction, since he'd just crashed into something he couldn't see. That would have made sense, except that when Janie looked up he was staring at her. Directly at her, no question as to that. Janie raised her hand, gaping in horror as a ghostly version of it began to turn solid and whole and very, very visible.

She scrambled to her feet, grabbing her sunglasses and jamming them back on her face. "Sorry, I . . . Sorry," Janie stammered. She ran off before the man could respond, before he could react to her sudden appearance.

Too late. A monster ran across Janie's path, talons scraping up pavement as it skidded to a halt. Completely blocking the subway steps. It turned its scaly head, beady eyes narrowing in.

Fear pierced Janie's heart. She wasn't invisible anymore, and even though she'd never experienced that particular gift before, suddenly without it she felt completely naked. She ducked, squeezing her eyes shut and throwing her arms over her head.

In hindsight, it wasn't the best move. But Janie wasn't a trained Hero, didn't know any combat moves, didn't even consider herself particularly brave. And so, faced with a threat she couldn't have even imagined the day before, the small, scared part of herself won out, and she curled into a ball like a helpless little mouse.

Timing and chance saved her. A flurry of movement gusted past, distracting the monster just as it was about to lunge forward and claim its prize. Janie peered through her fingers in time to see the monster whirl, snapping at this new foe. Unfortunately, its thick tail swung behind it; it caught Janie's side, sending her flying. She landed hard a few yards away, pain searing across her back and the palm of her hand.

Panic blanked her mind. For a moment, all she could do was lie there, the searing pain in her back and her hand overriding all but the hot tears spilling across her cheeks.

She wanted her mom. She was fifteen, dammit, too old for such childish impulses, but the need to be held overrode even the shame of that urge. She wanted someone to wrap their arms around her. Make soothing sounds against her hair. Tell her everything was going to be okay. Take the burden of choice out of her hands, fix the situation while she sat on the sidelines with a blanket around her shoulders and a mug of cocoa warming her.

So when a pair of hands gripped her shoulders, easing her over, it was at first a relief. Until the words reached her, a slap to jolt the life back into Janie.

"I told you to stay in the restroom!"

Janie shoved Clair off her. Fear and guilt flared hot into anger. "One of those things came in there!"

The lie came without thought. Spat in rage, it landed, sizzling, at Clair's feet.

Clair reeled back. For a second, Janie almost regretted it. Almost took it back. Almost told the truth. But then Clair whirled, grabbing Rip-Shift's passing wrist, stilling him as he tried to race by. She jerked her head toward Janie, still huddled on the ground like a broken bird. "Get her back to headquarters."

"But—!" Rip-Shift started. He was already motioning at the rest of the plaza, the monsters churning through the crowd, but Clair cut him off.

"The rest of us will take care of that."

Her face was already darkening, like some terrible storm cloud brewing on the horizon. Her fingers twitched, still wrapped around the sleeves of his black trench coat. Rip-Shift glanced down, at the exposed skin of Clair's fingertips, the proximity to his own naked wrist. His eyes widened for just a second, terror skirting around the edges, but then Clair's grip relaxed, her face softening.

"Just get her out of here," she said, her voice pleading, bordering on desperate. She met his eyes, her masked ones reflecting against the lenses of his sunglasses. "Please."

Rip-Shift nodded, and only then did Clair fully withdraw her hand. She broke away, launching herself into the battle as if she couldn't bear to look at Janie any longer.

Janie sat up straighter, gritting her teeth against the pain tearing through her back. She didn't want to be seen as small, weak, terrified—didn't matter that this was true. Already some muscle memory of the hero Jane was seemed to be pulling at her, telling her to stand her ground, stay and fight.

But Rip-Shift was already moving. He scooped her into his arms before she could even squawk in protest, cradling her like a new bride as he flicked one lazy finger and a rip split the skin of the world. "Trust me, you do *not* want to fight her on this one," he said. They plunged through a shimmering tear, leaving the screams of the plaza behind them.

THE GARAGE DOOR RATTLED AS JANE DRAGGED IT DOWN.
She caught her foot on the handle and pushed it shut the last few
inches, making sure the seal was firm against the cement, then
turned the stiff latch until it clicked into place. Even at the time,
garage door openers were plenty widespread, but Jane's parents
hadn't invested in one yet—in either world, apparently.

Her bike was already waiting for her on the driveway. As a
superhero, Jane kept up a vigorous fitness regimen, but it had
still been ages since she'd been on a bicycle. Briefly, she'd worried that her muscles would be sore against the unfamiliar seat
and motions, until she remembered that her teenage self had
ridden on them all the time, and this body belonged to her. She'd
probably be fine.

"Hi, Janie!"

Jane yelped, spinning around. Clair stood in the driveway, her
hair split into unevenly braided pigtails and a cautious expression on her face. She tucked her hands into the back pockets

of her jeans, where Jane knew she was hooking and twisting the fabric with her thumbs. It was a nervous tic she'd had as a teenager, one that turned the butts of all her pants saggy. Jane had almost forgotten about it.

"Are you . . . going somewhere?" Clair asked, eventually, after Jane had just stood there, hand on her bike handle, staring at Clair for several long seconds.

Jane's cheeks flushed as she looked away. She swung her leg over her bike. "Tutoring," she told the pavement beneath them. It was the lie she'd already prepared for Olivia, Paul, and the uninterested Allison, who'd barely glanced up as Jane passed through the house, calling out her intention.

"Oh." Clair reached up, scratching just below her ear. "On a Friday?"

"Yeah, well, you know—gotta hustle, if you wanna get ahead, right? Anyway, I . . . Oh," Jane said as things clicked into place. "*Friday.*"

For all the attention Jane had been paying to the sleepover two weeks from now, where they admitted their feelings and everything changed between them, she hadn't stopped to consider that the Janie and Clair on this world might have a slightly different schedule.

"Right . . . ," Jane continued, testing the waters. "I thought . . . I'm sorry, my schedule's so mixed up, I thought our next sleepover wasn't for a few weeks."

Immediately, Jane knew she'd done something wrong. Clair's brow drew together in the middle. "Janie . . . we do this every week?"

Jane rocked back in surprise. Every week? The most Jane's real parents would allow was once a month. But, as Jane was painfully aware, this wasn't really her past. And here, apparently, she was bailing on Clair.

Part of Jane considered staying. Just for a moment. Putting her bike away, laughing this mistake off. Popping in a movie and microwaving some snacks, and settling into the familiar memory of how these evenings were supposed to go.

But how could she possibly? Clair was *fifteen*. And sure, it wasn't like Clair would expect to get *up* to anything with her, that wouldn't start happening until after the night that loomed over Jane's timetable. But even before then, there had been such an easy intimacy between them. There was no way Jane would be able to keep Clair from realizing something was fundamentally different about her now—not when it was just the two of them.

Jane took a breath. She forced the words out, like knives coming up her throat. "Listen, I'm really sorry, but . . . can we maybe skip this one?"

Clair's face faltered, just for a second, before she caught herself. "Um . . . I mean, yeah, sure, if . . . if you want to."

"No, well, I don't *want* to, of course. Only, it's just, something's come up—an emergency—and I've got to go . . . take care of . . . the emergency."

One eyebrow ticked up, a look that so perfectly mimicked the woman Clair would become that it slayed Jane's heart. "A tutoring emergency?"

". . . Yeeees," Jane said slowly. "That's . . . exactly it. I said tutoring, and so, yes, it *is* a tutoring emergency. Big test coming up. Very unexpected. Anyway, I've gotta go."

She ducked her head, fumbling with her bike. It was the stupidest excuse she'd ever given, and Jane had made up a *lot* of dumb excuses over the years. But she couldn't walk it back, and she couldn't change it, so all she could do was try to outrun the shame. Jane kicked off, pedaling swiftly down the driveway before Clair could call her out on it.

A trail of thought bubbles scattered behind her. *Stupid stupid stupid stupid*, painting the road like a broken lane divider. In Jane's mind, Clair reaches down and picks one up and the regret lays like wet paper across her palm.

Jane stood up, her legs pumping the bike harder.

It's okay, she told herself. She'd fix this. All she had to do was find the woman who attacked them and force her to swap Jane back into her own body. Then whichever version of her that lived *this* life could step back in, and everything would be fine. It would be fine. There was no reason to worry that she'd be stuck here forever. Absolutely none. In fact, she'd be long gone by the time *the* sleepover rolled around.

She had to be.

Jane raced down the familiar roads, her bike a small shadow beneath a crowded twilight of her scratched-in thoughts.

It didn't take her long to reach the main stretch of town. Or maybe it just felt quick, the force of her fears making her pulse race. Jane slowed, pausing at a traffic light. A couple of cars flowed past, but at this time of night . . . There was a familiar joke that the town closed at seven, and it wasn't entirely without cause.

The light changed. She pedaled on.

It took only a few minutes to orient herself enough to find the parking lot where she and Clair had first appeared. Now that she understood what had happened, she was able to remember the grocery store from her childhood. The familiar paths she'd followed for years unfolded through her mind. She and Clair had applied for jobs there when they were sixteen, and Clair had gotten accepted but turned it down when they never called Jane back.

Clair. Jane's chest ached, all her breath suddenly squeezed from her lungs. She stopped for a second, leaning her head over the handlebars as if she was going to pass out. *Don't think about that,* she told herself, and the words superimposed over the image of her, alone, small, in the shadows of the Braddock's sign. *Don't think about that.* Right now, Jane didn't need to worry about her wife. Clair—the grown-up version, the one who'd been through all this alongside her—didn't need Jane's worry. Clair had the team and was more than capable of handling things on her end. In fact, they were no doubt working hard to figure out what had happened. They'd be back for her. They *would.* All Jane needed to do was hold on.

Hold on, and make sure she didn't screw up this version of the past too badly.

And so, for now, the car.

Jane should have thought about the car as soon as she'd realized what was happening, but she supposed she could be forgiven for being a little distracted by it all. Still, as soon as she'd seen the newspaper that morning, she knew she couldn't put off dealing with it any longer. She pedaled deeper into the parking lot, a sick sense that she was already too late settling over her.

Jane's heart raced and she picked up speed, only to have her fears confirmed: her car was already gone. Jane skidded to a halt, twisting her bike to catch herself. Nothing but a spray of safety glass remained, flecks glinting in the moonlight. Jane's mouth tightened.

She could have tried to come during the day, of course, but how would she have explained that? A nobody fifteen-year-old kid trying to cross a line of police tape, asking to sift through the wreckage of a futuristic car? Really, this attempt was doomed before it even began.

A shift in the corner of the lot caught her attention.

Jane may not have her powers at the moment, but that didn't mean she wasn't still attuned to changes in light and shadow. She was an artist long before she was a superhero, after all, and the world had always been a careful study of colors. Small differences were important, and right now, the palette of blues and deep purples and the sickly orange of the parking lot lights were swirled in a mix that should never have been.

Jane straightened her bike, pushing off quickly.

In retrospect, there were probably other, smarter, better courses of action she could have taken. No doubt she'd catalog them later, playing out whole issues of the way this evening could have gone better. The one where she pretends to be looking around the rest of the parking lot, slowly making her way over. The one where she circles around the building from behind. The one where she somehow has a taser, and can sneak up and catch her attacker off guard. The truly self-indulgent one: the rest of the team at her back, Jane's powers restored, as they charge forward and tackle their combatant to the ground.

Glimpses of these flashed through her mind even then, as she took the wrong course, but Jane ignored them. Fear and teenage bravado propelled her across the open space. Her youthful legs punched down on the pedals, tearing her across the night.

The muddled colors shifted. Whatever this woman's powers were, light did not obey her, and so, without preamble, when she spilled from the safety of the shadow she'd been hidden in, all the pinks and blues of her starry costume glittered brightly, a chunk of the night sky come to life.

The woman took off. Rounded the side of the grocery store in an instant. The woman didn't even stop long enough to force the door or pick the lock; one second she was barreling toward it, and the next it had already swung open, already let her inside.

Jane leaped from her bike and slammed the door open a moment later, following in her wake. She tumbled into a back hallway: cement floors, painted cinder-block walls; low lights caught a series of posters reminding employees of the importance of punching out and minimum wage laws, while one, near the bathroom, asked in firm block letters, *DID YOU WASH YOUR HANDS?*

There was no sign of the woman. Jane hesitated on the threshold. A door to the left, a door to the right. Beyond the hall, presumably, the grocery store spread out, the displays bedded down until morning.

"Oh, come on, Captain," a voice said. Jane spun around, but the words seemed to be coming from everywhere and nowhere all at once. They flooded the hall, currents pulling on Jane from every direction. "Surely you can work out a little puzzle like this. You've faced far, far worse than the likes of me, I assure you. As you will again. If you survive this."

If Jane had her powers, this wouldn't even *be* a puzzle. A quick infrared scan through the walls, the heat signature of her quarry lit up no matter where she ran. When she'd first gotten them, a part of Jane had been so afraid that she'd wanted nothing more than to be able to wish it all away; now, she wondered how she'd ever managed to live as long as she had before they manifested.

She didn't have time to waste on self-pity, though, so the end of the hall it was.

It was a choice made at random, but Jane felt on some level that it would be right. She pushed through a door into the main shop and nearly tumbled into a rack of pepperoni. A faint laugh drifted through the store, so at least Jane knew she'd made the right call.

She ran toward the sound. Through the aisles, into a side stockroom. Up a cold and barren stairwell, her feet slapping concrete as she vaulted the steps two at a time.

At the top, Jane burst through a door with an emergency exit bar. A trilling alarm like a school bell blared in her wake, but Jane didn't stop. Her shoes scraped over the gravel of a rooftop. Jane blinked, instinctively trying to shift her vision to handle the dark. But this body hadn't learned that trick yet, if it ever would, and her night vision remained normal, unremarkable, absolute shit.

A silhouette stood on the edge of the rooftop, framed from the lights of the parking lot below. Jane took off toward it. The figure darted aside, into the darkness, out of sight. On the roof, the night pressed in thick around her. Was she just not used to how normal people saw in the dark, or were there fewer lights reaching up here? She rounded a corner, maneuvering past . . . something large and boxy, part of an air conditioning unit maybe. For a second, she couldn't see at all, plunging straight into nothing but black. Then a light flicked on somewhere nearby—below—and Jane realized with a horrifying drop of her stomach that she was about to run straight off the rooftop.

Jane's foot slipped as she tried to come to a halt. Her weight shifted. Her glasses slid ominously down her nose. Her arms pinwheeled for balance, but found none. Panic seized her throat as she tipped forward. A scream started to spill out, when a strong arm grabbed her from behind.

"Easy there!" boomed a voice, deep and gravely. Not the woman she'd been chasing.

Jane stepped back, letting herself collapse into whoever had managed to rescue her. At this point, she did not even care, she was just grateful she hadn't splattered all over the sidewalk.

"T-thanks," Jane said as she slid free. She hurriedly fixed her glasses as she turned around.

Twin panels side by side, mirrored expressions staring in wide-eyed shock. In the corner of one, a speech bubble so small it was nearly a whisper: "Janie?"

"*Dad?*"

Jane gaped at the man in front of her. Her mind retreated back to the safety of lines and shading. It was Paul Maxwell, all right, but also . . . *not*.

Jane tried to be objective, to catalog what she was seeing as if sketching it for a poster. A tight bodysuit, vivid white with yellow sparkled accents like lightning bolts running up and down his arms. A shiny belt with a starburst buckle. A yellow cape trailing behind him. Jane cringed. He looked like someone wearing a bad Elton John costume for Halloween, not . . . whatever he was actually supposed to be.

Paul's face drained, his skin turning nearly as white as the mask around his eyes. "Oh my god. Janie, I . . . This isn't what it looks like, I didn't—I mean—It's not—*Shit*."

He clenched his fist, clamping down on his frustration, and for a second—just a second—it looked as though a burst of light was caught tight in the palm of his hand.

Jane gasped, dread stealing her breath. "Wait a second. Are you . . . are you supposed to be *Captain Lumen*?"

"It's Mr. Lightshow, actually," Paul said, the words straightening his spine. Then he frowned, as Jane's question caught up with him. "Who's Captain Lumen?"

"No," Jane said. She turned away from him, stalking to the middle of the roof. "No, that's not possible. You don't have superpowers. You can't, you didn't . . . you never . . ." She spun back. "Since when do you have *superpowers*?"

Paul sighed. He reached up, taking his mask off. His familiar face looked so tired, all of a sudden, and so much older—much more like the one Jane knew. The mask lay in his hands. Such a small thing, and so vital for keeping your identity hidden—but utterly useless when you stood face-to-face with someone you really knew. Paul scowled down at it, and in that instant he was so much the picture of Senator Maxwell that Jane's stomach twisted in a tight lurch.

But then Paul's expression slid. Anger turned soft. Pity and guilt, impossible expressions on that face, stepped up to fill the vacancy.

"I'm sorry, Janie. I never meant to keep this from you—from any of you—but . . ." A nervous laugh escaped him. "I mean, how are you supposed to break something like this to your kid? Where do you even start?"

"Believe me, I can handle this shit. What I don't understand is how it happened. *When* did it happen?"

Paul hesitated a moment, as if trying to decide if he should chastise her for the swear, or just answer the question. He shook his head slightly, shaking off the parental impulse. "Summer of '79."

"Just over twenty years ago," Jane whispered. Her eyes widened. She actually took a step back, as if distancing herself from Paul would somehow distance her from the truth. "No. What? No . . . But . . . that means *you* got your powers at basically the same time I got mine."

Paul raised an eyebrow. He glanced down at Jane, her gangly teenage body. "Honey, I think your math is a little off."

"No." Jane waved her hands, cutting him off. "Listen to me. Paul: this is going to sound crazy to you, at least at first, but I'm not your daughter. I'm not Janie."

She didn't blame him for the bark of laughter that escaped his chest. If anything, the disbelief only backed up his sanity. Still, she needed him to believe her. She straightened herself, drawing her shoulders back. Jane hadn't been an especially timid teenager, and from what she could tell, Janie wasn't a wallflower either. But there's a difference, however subtle it may be, between the overconfidence of a fifteen year old, and the age-earned ability to stand tall in the full knowledge of exactly who and what you are.

The first crack of doubt hit Paul's face. He tried to brush it off, tried to bury it beneath a mountain of *reasonable*, but it was there, a fault line buried deep. "Fine, I'll bite," Paul said, keeping his voice light enough to sound unconcerned. "Who are you supposed to be, then?"

"Okay, this is going to be hard for you, but I swear I'm telling the truth." Jane raised her hands, just a little, as if she needed to talk him down from a ledge. "My name *is* Jane Maxwell, I'm just not *your* Jane Maxwell. I come from a parallel world, one running about twenty years ahead of this one."

"Uh-huh. Twenty years, you say?" Paul said, clearly just playing along. "Then why do you look fifteen?"

"As best as I can put together, I must have been body-swapped with your actual daughter. And I don't know if she's, like, suppressed somewhere in my mind, or if she took my body, or what, but—"

"All right, Janie, this isn't funny. I know you're upset that I didn't tell you about my powers, and I get that you want to lash out at me—"

"I'm not *lashing out*," Jane snapped. She winced, shutting her eyes as she heard the petulance in her voice.

She needed something clear, something solid. Paul was watching her with the patience of a parent, waiting for her to wear herself out from her tantrum.

Jane tried to keep the frustration out of her voice as she said, "Look, if I still had my own powers I could maybe prove it to you, but I don't. But listen, would your fifteen-year-old daughter know her social security number? Or be able to explain the terms of her IRA? Or . . . oh!" Jane snapped her fingers. She stepped forward, looking Paul straight in the eye.

They were just about the same height, but the marginal difference didn't even matter, not now. Jane's true age and experience leveled the playing field, even if her physicality struggled to match it. The expression alone was enough to send a tremor down the fault line of Paul's disbelief, Jane could tell, but she needed to hit it with something a lot stronger if she was going to really get through to him. And now, she knew just the thing.

"Better yet," Jane said, and there was something cold and deadly and distinctly *adult* in the cut of her voice. She narrowed her eyes. "You're a lawyer. Ask me about my will."

The last of the humor slipped from his face.

A TIMER DINGED, AS IF JANIE WAS A TRAY OF BROWNIES
that had finished baking. She sat up from the bed, bracing herself for the same aches and pains she'd had when she first laid
down, only to find . . . nothing. Her body felt better than it had
since she'd arrived, and Janie vaulted to her feet with all the
enthusiasm of her fifteen years.

They'd brought her back to headquarters to deal with her
injuries. Janie had imagined being back in the lab, a first-aid
kit on the table beside her and maybe a scanner running over
her head to make sure she hadn't sustained anything serious.
Instead, they'd shown her to a small room with a bed and a chair
and a built-in dresser for her clothes.

A rejuvenation pod, they'd called it, like it was the newest
feature in some sort of spa.

She'd laughed when she'd first seen it. The bed in the corner was dressed in white linen, with a white arched canopy over it, images of soothing beach scenes and gentle forests projected across the fabric. What kind of joke was this?

Janie wasn't laughing now. She stared at her palm, the empty expanse of healed skin, as she stepped out into the hallway. How many times had this hand been beaten up and repaired again? How many scars would litter the skin she was borrowing, if they didn't have some fancy-shmancy piece of tech to knit it back together? Although the battle she'd witnessed had gone well, by all accounts, and the Heroes had brushed it off like it was nothing, Janie wasn't the only one of them who'd popped into a rejuvenation pod for a while.

It seemed that Janie was the last one to finish, however. The Heroes' voices drifted down the empty hallway, stern and concerned. Janie followed the sounds, running her fingers along the crisp white walls. They seemed to faintly glow, like panels on a spaceship. She found the Heroes in a lounge of some sort, a long curvy couch in the middle of the room, a giant fish tank across from it, a bank of windows overlooking the spread of Grand City.

Clair was, of course, the first to spot her.

"Janie!" She was already on her feet by the time she finished saying the name, rounding the couch and raising a hand toward Janie as if she was going to feel her forehead for a fever. Janie ducked aside, and Clair lowered her hand, cheeks tinted pink.

Cal nodded at her over the back of the couch. "Hi, kiddo. Feeling better?"

"I'm fine," Janie said, bristling at the "kiddo" moniker. She knew he meant well, but Janie would never get the Heroes to take her seriously if they kept thinking of her as a child. She climbed over the back of the couch, plopping down in the cushions, and pointed to a projection hovering over the coffee table: a spread of biographical data and a mug shot. "Is that who's behind the attack?" Maybe if she acted like she belonged, eventually someone would recognize that she did.

The glow of the projection caught the Heroes' faces. Uncertainty shifted between them, a silent debate, before finally Clair raised one shoulder in a resigned half shrug.

"Janie, meet Lester Trimble," Marie said, motioning toward the projection. "He and his brother call themselves Dog Squad, for reasons passing all understanding. They've been responsible for a series of high-profile robberies stretching from San Antonio to St. Paul, and now it seems they've made their way east. Just before you got here, we stopped them from making off with a diamond brought into the city for auction later this week. We turned his brother, Larry, over to the GCPD, and now as best as we can tell, Lester's out looking for revenge."

Janie leaned in, peering at the data. Lester had a narrow face, limp, mouse-brown hair hanging low across one of his eyes, and a detached expression, like even as his mug shot was being taken, he knew he wouldn't be in custody long. And apparently he'd been right, because look, here they were in Grand City, causing chaos.

She turned her attention to the biographical data. There wasn't a whole lot. Birthplace and age, last known location before they hit up Grand City, a list of previous targets. For powers, all it said was "hearing."

Janie pointed. "What's up with that?"

Marie glanced at the projection. "Seems self-evident. He has superhearing."

"Really?" Janie sneered. "How's that help him rob banks?"

"They go for things a *bit* more complicated than banks," Tony said.

"Don't be stupid," Marie added over him. "It's more useful than you'd think. As far as we can tell, Lester's the brains and Larry's the brawn. Imagine the sort of classified info you'd get, being able to hear the faintest whisper in a crowded street."

"More an issue for us," Keisha started, "is him eavesdropping on our plans out in the field. Doesn't do us any good to use comms, if he's listening in anyway."

Janie raised her hands, backing off. "Okay, okay. I was just asking."

Cal clapped a hand on her shoulder. "Don't mind them, Brainy Janie. They're just frustrated because we haven't come up with a plan to catch the bastard yet."

"Cal!" Clair cut him a pointed look, jerking her head in Janie's direction. "Language, please."

"Yeah, sure," Cal said. "Because we *never* called anyone a bastard in high school."

"I'm not offended by it," Janie said, trying to help.

Clair snorted. "You don't get a vote."

Of course she didn't. She turned back to the projection, but Clair was already reaching up to swipe it away. Lester's face, and all his info, crumpled into a ball of pixels before disappearing beneath Clair's dismissive hand.

"Anyway, it's late," Clair said. "You've had a long day, even with the rejuve pod. We should get you to bed."

Janie slumped back. "I suppose it's back to the hotel, then?" Not that there was anything wrong with the hotel, but come on: when compared to a literal superhero headquarters, there was no contest.

Only instead of immediately gathering Janie up like a toddler after a playdate, Clair's mouth pinched into a set line. "No." She glanced at Keisha, who gave her a nod of encouragement, and then said, "It's late, and you'll be safer here. It was stupid to leave in the first place."

Janie could barely believe it. She just sat there for a second, frozen in place, until finally Clair reached a gloved hand out for Janie, her exposed fingertips carefully spread to avoid contact.

"Come on. I'll show you to your room."

"NOT THAT DOOR."

Jane stopped, her fingers already gripping the handle to her father's old law office. *Parker and Maxwell,* said the gold on the glass. *Family Law.* Beneath that, smaller letters that Jane could have sworn she never saw before: *When you need to fight for what matters.*

Only, Paul wasn't standing by that door. Instead, across the hall, he dug out a key. He'd already changed out of his costume, ducking behind a dumpster while Jane had waited awkwardly at the mouth of the alley. Now a gray bag with a corporate logo hung against his back, as if he'd just come from the gym.

"Come on," Paul said as he shouldered the door open.

In her memory, the business across the hall was a dentist's office. As she stepped inside, Jane wondered where they'd gotten bumped to instead in this version of reality. She'd never been there, but she could picture what the waiting room must have looked like: the industrial beige carpet, the beat-up maroon chairs, the twisty toddler toy in the corner to entertain the youngest patients.

The front room did more or less match her vision. Jane supposed that made sense—if someone ever accidentally let themselves in, or broke in, or if the landlord ever stopped by, an empty waiting room was a lot less of a problem to find than a superhero hideout. Jane followed Paul inside, stepping through a circle of dusty chairs as they slipped down a hall toward the back office.

At the door, Paul hesitated. "All right, so . . . I should probably tell you, I don't work alone. You have to promise me that you're not going to tell her, though. Neither of us has figured out when to break the truth of this life to our families, all right?"

Jane nodded. She wasn't sure exactly which "her" she wasn't supposed to be telling, but it couldn't possibly matter. Jane was already keeping so many different secrets from everyone in this Jane's life, what was one more?

Paul took a breath. "Okay."

He swung open the door.

Jane saw him in profile first, a familiar line from forehead to nose bridge to chin. Not quite the version she was most familiar with, but close enough that her breath caught, just for a second, as she realized the "her."

Clair's dad spun away from the computer, his eyes popping wide as they landed on Jane. "Paul, what the hell? I thought we agreed not to—"

"It's not what it looks like," Paul cut in. He glanced at Jane and laid his hand gently on the back of her shoulders. He took a deep breath, and then he said, "This . . . this isn't my daughter."

Simon's brows scrunched together. It was a look that mirrored Clair so well that Jane almost laughed. "Excuse me?"

Jane stepped forward, out from Paul's grip. She stuck her hand toward Simon, making sure to hold herself tall. He'd stood up by now, nerves making him jittery.

"Jane Maxwell," Jane said, by way of introduction. "Short version is that parallel worlds are real, and I've been body-swapped into a version of myself twenty years younger than I actually am. Nice to meet you." She tried not to think about how, because Clair had been born when Simon and Donna were both so young, Jane was pretty much the same age as him. Even if she didn't look it at the moment.

Simon cast a wide glance over Jane's shoulder, his attention landing on Paul. "Is she serious right now?"

"Afraid so," Paul said.

"Huh." Simon's eyes slid back to Jane. He still hadn't taken her hand. He pushed his glasses up, leaning in to peer at her.

Jane leaned back. "Uh. Personal space?"

"It truly is remarkable," Simon said. He bopped Jane's nose. "You'd never be able to tell the difference, would you?"

"Yeah, that kind of goes with the whole 'body-swapped' thing," Jane said. She rubbed at her nose.

Abruptly, Simon stepped back. He collapsed into a beaten swivel chair taken from some office in the seventies. The metal and springs creaked under his weight as he spun back to the computer. The keyboard was already clacking beneath his fingers as he said, "I suppose that explains the readings from the other day."

"What readings?"

Simon didn't say anything at first, long enough for Jane to think maybe he was ignoring her. The light from three computer monitors spilled over him, casting a sickly blue glow over his face. He tapped at the keyboard for a while, clicking the mouse a few times, until a range of charts and spreadsheets filled the screens.

Finally, just as Jane wasn't sure she could take it any longer, Simon pointed to one of them. "Yesterday morning, our sensors picked up a spike in tetricore energy somewhere on Main Street, which is practically unheard of. We thought maybe it was related to Tiger Knight, a villain we've been tracking for the last few weeks. But he's been quiet lately, and by the time Paul got there, there was no sign of him—or anyone else. We did a sweep of the area, but so far, no trace."

Jane wasn't surprised. Whoever had brought her here, she was good, too good to leave obvious trails. Jane leaned in, checking the data for herself. Simon bristled a bit at her proximity, but Jane didn't care. The screen was full of data, most of it beyond her, but the timestamps seemed to match—at least as well as Jane could remember.

"Okay." Jane straightened up, planting her hands on her hips the way she did when she was addressing the Heroes. "So let's say this tetri-whatever energy is what my attacker used to swap me. How does that help us?"

Simon looked up with a crinkled brow. "What do you mean?"

"Well, there's got to be a way to reverse this."

Simon laughed. "I mean, yeah, maybe. It's theoretically possible. But I sure as shit can't do that."

"But you're supposed to be the science guy!"

"The what?"

Jane waved her hand around the headquarters, such as it was. The dim little office, the desk crammed full of boxy old computers. "The science guy. You know, hanging back, guiding the hero on comms, coming up with the tools and solutions? Oh, come on! I know you guys have watched superhero movies. You don't have as many as there are in *my* time, but you've at least seen Batman!"

"I'm not your dad's Alfred," Simon said, pushing the bridge of his glasses up with his knuckle.

"Technically, she's implying more of a Lucius Fox deal."

Simon grimaced. "Not helping, Paul."

Paul raised his hands in mock-defense.

"Look," Simon said. He turned his full attention to Jane, elbows on the cracked plastic armrests of his chair and fingers woven into a steeple over his lap. "Despite the presence of *some* enhanced abilities that science is yet to explain: there's comic books, and then there's the real world. Much as I'd love to wave a magic science wand around and fix your problems in a heartbeat, it doesn't work like that. I'm a *computer programmer*. I don't have advanced degrees in quantum theory and physiology or whatever else I'd need to untangle your . . . identity, from the physical flesh you currently occupy. Technically, it shouldn't have been possible to 'swap' you, as you claim, in the first place. We are our brains. End of story. Now, I'm sorry for your loss. But I suggest you find a way to make peace with it—because there's no way I can see to send you home."

"But—"

Jane's protest was cut off as Paul's hand settled heavily on her shoulder. "Come on, Jane. You heard the man. Let's go."

"YOU'LL HAVE TO FORGIVE SIMON," PAUL SAID AS THEY pulled out of the empty parking lot. "It hasn't been easy on him, since . . . well, since Donna."

Jane whipped her head around. "What *about* Donna?"

Paul took his eyes off the road. Just long enough to cut Jane a curious glance. Just long enough for Jane's heart to leap to her throat, and her hands to fly against the dashboard.

"You really don't know?" he asked as he returned his attention to the road.

"No." Jane pried her fingers loose, pulling them to rest in her lap.

A heavy sigh filled the car. Paul tightened his knuckles on the wheel. A faint sheen of light emanated from them, a soft glow that draped old shadows on his otherwise youthful face.

"Simon didn't like keeping secrets from his family," Paul said. "For me . . . I mean, I'd been living with these powers for, oh, maybe fifteen years by the time I met him. You were, what, ten when he reunited with Donna?"

"Yeah." That's how it worked on her world, after all, and there was no reason to assume the timetable would have been different here. It had been so weird for Clair—this sudden father figure appearing in her life after so long with just her and her mom. Made weirder by the fact that he actually *was* her biological father, both he and Clair kept secret from each other for years. It would have been one thing if Clair had a stepdad move in. That would have been better, in some ways.

Still, they'd managed to make it work. Simon had been so nice, and so patient. And Clair was . . . well, *Clair*. She'd find room in her heart for anyone worthy of it, in time.

"Simon wasn't supposed to find out about my powers, of course," Paul continued. "No one was, least of all my daughter's best friend's father. I mean, I barely knew the guy. Barbecues, birthday parties . . . he was a guy I shared a beer with as we watched you two from the sidelines."

Jane stared out the window. She could see it clearly, a rosier version of her own life. Jane and Clair in the foreground, laughing as they walked side by side toward the pool, neon towels slung over their shoulders. Their teeth are bright, their smiles reflecting in each other's plastic sunglasses. Behind them, present as the blocky shape of dads rather than drawn in any useful detail, are two shaded figures in twilight purple and gray.

"He got caught up in it by accident. I didn't even realize he'd be there, when I went in to rescue the hostages from Wilson Labs. This megalomaniac with some kind of tech-controlling powers was trying to infect the internet, and—anyway, it doesn't matter. Simon found out. And he told Donna."

Paul went silent. The car drew to a stop, a red light hanging overhead like a blood moon.

For one wild, terrible second, Jane's heart stopped, imagining her father taking matters into his own hands. Silencing Donna, by force, to keep his secret. Maybe he hadn't meant for it to go that far, maybe he'd driven over hoping he could talk to her. A panel of Donna's face, twisted to the side as it was struck by an unseen hand, the page tinged with red.

"I mean, I didn't know what I expected, but she was *all over* the idea," Paul said finally, the car starting up. The pages of horror tore from Jane's mind as surely as if they'd been tethered to the stoplight. Her cheeks burned, disgusted with herself for even thinking it.

Donna's enthusiasm for superpowers may have surprised Paul at the time, but it didn't surprise Jane now. She'd always been so proud of Clair, running around saving the city.

"So what happened?" Jane didn't really want to know, didn't

want to see some terrible fate splash across the pages of her imagination, not for Donna. But she was in too deep by this point.

"She thought she could help. She'd always had this . . . this *way* with people, you know? Like she could make your whole day better with a simple hand on your shoulder, a reassuring word. And you *believed* her. Even if you knew it should have sounded like some bullshit platitude, you believed her."

It was true, though Jane had never thought about it quite like that. It was a trait she more often attributed to Clair, but Clair had to learn it somewhere.

"Anyway, long story short: we told her not to, but she followed us to this warehouse where I was trying to take down a mad scientist. He was conducting experiments with a serum that would heighten a person's strength and sensory perception. Thought it would give soldiers better reflexes, but in reality, those benefits came with a healthy side dose of crazy. He'd been experimenting on convicts he'd broken out of prison."

Paul paused, took a deep breath. They were almost home by now, the streets outside too comfortable for the conversation they were having.

"And Donna goes in, masked up, in this costume she'd put together for herself. I think she thought she could talk sense into him."

Jane flinched. She'd written enough comics to see how this story was going to end. A rescue attempt gone wrong. Donna, tied to a board and threatened with the serum as Mr. Lightshow and Simon raced to save her. In the safety of panels, they would have made it, swooping in at the last second. In real life . . .

"He killed her, didn't he?"

The words sat thick between them, Jane's speech bubble so weighted with her assumption that it lay in a sad puddle on the console between their seats. God, poor Clair.

Instead, a bitter laugh broke the stillness of the car, jarring Jane from her sorrow.

"That would have been nice," Paul said. "But no. He tried to drown her in a vat of the serum. We got to him before he could finish the job." His face turned sour. "Sometimes I think it would have been kinder if we'd failed."

They pulled into the driveway. Paul cut the engine.

"But," Jane said. "Wait, but if the serum drove people crazy—"

"She's in the Cedarcreek mental health center." Paul turned to her, his face suddenly even more serious than it had been throughout the story. "And Jane, whatever you do, you've *got* to keep this to yourself. I'm trusting you, because I know you can handle secrets. Clair thinks her mom is in rehab. Simon couldn't bear to tell her the truth."

Jane sat back in her seat, dumbfounded. "You expect me to just *lie* to her?"

Paul tossed her a weathered expression. "You're already lying to her, Jane. Sometimes we have to lie to protect the people we care about." He took the keys out of the ignition, popped up the lock on the door. "You're supposed to be a superhero—surely you've figured that out by now."

JANIE SLID INTO VIEW OF THE MIRROR, THE REFLECTION
of her shoulder bumping the frame as her socked feet came to a
halt. She cocked her hip, adjusting the necktie that wasn't even
remotely tied correctly, but whatever—she wasn't wearing her
glasses, so it looked fine to her. "The name's Maxwell," she said
in a voice that was aiming for sultry, but instead landed like a
pile of wet socks. "Janie Maxwell."

She still couldn't believe all this stuff belonged to that other,
grown-up version of herself. The suite was massive, with a living
area, separate bedroom, and private bathroom. Clair had shown
it to her the night before, a tiny pinch on her face as the door slid
open and the living area revealed itself. *"It . . . hasn't been used in
a long time,"* Clair had said. Janie had bounded in ahead of her,
eyes alight while she took in every detail. She could tell there
was more to that statement than what it meant on the surface,
but at the time, she wasn't inclined to dig deeper.

Besides, the suite was so cool that Janie couldn't bring herself to care. Even if there was some nefarious secret behind it, it didn't change the fact that Janie was currently standing in a place straight out of *The Jetsons*.

Still, exhaustion had caught up with her before she'd really gotten to explore. Now, though, was a different story. Janie had woken up a little before six, her body snapping into consciousness without her permission. At first, she'd just laid there, stubbornly refusing to throw back the covers and pad out of bed at such an inhuman hour. But then, well . . . the truth is that, weirdly, she wasn't as tired as she should have been? And the suite, and all the secrets it potentially held, was more than she could resist. That must have been all it was, this weird alertness. Like a kid waking up early on Christmas, ready to tear through her presents.

Unfortunately, she hadn't found out as much as she'd have liked. Janie had already explored every dresser and drawer in the suite, and weirdly, the version of herself that had once lived in these rooms hadn't left anything meaningful behind. The paintings on the walls looked like something you'd find in a waiting room. There were no books or art supplies anywhere. In the bathroom, Janie had found a curling iron, a pack of contact lenses, an electric toothbrush, and a scary-looking device that was either a medieval torture tool, or possibly something involved in hair removal, it was hard to tell. There was also a dusty circular case half filled with expired birth control pills, which Janie very carefully dropped back in the drawer and backed away from as if she'd been caught with porn.

Actually, porn would have been more interesting. At least that would give her some clue as to what sort of person she'd grow up to be. As it was, the rooms seemed designed to fit a Generic Adult Woman. Even the magazines on the end tables, years out of date, were a suspiciously balanced mix of fashion and home design, their pages crisp and unthumbed.

The closet, at least, was more fun, if still not particularly illuminating. Lots of silk blouses, tailored pants, rows and rows of heeled shoes. Janie had spent the last hour or so trying things on, dancing around to the mix of nineties songs she'd found while scrolling around the computer screen by Jane's bed. *Her* bed.

Now she tugged the improperly done tie from her neck, tossing it onto the sheets as she made her way back to the closet. The one thing she *hadn't* worked up the nerve to try on yet was the red leather superhero suit, hanging limply at the far end of the closet. Janie eyed it every time she shuffled through the clothes, hesitating whenever she reached for it.

Instead, she peered onto the top shelf, raising on her toes before realizing she didn't need to. Her new body was constantly surprising her, taller and stronger and larger than she was used to. She nudged aside a few plastic storage bins, reaching for the very back corner, when her fingers brushed against something cold and metallic.

She drew the box out. A palm scanner filled most of the top, a thin layer of dust settled over the screen. Janie brushed the back of her sleeve across it. She laid her palm flat on the surface. The box hummed, a sweep of light tickling the powers running just beneath her skin.

The box gave a soft *beep*. The palm scanner turned green. A latch at the front clicked open.

Janie raised the lid.

She was expecting something secret, something tantalizing, but the first thing that met Janie's glance was a piece of paper filled with sketches of a superhero costume. Purple marker shaded most of the outfits. Janie lifted it up, examining the various stages of designs: cape, no cape, different belts and seam lines and footwear options.

Beneath the papers were a few fabric scraps, presumably from the creation of the costume in the sketches—they were the same purple, though much more shimmery in real life, the exact hue shifting as Janie held it to the light. Some matching purple makeup. A single photo: Jane's grown-up face, framed by a bathroom mirror, one of the space-age cellphones of this era held up to snap the picture. Her eyes were surrounded by a sweep of glittery purple makeup, and a twisted little smile turned up the corners of her lips.

A chill ran down Janie's spine—there was something about

the expression staring back at her, a vision of herself she didn't recognize. Janie knew that the grownup she'd replaced was still a stranger to her, but there was something . . . *else* in this photo. Something cold. Something Janie didn't want to touch. She stuffed everything back into the box, and the box back into the closet where she'd found it.

Her stomach growled. Janie laid her hand across it as she spun around and headed off in search of both distraction and breakfast. They'd passed a kitchen on the way to her rooms last night. Janie found it easily enough, then drew to a halt in the open doorway.

Clair was already there, as if Janie had wished her into existence. Seated at the table, a paper-thin laptop open in front of her and a bowl at her elbow, full of what looked like yogurt and granola and some kind of little black seed. Clair glanced up and, for a split second, her whole face started to brighten, eyes sparkling in recognition. But then, so quickly Janie could almost convince herself she'd imagined it, Clair blinked and the look was gone. Replaced by a forced smile and professional voice. "Janie. Good morning. Can I get you some breakfast?"

She stood up even as she was asking the question, like she already knew the answer. She shut the laptop and moved over to the cabinets.

Janie settled at the table, perching awkwardly atop one of the kitchen's odd little egg-shaped chairs. Did she want anything? She suddenly wasn't sure, but refusing felt too weird. "I don't suppose you have any donuts?"

"For breakfast?" Clair turned around. "Didn't we already go over what happens with that whole pizza-and-cake nonsense?"

"I'll risk it."

Clair hesitated, biting her lip as she studied Janie. Janie thought for sure Clair would keep arguing, but instead she pulled out her cellphone. Maybe she was still feeling guilty because she thought she'd put Janie in danger yesterday. Never mind that it wasn't actually her fault—Janie wasn't about to correct her. Especially not if it got her free stuff.

"Just don't come crying to me when you feel like crap later," Clair said, tapping out something on her cellphone.

Janie sat up straighter, practically bouncing in her seat. "Great! So . . . can we go?"

Clair glanced up. "Go?"

"To get donuts."

A laugh slipped across the table. "Oh, honey, no. We'll have it DoorDashed."

Clair turned her cellphone around. Images of donuts and coffee, what looked like some kind of order screen, reflected back at Janie.

Her eyes widened. "You can get *donuts* delivered? The future is *awesome!*"

JANE, MEANWHILE, DRAGGED HERSELF OUT OF BED AT 6:30. Oddly bleary-eyed, her body sluggish in a way she hadn't felt in years, but dammit she was *up*. She stumbled from her bedroom, drawing the tangle of her hair back into a low, loose ponytail. She hadn't bothered to put her glasses on yet, still folded neatly in their case on her bedside table. She didn't need them; despite living on her own since college, Jane could still close her eyes and draw every step of this house from memory. Her toes sinking into the carpet in the upstairs hall. A low angle looking up the stairs as Jane descends, caught midyawn; one hand trails along the banister, the other covers her stretched mouth. At the bottom, she would need to make a U-turn and shuffle fifteen steps to the kitchen threshold.

Her parents were already there. The warm smell of coffee and the lingering lure of an egg-white omelet made Jane's stomach lunge ahead of her. Jane wasn't normally hungry when she first woke up, but she wasn't about to question the rage clawing at her stomach. She rubbed her eyes as she stepped through the doorway.

"Morning," she said, her voice thick with sleep. "What's for breakfast?"

Even through the blur of her morning eyes and lack of glasses, Jane could see the double take Olivia did at the sight of her. "Two mornings in a *row*? Honey, are you feeling all right?"

Paul raised his head, curling his newspaper down, dad-style. "Cut her some slack, Liv. She's making an effort."

"An effort to get something," Olivia said. She leaned against the kitchen counter, one hand on her hip. "All right, kiddo, let's hear it. What are you buttering us up for?"

"Were you always this suspicious?" Jane said, ignoring the question as she dug into the freezer for a box of Eggos. "I don't remember you being suspicious."

"I'm suspicious when my daughter *suddenly* just *decides* to start getting up before noon on a Saturday, yes. I'm suspicious when she *just so happens* to take it upon herself to put in an effort for no apparent reason."

Paul cleared his throat. "Liv."

Olivia put her hands up in absolution. "I'm just saying."

Jane turned away, popping the frozen waffle into the toaster oven and twisting the knob to medium.

It was weird—Jane's mother could see right through her, yet there was something about this version of Olivia Maxwell that felt *shallow* by comparison. Like she was posing for a mom portrait on the cover of a comic book: styled to be just *slightly* out of fashion so she'd look "mom-like" without crossing into frumpy; a styrofoam cup of coffee in her grip and a perpetually harried look about her face. The look was right. The acting was right. But there was a shrewdness to Jane's mom, as well as the Mrs. Maxwell in her adopted reality, that was somehow missing. Something in the gray eyes, the way they sized Jane up without really seeing her.

There's no way Jane's real mother would have bought this act. Jane had nothing solid to base this on, but she felt it. It was like this version was a copy that had been drawn by laying tracing paper over another picture—all the right outside angles, but without any of the interior circles and lines that had been used to form the original.

"Right, well, I've gotta run," Olivia said finally. "I've got two showings this morning, then an open house at noon. You've got the kids?"

Paul stole the tiniest glance at Jane. He nodded. "I've got the kids."

"All right, then." Olivia darted over, giving him a fast kiss. "Love you."

"Love you more," Paul said.

Jane looked down at the counter. Olivia raced by, ruffling Jane's hair as she went. "Be good!"

The absence that fell in her wake stretched between Jane and Paul, stilted as the ticking of the toaster. She did not dare risk looking up at him, for that might inspire the need for conversation. And despite the revelations from the night before, him learning her identity and her learning his, this was still Paul Maxwell, and still Jane. She turned her attention to the toaster oven instead, leaning her elbows on the counter as she watched the glass fog up.

Paul folded his paper and set it aside. "Seriously, though, as much as I'd love to have one daughter I didn't need to drag out of bed in the morning, you're going to have to start behaving like a teenager if you want people to buy this act of yours."

"Whatever," Jane said under her breath, and Paul laughed.

"That's better."

A muscle in Jane's cheek twitched, her lips itching at the edges. Jane bit the inside of her cheek, fighting it back into place. *Nope* said the text block hovering near her head. His false, homey-dad routine would not win her over that easily.

The toaster oven *dinged*, the sound bubble jagged around the edges. Jane's slim hand reaching forward, seen close up and in profile: there's a series of hair ties around her wrist, her navy-blue painted nails chipped around the edges. This youth of hers was as false as the pages of a comic, a lie slapped over her reality to make it easier for readers to digest. A circular panel, edged with the pattern of the plate she'd taken from the cabinet, surrounds a portrait of her buttering her Eggo: her head down, the loose edges of the bangs she's growing out hiding most of her face. Morning sunlight streams in from the window beside her, catching only the outermost, superficial side of herself.

Jane took a bite, the slightly burned Eggo crunching in her teeth. She slid down the length of the counter, reaching for a mug on the little wooden mug-tree that she'd painted for her mom in second grade.

"Hey!" Paul jumped up, snatching the clear glass mug from her hand. "What do you think you're doing?"

"What? I don't need to pretend around *you*."

"Nope. You're still in my daughter's body. I won't let you stunt *her* growth, either."

"You know, lots of kids in my era drink coffee now. They're doing just fine."

"Good for them." Paul set the mug down, opened the fridge, and poured Jane a quick glass of orange juice instead. "But this is now. And these are my rules."

He held the glass out.

Jane took it—with extreme caution, pinched between her fingers. Hey, if Paul wanted teenage authenticity . . .

She took a tentative sip. The citric acid hit her tongue, puckering her eyes shut.

"So . . . ," Paul said, "what's it like?"

"What, the juice?" Jane tipped her glass toward him. "Trade you, if you want to find out."

A smirk crossed Paul's face. "No, smart ass. Where you're from. *When* you're from."

Jane set down her glass. "You're asking me to tell you about the future?"

"Not at all," Paul said. "I'm asking you to tell me about *you*. If I'm following this whole parallel worlds thing, there's absolutely no guarantee that anything in my Janie's life is going to turn out like yours."

Jane's mouth twisted up, as if she'd taken another sip of her orange juice. Panels boxed in her face: various angles of her and Clair's hands held by their sides, their fingers twisted together, caught in the dappled sunlight coming through the dying leaves of the oak tree.

Jane shook her head to clear the images. "I just don't think we should be talking about this."

"Oh, come on," Paul said. "Where's the harm?"

"I don't know," Jane snapped. She rolled her shoulders, as if the feeling inside her could be shrugged off. "Maybe there isn't any, but I just—I don't want to talk about it."

Paul scoffed. "Throw me a bone here, Jane. I'm not asking

much. You must have a job, right? Maybe a house? Or—wait, do I have grandkids?"

"I *said* I don't want to talk about it."

"Why not?"

"Because you're *dead*, all right?"

She stole a fast glance to the side. Paul had frozen in place, the dishes he'd started to retrieve from the table hovering halfway into the sink. He quickly set them down, his hand on the counter for balance. He couldn't bring himself to look at her.

Jane didn't know why she said that. Her real dad, back on her original Earth, could easily be called "dead to her," but he was still very much alive. Technically. So was the one on her adopted Earth, who still thought Jane was that *other* Jane, the one who in reality had turned into UltraViolet. In fact, Jane didn't know a single world in which any version of him had actually died.

Paul cleared his throat. "Janie, I—"

"It's fine," Jane said. "It was a long time ago. Besides, I need to take a shower. I have a Homecoming committee meeting this morning."

"Do you need a ride?"

The question was soft, barely above a whisper. There was something so hopeful in his voice, it nearly broke Jane's heart. For a split second, she almost considered letting him take her. But this was *Paul Maxwell*. No matter how convincing he sounded, she couldn't let herself forget that.

"No." Jane dropped the unfinished Eggo in the trash, the butter instantly soaking into a pile of coffee grounds. "I'll take my bike."

TWENTY MINUTES LATER, CLAIR'S CELLPHONE CHIMED. She glanced at it and then stood up, nodding for Janie to come with her. "Donuts are here."

They rode the elevator down to the lobby together, accepting the package straight through the passenger-side window of the delivery driver's car.

Janie leaned over. "Don't you need to tip him?" she whispered, but the driver was already rolling up his window.

"Oh, I already did. It's all in the app." She handed the box to Janie, then marched back to the building as Janie watched the driver pull away.

Janie was about to follow, when a limo rolled up to the curb, seamlessly taking the place of the donut driver. Janie stood there, gawking. Sure, they were in a fancy part of Grand City, but you still didn't exactly see limos lining up at every building. She wondered if it was a celebrity—not that she would recognize them if they were, since she doubted any of the movie stars she was familiar with were still at the top of their game. It would still be cool.

The back door popped open. A shiny black dress shoe and the cuff of an expensive suit reached toward the sidewalk.

"Not *now*," Clair muttered, stepping beside Janie.

Paul Maxwell got out of the back of the limo.

A grin burst out of Janie. "Dad!" She started to surge forward, only to run into the barricade of Clair's arm. Clair tapped Janie's wrist, a single finger dipping against her skin—barely even touching, just long enough for the word *No* to enter Janie's mind.

No? No, *what*? No, this wasn't her dad? Janie turned back. The man was straightening his suit jacket, smoothing out a startled expression as easily as the creases. But while he may have been caught off guard by Janie's greeting, it was definitely her dad. Older, yeah, sure. He looked more like Grandpa Maxwell than Janie was used to, but that was only to be expected. A twenty-year time difference would have put him in, what, his sixties by now? Yet the silvery hair, leaning more toward salt than pepper, only lent him an air of distinction in his old age. And he was clearly doing well for himself: the limo and quality of the suit spoke to that, long before an honest-to-god *bodyguard* stepped out of the car and stationed himself behind him, sunglasses and little earpiece and everything.

Her dad crossed the sidewalk. Clair stepped in front of Janie, not enough to completely block her, but clearly signaling her control of the situation.

"Senator," Clair said as he approached. "We weren't expecting you."

Janie's eyebrows shot up. *Senator?* She supposed that explained the little American flag pin on his lapel (and the body-guard, now that she thought of it), though she'd never known her dad to have political aspirations.

Yet there was no denying it. Her dad, the *senator*, drew to a stop several feet from Janie and Clair.

He brushed off her comment with a quick shake of his head. "I don't have time to ask what I did to piss you off. Is the rest of your little team around? We need to talk."

The remark was directed at Clair, but Janie stepped back as if it had reared up and bitten her. Not so much the words themselves—though Janie had never heard her dad be *snide* before—but the tone. Light, detached, and utterly disinterested. He had one hand in his pants pocket, his suit jacket tucked behind the arm, while the other hung by his side as he brushed his fin-gers against each other. He wasn't quite looking at Janie or Clair, but wasn't obviously *not* looking at them, either. The whole thing reeked of a performance, like he alone was up on stage. Janie found herself glancing around the street, at the cars and foot traffic gliding idly past.

Clair, on the other hand, wasn't thrown by his behavior in the least. She continued to stand between Janie and Senator Maxwell, a human shield. Suddenly the morning air reeked of sharp cologne and too much sugar, the box of once mouthwater-ing donuts sagging in Janie's hands.

They didn't say anything. Not as Clair cut back toward the building and across the lobby, not as she entered her retinal scan and ID code to allow them access to the elevators. Janie raced after her, feeling lost, but Senator Maxwell strode forward with purpose, somehow in the lead even as he literally followed.

The elevator doors slid shut, sealing them off from the outside world. Clair had her cellphone out, tapping what was probably a heads-up message to the rest of their "little team" as they rose, with painful slowness, up the many levels of the building.

Janie snuck a glance at Senator Maxwell across the top of Clair's dipped head. What had happened to him, to make him react so dispassionately to his own daughter? Had *Jane* done something to earn her father's spite?

She chewed her lip all the way to the top floor. When they finally came to a stop, the doors whispering open, Janie was the first to dart out into the hall.

She thought they'd be heading to the kitchen or the lounge, but instead Clair turned left, making a straight line for the command room. Janie's heart skipped—was she really going to get to see it? The security keypad turned green for Clair, and she waved them in behind her as a soft-spoken computer voice, buttery smooth, chimed overhead. *Welcome, Clair. Welcome, Jane. Welcome, AUTHORIZED GUEST.*

Janie did her best to suppress a giggle. But then her amusement was cut off, her breath catching as the room unfolded before her. While a part of her had known that the heart of a real-life superhero headquarters had to be cool, she had no idea just *how cool* it would prove to be.

The room was bathed in a soft blue glow, mainly provided by a solid bank of computer screens that took up the entire far wall. There were no windows. In the center of the room, a curved conference table, reflective black, was surrounded by tall-backed chairs. A projected map of Grand City rotated lazily above it, each of the buildings rising up in perfectly miniaturized 3D. It felt like stepping onto the bridge of a starship.

A gentle nudge on her back snapped Janie out of it. Right: she supposedly saw this all the time, there was no reason for her to be impressed. Janie stepped forward, dropping the donut box on the table as if this was nothing.

Tony, mercifully, stepped forward and helped himself to a sugary-crusted donut, winking at her to break the tension. He, along with the rest of the team, had changed into their superhero uniforms—somewhat hastily, if the quick tuck Keisha gave her shirt was any indication.

"Not exactly what I'd pictured," Senator Maxwell said, taking in the room. His hand rested across the back of one of the chairs, staking a claim.

Janie glanced at the rest of the Heroes. Was it possible this was the senator's first visit to the headquarters? Janie couldn't imagine a world in which her parents were cut out of such a central part of her life. But then she'd never considered the ramifications of superpowers before. Not *really*. Maybe he'd been kept separate to protect him from those who'd wish Captain Lumen harm.

"What can we do for you, Senator?" Cal, in full Deltaman gear, said. He strode to the middle of the room, assuming a position of authority above the rest of the group.

Dressed up like that, the full weight of his superhero identity looming, it was easy for Janie to see why the team had established their rule of only thinking about each other as their superhero identities when on the job. In the moment, he didn't even *look* like Cal anymore, either the one Janie had left behind in the world of her adolescence or the grown-up version she'd met here. Standing tall, black bodysuit sculpted against him, utility belt glinting with a variety of weapons and gadgets, face partially obscured by the hood of his cape, a smear of grease paint around his eyes, it was impossible to see anything but a superhero.

The same went for the rest of them. Who would have thought that some blue spandex over the face, a denim jacket and neon tutu skirt, hardened skin beneath military pants and tank, and a black Matrix trench coat would transform each of her friends so completely?

Senator Maxwell turned, his attention landing on Deltaman. Could he even tell whose face was hidden beneath those shadows? He glanced at the uniform, as if sizing Deltaman up, before taking his cellphone out of his pocket and handing it over.

Deltaman swept his fingers across the screen and Janie watched, barely containing a gasp, as the image jumped from the cellphone to the giant screens covering the wall. A shaky video started playing, as if it had been captured on a camcorder. Screams and chaos, people running everywhere. Janie recognized the fight she'd followed Clair into. One of the lizard men— a Shadow Raptor, Clair had called it later—leaped across the screen, the camera swinging to follow its path.

"Whoa," a voice in the recording said. "Do you see that?" An arm appeared from behind the camera, pointing across the open plaza, and then the image jumped several times, zooming in tighter and tighter on a small figure in the corner. A figure falling onto her butt, the image of her slowly shifting into view as she seemed to appear out of thin air. Janie went cold as, on screen, she watched her sunglasses fall from her face, watched herself scramble to collect them. The version of her on film glanced up as she hauled herself back to her feet, and this is where the video stopped, freezing the moment on a blurry but obvious truth: her own face, Jane Maxwell's face, looking back toward the camera.

For a second, everyone was silent. Then Clair's voice, clear as a bell, cut through the chill of the room. *"Fuck."*

"Has it gone viral yet?" Pixie Beats asked.

Granite Girl was already typing at a keyboard below the bank of computer screens. "I don't see anything on social media."

"That's because it's not on social media," Senator Maxwell said, whatever that meant. His words clearly had an impact on the rest of the room though; Janie saw them visibly let out a breath. Senator Maxwell scoffed. "I wouldn't be so relieved. If I don't deliver $10 million in crypto to someone calling themselves 'Dog Squad' by midnight Monday night, they'll post it."

"Fuck," Clair repeated, and Janie startled. When did Clair become such a potty mouth?

"Wait, Dog Squad?" Rip-Shift asked, while Deltaman added, "So it's blackmail."

The senator nodded tersely.

Granite Girl was already on it. She grabbed the cellphone from Deltaman, setting it beside her keyboard. Strings of code and numbers spread up the giant screens above her. It was all gibberish to Janie—she wasn't the most techie of her friends even in her own era, never mind working with stuff from the future.

She leaned over, whispering to Clair, "What's she doing?"

Clair ground her teeth for a moment in silence. "If I had to guess," she whispered back finally, her voice weirdly clipped, "I'd say she's trying to backtrace the file, see if she can hack the originating server to delete the footage."

"Okay, cool."

Clair huffed. "No, Janie. It is not 'cool.' If this video gets posted, the whole world will see Jane turning visible, exactly the same way Captain Lumen does. It'll take *two seconds* for people to figure out it's been her all along."

"I didn't mean it like—"

"Damn," Granite Girl said, cutting her off. "I've got to hand it to Lester, he's *good*. He's obscured his tracks through so many levels of encryption and relays, there's no *way* to trace it back to the source."

"Are you actually admiring a supervillain?" Clair said.

Granite Girl shrugged. "I appreciate artistry when I see it. Even if it fucks us over."

"So it's settled, then." Senator Maxwell marched over, snatching his cellphone back.

"Hey!" Granite Girl said, but it was Rip-Shift that stepped forward, Rip-Shift that put his arm out and blocked the senator from leaving.

"What's settled?" he asked.

"I pay up," Senator Maxwell said, sliding his cellphone back into his breast coat pocket.

A collective groan rippled from most of the team.

Deltaman clapped a hand on Senator Maxwell's shoulder. "Bad idea."

"Seriously," Pixie Beats said. "Never give in to a blackmailer."

Senator Maxwell slid out from Deltaman's grip. "Well, *thank you* all for your opinion," he said, not sounding remotely grateful, "but this really isn't up to you. I'm the one they contacted. I'm the one whose daughter is being used against him."

He didn't look at Janie, but somehow it would have been better if he had. Laying the blame where it belonged. Her stomach squirmed, even as Clair stepped forward.

"You're not the only one with something to lose here, Paul."

The corner of Senator Maxwell's lip twisted up. "No, but I am the one who's being asked to do something about it. I only came here to see if your team had a better option, but clearly your tech isn't up to the job."

"Hey!" Granite Girl said again.

"Senator," Deltaman said. He pushed himself between the senator and Clair, physically blocking the glower openly passing between them. "I'm asking you to think this through. There's no guarantee they won't release the video anyway, once they've gotten your money."

"They won't."

"What makes you so sure?"

Senator Maxwell stepped back, spreading his arms wide. His suit jacket rode up, its chest pulling open to draw attention to the patch of his impossibly white shirt beneath. "I'm a senator in the United States Congress. You really think they're going to give up that kind of leverage?"

"And you want to *give* them that leverage?" Windforce cut in, as cold as the gusts he controlled.

"I don't want to give them anything," Senator Maxwell said. "But at least if I keep paying, they'll keep silent. Eventually, either one of you supposed 'geniuses' will figure out how to delete the footage, or they'll get sloppy enough to get arrested. In the meantime, everybody's secrets stay secret. Unless someone in this room has a better idea?"

Silence pressed down on their shoulders. Janie glanced at the rest of the Heroes as they ducked their heads or rubbed the back of their necks, looking more like chastised schoolchildren than towering figures of virtue.

"That's what I thought." Senator Maxwell straightened his suit jacket, tugging at the sleeves. He still did not look at Janie. "I'll see myself out."

JANE IS TRAPPED IN THE MIDDLE OF A DEMON PIT.

They encircle her as an ancient ritual, each demon a point on a pentagram and Jane the unwitting sacrifice in the middle. The page looks straight down at her, her face turned up and slightly to the side in order to be identifying. Candlelight casts jarring shadows across her features, so it's impossible to tell if she's praying for rescue or plotting her own escape. The outside edge of the page is covered in speech bubbles full of heavy slashes, implying a wash of chants without actually naming them.

A glob of ink disrupted the shading Jane was adding, and she swore under her breath.

All she had to work with were cheap Bic pens, so she was making do the best she could. Jane herself had long since invested in a set of art pencils by the time she was this age, but if her younger parallel self had done the same, Jane couldn't find them. The sketches in the rest of the book looked like they'd been drawn in a standard No. 2 pencil, and Jane had forgotten to make sure she had those in her backpack.

It was fine. It's not like she was using this for anything other than to pass the time while Emily and Amber, from the student council, droned on in the center of the room about timetables and ticket sales.

Jane kept her head down, her forehead leaning on her fist as she doodled in the sketchbook balanced on her lap. She pushed her glasses up with her thumb and then added another line, shading in the horns of the demon in the heart of the pit—a demon with a *coincidentally* similar hairstyle to Emily's.

God, Jane hated high school.

Somewhere in front of her, a girl cleared her throat. Loudly, and with great exaggeration.

"Janie? Any thoughts to contribute?"

Jane looked up. The demon pit faded from her mind, replaced instead by her own personal version of hell: a cluster of perky blondes and wannabe-jocks, desks dragged into a circle "so that everyone has a chance to contribute." Jane had a seat two rings back from the center, hoping to keep out of sight. But apparently Emily and Amber took their Homecoming duties as seriously as it would look on their college application letters, and now everyone had swiveled their heads to look straight at Jane, Emily's beaming white gaze shining a spotlight on Jane's quiet corner.

"Um," Jane said. "Not really. I mean, it all sounds good."

A series of titters broke the room. Clearly the wrong answer. If Jane was still *actually* a teenager, she may have been embarrassed —even mortified—by getting caught out like this. Luckily, Jane had been away from high school so long that the idea of caring what any of these people thought of her was a joke.

She turned back to her art without waiting for the conversation to move on.

The sketchbook had been wedged between two of Janie's textbooks, crammed into the bottom of her backpack. Jane had only found it because she'd been pretending to look for something when she first sat down, in order to avoid talking to anyone.

Jane knew the brand immediately. Something she used to buy at Walmart during back-to-school season, a whole pile of them for just five dollars. The paper was okay, not great, but at the time quantity was far more important than quality. Young Jane had gone through paper like nobody's business, to the point where she'd quickly been banned from pulling from the stash of her dad's printer paper when she was just seven years old. At the time, they'd bought her stacks of faded construction paper. The Walmart sketchbooks, then, discovered halfway through middle school, were a treasured step up.

The pages were filled with pictures of girls, in all different poses. In her own youth, Jane had told people she wanted to be a fashion designer, despite the fact that she perpetually dressed like the baby gay she was. It had taken Jane a while to find a blank page.

A shadow fell across Jane's sketch. The demon pit turned ever darker.

Again, Jane probably should have been embarrassed. Again, it was more effort than Jane could muster. What difference did it make if a bunch of literal children realized she was bored by their meeting?

Rather than being insulted by the drawing, though, Emily's face lit up at the sight of it. More than that: she actually *clapped her hands*, and gave a tiny hop where she stood.

"Ja-nie!" Emily squealed, drawing the name out. "Why didn't you say you were an artist? You could help with the setup!"

Jane glanced down at the half-finished drawing in her lap. Her heart knew how to craft the lines and forms she was used to, but the untrained muscles in her arms and fingers didn't. The result was, to Jane's eye, a shoddy imitation of the craftsmanship she was used to—this weird mishmash of amateur and professional that somehow ended up being neither and both. She'd never have allowed such a mess in her studio back in her own life, but here, apparently, it would more than suffice.

"Oh," Jane said, leaning over to cover the page with her arms as best as she could, "I don't know. It's not something I really share with people."

Emily was not dissuaded. "We're not asking you to enter something into an art show, Janie. We're just talking some banners, maybe a drawing we can put on our flyers. I promise, if you want, no one outside of this room will even know you're the artist behind it."

"Yeah, no, it's not that," Jane said. "It's just, I don't really . . . do that sort of thing."

Emily crossed her arms. "What sort of thing? Contribute? Put in effort? Show your support to the classmates who make your high school career possible?"

It was all Jane could do to bite down on the laugh working its way up from her chest. "Yeah. That's it, exactly."

Emily blinked, as if genuinely puzzled by the sarcasm. "Why are you even here, then?"

It was a good question, one Jane had wondered herself more than once since setting foot in this room. There were so many things she needed to be doing, in order to figure out how she'd gotten here and (hopefully) how to send herself back.

"Got sent to the principal's office," Jane said. "They told me this was better than detention."

The haughty expression on Emily's face faltered. Just for a second. A jostle, not a collapse. Her nose wrinkled. "This is a privilege, Janie. I'm sorry you can't see that."

Jane's cheeks heated as she turned back to her sketchbook. She may look like a child, but she was still an adult. Who was she to be mean to a teenage girl—one who probably had her own shit to deal with, piles of hidden insecurities that Jane could be pissing all over and not even realize it? Jane wanted to blame the hormonal cocktail swimming in this teenage body, kicking her snark into high gear. But was that truly an excuse for bad behavior? An eternal question, she supposed: how much of teenage angst was chemical and how much was the transient nature of youth, realizing that the world was a lot shittier than the story her suburban upbringing had sold her?

By the time she could even think of being the bigger person and apologizing for her pettiness, though, Emily was wrapping up the meeting. "Okay, so be sure to get those updated flyers out by the end of the weekend, yeah?" she told one of the other students. Jane glanced at the clock over the door just once before stuffing her sketchbook back into her bag and hightailing it out of there.

She was just passing the library when she saw it. A paper taped to the door, tall block letters written in thick marker:

Summer brain giving you reentry troubles? Tutoring available now!
Beneath that, an extremely crude drawing of what Jane sincerely hoped was supposed to be a rocket ship.

Jane slowed, shifting the weight of her backpack strap. Although it was Saturday, there were still pages and pages of homework dragging the bag down against her back. Homework that, despite her best efforts, Jane could barely remember how to do. Sure, she planned to get out of this situation—reunite with her team, find a way to reverse the effects of this body-swap, set everything right again—but how long would that take? And in the meantime, her grades would tank with every passing test. She shut her eyes, the memory of Emily's hurt face staring down at her. Jane knew better than anyone that what happens in high school does, potentially, have consequences, and even if *she* wasn't planning to stick around long enough to deal with the fallout, that didn't mean there wouldn't be any.

Jane sighed as she pushed open the library door. It may not be her *first* choice, but she could, at least, be an adult for once. She could do one thing right.

"OKAY, SO WHAT ARE WE REALLY GOING TO DO?" KEISHA
said once the senator was gone, the door *shushing* shut behind him.

"Not sure yet," Clair said. The team tightened, forming a ring around the conference table. Clair took a deep breath and spread her hands. "All right, give me any and all ideas. Nothing is stupid at this point—except Paul's."

A low chuckle broke the tension.

Janie hung back, leaning against one of the few slices of wall not covered by screens. If she was lucky, they'd forget she was even here. Personally, she didn't see what made Senator Maxwell's plan so awful. Risky, yes, sure, but wasn't everything the Heroes did every day?

"I think before we can even think next steps," Keisha said, "we need to figure out what's really going on here. Why is Dog Squad suddenly in the blackmail game? It's not their typical M.O."

"Does it matter?" Tony said. "The problem's the same no matter their motive."

"Unless their motive helps us identify their next moves."

"Assuming we guess it right," Clair said. "At this point, the best we'll do is speculate, and who knows if we're even remotely close to the truth. We can't afford to waste time exploring a scenario that may be completely off base."

"Fine, but even if we abandon their motives, Dog Squad is still our best way in," Keisha said. "If we can't trace the *message*, maybe we can trace the *messenger*."

"She's right," Devin said. "I can do a few sweeps of the city, see if I spot any signs of recent Shadow Raptor activity."

Clair nodded. "All right, that's fair enough. In the meantime, Keisha, Tony, why don't you hit up some of the seedier parts of town, see if you can't shake loose any information. Lester's breeding new Shadow Raptors, he has to be getting his supplies somewhere."

"I'd like to stay here," Marie said. "While they're hunting him IRL, I can keep a script running to search the internet for any sign of his recent activities. Plus, I've still got some ideas I'm working on for the Janie Problem."

Janie looked up sharply. "*Excuse* me?"

Marie turned and shrugged, unapologetic. "You're still squatting in a body that doesn't belong to you. The scans we ran haven't handed us a solution on a silver platter, but that doesn't mean we don't keep trying."

"That's perfect," Clair said, cutting in before Janie could respond. Janie crossed her arms.

"We should also see what we can get from Larry," Cal said. "He may be in prison, but that doesn't mean his brother didn't tell him anything before shit hit the fan."

"Good," Clair said. "I'll go."

Cal's face tightened. "I was thinking I could do it."

Clair curled her fingers, one by one, and then spread them again. "He won't volunteer that information. Besides, we still need someone to run through his local known associates."

"*What* known associates?" Cal asked. "These two clowns had barely arrived before Larry landed himself in jail."

A flick of Clair's wrist, and a fresh projection floated over the conference table.

Cal leaned in, squinting as he read the file. "You're kidding, right? This isn't a *known associate*, this is an elderly aunt he probably hasn't seen in twenty years."

"We don't know that."

"But we can reasonably assume," Cal said. He sneered. "She's probably got an apartment full of cats. What information could she possibly have?"

"That's what you're going to find out."

"Clair, I—"

"It's not up for discussion. We need someone to check it out. Work your 'charm' on her. And don't complain, you just drew the short straw this time."

"And every time," Cal mumbled, his shoulders bristling.

"Okay, so are we good?" Clair turned, assessing the rest of the Heroes, who all nodded their agreement. "Good." She tapped the table, as if adjuring court. "All right. Let's do it."

"Wait!" Janie said. "What about me?"

The Heroes turned, controlled faces looking back at her.

"What *about* you?" Clair asked.

Janie fought against the rush of heat to her cheeks. She stepped forward. "I want to help. I know I'm not, like, a fully trained superhero, but I can still be useful."

Cal raised an eyebrow. Not entirely agreeing—but not ruling it out, either. He tossed a look to Clair, who immediately shook her head. Janie gritted her teeth. She was starting to hate the way that Clair was just *in charge* of her for some reason, everyone deferring to her judgment. But what was Janie supposed to say, without sounding like a whiny child?

"No," Clair said. "You're not getting involved."

"Clair," Keisha said. "Come on. She's a big girl. There's got to be something we can give her."

Devin raised a hand. "She could maybe help Marie?"

"No way," Marie cut in, and a rush of gratitude flooded Janie—finally, someone who believed in her—until Marie added, "I'm not babysitting."

So much for solidarity.

"No one said anything about babysitting," Devin said. "She can . . . I don't know. Get you coffee or something."

"I have a state-of-the-art automated espresso machine in the lab. I don't need an intern."

"Yeah, but the point—"

"The *point* is to keep her occupied so she's not causing trouble," Marie said. "That's babysitting. That's the literal definition of babysitting."

"I can take her."

The team paused, their heads collectively turning in Cal's direction.

"What?" he said. "We all know I got the training-wheels assignment. There's no reason she can't come along and listen to me talk to some old biddy."

It was sound reasoning, as far as Janie was concerned, if a little insulting.

Unfortunately, Clair would not be moved. "No. I'm sorry, but no."

"Oh, come on," Cal griped. "You and I both know it's perfectly safe."

"We actually *don't* know that," Clair said. "What if Dog Squad actually *did* make contact with their aunt? What if they're monitoring the place? What if Janie gets separated—"

"I'll protect her," Cal said, and there was something so determined in his voice that it actually stalled the argument for a moment, both Janie and Clair rocking back under its impact. The rest of the team looked away, clearly not wanting to get involved.

Cal took a step toward Clair. For a second, she raised her hands in defense, as if expecting him to strike out or something—but all he did was hold his own hand out, palm up, between them. Offering.

"Clair. I promise, I'll keep her safe."

Janie held her breath as Clair considered the vulnerable skin in front of her. What Cal planned to share through Clair's empathic powers was anyone's guess. It wasn't clear at first if Clair would even accept this offer—maybe she didn't even know, herself. But then, tentatively, Clair reached out and laid the bare tips of her fingers against Cal's open palm.

She drew back almost immediately, as if she'd been burned. But it was clearly enough, because she looked at Janie, studying her intently for a moment, before turning back to Cal.

"You'd better."

THERE WAS NO LIBRARIAN ON SATURDAYS, SO IT TOOK Jane a few minutes to track down this mystery tutor. A second sign, taped to the checkout desk, simply read "TUTOR" and pointed with a sloppy arrow to the left.

Jane heard him before she saw him. A choppy drumbeat, the end of a pencil tapping against a table. The sound trailed from the open door of a study room, a wild snake of a sound bubble with *tappity-tap-tap-tap* markings. Jane twisted around it, letting it flow over and past her as she followed it to its source. There was something vaguely familiar in the pattern, like a back issue she'd forgotten she'd already read years earlier.

She rounded the final corner. Drew to a sudden stop in the open doorway.

Cal glanced up. He blinked in surprise, just for a second, before his face broke into a wide grin. "Brainy Janie!"

Jane flinched. She never thought she'd miss being "Main Jane," but she'd certainly take it over this version of the nicknames Cal insisted on giving people. Jane pointed at him. "I thought *you* were the one who needed tutoring."

"In *math*," Cal said, the *duh* practically dripping from his words. He did not appear offended by her confusion, though. He leaned back in his chair, far enough to prop one of his shoes against the edge of the table. "You should be flattered. I got the idea from you. When you bailed on me—"

"I didn't *bail*—"

"—I figured, hey, I may be doomed in Geometry. But that doesn't mean I can't make a few bucks off the rest." He spread his arms wide, gesturing to the books spread across the study room table as if he were lording over his own tiny empire.

In truth, it wasn't *that* outlandish of a realization. Cal had plenty of faults, in any version of reality, but he wasn't outright stupid. That's what made it so frustrating to deal with him, when he was at his most base. It's not that he couldn't grasp the concepts of patriarchy and privilege; it's not that he wasn't capable of understanding what he was doing wrong, when he pushed the line too far. It's just that he usually didn't take the time to care about bettering himself.

But he'd always done reasonably well in school, Jane had to grant him that.

Cal took his foot back off the table. He picked up his pencil, the eraser hovering over an open notebook but not yet resuming its drumbeat. "What are you doing here, anyway?"

Jane gripped her backpack strap. It was one thing to ask for help when she figured she'd be paying a total stranger. Going to her friends—going to Cal, in particular—was not only a much more embarrassing prospect, but a risky one as well.

Did she have any other choice, though? She needed to catch up, and she didn't exactly have Google and YouTube to turn to yet. Even if the answers existed on the internet, tracking them down in this era would be impossible, especially for someone spoiled by modern search algorithms.

"It's like your sign said," she offered eventually. "Reentry troubles. It's . . . been a while since I had to do homework."

Cal just barely stifled a laugh. "Weren't you the one who was bragging just a few days ago about how easy German was this year?"

"Look, do you want to help me or not?"

The humor slipped off Cal's face. He put a hand to his chest. "Always. My Brainy Janie needs a hand, I'll be there for her. You know that."

"Thank you," Jane muttered, feeling oddly chastised.

"But it *will* cost you." Cal snapped his fingers and pointed across at her. "There are no free rides on the Cal Knowledge Train."

"Of course." Jane pulled her backpack around, already groping for the change purse where she kept her lunch money. "What are your rates?"

Cal shook his head. "Nope. A trade: whatever subject you need, for math lessons from you."

Jane froze, her hand still stuffed into her backpack. "Ah."

"Don't tell me your summer brain ate that crazy math skill."

"No, of course not." Jane spoke with confidence, as if surety would make up for the severe gaps in her knowledge. "Deal. Math lessons. No problem. But we have to start with mine."

Mainly because Jane needed time to *learn* the math before she could even begin to teach Cal—or better yet, find a way out of the deal before she had to make good on her promise. But he didn't need to know any of that.

Cal shrugged, oblivious. "Suits me."

He shoved out the chair nearest him with his foot. It slid crookedly, barely even leaving room for Jane to sit, but she pulled it out the rest of the way and took her place.

A grin broke over Cal's face. Surprisingly genuine, like he was actually looking forward to this. "So where do we start?"

Jane pulled each of her textbooks out of her backpack, piling them up on the table between them. It wasn't all her subjects, there was only so much she could lug back and forth from her locker in one go. Still, it was a start.

"The beginning," Jane said, slapping her hand down on the stack of books. She met Cal's eyes straight on, daring him to question her. "Teach me everything."

Cal glanced at the pile. He twisted them toward him, just enough to take in the handwritten label on each of their grocery-bag wrapped spines. For a second, Jane was worried she'd gone too far—that she'd scared him off, or tipped her hand, or stretched his tutoring abilities past the breaking point.

But just as she was about to take a breath and tell him to forget it, he nodded.

"You got it."

THE AUNT, IT TURNS OUT, DID INDEED HAVE CATS. CATS,
and a decorating style that was far more . . . *expressive* than Janie
was used to.

Cal sat back on the couch, letting a cat with long white fur
step onto his lap. It sniffed and then headbutted his open palm.
He scratched it behind the ears as he cracked a grin and said,
"So. You like pussy, huh?"

The aunt (she'd introduced herself at the door, but Janie had
been too overwhelmed to process names) barked a sharp laugh.
She raised one bony hand, bangles clacking down her arm as she
motioned at the walls. "Occupational hazard, I'm afraid. I'm an
artist, and my wife was a sex therapist before she passed, bless
her soul. It comes with the territory."

Janie took a sip of the water she'd been offered. The glass
was sweating almost as much as she was. She kept her eyes
fixed forward, on the aunt's face, to avoid accidentally looking
at the . . . art. Or more precisely, the naked women, and naked
women's body parts, in the art.

The aunt smiled at Janie.

She had been reluctant to let them into her apartment, at first. *I don't talk to cops,* she'd said before they'd even introduced themselves, and Cal had laughed and assured her that he didn't either. That had only hardened her expression, taking in his close-cropped blond hair and crisp jeans. She was about to close the door in his face when Cal leaned in, whispering something against her ear. Janie couldn't hear what he'd said, but whatever it was, it must have been good: the aunt's face had gone slack, then burst into a wide smile as she suddenly changed her mind, quick as a switch being flipped.

Must be nice, Janie thought to herself as the aunt ushered them in, to have that kind of power over people. They were led into the aunt's living room, plied with offers of food and tea and finally water, if nothing else.

Now Janie ran her thumb through the condensation on the glass, tracing tighter and tighter spirals. There was an emergency flip phone in her pocket Clair had given Janie before she left, preprogrammed with the Heroes' numbers. Janie was only supposed to use it if she found herself in the middle of a disaster Cal couldn't save her from. Janie wondered how much trouble she'd be in if she used it to bail on this mission she'd begged to be allowed on in the first place.

Cal glanced over, a surprisingly sympathetic expression on his face.

"Actually," he said, turning back and interrupting whatever the aunt was saying, "you know what? I think I will take one of those lemon bars. And tea sounds great, thanks." He leaned forward, squeezing her hand. "Take your time."

The aunt blinked. "Of course. Excuse me, I'll be back in a few minutes."

She shuffled off to the kitchen, shaking her head as if trying to clear a fog.

As soon as she was gone, Cal leaned over, lowering his voice. "You okay?"

"Yeah, duh," Janie said. Too quickly. She set her water glass on the coffee table and leaned back on the couch in an effort to appear nonchalant.

"You know, if this is too much—allergies, or whatever," he said, raising his hand from the cat, bits of fur drifting into the air, "we can go. Just say the word."

Janie wedged a smile onto her face. "Nope. All good. I was just . . . ," she trailed off, something odd catching the corner of her eye. Janie sat up straight. "What was *that*?"

Cal looked around the room, clearly dumbfounded. "What?"

"You didn't see it?" Janie got to her feet. "It was . . . I don't know. Not a color, exactly, but . . . *something*."

She hated how unhelpful that was, but honestly she didn't know any words to describe it. A wave of something she could see, but not something she could ascribe a solid adjective to. It was red, but not red. It was a bubble, but not a bubble. It made Janie's head hurt trying to find a way to explain it—and there it was again. Rippling out from the corner of the room, faintly at first, but now it was picking up intensity.

"Here." Janie strode over and picked up a circular object sitting on a shelf by the window. The not-color was so *bright*, pouring off the thing in pulsating waves that ballooned out to fill the room. Janie flinched back from it, even as she held it out to Cal. "It's coming from here."

"Oh. That's nothing. A myMind—you talk to it. It tells you the weather and sets your calendar and shit."

"Seriously? Like the Star Trek computer?"

"Yeah, sure."

Sweet Roddenberry's ghost, what *didn't* the future have? Janie tried to look at it, but the not-color seared across her eyeballs.

"Is it supposed to be going this nuts, though?" Janie squinted through the pain. Waves radiated out in rapid pulses, drowning the room. "Whatever it does, it's going crazy."

"I'm sure it's fine."

"I don't know. I don't think it's supposed to be like this. It's like it's—"

The not-color flared, bright enough that Janie yelped and stumbled back as if it had burned her. The myMind slid from her fingers, thunking to the carpet. The light bubbles were all she could see now, just waves and waves of the stuff, pouring over and through her, down her throat as she tried to cry out.

Somewhere, distantly, she thought she heard someone shout her name, but it was too far away, shrinking beneath the oppressive onslaught of whatever this was. Janie's world spun, whispers of a voice not quite her own shuffling around in the back of her mind.

She might have passed out, or she might have just hallucinated the blinding light so long that time passed without her noticing. By the time she came back to herself, Cal was setting her down on the front steps of the building.

"It's fine," he kept saying to concerned passersby, "she's good, we're fine," and for some reason, no matter how worried they looked as they approached, they believed him, drifting off like moths.

"Are you okay?" Cal asked. He crouched in front of her, feeling her forehead with the back of his hand.

Janie swatted him away. "I'm fine. Just a headache."

"It didn't look like a headache." He straightened up, towering over her. "Should I call Clair? I'm sure she'd—"

"*No,*" Janie said. She fixed her glasses, crooked from when Cal had probably had to carry her down the stairs. God, how humiliating. "I swear, Cal, I'm fine. Come on, we should probably get back upstairs before we ruin our welcome."

Cal waved this idea off. "Nah, that's a total dead end. I knew it from the instant we got here. Clair must have, too, deep down, or else she'd never have agreed to let you come."

Janie's mouth soured. She hated the reminder of how useless the team thought this mission was, but, on the other hand, it meant she didn't need to return to the naked-lady apartment with Cal, and that was . . . good.

"Right." Janie drew herself to her feet, careful not to sway. "Okay, well. I guess we should get back, then." She started walking, hoping it was the right direction.

Cal fell into step beside her. "You know Clair's just looking out for you, right?" he said finally. "I get that it's frustrating, but sometimes we need to act in a person's best interest, even if it's not something they'd choose for themselves, and—" Cal drew himself short. His face turned sour, as if the words were distasteful. "Actually, screw that. You should be allowed to help, if that's what you want. Just . . . make sure you're ready for it, that's all. It can get messy, this life."

"Is it really that tough? Doing your job, I mean. Being a"— Janie glanced around, then leaned in and lowered her voice— "superhero."

Cal smirked, but somehow it wasn't unkind. He stepped wide around a flower display outside a shop. "It can be. You don't go into this looking for an easy lifestyle. But it's not the job that gets me, not really. The others don't understand. They've got this perfect little club going, but if you're not exactly what they want from you . . ."

"I thought you were part of the team."

"Oh, I am," Cal said. The smallest frown creased his brow. "On paper. But the others have powers, and while no one ever *says* that makes them better heroes than me, you know that's what they're all thinking."

"I'm sure no one thinks that."

"Ha, no, they definitely do." He reached beneath his shirt collar, drawing out a set of dog tags that clicked together as he held them up for Janie to see. "But I served two tours of duty in Afghanistan. Did you know that? I was a fucking Marine. Got a medal once for charging into a building that was about to collapse, to rescue some civilians. Don't get me wrong, I'm not saying the rest of them don't put their lives at risk when they're out there protecting the city, but this gig's got *nothing* on the shit I saw over there."

"I'm sorry." Janie really didn't know what else to say. She tried to imagine the Cal she knew doing that—but as much as he was a friend, she just couldn't see it.

Cal tucked his dog tags back under his shirt, indifferent. "It was better before I lost part of my memory. We may have had our differences, but at least we were a *team* in those days. Now it's like they barely even trust me to put the dishes in the sink."

"*Do* you put the dishes in the sink, though?"

A bark of a laugh. Cal lifted his hand and tipped it back and forth like scales settling. "Jury's still out, honestly."

Janie smiled, but then the feeling soured on her tongue. It had felt natural, normal even, to make a joke about his ability to keep up with a household chore, but now she wondered if she'd too easily ignored that little bomb he just dropped. *Before I lost part of my memory.* Cal didn't often open up about things that actually mattered.

"What happened?" Janie asked carefully. Trying again. "With your memory, I mean."

Cal sat with the question for a moment. "I don't really know. I went to bed one day, everything's fine. Next thing I know I'm waking up in a rejuve pod, and the team tells me it's a few years later and that I got hit with some kind of blast from a baddie that may have impacted my memory. Which was the biggest fucking understatement bullshit I've ever heard."

"You don't remember *anything* between?"

"Nothing worth it. There are bits and pieces. Sometimes. Some of it's come back, stupid stuff like half a memory of one birthday I'd otherwise forgotten, but otherwise, nope. I've got zip."

Janie looked away. She couldn't imagine having that much of your life just gone. On some level, perhaps, it wasn't entirely dissimilar from what she was going through now: suddenly being years in what may as well have been the future, everyone else full of history, so many comments and inside jokes going over your head. But they hadn't been *stolen* from her. It was a subtle distinction, perhaps, but one Janie hadn't even realized was a comfort until now.

When she reached over, wrapping her fingers around his arm, she didn't even question it. Just gave it a squeeze.

"It's nice getting to talk to you."

Cal glanced down at her hand. Smiled. "Yeah. You too, Brainy Janie. You know, it's funny—you're a lot more like the Jane we used to have. Our new Main Jane doesn't like me very much."

"New Jane?"

"Yeah. You know, the one you replaced . . . ?"

He glanced at her for a second, clearly waiting for the recognition to click, the moment when her face changed.

"Oh," Cal said when she offered nothing. He slid his arm from her grip. "They didn't tell you, did they?"

"I guess not?"

"Right. Yeah, I suppose there are a few things they skipped in your Welcome to Our Earth speech." He ran his hands over his cropped hair. "Okay, so . . . I can't give you the details, because this happened during that memory gap, but apparently the Jane you swapped bodies with came here from yet *another* parallel world. I think the deal is that we brought her here to help solve a crisis, because our Jane was missing and we needed a Captain Lumen? Either way, she never ended up going back. Decided to pick up the whole superhero thing and stick it out with us."

"What?" Janie stopped in the middle of the sidewalk, trying to process this. She knew that superheroes had to keep some secrets, but that was kind of a lot to leave out. Jane wasn't even this world's original Jane? Janie's mind swirled, trying to piece it all together. On the surface, what Cal said made enough sense to at least follow the line from dot to dot.

But she could tell, even just from this fragment, that there was so much *more* to what had happened. She would have suspected him of skimming over it, hiding details because Janie was too young, too inexperienced, too . . . not their Jane. Except that, by his own admission, there was a lot about this situation that even he didn't know. And Janie would never be sure, but she couldn't help but wonder if part of that wasn't by design. There were too many gaps, too many variables that didn't add up at the end of the equation. Cal had never been great at math, always forgetting to account for numbers that had been left aside in parentheses.

Janie, on the other hand, always accounted for all the pieces.

"But . . . what about your original Jane?" Janie asked finally. "Where's she?"

A wrinkle drew itself between Cal's eyebrows. "I . . . don't know." Cal's voice had gone oddly soft, like he was puzzling something out and speech wasn't really part of the mental process. "For some reason I never thought to ask . . ."

But then, like someone had snapped their fingers, the moment was over. He blinked, shook his head. His easygoing grin was back, so bright it was hard to imagine it had ever left his face. He turned to her, snapping his fingers. "Hey, you want some ice cream before we head back? I know a great place."

For a moment, Janie could only stare at him. She wanted to

dig in further, to see if she could bring back that window of hesitation, but . . . something told her not to poke at it too much.

Besides, she had a feeling Cal wasn't the one she needed to press for answers at this point. "Sure," she said, filing this away for later. "That would be great."

THEY WORKED IN THE STUDY ROOM FOR SO LONG THEY lost track of the time. In fact it was Cal, not Jane, who eventually looked up at the clock and realized they were already running late.

Jane blinked, raising her head from the stacks of textbooks, worksheets, and spiral-bound notebooks. "Late for what?"

"We're supposed to be at Tony's?" Cal said, searching Jane's face for signs of recognition. "Movie night? Remember?"

"Right. Of course." Jane stood up, hastily stuffing notebooks back into her bag and cursing this world's version of herself for making so many plans. She didn't remember her friends being this organized, scheduling hangouts and movie nights days in advance, but she supposed it could have easily been time playing tricks with her memory, and not necessarily the difference between her parallel selves.

Outside, they discovered that they'd used the same bike rack. "Might as well ride together," Cal said, and Jane couldn't find a way to argue. They were going to the same place, from the same place. Trying to avoid each other would just be weird, and besides—they were friends, weren't they? Just because Jane couldn't remember hanging out with a younger Cal one on one, not surrounded by the buffer of the rest of their group, didn't mean they shouldn't. Plus, this version of Jane used to tutor him in math. There had probably been plenty of times when they'd ridden somewhere after school together. It wasn't weird, she told herself, as she hitched onto her seat and checked her brakes.

When they arrived at Tony's house, they dropped their bikes into the pile gathered in the driveway. They didn't even knock at the front door, just let themselves in, Cal hollering a hello as he clambered over the shoes in the foyer and vaulted up the split staircase to the main floor.

Jane hesitated in the doorway behind him. For Cal, it had only been, what, a couple of weeks since their last movie night? But for Jane, it had been years since she'd stepped through these doors—not since they all graduated from high school and moved on with their lives.

The friends were already gathered in the circle of the living room, dining room, and kitchen. Devin's head popped over the half-height wall overlooking the foyer as Jane climbed the stairs, shouting her name. "There she is!"

Jane nodded a hello, a stiff smile on her face. Weird that she felt more comfortable at an art-gallery fundraiser, helping Clair squeeze out donations for the museum she worked at, than here in the company of her oldest friends—the same people who, as adults, she spent every day fighting crime with.

But that was the thing: as *adults*. Here, they were still the furthest cries from their superhero personas they would ever be. Jane hovered in the hallway just outside the living room and kitchen, the rest of them acting so clichéd it was impossible not to see them as cartoon characters. There was Cal, already in the thick of things, one hand raised in a crude gesture, the other stuffed wrist deep into a bowl of radioactive-orange Cheetos. Keisha was curled onto the sofa, reading a book as she kept half an ear out to the rest of the conversation floating around her. Marie, out of sight in the dining room; nonetheless, her speech bubble floated into view, muttering something about frosting.

Tony, meanwhile, was in the kitchen with his dad, the two of them grating cheddar cheese over a tray full of potato skins.

"Ah, Janie," Tony's dad said as he shifted back to life, lines fading away into real shadows. "We were starting to think you wouldn't make it."

"Hi, Mr. Anderson." Jane was grateful, at least, that her reduced stature and the spread of angry zits across her cheeks instinctively brought back some old habits—these days, she called all her friends' parents by their first names, could barely even remember a time when she didn't. But now she *was* back in that time, the nebulous stretch of what may as well be her past, and old habits, it turned out, died hard. "Thank you for having me."

Mr. Anderson grinned. "Anytime, Janie. You're good kids. We're happy to have you."

Jane blushed. She moved through to the dining room. Tony's family had cleared the table, homework and bills and a random sweatshirt shoved onto a chair to make space. In the open territory, they had filled the gap with food. There was enough here to feed a small army, so if they were lucky it should barely cover the hunger of seven ravenous teenagers. Even Jane's stomach growled as she took in the spread before her: giant plastic bowls filled with every flavor of chip and cheese puff available; a bubbling casserole of some kind of cheesy dip, orange grease pooled along the edges; a tub of store-bought sugar cookies; bags of ripped-open candy, M&Ms spilling across the tablecloth; and, naturally, three giant trays of Marie's signature chocolate chip cookie dough cupcakes.

It was hard for Jane to remember, sometimes, the environment Marie had grown up in, and the kind of person she'd been forced to be. Her parents were deeply, *deeply* religious, and there was never a shortage of baking in the Miller household, for bake sales and church events and just because Mrs. Miller felt it was important to bring food when you were invited somewhere. As a result, Marie had rarely turned up to a gathering without plenty of sugar and carbs on hand—the only benefit her friends saw to the upbringing Marie raged against in private. Really, it was a wonder she was allowed at these movie nights at all, a hard-won victory Jane had nearly forgotten about. Though Marie would still need to be home by nine, Jane remembered suddenly.

Jane stepped forward, picking up one of the cupcakes from the tray. It looked and smelled *amazing*, though Jane hadn't actually tasted one in years. Even the Marie from her original world, the one who hadn't become a superhero but had instead built a tiny internet empire for herself with her cooking blog, still refused to make the old recipes her mother had taught her.

But either version of the future was still a long way off. Right here, right now, Marie would be making cupcakes for the next several years. And Jane, for one, planned to enjoy the fruits of these labors as long as she was here. Especially since the stomach of this borrowed body actually allowed her to eat all this junk without getting a carb hangover the next day. This free ticket was a weird and unexpected gift, one she still wasn't used to accepting. But if the smell of Marie's cupcakes wouldn't tempt her into indulging, literally nothing would. Jane peeled the paper back and bit in, sugar and fat exploding across her tongue.

When she was done, she wiped the last bit of frosting off her face with her thumb. The sugar was hitting hard now, a rush of wildness sweeping over Jane as she surveyed this gangly group of her friends. They were so young, their futures still a murky, unknowable shape that pulled at them with a yearning so fierce it almost ached. The need to know how everything would turn out used to gnaw at Jane, so much that at times she thought it would drive her mad. There was no way to know, no way to be sure.

Until now.

Jane grinned. "You know," she said, a tease in her voice, "I bet Sean Bailey would really love these cupcakes."

She said this simply, plainly, setting it in the middle of the table as if it was another snack for the group. As Jane had expected, they dug into it with all the ferocious appetite of gossip-hungry teenagers. All heads whipped toward Marie, whose cheeks bloomed a sudden, furious red.

"Sean from chem lab?" Keisha asked. Her eyes widened in delight as Marie's cheeks deepened even further. "Oh man, you *like* him!"

"Do not!"

"You so do!" Keisha said with a laugh. "You should ask him out!"

"Ask him to Homecoming," Jane offered. Sean and Marie had gone to Homecoming in her own world, though she couldn't remember who'd asked whom. It wouldn't last, but she thought they'd had fun that one night, anyway.

Marie blushed furiously. "I couldn't." She picked up one of her own cupcakes, stuffing her face.

"Aw, come on!" Keisha said. "Why not?"

"Keish," Clair said softly. She laid a gentle hand on Keisha's shoulder, quieting her. "It's fine. If she doesn't want to, she doesn't want to. Besides, I can think of someone else who's *much* more desperate to ask out their crush." Clair glanced over, catching Jane's eye—just for a second, and then a second too long.

No. Jane's world spun out from underfoot. Was this what she got for meddling, then? Some karmic kickback, the universe punishing her for teasing them by proving that even now Jane couldn't have all the answers? It felt impossible that Clair would choose *now* to make her move, so casually, in front of all their friends, and yet—for one wild second, Jane was sure it was going to happen.

But then Clair turned away, grinning as she said, "Devin. *How* long has he been pining over Jess now?"

Jane let out a nervous laugh. It blended into the group as several squeals and oohs scattered over the table.

"Yes, *please*, just do it already," Tony said, tipping his head back in frustration. The rest of them laughed in agreement, even as Devin waved his hands in repeated X motions as if warding off a demon.

"It's not that easy!" he said. "She's . . . You guys have no idea. I've got to do it *right*."

"Yeah, yeah." Clair waved a cupcake in dismissal. "That's what you've been saying since the two of you met at star camp."

"Astronomy camp," Devin corrected automatically.

"Right. I keep telling you, if you like a girl, you've got to just *say it*. Be bold!"

Heat threatened Jane's cheeks. She tried to will it away, resting her hand over Devin's instead.

"Don't worry, Dev. You'll do it, and it will be amazing. Trust me. She's going to love you once she gets to know you."

Marie folded her empty cupcake wrapper. "Look at the Love Prophet over here. You've never even had a boyfriend. What makes you so smart?"

Jane ignored the heteronormative assumption. "I just have a feeling."

A feeling, yes, but also a string of memories. In her own world, anyway, Jess would turn out to be Devin's first serious girlfriend, dating him all the way through the beginning of senior year. In the end, she'd break his heart, but that hurt would pave way for him to meet Claudia, and then Angela, and a string of others who would move in and out of his life with a happy regularity.

Jane reached for another cupcake, her hand sliding off Devin's.

"Okay, enough of this sappy crap." Tony grabbed a bowl of chips from the middle of the table. "Are we going to watch a movie tonight, or what?"

"Hell yeah!" Cal said, keeping his voice low so that Tony's parents wouldn't hear the swear. He followed Tony into the living room, flopping deep into the Andersons' couch.

The rest of them trickled in, tossing pillows around as they claimed spots and made themselves nests. A tangle of bony teenage limbs knotted themselves into a puppy pile. Tony pulled his copy of *The Matrix* from a cabinet full of VHS tapes. It was the same movie they'd been watching every time he hosted movie night since it came out last year, but nobody was going to complain—not only was it Tony's house, Tony's pick, but at this point *The Matrix* was still hands-down the coolest movie this fresh-faced group of nerds had ever seen. Tony, in particular, would latch on to it with such gusto that his obsession still hadn't wavered by Jane's time—still occasionally introducing himself as "Mr. Anderson" in his eerily authentic Hugo Weaving voice.

Jane settled into the corner of the couch, drawing her feet up onto the cushion with her. Sugar and a youthful giddiness had seized her, and she found herself oddly looking forward to this experience. Despite Tony's fanaticism, it had been *years* since Jane had last watched the movie, and she was curious if it would still hold up.

Clair settled in beside Jane. Their warm shoulders knocked together. "We should have invited Hailey," Clair said. "She really loves this movie."

A shard of happiness broke off Jane's mood. She shifted deeper against the couch's armrest, away from Clair. "Whatever. Everyone likes *The Matrix*."

"No, but she knows all sorts of behind-the-scenes stuff about it," Clair said, turning to Jane. "She's, like, a Matrix trivia *expert*. She could probably give Tony a run for his money."

"Not freaking likely!" Tony shouted over his shoulder. He had already slipped the tape free of its sleeve and was popping it into the VCR. The TV stood, muted behind him, framing his face with a backdrop of the Home Shopping Network.

Jane's mouth soured. "She can't know *that* much," she said, her voice dismissive as she popped open a Sprite from the collection on the coffee table.

"You don't know that," Clair said. "You've barely spoken to her."

"Don't need to. There's no way she's that much of a hotshot."

"Yuh-huh. She knows *all* about the production, the casting, the script—"

"Bet she doesn't know it's a trans allegory."

Clair's nose wrinkled. "A what?"

Jane froze. She shouldn't have said that, should she? Her mind spun back, trying to remember when the Wachowskis had come out. Nowhere near this long ago, that was all she knew for certain. More broadly, was the shorthand phrase "trans" even really in use yet? Jane cast her mind back, trying to dredge up the early naughts. She must have known about the concept of a transgender person in those days, right? It felt impossible not to, but she also knew how sheltered her childhood had been when it came to queer culture and history.

"You know what, never mind," Jane said. "Not relevant." She took another long drink, chugging most of her Sprite from its can. When she was done, they were all still watching her, so she dropped the can on the coffee table and said, "Let's do this!"

The rest of the group's attention broke, returning to Tony and the TV. It was fine, Jane told herself. There was no way for Clair to know why Jane was acting weird, and besides, by the end of the night, she'd forget all about it. Jane fixed her attention on the TV, the green Warner Bros logo covered in Matrix code. But she could feel Clair's gaze on her, all through the opening scene, and when Jane glanced over, Clair's face was scrunched as if there were words dissolving like sour candy on her tongue.

What? Jane mouthed, and only then did Clair turn away.

SUNDAY DRAGGED ON WITH PAINFUL DOMESTICITY.

There were no updates about the scans Simon was running. No further moves Jane could think to make at the moment. She'd tried to study more, reviewing old homework assignments, but her brain was fully mush after yesterday's tutoring session. So instead of doing *anything* useful, Jane spent most of the day curled up in the Maxwells' living room, curtains drawn, slumped on the couch as she worked her way through all her old favorite video games. She hated spinning her wheels under such desperate circumstances, but what else was there to do? At least the nostalgia and dopamine hits gave her an artificial sense of accomplishment, a balm for her real-life failures.

No one bothered her. Whether because Paul kept them at bay, covering for her, or because a teenager wasting her weekend mashing buttons was normal, Jane couldn't be sure. And, at the moment, she wasn't sure she cared.

By afternoon, the house had emptied out. Mrs. Maxwell had an open house to run, Allison had plans with friends. Paul spent the morning working in the yard, raking and bagging the leaves and then running the mower over the lawn for one last cutting of the season. When he was done, Jane heard him head upstairs, shower, and then close himself away in the spare bedroom that served as his home office.

"Useless lump," Jane muttered to herself. She punched a button, sending Sonic into a whirling spin dash across the TV. Paul, at least, should have been out there doing something. Patrolling the streets. Looking for clues. Knocking heads together until some criminal element talked—Jane's attacker must have drawn the attention of the seedier elements of society by now, surely? And fine, Paul had at least called in a favor and gotten Jane's car demolished for her.

It wasn't enough.

He clomped down the stairs a few hours later, just as the light piercing the edge of the living room curtains began to fade. A familiar gym bag was slung over his shoulder.

"I'm heading out," he called from the front hallway. "Tell Olivia she can start dinner without me, okay? I'm not sure how long I'll be."

Jane threw her controller down. She launched across the living room, sliding into the hall on her slouchy socks. "Did you get a lead?"

Paul startled. He frowned down at her. "No, I didn't get a lead. This is something else."

"Like what?"

Paul studied her for a second, uncertainty flickering across his face. If she was really his daughter, really fifteen, he'd refuse to tell her. Keep her home, find some chore for her to do. But she wasn't. And as hard as it must have been to see her as an equal, her experience couldn't be denied.

"Something I've been trying to track down for a while," he said after a moment. "There's a new street drug spreading through Grand City. They call it Whisper, pretty nasty stuff. It'll get you high as a kite, but unfortunately it also makes most people incredibly susceptible to suggestion. *Any* suggestion."

"Like convincing a girl to have sex when she might say no?"

Paul winced. Whether at the concept, or the ease in which the words tumbled out of what looked like his teenage daughter's mouth, it was hard to say. Jane could see him steeling himself, one bit at a time, before he spoke again. "That . . . does happen. Yes. But kids are also daring each other to do all kinds of nonsense on it. Some of it's not the worst. Until they started holding up banks and driving the wrong way down highways. I don't think either of us wants to see what it has the potential to escalate to next."

"Yeah, sure." Jane crossed her arms, leaning against the living room archway. "And you've got a lead?"

"I've got a lead," Paul confirmed. "A contact of mine says there's a regular pickup down by the docks, and the next one's supposed to take place today. I'll intercept the seller, see if I can get any answers out of him."

"Great. When do we head out?"

A single eyebrow quirked toward Paul's hairline. "We?"

"What, you expect me to just sit here and watch you go without backup?"

"Jane . . . I'm not trying to be rude, but what exactly do you think you can offer out in the field in your current state?"

Jane rolled her eyes. It was so typical of Paul, to dismiss her because he couldn't see her usefulness. She brushed a spray of potato-chip crumbs off her sleeve. "Experience, for one. Fine, I'm in a child's body. That doesn't mean I can't be useful. You're going to stakeout a drug deal, right? I've done that a hundred times. Even if all I do is sit back and observe, you have no idea what I might spot that you'd otherwise overlook."

Paul's face soured. Part of her couldn't blame him. The idea of taking orders from a kid—from *his* kid, as far as it looked from the outside—couldn't be an easy pill to swallow. But Jane wasn't going to back down. Of the two of them, she was clearly the senior superhero. Even though she'd only been Captain Lumen for a few years, her training and experience far outstripped anything Paul had put himself through.

"All right," Paul said finally. Jane barely resisted the weird urge to pump her fist in triumph. As if sensing this, Paul raised a finger. "But *only* if you promise me you'll stay out of any actual conflicts. In fact, if a fight of any kind breaks out, I want you to run the other direction as fast as your legs will carry you, you understand? Your first and only priority is to keep my daughter's body safe. Deal?" He held his hand out.

"No problem," Jane said. She slapped her hand in his before either of them could change their minds.

TURNS OUT, NONE OF THE HEROES' INVESTIGATIONS yielded anything useful.

Janie turned the flip phone over in her hand. Cal hadn't thought to take it away from her yesterday, and she wasn't about to remind him. It could "only" call and text, Clair had told her when she'd handed it over, as if that wasn't the *entire point* of a phone. Honestly, sometimes Janie wondered if the magic of future tech was making people stupid. Like Janie, a *teenager*, wouldn't know how to use a *phone* to full effect.

It had been stupidly easy. A quick call to the 411 directory. Senator Maxwell's personal phone number was a private listing, of course, but his office was a matter of very public record. Janie had scribbled the number onto her palm, dialing it a moment later. As soon as one of his aides had answered, she'd spat into her open hand and smudged the ink off—she wasn't going to leave evidence.

Getting the aide to actually *listen* to her was a different matter, of course. He kept insisting that, if Janie was *really* the senator's daughter, surely she had his number? Which she couldn't really argue with, but she wasn't trying to get the number from him. All she'd wanted was for the aide to pass along a message. Surely that wasn't too much to ask, and yet, he'd been downright rude. She wasn't sure at all that he'd do as she asked, despite how much she'd begged him. But a few hours later, a text had popped up on Janie's cellphone. *If this is really you, you'd better have a good reason for the runaround.* Which wasn't exactly the loving reaction of a concerned father, but she'd take it.

Now she flipped the phone open, finding the text again.

Senator Maxwell answered after the third ring.

"Hi, Dad," Janie said, before he'd even gotten a chance to speak. If she was going to do this, she had to do it fast, before she lost her nerve. "Listen, I know you didn't exactly get the most, um, friendly response to your suggestion? You know, about . . . the video? But I was thinking, and I'd feel better if you had one of us go with you when you made the drop-off."

Half a lie. Janie would, in fact, feel better about this deal if even one of the Heroes watched over her dad while he did it. However, in the absence of any of them being willing to, she'd have to make do as best she could. Janie still didn't know if her presence would make things better—but she could, at least, watch from a safe and invisible distance and see where Lester went *after* the deal. After all, if there was one thing teenagers were great at, it was sneaking around.

Never mind that Janie had always been too responsible to practice that particular skill set. The knowledge, she felt sure, was in her somewhere.

"You?" Senator Maxwell asked, breaking the silence. Janie did not confirm this—she didn't feel the need to, the question coming across more as a way for him to consider the situation than to verify his assumption. "I suppose it could work."

"Then you'll set it up?"

"How did you get the rest of your team to agree to this?"

Janie bit her lip. She was hoping he wouldn't ask about that. She wasn't exactly keen to admit that this was her idea, taking matters into her own hands since the Heroes' efforts clearly weren't cutting it.

But Janie's dad had always been able to see through her. She shouldn't have been surprised that Senator Maxwell could, too.

"Oh, I see," the senator said after a moment. "They don't know. Do they?"

"Not exactly."

The slightest pause. Then, "Not even Clair?"

"Especially not Clair."

A chuckle broke over the phone line. "Betrayal, Jane? I'm impressed. I didn't think you had it in you."

Janie bristled. It wasn't *betrayal*, she wanted to argue. She wasn't hurting them—in fact, if she and her father were successful, the rest of the team would probably thank them. Somehow, she didn't think the senator would see things her way, though, so Janie stayed silent. Letting him think what he wanted.

Finally, the senator took a breath. "Very well," he said. "I'll set it up."

THE MEET WAS SCHEDULED TO TAKE PLACE BY THE docks, in an out-of-the-way lot behind a cluster of warehouses. As Captain Lumen, Jane had been there dozens of times before—even in her era, on her Earth, this was still a popular spot for illicit activity. So when they'd arrived, parking at a safe distance, Jane didn't even hesitate, heading for where her team had long since determined was the best vantage point.

Paul fell into step behind her. She couldn't tell whether he was deferring to her greater experience as a superhero or just didn't feel like arguing, but frankly it didn't matter. For the first time since this body-swap happened, Jane was feeling properly like herself again. Even if she still didn't have her powers. Even if, instead of a superhero suit, she was cloaked in an old Sutton University hoodie that was about three sizes too big for her. Jane had selected it for its dark red color and absurd size, hoping the monk-like drape of a huge hood over her head would obscure her identity. She didn't remember having one when she was younger, but apparently Janie had loved it, the fabric as soft as an old teddy bear. And sure, technically, she shouldn't be out doing something like this without a real uniform, but Paul had balked at the idea of outfitting Jane properly. *I don't want you getting too involved in this*, he'd said—plus, neither he nor Simon were exactly skilled with a sewing machine, and unless Jane wanted to swing by Walmart and pick up a Halloween costume . . .

She supposed that even a black plastic mask might have been a good idea, but Jane's professional pride had bristled at the thought. The hoodie would do, enough for tonight at least.

A few minutes later, they'd climbed on top of one of the shipping containers. Over the edge, she could see their target had already arrived, his car idling beneath a streetlight as he waited for his dealer.

Paul, meanwhile, was pacing the length of the shipping container, muttering under his breath. Jane stretched her legs out in front of her, crossing them at the ankles. Their target was still waiting, which meant they had time to kill, and clearly Paul needed some kind of distraction, so as he opened and shut his palm, tiny bundles of light flaring to life and then extinguishing, Jane asked, "How *did* you get your powers, anyway?"

Paul's eyes widened. He sucked in a breath, letting it out slowly between pinched teeth in a whistle. "Hoo boy."

Jane raised an eyebrow. "That bad?"

"That embarrassing," he said with a small flinch. It had worked, though. He'd stopped his pacing, and now he folded himself so that he could settle in beside Jane. "This is a conversation I really didn't plan to have until you were older, but"— Paul glanced beside him, a rueful smile on his face—"I suppose you are now, so there's really no harm in admitting this. I was, uh . . . looking for a place to get high?"

A laugh burst out of Jane, cutting through the night. "Excuse me?"

"Don't judge. I was in my senior year of law school, exams were coming up. Your mother and I just had a big fight, some stupid shit, I don't know. I was being an idiot, but what else was new in those days?"

Jane sat back, shaking her head. She tried to picture it. A young version of her dad, drawn from reference photos of him back in college in the seventies. An orange-and-brown polo shirt in an oversized diamond pattern, tan corduroy pants. His hair is a little longer than Grandpa Maxwell would approve of, the front sweeping across his forehead, feathery ends trailing past his ears. A joint is pinched between his fingers as he leans back against an open-faced cabinet full of records, an amplifier, his turntable.

"Well, I couldn't smoke in the apartment, your mom hated it, so I got in my Oldsmobile and just . . . started driving. I thought about lighting up in the car, but she'd smell it when I got home. I finally ended up parking by this old factory, you know the empty one down past where the post office used to be?"

Hairs raised on Jane's arms. Oh, she knew the one, all right:

imposing brick walls towering above an overgrown field like a medieval fortress; faded white letters catching the moonlight, *ChemWerks Industries*. Mirrored panels, rendered in deep blues and grays—Jane and her friends arriving on scattered bikes, a young Paul turning his boat of a car carefully into the abandoned parking lot. The same pale moonlight spilling over the same broken pavement, catching Jane's sneakers as she dismounts, Paul's white snakeskin loafers as he gets out of his car.

Paul coughed. "I, uh . . . I sat on the trunk for a while, just, you know, smoking. Staring at the stars and shit. Contemplating my pathetic fucking existence." He fell silent, his mouth twisted up, remembering.

Jane studied his face. The white of his mask and suit glowed like their own moon, so ridiculously earnest. It was such a far cry from the Paul Maxwell she knew—even the Paul Maxwell from when she'd been fifteen. That one never would have taken the time to put on a costume and spend his nights patrolling the city for evildoers. Never would have sat and told his life story to his daughter, no matter what version of her was sitting beside him on an old shipping container. The Paul Maxwell of Jane's teenage years practically *lived* at his law office, and on the rare occasions he wasn't working, he was in the city making connections with hotshot lawyers on slick, shiny corporate career tracks. That Paul had never been happy with family law, always longing for something bigger, bolder . . . "braver" was the word he used, whenever he talked about it.

"Anyway," Paul said, breaking both of them out of their respective pasts. "When I finally got up, I was just about ready to go when I spotted this . . . this *glow*. Coming from the field beside the factory."

Green light, peeking up through the top of the tall grass. It's so subtle at first, nearly washed out by the haze of the city behind it. Maybe your eyes are playing tricks on you, you think, except of course the grass itself is oddly vibrant, a patch lit up as rich as a golf course lawn in the middle of summer. Clair's voice, a spotlight hovering near the top of the page. *Look!*

"It's hard to describe it," Paul said, "but there was this . . . weird little *device*, hooked up to the factory's generator. I mean, the place hadn't been used in a few years by this point, there's no way this was supposed to be here. Plus, it looked like something out of Star Trek, like they'd taken a shitty, glow-in-the-dark beach ball and hooked it up to some wires and pretended it was alien tech."

Jane frowned. The way she'd always drawn it had looked a lot sleeker: a pulsating orb in an intimidating metal base, black reflecting green, spiky arms reaching up to hook the power core in place. But, she was forced to admit, his description of the real thing—as opposed to the cooler version that lived in her comics—wasn't entirely off base.

"I really don't know what compelled me to touch it—other than the fact that I was high." Paul looked down at his hands, opening them until a faint glow could be seen creeping along the well-worn lines of his palms. "I got such a jolt, it threw me back and knocked me out cold. I still don't know how Olivia found me the next morning, but she was *livid*, I mean, understandably. I tried explaining it to her, but the device was gone, not even a single mark left in the dirt to prove it had been there."

The shadow of a silhouette falling across the younger Paul's face. He's lying on his back in the dirt, squinting up at whoever is above him, hash marks sketched into his cheek to show dirt and bruising.

"That's exactly what happened to us. Minus the getting high part," Jane added when Paul shot a look at her, startled and disapproving.

"I should certainly hope so."

Jane rolled her eyes. Paul had always been such a hypocrite, yet somehow this swell of parental concern quelled her usual impulse to call him out on it.

"No, but don't you think that's weird?" Jane asked instead. "Why would there be an orb sitting behind the *same* factory, in the *same* way, on two separate parallel worlds, but twenty years apart from each other? And each just in time for a Maxwell to find them?"

"But they weren't sitting there twenty years apart."

"Um, yes, they were? Otherwise, your Jane would find it, not you."

Paul shook his head. "No, listen. According to you, you got your powers at the same moment I did. That means they *were* sitting there at the same time, relative to each other. Just . . . at different points in our internal timelines."

Jane's eyebrows shot up beneath the shadow of her hoodie. That was a good point. "You think someone jumped between the worlds, placing them?"

"Maybe? Or it could just be a coincidence."

"Maybe," Jane said, though she didn't believe that for a second. She'd been in this game long enough to know that if something smelled like an evil plot, it probably was.

But if it had been intentional, then what? As far as Jane, or any of the other Heroes of Hope knew, they had been the first and—up until now—only people to have gotten their hands on world-hopping technology. The thought that someone else had beaten them to it, and by nearly two decades, was . . . unsettling, to say the least. What other changes had been made? Were the villains the Heroes fought over the years even from their world?

"Course, I had no idea at the time that I'd gotten superpowers," Paul said finally, breaking through Jane's thoughts. "They didn't manifest themselves until years later—by then, I'd already gotten married, had a couple of kids, settled down . . . I thought my life was set, you know? Like, I'd really *made* it by then, or at least was on the verge of it. There was even talk that I'd be making partner in a few years if I played my cards right."

That much Jane didn't need explained. Once her dad had gotten his sights set on a career advancement, there was no holding him back. It hadn't mattered how hard he needed to work, what kind of sacrifices with his family he'd needed to make. *I'm doing this for you!* he used to shout at Jane's mom, when they thought they were far enough away that their voices wouldn't carry to Jane's ears. But they did. They always did.

"But then I got these powers," Paul said, his voice melty with reverence.

Jane looked up. He was looking at his hands again, but this time the glow had increased, small orbs of light hovering over his palms. It reflected off his face, turning his expression angelic.

"I know this is probably going to sound stupid, but they honestly saved my life."

Jane sneered. "Why, because now you were *special*? Got to go around and get a rush out of people cheering for you?"

Paul looked over, startled. The orbs winked out. "Because they brought me back to my family." He took a breath, plunging on before Jane could snark him for it. "It was shortly after I'd first gone out patrolling. Your mom was giving you girls breakfast— I was supposed to have already left for work, but I'd overslept because I'd been out so late. I remember I was *pissed* when I first woke up, I wasn't even going to have time to shower, but then I stepped into that kitchen, and you looked up and grinned at me, and . . ." He shook his head. When he spoke next his voice was softer, awed. "Time just . . . stopped. And suddenly I could see it *all*, this life that I had set myself on. All the long days in the office, the missed school plays and ball games and birthdays, it's like they just hit me all at once, you know?"

Oh, Jane knew.

She could see those moments herself, each one lined up in a montage of old-man's regret. Paul, rendered in vaguely green-tinged sepia to give the panels an edge of existential despair. A series of panels showing him at his desk, grabbing coffee from the break room, back at his desk; each hunch of his shoulders growing steeper, the lines of his face eroding deeper and darker tracks.

And below, Jane growing up: clutching a picture book on her first day of school; wobbling on a bike just rid of training wheels; standing on stage for a talent show, the spotlight pinning her in a pool of nervous sweat. In each one, a shadow where her dad should have been.

She knew them because she'd lived them.

But then, bursting across the panel boundaries, a cherubic version of her own tiny cheeks wresting attention away from that reality. Toddler Jane, brown hair falling in loose tangles around her face, one chubby hand gripping a rubber spoon as she sat on a booster chair at the table. Her eyes are lit up like a Disney princess. *Daddy!*

It was supposed to be sweet—moving, even. Inspirational.

The cautionary tale of a man who'd almost lost it all, having his own fucking *It's a Wonderful Life* moment. Paul was practically beaming at Jane now, hints of actual light threatening to spill out from his collar.

How was she supposed to explain to him that, at this moment at least, she hated him far more than the dad she'd long since left behind?

A door slammed in the distance. "Yo, yo, my man!"

The voice broke through just in time. Jane and Paul snapped to attention, peering over the edge of the shipping container. Jane folded up Paul's reminiscence, tucking it away like stuffing a comic into a backpack.

The mission was back on.

THE SCENE BELOW, RENDERED FROM A DISTANCE. DARK, men-shaped smudges, bridged as they slapped hands in greeting. Only a single streetlight is working in the whole parking lot, and the one who was waiting had positioned the nose of his car beneath the sweep of the beam.

"Right," Paul said. "I'm going in."

"Hang on." Jane grabbed his arm, stilling him before he could stand. "There are two of them, and only one of you."

"I've faced worse odds."

"Yes, and I'm sure you love showing off your bravado—but you know the best way to beat odds when they're stacked against you?"

"You're not coming with me."

"I never said I was." Though really, would it have been so terrible if she did? A teenage body, yes, not nearly as fit as it should be, but with Jane at the helm . . . But no. They had a deal.

"I was going to say, you go in with a plan. Maybe turn invisible and sneak up on them or something."

Paul frowned. "I don't have invisibility powers."

"Not directly, no, but if you bend the light around you, it can cloak you just about as well."

A bubble of silence welled up between them, held like a breath.

"What's wrong?" Jane asked.

Paul squirmed. "I've . . . never done that."

"Are you *kidding* me?"

"Hey now," Paul said. "I didn't have a whole team studying how this stuff worked and helping me understand my powers. Most of the time, it's just been me. Trying my best."

Jane bit back a sigh. She tried to tell herself it wasn't his fault and, when that failed, that there was no sense wasting time yelling at him about it. She could chew him out later, if she wanted. For now, they needed a different plan.

"Okay, but maybe there's a way we can rig up some kind of distraction? If we—"

"There's no time," Paul said, vaulting to his feet. "I've got to act, or they'll get away."

"No, but Paul—*Paul!*" Jane said, but he was already gone. "Goddammit." She turned back, peering over the edge of the shipping container once more.

A minute stretched on. Jane couldn't see him. For once, that was a good thing—it at least meant he knew how to keep himself hidden as he approached, even if he wasn't technically invisible. Inky-blue panels slotted themselves in her mind, Mr. Lightshow reduced to a slip of seventies-glam moonlight as he slips between shipping containers.

But while discretion was always a good thing, Paul was taking too long. In the pool of lamplight, Jane watched the drug deal begin to wrap up. A curled bundle of cash passed between them, then the slap of product into palm. Jane had staked out enough of these to know neither party would be sticking around long. They needed to act now—or even better, a second or two ago. The men were stepping away from each other, and still no sign of Paul.

Jane shoved her glasses up her nose. "Screw this." She scrambled to her feet, making sure her hoodie was tugged forward enough to throw her face in shadow. The last thing she needed was for her attackers to see a fifteen-year-old girl facing off against them. There was a ladder bolted to the side of the shipping container, and Jane began to scramble down with all the cocky confidence of her body's age.

The sounds of a fight breaking out covered the slap of Jane's sneakers hitting the pavement. Throaty bro-voices barked through the empty night, set against the percussive beat of fists hitting flesh. By the time Jane rounded the corner and peered into the fray, Paul had already disarmed one of them and was currently body checking the other, locked against him like rams butting heads.

Unfortunately, that left the disarmed one free to do whatever he wanted—and what he wanted, apparently, was to get the hell out of Dodge. He leaped into his car, the engine turning over with a roar.

Now, if he was the one who'd been waiting while Jane and Paul reminisced on the top of the shipping container, Jane probably would have let him go. That one was the buyer, after all, and if he'd had any useful information to be gleaned, they wouldn't have sat around waiting for his dealer to show. The whole point had been to wait for the dealer, to bust in there and scare him into giving up the next link in his supply chain—not to stand idly by and watch him peal away in a puff of exhaust.

There was no way Jane could catch up with his car on foot, not even if she'd had her toned and trained adult body. Even if she could, what did she think she was going to do, leap onto the roof and fight her way in through a conveniently open window? No, that was nonsense—the stuff of comic books and action movies, not a real world in which Jane was operating in a child's body, without a single shred of powers to be found. She needed some way to stop the car. High-tensile wire, or a spike strip, or something else to pop the tires. But there was nothing, she had no resources, and in the breath it took her to run through this lightning-speed checklist in her mind, the car had already gained an impossible distance.

And then Paul or the drug buyer yelled, still tussling, and one of their feet lashed out, grappling for balance against the cracked parking lot. It connected with the gun Paul had previously wrestled from their grip, sending it clattering in Jane's direction.

Jane had never been one to waste an opportunity in the field. She raced forward. A close-up of her hand as it snatched the gun from a patch of scrubby grass that had broken through the asphalt.

It took three shots to hit her mark, three identical panels of the gun going off in profile. Despite Cal's training, Jane had never been the most skilled of the Heroes when it came to guns, and the weight and kickback of this particular piece were more than Jane's teenage arms were prepared for. But she only needed to get lucky once.

The tire popped. The car veered. Most of the page is Jane running as the car lurched to a stop.

She did, at least, manage to get one solid punch in as the dealer got out of the car, spit and an imagined tooth flying in the close-up. Triumph and knuckle pain surged through her as he stumbled forward, catching himself against the open door. But her victory was short-lived.

Jane saw it coming, sketched out in her mind in the split second before it happened. His arm snapping out, a bat to swing at Jane. She tried to leap aside but her reflexes were too slow, his reach too great. His forearm cracked against Jane's ribs, sending her back against his car. He spun toward her, and his other arm blocked against her neck, pinning her to the back door. The gun she'd used to shoot the tires went flying, knocked from her grip. Her spine screamed at her as the force of his arms bent her backward, her shoulders leaning over the roof of the car.

Her hood slid back. Piss-yellow lamplight spills over the pained wince of her youthful face, framed large on the page.

The dealer's arms loosened their hold against her, just a fraction. Probably more in surprise than any sort of kindness as he realized he was up against a gangly teenage girl.

His face contorted. Confusion and disgust. "What the shit is this?"

Jane tried to use his distraction against him. A foot, lashing out, attempting to hook his legs, but his body suddenly felt ten times larger than hers, his own legs planted firm as oaks. Jane's heart kicked up into her throat and her vision blurred, her head swimming in unfamiliar terror that not even comics could find purchase in.

"Let her go."

Relief at the sound of Paul's voice flooded Jane, souring quickly as she hated herself for the impulse. She was supposed to be a Hero, dammit, not the innocent damsel they swept in to rescue. Jane jerked, hoping the distraction of Paul's arrival would have loosened the dealer's grip, but nope.

The dealer turned his head. Paul was standing a few yards away, the same gun Jane had lost held fast in his grip. Jane had no idea where he'd learned to handle firearms—Jane's own dad, for all his faults, at least was not a gun fetishist—but Jane's trained eye could see that he knew what he was doing.

The dealer probably could, too, but the sight of it did nothing to intimidate him. "Or what? You think I'm scared of some dope in a leisure suit?"

"You were scared enough to run."

The dealer spat at the ground, the wad splatting disturbingly thick by Jane's feet. "Orders. I had to protect my product."

"Whose orders?"

A bark of a laugh, spat in Jane's face. "Man, I don't gotta tell you."

Paul took a single step forward, the gun trained on the dealer's face. "You sure about that?"

The dealer cracked a slashed grin. "I'm sure. I read the papers. Your type talks big about 'fighting crime,' but y'all don't have the balls to actually get into a *real* fight." His upper arm loosened from Jane's sternum, but only long enough for him to wrap his fingers tightly around her throat. "So you drop that little water pistol, or I snap this poor girl's—"

He did not get to finish his threat. The crack of his gun ripped the parking lot in half, ripped the dealer's hand from Jane's throat. She staggered forward, gasping, as he staggered back.

Blood poured from his leg as swears poured from his mouth.

Before Jane could process what was happening, Paul had raced forward, and a swift punch sent the dealer to the ground. Paul slammed his foot down on the dealer's chest, his gleaming white boot flecked with red.

"Is this *ballsy* enough for you, asshole?" Paul shouted as he leaned over to shove the gun in the dealer's face.

"Lightshow, *stop!*"

The words tore from Jane's throat, already raw from the grip that had squeezed down on it. She lurched forward, grabbing Paul's arm, but he shoved her off—probably with more force than he'd meant, and her ass hit the broken pavement.

It was her involuntary yelp that finally stole Paul's attention from the dealer. For a second, he straightened up, as if seeing how far he'd gone. He glanced at Jane, at the gun in his hands, horror just beginning to cross the face behind his mask.

But then the dealer reached up, probably trying to grab the gun away from Paul in his moment of distraction. Unfortunately for the dealer, Paul's boot was still pinning him in place, and his attention, it seemed, was not *quite* so distracted as that. Paul swooped in an instant, a backhand from the fist still holding the gun. The dealer's head knocked back, striking pavement. A groan of pain slid from the side of his mouth, pooling on the ground beneath his ear.

Paul grabbed him by the collar, lifting him just enough to whisper threats across the night. And though Paul's voice was too quiet to reach Jane's ears, she knew by this point they'd be effective, that the dealer would give up the next link in their organization. Sure enough, a second later the dealer's lips started moving, and Paul nodded, satisfied by what he heard.

His business done, Paul stood, turning his attention back toward Jane. He reached out, probably hoping to help her up, but Jane swatted the offer away as she drew herself unsteadily to her feet.

He did not seem to notice the slight. In an instant he'd drawn his keys from the pocket of his suit, tossing them across to Jane. "There's rope and a first-aid kit in the trunk," he said, already turning away from her. He hauled the dealer upright, dragging him around until he could be propped against the side of the car.

"We'll leave him here and drop an anonymous call to the police. They can deal with him from there."

SO THE PLANS WERE SETTLED WITH SENATOR MAXWELL, and that took one thing off Janie's to-do list. Now it was time for the second. Properly armed, Janie let herself into the labs.

Welcome, Jane.

"How's it going?" Janie asked.

Marie didn't even look up. She was hunched over a magnifying device as she poked at the innards of a gadget splayed open in front of her. "If we'd made a breakthrough, you'd know."

"Yeah, I wasn't coming here to bug the two of you." She stepped deeper into the room, careful not to spill the coffee she'd brought with her. "Where is Devin, anyway?"

Marie blinked as she finally raised her head. She glanced around the lab, as if she'd forgotten where she was. "Went to sleep, I think. He's got this weird thing where he thinks he's a more functional human being if he pauses to rest." With a side eye toward the cups in Janie's hands, she added, "Weak, if you ask me. Is that coffee?"

"Yeah," Janie said, and before the word was even fully out of her mouth, Marie had grabbed both of the coffees and raised one to her lips. The other, she set down on the counter by her elbow.

"I wasn't sure you'd want it, what with your state-of-the-art espresso machine you keep bragging about."

Marie pulled a face. For a second, Janie worried she'd made the coffee wrong—she didn't exactly have tons of experience—but Marie turned her evil eye upon the espresso machine instead. "We're not on speaking terms. It thinks my heart rate is too high for additional caffeine. *And it's wrong*, I might add!"

A shrill beep came from the corner of the room, making Janie jump. *"Caffeine intake parameters outside of accepted range."*

"You're outside of accepted range."

Janie stepped uncomfortably to the side. "Please tell me that coffee maker isn't, like, actually alive."

Marie's gaze unfocused as she stirred her drink with a nearby screwdriver. "There's considerable debate about the nature of sentience in the AI community. But no," she added when Janie's eyes widened in alarm, "this one is decidedly not. Just programmed to monitor my coffee habit, and locked by an encryption protocol thanks to Devin's mother-henning. Say, I don't suppose you'd like to use Jane's ability to manipulate wifi and get me access to the system . . . ?"

Janie's stomach twisted. *Jane's* ability. Like these powers didn't even belong to her.

"Not sure I'd know how." Janie tried to keep the edge of bitterness out of her voice, but wasn't entirely sure she succeeded.

"Shame." Marie raised her cup toward Janie in a salute. "Still, thanks for the fuel."

"Yeah, of course." Janie waved off the gesture as if it was nothing. The last thing she wanted was for Marie to think she was *trying* to be nice. That could make it look as if she was buttering Marie up for something. Even if that was, technically, kinda sorta what Janie was doing.

She cleared her throat. "Um, speaking of my powers, though: I don't know if Cal mentioned it, but there were these weird . . . bubbles, I guess, around some sort of assistant device in that aunt's house?"

"You know you don't need to phrase everything as a question, right?"

"Marie. Come on, this is important."

"Which is why I'm listening," Marie said. "Just thought I'd offer a bit of friendly advice along the way. Nobody's going to take you seriously in life if you don't take yourself seriously first."

Janie rolled her eyes. "Are you going to help me or not?"

Marie set down her cup and picked up a slim computer screen instead. "Bubbles?"

"That's the best way I can describe it. They were, like . . . coming off the assistant thing in waves? Cal didn't think it was anything to worry about, but I don't know. They were even outside."

"I mean, if you're talking about a myMind, there would be more of them outside. They're actually part of phones and watches now. Could have been everyone syncing to an update."

"I don't think so. That doesn't *feel* right. I just . . . don't know why."

Janie lapsed into silence. If she could just *understand* her powers more; how they worked, what all the jumbles of images and sensations meant, how to manipulate them. But so far no one, least of all Clair, was interested in giving Janie the training she needed. Didn't they understand? Even if they weren't going to allow her out in the field, she couldn't just have these abilities and not know what they were. It was like having an arm without being allowed to learn how to wield a pencil or paintbrush—not even knowing that these digits could grab objects and manipulate the world around them.

"Well, there's one way to isolate them," Marie said. She crossed to the other side of the lab, where she rummaged around in a drawer for a moment. When she came back, she handed Janie a pair of retro-looking sunglasses.

"What's this?"

"*This* is a multispectral retinal scanner." Gently, Marie removed Janie's glasses, setting them aside on one of the lab tables. "The front of it projects a variety of beams along the electromagnetic spectrum, from light all the way to radio waves, while a sensor on *your* side records your pupil reactions. I've been trying to get Jane to let me use this on her for *years*."

"Why hasn't she?"

Marie shrugged. "She says she hates feeling like a science experiment. Which is the stupidest reason, if you ask me—who *doesn't* want to advance our understanding of the universe?"

"Um, yeah." In truth, Janie kind of agreed with the other Jane on this one, but if playing lab rat would get Janie some answers . . .

Marie slid the sunglasses into position on Janie's face. She tapped the frame, and instantly a teal user interface popped up across the lenses.

Janie sat back, startled. "Whoa."

"Cool, right? So I'm going to start up the sequence, and all you have to do is give a shout when you see something that looks like your 'bubbles,' got it?"

"Got it."

"Good." Marie picked up the coffee Janie had brought her and settled onto one of the stools scattered around the lab.

The screen lay on the counter in front of her, and Marie tapped a few buttons on it. "We'll start with ranges we know you're familiar with."

"Okay."

"So this is wifi," Marie said. "If the myMind was getting an update, it would have done it over this frequency."

The world around Janie shifted. Janie sucked in a breath.

It was . . . sort of bubbly. Waves were, at least, emanating from Marie's screen, as well as half a dozen other gadgets and spots around the room. Thin layers from outside sources even crowded into the lab, washing over everything in a chaotic jumble. God, it was so *busy*. She barely even knew where to look.

But it wasn't the same thing Janie had seen, not quite. "No. It wasn't like this."

"Interesting," Marie said, and she really sounded like she meant it. "Okay, what about this one?"

"Nope."

Marie made a *hmm* sound under her breath. She tapped the screen again, and again the world shifted around Janie. Also not the way she'd seen it before.

They sat in silence for a while, Marie working her way through the different parts of the spectrum, giving Janie just enough time to look around and shake her head—again and again and again, no no no—before she moved on to the next one.

It was boring, sure, but at the same time, it gave Janie a perfect excuse to look around Marie's lab without getting yelled at. Most of it was filled with sciencey stuff that she didn't have the faintest clue what it did. Janie pointed to a few to kill the time, letting Marie babble on about a prototype device to more efficiently extract caffeine from coffee beans without losing flavor, or her tool to detect shifts in the timing between universes.

Splayed in the middle of the main workstation was a series of circuit boards wired up to what looked like some sort of fancy crystal. "And this?"

"Hopefully, your way home," Marie said. "The working theory is that it'll have the right kind of energy to jolt your mind back into your own body."

Janie shifted on her stool. "Will that work?"

"We'll find out, won't we?" She tapped her screen, switching frequencies. "This one?"

"No."

Janie twisted her fingers in her lap. Suddenly, she wasn't interested in the tech anymore. She let her attention drift to a high shelf, where a cactus was dressed up with a cowboy hat on the tips of its spines. Beside it, what looked like a Venus flytrap was planted in a coffee mug. Janie squinted at it. The mug was printed with a photo of Marie and Tony at some amusement park, heads sticking through one of those plywood cutouts where you get to pretend to be cartoon characters or Presidents or dogs. In this one, they're posed as astronauts in space, heads poking through helmets, painted bodies floating in an open void.

"So . . . are you and Tony . . . you know . . . ?" Janie raised her eyebrows.

Marie looked up sharply. "Why would you ask me that?"

Janie pointed at the mug. "It just looks like you're really . . . close . . . these days. You never seemed to like him, back in my time. Not *like* like, anyway."

"That's because I don't." Marie turned and raised onto her toes, barely reaching the shelf as she twisted the mug around. "I don't '*like* like' anyone. I'm not twelve."

"I just meant—"

"I know what you meant. And I get that you're trying to fit into a really weird situation, but let me make one thing clear: I'm not your friend, Janie. Tony and I have known each other longer than you've been alive, and you wouldn't be able to understand the dynamics between us even if I drew you a diagram."

Janie raised her hands in defense. "Okay, okay. I didn't think—"

"We're done here." Marie stepped forward, pulling the glasses from Janie's face.

Hair trailed across Janie's nose, dragged from the ear stem. Janie took a second to pull it back, tuck it all behind her ears, smooth it down. She slid her real glasses back on, the world coming back into proper focus.

Marie had already turned her back on Janie. She stood at a counter along one of the walls, tapping at data on her screen and occasionally flicking her wrist so that a string of equations flew up to project across the wall instead.

"I wasn't trying to upset you," Janie said finally.

"You didn't. But I really do have a lot of work to do, if we have any hope of getting you back to your own body."

Janie slid from her stool. She was sure that was technically true, but she also knew a dismissal when she heard one. Still, she'd probably pushed her luck as much as she should for now. "Okay," Janie said. "Thank you for helping look into the bubbles —even if we didn't find anything yet. I feel better just knowing you're working on all of it."

Marie's shoulders dropped. She tipped her head back, as if gathering strength from the ceiling, and then she turned around.

"Janie. This isn't a comic book. I know you're probably still young enough to think adults know what they're talking about, but the truth is, most of the time we don't. We're doing our best, but there's no guarantee *any* of this will work. Do you understand?"

"Of course," Janie said quickly.

"I'm not trying to scare you," Marie added, as if Janie hadn't said anything. "But I don't make false promises. The truth is, you might need to learn to live with things as they are."

As they are. Janie looked over at a reflective surface on one of Marie's weird gadgets. Her grown-up face stared back at her. Truth is, she was getting used to it. And while she wished they'd actually let her practice her powers, she was getting used to them, too.

Marie had meant her warning to be something Janie needed to brace herself for, a worst-case scenario she might one day need to grudgingly accept. But suddenly Janie wasn't so sure that was true. In fact, if Jane really wasn't going to get her body and her life back, there were plenty of things Janie could think to do with them.

SILENCE FILLED THE DRIVE HOME, NOT EVEN THE SOUND of Paul's classic-rock station slipping from the radio. Disapproval radiated from both the front seats, blasting hotter than the warmth spitting feebly through the dashboard vents. Jane reached forward, adjusting the vent anyway, cupping her hand around the air pushing against her palm.

She didn't know what right *he* had to be angry, but if there was one constant stretching across the universes, it's that Paul Maxwell would always find a reason to both disapprove of and disappoint Jane. So she let him sit in resentful silence, grinding his damn teeth, all the way until they'd pulled into the driveway and cut the engine. Finally.

"Just a minute, Jane," Paul said as Jane reached for her door handle. He wasn't looking at her. His hands were still on the steering wheel, his grip tightening and loosening as he tried to steel himself. He took a deep breath. "You're grounded."

A laugh burst out of Jane's chest before she could stop it. "Excuse me?"

"You heard me." Now he turned, his face a mask of dark shadows slashing over his features. "You'll still go to school, but I want you straight home after. No more heroing. No more visits with your friends. When you're not in class, you're to be in your room, doing homework and studying to keep Janie's grades up."

"Where's this coming from?"

"You crossed a line tonight, Jane."

"I'm not the one who *shot* someone!"

Paul's temper kicked in, fast as a gunshot. He slammed the steering wheel so hard the whole car lurched. "He was threatening my daughter! My daughter's body," he quickly added, his correction a paper cut Jane firmly denied the sting of. Paul took a breath to steady himself. "He was threatening my daughter's body. Something he never could have done if you'd *listened* to me and stayed put."

"I know what I'm doing."

"Sure," Paul said, a hint of disdain twisting his voice. "And under normal circumstances, I'm sure you could have waltzed in there all la-di-fucking-da and wiped the floor with such petty criminals. But in case you haven't noticed, these aren't normal circumstances. Janie's a great kid, but she's not exactly the most physically active. It's not fair of you to expect her muscles to take the same abuse you're used to putting on your own."

Jane opened her mouth to protest, rage kicking at her stomach. But just as she was taking a breath, she forced herself to stop. He may well have been right that she'd overestimated her current abilities—even now, her shoulder was screaming at her from the punch she'd thrown, and while her legs weren't protesting yet, she could well imagine the soreness awaiting her in the morning —but that didn't erase the damage of Paul's overreaction.

Paul's face softened. As if it was *his* absolution that mattered. "Look, I get it. You're used to being in charge, to having all your powers and your training and your team at your back. It can't be easy to suddenly lose all that. I'm just saying . . . you've got to pace yourself here."

He reached out, attempting to rest a concerned, fatherly hand on Jane's shoulder. Jane flung the gesture aside.

"Don't touch me! You're not my dad. You don't know anything about me, or what I'm used to, or what I'm going through. And you sure as shit don't get to exert some puffed-up sense of authority over me. Not after what you just pulled."

She kicked the car door open, stalking out before he could grab her.

"Janie—Jane!" Paul leaned across the seats, shouting out of Jane's open door. "Where do you think you're going?"

"Clair's," Jane said. She flipped her hood back up, blocking most of her face from view as she started to turn away. "Screw this 'grounded' bullshit. I'm not your daughter. I never will be."

**THE SUDDEN BOOM OF CLAIR'S VOICE TORE JANIE FROM
SLEEP.**

"Get up," Clair said, switching on lights as she strode across
the bedroom. "Get dressed. There's a problem at your office."

Janie groaned. She rolled over, blinking sleep from her blurry
eyes and shoving her hair off her face. "My office?"

Clair moved to the closet. "You run a comics publishing company," she said over her shoulder. Hangers *shhnk*ed across their
bar. "And I'm still piecing together what the crisis is, exactly, but
they're blowing up your phone on Slack this morning."

"I don't even know what half of those words *mean*."

"Doesn't matter." Clair pulled out a blouse, wrinkled her
nose, put it back. "The point is they need Jane, and you're the
next best thing we've got at the moment."

"Me?" Janie scrambled up, sitting in a tangle of sheets in the
middle of the bed. "No, but . . . there's got to be someone else
who can handle it."

"You mean like a business partner? Cofounder? Someone you trust your company with like it's their own?" Clair flicked through the blouses. "Yeah. And she's currently on vacation, hiking in the mountains. No cell service."

"What?"

Clair took a shirt off its hanger, laying it over her arm as she moved deeper into the closet. "You—that is, Jane—told her to go. Blue hasn't had a day off in literal years. In Jane's defense, she wasn't exactly planning on being body-swapped with her childhood self this week."

Janie hopped off the bed. "But I don't know anything about running a business!"

"That's why you're not going alone," Clair called from the closet. She strode out, pants and shoes added to her collection. She shoved the ensemble into Janie's arms, then dug something out of her pocket. A necklace with a bold, abstract pendant swung from Clair's finger. "You'll be wearing a hidden camera and an earpiece. I'll walk you through whatever is going on over there."

"Do *you* know anything about publishing comics?"

Clair let out a *pfft* of dismissal. "Janie. I'm a literal *superhero.* I've helped save the city from destruction more times than I can even remember. I think I can handle whatever Dream Sequence has to throw at us."

Janie raised an eyebrow. She didn't want to be nasty, but even she, at fifteen, could see how ridiculous that assumption was, for what did one really have to do with the other?

"Also, who do you think has been running the show the last few days?" Clair said as she turned Janie, forcibly, by the shoulders. "I'm logged in to Jane's Slack and email accounts—so far, no one's known the difference."

"But—"

"Get dressed." Clair shoved Janie into the en suite bathroom. "Brush your hair. Put the necklace on. I'm going to sort through this mess as much as I can in the meantime."

* * *

JANE RETURNED TO THE MAXWELLS' HOUSE ONLY LONG enough to grab her backpack. She'd showered at Clair's, borrowed a clean shirt and a pair of jeans, ran one of Clair's combs through her wet hair. She knew where Clair's family kept their supply of spare toothbrushes, freebies from trips to the dentist, in a cheese box in the linen closet. Really, there was nothing at "home" Jane needed, except for her schoolwork.

Paul was already gone for the day when Jane raced through the house. Olivia shot her a suspicious glare, but said nothing— Jane didn't know what excuse Paul had given, but at least whatever it was, it didn't warrant questions at the moment.

Outside, Allison was idling in her car. She'd been reading a book, the cover curled back around the spine, but when she spotted Jane she stopped and rolled down the window. "You coming?"

Jane shook her head.

Allison tossed her book onto the seat beside her. "Look, I don't know what kind of fight you had with Dad, but don't be stupid. You already missed the bus—if you walk, you'll be late. Get in the car."

She got in the car. The slam of the door was the final punctuation at the bottom of the page. Flip to the next, and a montage of Jane's morning passed without commentary: a featureless silhouette of her back as she funneled with the rest of the herd through the front doors; a teacher adjusting her glasses as she stood in front of a chalkboard, half a mindmap with "+ Juliet" visible behind her; Jane's head in profile, chin resting on her fist as she scribbled notes into her binder; a stack of books on the floor in front of her locker, pinched between the ankles of Jane's ratty sneakers.

Jane, sitting small in the middle of the school's courtyard during a free period.

That made it sound fancier than it was—by design, Jane assumed. In reality, the courtyard was just an open space inside the main doors of the school. Too big to be a foyer, too cramped to be an architectural highlight. There were no high walls of windows or grand skylights, no crisscrossing overhead beams or interesting pillars cutting jaunty angles. Just a large, gray nothing, jammed with a handful of folding tables stolen from the cafeteria, broken plastic chairs, and a struggling tree in a cement planter too large for the room.

It was here Jane had parked, on a slab of bench that curled around the outside of the planter. It wasn't the most comfortable seat in the courtyard, but she'd always liked it: if she leaned her head back and squinted, she could pretend the leaves above her were outdoors, that she was stretched out on the grass beneath the oak tree by the river behind her house.

Daydreams would have to wait today, though. Instead, Jane sketched the room. She was supposed to be getting a jump-start on her homework, but her brain was exhausted, rebelling against the sheer volume of information she'd packed into it over the last few days. She'd opened a blank page to start a new version of her English essay, but instead her pen had started mapping out the lines and perspectives around her. It helped to ground her against something she could see, rather than the usual imagined worlds inside her mind. Because every time she retreated there today, all she could picture was her dad's vengeful face, towering over her by the docks. And fine, so it hadn't really been her dad, but it was still the face of Paul Maxwell. Still the one that was supposed to have watched over her in her youth, still the one that had, instead, sat expressionless at the kitchen table when she'd come out, still the one that wouldn't look at her the next day when he packed up and left.

Her pen scratched absently across the paper, tracing out that same face. Jane ripped the page from her notebook, crumpling it into a ball and tossing it across the foyer toward the nearest trash can. It flew between the heads of several passing students, who turned and shot her a dirty look. Jane tipped her head back against the planter just as a familiar set of voices resolved themselves from the surrounding din. ". . . but even if she does, it won't matter," Marie said.

"No, listen," Devin said, continuing an argument, "the stats don't lie. I'm telling you, Lightshow's going to need to majorly up his game if he wants to keep up with this new chick."

Jane looked over as her friends rounded the planter. Devin and Marie, with Cal wedged between them, a rope of black licorice hanging from his lips. Marie peeled off from the group and sat beside Jane.

"I don't know, dude," Cal said around his licorice. He staked one foot on the planter's bench, sprawled even while standing. "There's no proof she's good."

Devin rolled his eyes. "She was chasing a *baddie*."

"Unless she *was* the baddie. Think of it!" he added over both Devin and Marie's scoffs. He took the licorice from his mouth, waving it to make a point. "Did we see her catch anyone? No! And look at her outfit!"

"What about her outfit?" Marie asked, her voice laced with skepticism.

"Oh, come on. Skintight red leather? Someone's going for vixen, for sure." He ripped off a fresh piece of licorice, as if that settled things.

Jane sat forward, the notebook nearly sliding off her lap. Jane slapped it against her legs as she asked, "What are you guys talking about?"

"Just the latest X-Capes post," Marie said with a dismissive wave of her hand.

"Am I supposed to know what that means?"

"Dude!" Cal said. "Grand City X-Capes! I told you about it over the summer! It's only the greatest site ever."

"X-capes tracks all the latest superhero activity," Devin added. "Get it? Like 'escapes'?"

"Delightful," Jane said flatly. "What's the URL?"

"No, dude," Cal cut in before Devin could give it. "It's like ex-*capes*. Like it's run by someone who used to be a Cape—a hero."

"That's never been proven," Devin said. "No one knows who runs it."

"Exactly! No one knows, *because he's got an identity to protect*."

"Guys, it doesn't matter," Jane said, but Devin was already arguing back, voice raised over Jane's.

Marie laughed under her breath. "Don't bother, they'll be at this forever." She took Jane's notebook and pen from her, then scribbled a GeoCities address on the top of the page. Jane raised an eyebrow—even in this era, that was an outdated website host, and she didn't have high hopes for the quality of their content.

"Thanks," Jane said anyway. She gathered up her stuff and squeezed past Cal, still taking up too much space on the planter. He reached out after her, but she was too fast for him.

"Wait, wait, Brainy Janie! Where are you going?"

Jane spun around, walking backward. "To the library." She clutched her notebook against her chest. "I need to figure out who's right about this new hero."

JANIE MANAGED TO KEEP HER COOL RIGHT UP UNTIL THE moment she was faced with the glass doors to the office. *Dream Sequence Comics,* it read in a slim font. A speech bubble surrounded it, encircling both the letters and the faint reflection of Janie's head.

"Nope," Janie said, turning away. "Can't do this."

"Janie," came a warning voice in her ear. Clair, nestled safely in the command room.

"No," Janie said. "This isn't going to work, I don't—"

"Janie!"

From behind her this time. Janie drew to a halt, cursing under her breath. She screwed on a smile as she pivoted on her heel.

"Heeeeey," she said, pointing at the woman who'd opened the door to call out to her.

"Sara," said Clair in her ear.

"Sara," Janie repeated. She nudged her glasses up her nose. "Hi, Sara. How's it going?"

Sara looked at Janie like she'd grown two heads. "Not great. You did get our messages, right?"

"Yes," Janie said, with far more speed and confidence than she actually felt.

Still, it was true. To some degree. Clair had been the one to actually read them, but she'd done her best to bring Janie up to speed. As she explained it, there was some sort of copyright issue: apparently, one of the stories they'd been publishing used to belong to another comics company, one that had gone under years ago. Which was fine, Dream Sequence had done what they'd needed to pick it up—or so they thought.

Only now there was some sort of movie deal, and the heirs of the original publishers were claiming Dream Sequence didn't have the right to sell to a movie studio. And backing out wasn't an option because, according to Clair, the money from the deal had already been reinvested.

In short, Clair had said, if Dream Sequence *didn't* own the rights and couldn't settle, they were completely screwed.

"And what am I supposed to do about that?" Janie had asked, but Clair was already rushing her out the door at the time, into Tony's idling car. He'd dropped her off at a sleek office downtown about half a twist of Janie's stomach later, and handed her a nearly invisible earpiece that, along with the hidden camera in her necklace, would connect her to Clair back at headquarters.

Now Janie fiddled with the heavy pendant as she followed Sara into the office. Janie's eyes widened, taking in the place. She'd been picturing . . . well, an *office*. Gray cubicles under fluorescent lights, wilted plants dotting the corners of the room, nothing in the air but the heavy clack of keys and the whine of a giant printer by the window.

Instead, she found an open room with a high, exposed ceiling. Clusters of freestanding desks surrounded a central ball pit, currently threatening to swallow the two employees who were sitting in it, only the tops of their heads and their laptops visible. One wall was full of nothing but a giant mural, characters of all shapes, sizes, and colors interacting and floating through a dreamy expanse. Another wall housed an array of snacks. And in the corner, two offices cut off from the rest of the room by giant panes of glass. Sara was striding to one of these, and Janie hurried to catch up.

"So it's not great," Sara said as Janie paused by the door. Her own name, painted in frosted, handwritten letters, shone from the glass. "They're talking two mil to start, plus a percentage of the movie revenue—which the studios did *not* agree to, and are saying any additional change is coming out of our earnings."

Janie paused, running her fingers across the name on the glass. *Jane Maxwell - CEO*. Her head swam, just taking it in.

"Jane?" Sara doubled back, grabbing Janie by the elbow. "Look, I don't know what's wrong with you today, but you're not going to have this sweet office much longer if you don't snap out of it and *pay attention*."

"Right. Yeah, no, I'm totally here. I'm focused." Janie clapped her hands together. "Let's do this!"

"Tone it down," the voice in her ear said, and Janie nodded, which didn't help.

Sara raised an eyebrow. "O-kay." She motioned over her shoulder with her thumb. "I'm gonna leave you to it. We've managed to get you a meeting in twenty minutes with Dave Shapiro—the grandson. He seems the most receptive to reason, but *don't* push it."

She handed Janie a slim screen that looked like a larger version of the cellphones Clair and the others carried around. It was already displaying a lot of scary-looking numbers in a spreadsheet, and Janie made a "hmm" noise as she looked at it, trying to appear as if they meant something to her.

"Cool. Thanks, Sara," Janie said. She tossed a salute, which she hoped looked pretty jaunty, but Sara only backed away, letting herself out.

Clair's voice clipped through the earpiece. "Can you maybe *not* make a complete ass out of yourself for two minutes?"

Janie turned away as the office door shut in Sara's wake. "Don't blame *me*. You're the one who threw me into this with no idea what I'm doing."

"A decision I'm starting to regret."

"You and me both," Janie muttered.

She moved over to the bank of windows, the view of Grand City spread out in a dizzying display. A framed photo on the wall caught her attention: Jane and a woman with spiky pink hair, grinning in front of the Dream Sequence office building.

"Who's that?"

The slightest pause, as Clair probably consulted her end of the video feed. "That's Blue. Jane's business partner."

"Why is she called Blue if her hair is pink?"

"Because that's her *name*," Clair said. "Can you please just sit at your desk? People are going to think it's weird if you're staring at photos all day."

"Okay, okay." Janie stole one last lingering glance at the photo before turning away.

Her desk.

There was no doubt it belonged to the boss. Although it lacked the heft and austerity Janie was used to seeing in pictures of posh corner offices, something in the slim lines and glass surface spoke with the same degree of power. A white-and-teal office chair sat behind it, framed by a series of art prints hanging on the wall.

Janie approached with caution. She felt very much like she was snooping in the principal's office, suddenly, the situation ballooning up and threatening to swallow her whole. What had the Heroes gotten her *into*? She didn't know the first thing about running a business, that much was painfully obvious. Even faking it felt like way more than she was capable of. Her hand hovered over the top of the chair, as if touching it would somehow make this whole situation more real than it already was.

"Oh for god's sake, it won't bite," Clair said, and Janie's cheeks heated. She sat, quickly, before she could change her mind. She crossed her arms.

"What am I supposed to do now?"

"Nothing," Clair said. "I'm already messaging your lawyers. What we really needed from you is to make an appearance. It's already been causing stress having both Jane and Blue out of the office lately, but at least things have been running okay. If they didn't see anyone during a crisis, though, they'd start to freak."

"So I should just, like, sit here?"

"Pretty much. Pretend to use Jane's computer—make it look like you're working. I'll have something for you in a bit, and then you can go out and tell them it's all going to be okay."

Janie picked a pencil off the desk, twirling it between her fingers. "And if it's not?"

"It will be," Clair said, and there was something so fierce and protective in her voice that Janie almost believed her.

Janie set the pencil back where she'd found it. She was

tempted to steal some paper from the printer and doodle, but she doubted that would look like she was solving a huge legal crisis. Instead, she wiggled the mouse, waking up Jane's computer.

A web browser was already up, some sort of furniture shopping website open from the last time Jane must have used it.

Janie's spine tingled, realizing what was in front of her. The internet. Moreover: the internet of the future. Unchecked and unguarded, and sitting right at Janie's fingertips.

Janie shifted in her chair. She twisted her body so the view from the necklace camera was facing away from the screen. She hoped her posture didn't look too weird to the employees in the rest of the office, but she'd deal with that if it meant she could nose around a little. Clair must have been *really* distracted by the crisis, to have so obviously not thought this situation through.

For one split second, a flash of guilt coursed through Janie. But if Clair was going to slip up like this, there was no way Janie *wasn't* taking advantage of it. Quickly, she moved the cursor to the navigation bar, and found the modern-day version of Yahoo! It didn't exactly look like the search engine she remembered, but what did these days? It would still work. Janie held her breath and typed "jane maxwell" into the search box before she could talk herself out of it. She was about to click on the search button when a drop-down menu slid down from the box, displaying a string of lines with her name in bold, then a bunch of seemingly random words after it:

jane maxwell comics
jane maxwell bluewillow series
jane maxwell dream sequence
jane maxwell twitter
jane maxwell comics in order
jane maxwell net worth
jane maxwell instagram
jane maxwell quotes

Janie's hand froze over the mouse. Were these . . . were these all phrases that somehow applied to *her*? Obviously "comics" and "comics in order" made a certain amount of sense, and her company was called Dream Sequence. She supposed "bluewillow" could be a comic she published. She could see, too, how "net worth" and "quotes" might have been tied back (though why anyone would be interested in how much money she had was anyone's guess), but some of the phrases were absolute nonsense. She wasn't a bird, so why anyone would pair her with "twitter" was a mystery, and what was an "instagram," anyway?

But it wasn't any of those that her eyes kept being drawn to, not really. Those were the safe phrases, the ones she made herself curious about because the one she was *really* interested in, the very last one in the list, was too electric to even dare to touch.

jane maxwell wedding

She swallowed, her throat dry as sketch paper.

She was about to click it when something buzzed in her pocket. Janie yelped, practically leaping out of her seat.

Immediately, Clair's voice in her ear: "Janie? What's wrong, are you okay?"

"Yeah—yes. Sorry, I'm fine." She quickly closed the browser, hoping none of the screen had shown as she'd jumped.

Her pocket buzzed again, but this time Janie wasn't feeling quite so jittery from snooping, and recognized it as the emergency cellphone Clair had given her. She slid it from her pocket. *2 New Messages,* the screen read, and then below that: *Dad.*

A quick glance up. Nobody from the office was paying her any attention, no word from Clair reprimanding her through the comms. No one seemed to have noticed and so, keeping the cellphone low, out of sight of both the camera around her neck and the office beyond the glass, Janie opened them.

They replied, the first message read.

Told me to meet them. Thirty minutes, Regent Park.

Janie's stomach squirmed. This is the news Janie had been waiting for, proof that their plan was working. But why did it have to be happening *now*?

The cellphone buzzed in her hand, a new message popping up.

You coming?

THE BELL RANG OVERHEAD. JANE ENTERED THE TUMBLING
flow of students as they pinballed from one class to the next,
stuffing a set of printed pages into her back pocket. The librarian
had grimaced as she handed them over, *You know these people are
nothing but trouble, don't you?* and Jane had nodded, because the
librarian wasn't wrong.

Rather than following the usual path to her next class, though,
Jane cut a left and raced up the stairwell. She wasn't that familiar
with Allison's schedule, but at least she knew where her locker
was.

Jane reached her just as Allison was drawing a fat textbook from her locker, the brown paper wrapper covered in tiny
checkerboards.

"Hey, Allie," Jane said. She'd rushed through the halls so
she'd purposefully be just a little out of breath. "I need your
keys."

Allison's face was impassive as she slammed her locker shut. "Um, that's a no."

"*Pleeease?* I forgot my English essay in the car this morning, and my teacher's going to kill me if I don't hand it in on time."

"Then you shouldn't have forgotten it. It's not my fault you don't keep track of your things."

"I know, but I *really really* need it," Jane said, staining her voice with every bit of whine she could muster. Would it be too much if she cried? Probably. "Come on, you *know* how much I've been struggling with schoolwork lately." At least that much wasn't a lie. "This is my last chance! If I don't pass—"

"Oh my god, *fine!*" Allison spun the dial of her locker again, huffing under her breath as she tracked the numbers. When it popped open, she yanked her backpack forward, rummaging in the deep pockets. "Here." She slapped a set of keys into Jane's waiting hands.

"Thank you, thank you, *thank you!*" Jane went to throw her arms around Allison's shoulders, but Allison slapped her away.

"Just get out of my face."

Jane gave Allison a thumbs-up as she turned away. She hit the stairs, picking up the pace as the bell rang and the crowd thinned around her. The last thing she needed was to be spotted by a teacher—she had to get out of there, and quickly. Luckily, there was an exit near the stairwell. Jane glanced over her shoulder and slipped out before anyone could see her.

She was nearly to the car, confidence boosting her speed, when a voice cut in front of her. "Where do you think you're going?"

Jane froze. Of everyone who could have caught her out, she wasn't expecting it to be Keisha.

"Heeey," Jane said as she turned around. She pointed her thumb over her shoulder. "Relax, girl. I'm just getting my English paper."

Keisha marched forward over the dead grass. "It doesn't look like it."

Jane looked down at herself. "What does it look like?"

"Like a girl on a mission."

"Um, yeah?" Jane said. "A mission not to fail my essay, which I spent, like, all night working on."

Keisha crossed her arms, cocking her hip. "Nah. There's something going on with you lately, Janie. I don't know what, but I know you're not getting no essay."

Jane took a step backward, closer to the car. "Of course I am."

"Where is it, then?"

"Excuse me?"

Keisha jerked her chin toward the car window. "Your essay. If you left it in the car, where is it? There's no papers on those seats."

Jane turned, looking over her shoulder. "Huh. Must have slipped underneath."

"Oh my god, you're such a terrible liar," Keisha said. "You know you can talk to us, right? We're your friends."

"And I appreciate that, really. But I swear, Keisha, there's nothing going on."

"There is, though! You're not eating right, you're constantly acting surprised at the normalest things, there was that weird crap at the party, you keep ditching Clair—"

"I'm not ditching Clair!"

Keisha shook her head. "Yeah, but you so are. And now you're trying to cut class? It's like you're not even *you* anymore."

Jane bit her lip. She was so used to being enamored with Clair that sometimes she forgot that other people were capable of being whip-smart and observant, too.

"Keisha . . . I really appreciate you looking out for me, but I'm *fine*, I promise. There's nothing to talk about."

"Bullshit. Now you're gonna tell me what's *really* up with you, or I swear I will march right back in there and tell Allison exactly what I know."

"Oh, come on."

"I mean it!"

"There's *nothing* going on, okay? I don't—"

Keisha shrugged. "I warned you."

"No, wait!" Jane surged forward, grabbing Keisha's wrist. "Okay! Okay, I get it, just . . . get in the car. I'll explain on the way."

This was a terrible idea. Jane knew it, as soon as the words were out of her mouth, but what other choice did she have at this point? This situation really *was* turning Jane into a terrible liar.

Even though this was what Keisha said she'd wanted, she hesitated. "You don't even know how to drive."

"*Janie* doesn't," Jane corrected, turning back to the car. She stuck the keys in the lock and twisted, once and then twice to open all four doors. "But like you said . . . I'm not exactly her these days."

COULD SHE PULL THIS OFF?

Janie wasn't so sure. For all the swagger she liked to imagine in herself, a rebel with a cause, the truth is Janie had never misbehaved in her life. Not *really*. She knew other kids her age sometimes skipped class, smoked, stole beer from boxes in their parents' garage. Janie, however, still felt guilty for the time she took an emerald-inked Bic pen from her third-grade teacher's desk without permission. Yes, okay, so it was from a box of like fifty other identical pens—it was still *stealing*. Technically. Sort of.

But this wasn't hurting anybody. No, if anything, helping Senator Maxwell pay the blackmailer's demands was fixing a problem, and one of Janie's own making. Really, she owed it to the team to act.

Pick me up at my office?

If Janie had her own cellphone at home, she'd have been able to type this much faster. She knew kids who sped through texting, each letter memorized to how many times they needed to press the number on the keypad. Add that to the list of reasons Janie deserved one, if she ever got back.

Senator Maxwell's reply, by contrast, came in immediately. *Ok.*

So now all Janie had to do was sneak out. While wearing a necklace that tracked her every move. With Clair listening to every breath she took. Yup, no biggie.

Janie swiveled in her chair. She knew what she needed, she just wasn't sure she'd be able to find it in this sea of colors, paintings, and unfamiliar office equipment.

"Where are you going?"

"I'm hungry," Janie muttered under her breath. She wasn't, but she figured it was the easiest lie.

The sigh in her ear was heavy, but Janie was used to this older version of Clair judging her eating habits by this point. "Fine. But at least try to look concerned while you're getting your snack, all right? You're supposed to be dealing with a crisis."

Janie made a low *mm-hmm* in her throat, covering it with a cough fast on its heels.

She wound her way through the office. Turns out, what she was looking for wasn't actually that hard to spot, which Janie supposed made sense. All she had to do now was find a way over there.

The snack bar was . . . disappointing. A serving bowl of proper rabbit-food salad and a tray full of cheeses, grapes, and something like tiny salamis, bowls of huge, ripe olives between them. Janie was grateful she wasn't *actually* hungry, though for the sake of show, she did pick up a plate.

Her target was still in her sights. She kept half an eye on it. Not that it would move, but it felt better to ground herself as she scooped food onto her plate at random. If Clair was paying attention to what Janie was dishing up, if she had any sort of commentary on Janie's choice, for once she kept it to herself.

Snack in hand, Janie took the long way back toward her office. Partway there, she caught the toe of her shoe and tripped, sending her plate crashing to the hardwood floor. Three employees rushed over to help her, *Are you okay?*s and *What happened?*s spilling to mingle with the mess of Janie's food. "It's fine, I'm fine! I'm sorry," Janie kept insisting, even as paper towels were called for, a trash can, a mop.

She stood up, letting them fret and fuss over the mess at her feet. And now the whole office was distracted, but nowhere near as distracted as they were about to be. A sharp thrill raced up Janie's spine.

After all, a tiny part of her had always wanted to pull a fire alarm.

She did not let herself stop to think. Just reached behind her, going by feel. Her fingers wrapped around the slim lever, and all that was left to do, like the letters said, was *PULL DOWN*.

The overhead lights cut out, emergency flashers spinning near the ceiling. The wail of the alarm was so loud that Janie could barely hear Clair asking *What the fuck?* in her ear. Janie didn't answer her. She had already wrapped her fist around the pendant, blocking the view of the camera, and was digging the comm out of her ear. She dropped both of them in a trash can in the stairwell.

She met Senator Maxwell at the curb. His limo slowed to a stop. He pushed the back door open himself, not even waiting for his driver to come around as he boggled at the sea of people pouring from the building. "Jane? What's going on?"

"Just drive," Janie said as she slid in beside him.

Senator Maxwell studied her for a moment. Could he see the misbehavior, written somewhere on Janie's face? He was still her dad, after all, and Janie had always had trouble keeping secrets from her dad.

But before Janie had completely sweated it out, the senator sat back in his seat, smoothing his suit jacket. "You heard my daughter," he called forward to the driver. "Let's go."

"YOU EXPECT ME TO BELIEVE ANY OF THAT?" KEISHA ASKED.

Not really, Jane thought, the bumpy edge around the words overlapping her larger, smoother speech bubble as aloud she said, "You asked."

"Because I wanted the truth. Not to be fed some *Freaky Friday* crap like I'm twelve. You know I never even liked that movie."

Jane sighed wistfully. "Oh man, Lindsay Lohan was so great in that one."

"Janie. Lindsay Lohan wasn't even alive in the seventies."

"It's called a remake? Trust me, you'll understand when they film it in a few years."

"Yeah, all right," Keisha said in a tone that was clearly humoring her. She unfolded the paper Jane had given her as they'd set off, the printout with the shitty, low-res photo of Jane chasing her attacker. "You realize this webpage is worse than a tabloid, right?"

"I'm not saying they're a bastion of journalistic integrity," Jane said. "But if they could snag a picture of me, then maybe someone else managed to, as well."

"Okay, but even if I believe you—which I don't—what difference does it make? If this is really you, why do you need a picture of what happened?"

"Because I only know what happened until . . . ," Jane trailed off, motioning at her gangly teenage body. She returned her hand to the gearshift. "What I'm interested in is what came next."

In some ways, that was the worst part of this whole situation. She'd run behind that convenience store with Clair. They'd both confronted the woman who'd attacked them. Jane had ended up in her younger body, sure, and that was terrible and frustrating, but what about Clair? And, slightly less important but still a question that lingered heavily: what had happened to the body her mind had abandoned?

Jane slowed the car, easing around a jogger. He glanced in as they passed, scowling slightly, but Jane just gave him a cheery wave, like she was plenty old enough to be behind the wheel.

"Oh man." Keisha slid down in her seat, shielding her face even though they'd long since passed out of the jogger's field of view. "We are so gonna get grounded for this."

"Relax. We play this right, we'll have the car back before Allison even notices it's missing."

"Janie, you're driving without a license!"

Jane laughed. "Trust me, I've been driving longer than you've been alive. I know what I'm doing."

"Mm-hmm," Keisha said, her voice flat and appeasing.

"You still don't believe me."

Keisha didn't say anything. She didn't have to.

They turned onto a side street, no traffic ahead of them. Jane glanced at the dashboard. She'd been getting a feel for the car for about ten minutes now, and it sure as shit wasn't anywhere near the beautiful beasts she'd gotten used to driving, but it had been kept in good condition, the engine running smooth and strong for what it had to work with.

"You want proof?" She checked her mirrors one last time. Still quiet, out of sight from the main roads.

Jane shifted gears and gunned the engine, yanking the hand-brake to toss them into a donut. Before Keisha could argue, before she could tell Jane there was no proof that would convince her.

Keisha screamed. Jane couldn't blame her, but she ignored the freakout in the seat next to her as she straightened out the shaky car—now completely one-eighty from the direction they'd been going in—and took off like a shot down the empty street. The speed pressed Jane back, melding her with the car, and she focused on the familiar feel of the wheels against the pavement, the rumble of the engine.

"What the *freakin' hell!*" Keisha shouted once Jane let off the gas, easing them smoothly into the flow of traffic once more. "What was *that*?"

Jane shifted lanes. "Proof."

"Of *what*, your complete insanity?"

"You've been my friend for years, Keisha. When would I have learned to drive like that? Have I ever even taken driver's ed before?"

"No, but—"

"I know. It's a lot to take in. And I'm sorry, but I need you to believe me. Because in just a second, I'm going to pull up in front of a convenience store to steal their security footage, and I can't have you running off to call the cops. Or my mom."

Silence filled the car. In her peripheral vision, Jane could see Keisha staring at her, wide-eyed, though it was impossible to tell what kind of stare it really was without Jane taking her own eyes off the road.

Jane wanted to give Keisha longer to consider this. She knew how impossible it sounded, even in a reality where superheroes were already a thing. Jane remembered, sharply, how absurd the concepts of parallel worlds and powers were to accept, when she first learned about them. She hadn't handled it well, and she wanted to be a better guide for Keisha, ease her into this reality, but they were already here. Jane slowed the car and spun the wheel, nosing them into the parking lot. Cut the ignition. The engine ticked in silence.

She took a breath. "Okay, well. Wish me luck."

A warm hand wrapped itself around Jane's, still on the gearshift. A braided friendship bracelet on Keisha's wrist caught the light, one color to represent each of the friends. She'd made them over the summer, Jane remembered suddenly, and given one to each of them, despite the fact that they were in high school now and too old for camp-made crafts. None of the others wanted to wear theirs, though Clair would sport it occasionally just to be nice. Only Keisha tied it on and left it there until it fell off in senior year.

"Stop." Keisha's voice was bold and steady, not a trace of the terror Jane expected. "Superhero or no, don't be stupid. You're gonna pull this off, you need a distraction."

"Are you sure? I don't want you putting yourself in danger with some wild scheme."

Keisha snorted. She pointed at the building, then at herself. "Convenience store, Black girl. Ain't nothing wild about this plan. Trust me, they'll be distracted the second I walk in the door."

16

JANIE HAD NEVER RIDDEN IN A LIMO BEFORE.

The closest she'd come was when her grandfather died and the funeral home had driven the family to the cemetery in a very nice town car. Janie had been secretly disappointed it wasn't something fancier, but even at twelve she'd known better than to complain about the ride. Even though she wasn't actually *that* upset about Grandpa Maxwell, considering she'd only ever seen him two or three times in her life. Her dad was depressed enough for the both of them, and Janie hadn't wanted to add to his burden. She'd scooted next to him, letting him wrap his arm around her shoulders, leaned her head against his own.

How weird, then, that she was taking her first actual limo ride next to him again. Or not really *him*, but still. She couldn't quite wrap her head around the fact that he'd become a *senator*, that limos were apparently normal now. While Janie knew that some people rode limos all the time, for the Maxwells they'd always been aspirational, something people splurged for at funerals, yes, but also proms, weddings . . .

Jane Maxwell wedding.

Janie turned away from her dad, her cheeks suddenly hot. She knew she shouldn't be thinking about this. Not while they were on their way to deal with dangerous criminals. And yet, in this temporary slice of quiet, it was impossible not to.

Was she actually *married* in this world? Or at least engaged? She glanced at the ring finger of her left hand, as if somehow she could have missed a diamond ring sitting there. She tried to remember if she'd been wearing one when she first zapped into this body, but she'd been so freaked out and confused, it would have been impossible for her to notice something as small as that. And then she'd passed out, and by the time she woke back up again, someone had changed her into sweats. It would have been easy enough to slip a ring from her finger at the same time.

Janie's stomach twisted up. If she *was* married (or engaged, or whatever), then why hadn't someone said anything? And where was this mystery man, if he even existed? Wouldn't he have cared that his wife hadn't returned home yet?

Unless he was one of them. The thought struck Janie so hard she nearly passed out. It felt absurd, on the surface, but . . . it *would* explain why Clair was so adamant that Janie not be told anything about her future, wouldn't it? She tried to picture them: Tony and Devin and Cal. She couldn't imagine herself with any of them, but it made more sense than a random stranger, didn't it?

Janie glanced sideways. There was one person who could tell her. Except she couldn't ask him, not without revealing the truth of her body-swap. And while Janie trusted her own dad with just about anything, there was something in this version of Paul Maxwell that held her back. He wore a coldness around his shoulders, unfamiliar and not entirely safe. There was no way for her to know how he would react to the news that she wasn't his real daughter. Besides, even if she was willing to take that chance, she couldn't risk that he'd refuse to go through with the mission with someone he didn't trust. At the very least, her curiosity would need to wait until they'd dealt with the blackmailer, gotten the video back in their own hands.

The silence was driving her crazy, though, so she latched on to something that felt safer instead. After all, this version of her dad may be a senator now, but he'd started his career as a lawyer. And a really good one, at that.

"Can I get your advice on something?"

She supposed that Senator Maxwell was too well versed at hiding his surprise to let his mask slip—still, Janie thought she detected just a hint of it around the edges. But he smoothed it out in an instant, so quickly Janie wondered if she'd imagined it. When he spoke, his words were as crisp as his suit. "I'm listening."

So Janie told him about the trouble at her company. Jane's company. Whatever. As best as she understood it, anyway, which probably wasn't quite right, but surely it would be enough to convey the general problem.

Senator Maxwell did not ask questions, did not interrupt. Instead, he poured himself a drink from a crystal decanter, sipping and listening and staring out the window as the city rolled by.

When she was done, he didn't say anything. He rested his glass on his knee, spinning it gently for a moment.

"Well?" Janie asked, after the silence had stretched out to the point of discomfort. "What do you think I should do?"

The senator tapped a finger against his glass. "Are you asking me as your father, a lawyer, or a senator?"

"All of them, I guess? I don't know, whoever has advice for me."

"Hmm." Senator Maxwell took another sip. "As a lawyer, I'd need to review the contracts. There may well be a loophole, it just depends on how good *your* lawyers were when they drafted the agreements."

"It's your firm." Janie had seen that much, at least, on the screen Sara handed her when she'd shown Janie to her office. *McAlister, Roth, and Maxwell.*

"Then you should, at least, be able to avoid complete disaster —though I'm given to understand some of the new blood isn't quite as ... *thorough* as I used to be. I've been thinking about having them take my name off, truth be told. But it should still be enough."

A breath of relief escaped Janie's chest. Maybe she'd been right to ask him.

"That said . . . you're a Maxwell, Jane. You want this situation to go away, it can go away."

Janie sat back, suddenly unsettled. He was making it sound like they were the Mafia. And, sure, okay, Senator Maxwell had certainly risen to power, a position Janie couldn't imagine her own dad climbing to. And there were the jokes about politicians not being trustworthy—but they said the same thing about lawyers, and her dad had never been anything but an upstanding man.

And yet. Looking across the limo at him, Janie couldn't shake the feeling that not only did the senator mean what he said, he was almost . . . eager, maybe, about the idea of Janie taking him up on it. Janie shivered, remembering the way he'd reacted to this whole plan in the first place. *Betrayal, Jane?*

Senator Maxwell glanced out the window. "We're here."

The limo rolled to a stop, so smoothly the senator didn't even spill his drink. He set his glass down, pulled an unassuming envelope from his breast pocket. The door opened and he unfolded into the bright light of day.

Janie followed him out. She tried to tell herself the shakiness in her legs was just the nerves of running away from the Heroes, the idea of making a trade with a criminal.

She almost believed it.

The instructions were for Senator Maxwell to order a cup of coffee from a nearby food truck, then sit on a particular bench with the envelope in his left hand and the drink in his right. Janie, meanwhile, was supposed to hang back. Find a quiet spot to turn invisible, then keep an eye on the situation from a distance. Once the blackmailer showed up to collect his money, Janie would follow him, texting the senator the address of wherever he went next.

As plans go, Janie felt pretty confident in it. She'd been practicing over the last few days, and could control her invisibility more often than not. With the importance of what they were doing, she felt certain she could manage it, and sure enough: tucked behind a cluster of bushes, crouched low where no one could see her, she drew the light in and watched her hands disappear. When she stood back up, no one seemed to notice her. She crossed the park just as Senator Maxwell was approaching the bench. Janie stopped beside a tree, steadying herself against the bark as she stood watch—she found it slightly disorienting not to be able to see herself move, and grounding herself against a physical point of touch helped. Already a swell of pride was beginning to warm her chest. The rest of the Heroes thought this was a bad idea, but look how well it was going already! They'd be so proud when she returned later, probably even proud enough to forget that she'd snuck away from them in order to pull this off. She couldn't wait to see the look on Clair's face, particularly. Proof that Janie wasn't just some dumb kid.

This confidence stayed with her for several long minutes as both she and the senator waited patiently to see what would happen next. It lasted, in fact, right up until something pressed firmly into the middle of her back. She did not need to turn around to understand it was a gun.

"Stand down, Captain Lumen," came a stern voice. "Or should I call you Jane Maxwell?"

JANE WAITED IN THE CAR AS KEISHA STROLLED INTO THE convenience store.

By Jane's own time, of course, she'd long since become "woke" to systemic racism and white privilege, but even so, seeing it in action back in a time that had felt like a simpler, less problematic past was . . . eye-opening, to say the least. Jane remembered this time of her life with the lazy, idyllic haze of nostalgia: a time when everything felt easy, hopeful, free of the cares and responsibilities of the full brunt of adulthood. Sure, teenage angst had colored it at the time with a thin film of cynicism and world-weariness, but that had long since faded away from her now technicolor memories. When Jane thought back to the year 2000, she pictured summer vacation, her first kiss, hours spent under the oak tree with Clair. All her greatest hits, printed and bound in a single issue. And sure, reliving this time was . . . not quite as relaxing as she'd imagined it would be, but still. Most of that could be attributed to the bizarre circumstances of finding herself here in the first place, the struggle to get back.

Now she was watching through the convenience store window as Keisha milled idly at the magazine rack, thumbing the covers of *Seventeen* and *Cosmo*, exactly like Jane or Clair or Marie might have done at that age. Only instead of wandering in peace, giggling and playing games in the aisles with barely a glance from anyone, Keisha had the full and undivided attention of the man behind the checkout counter, and it was impossible to ignore the fact that Keisha had been living with this her whole life. And she *knew* this would happen, and she'd gone in anyway, because what other option was there? Don't shop at all?

Jane's stomach soured as the convenience store clerk rounded the counter, intent on Keisha as she moved to the spinning rack of single-serve chips.

This was her chance.

Jane slid from the car.

A bell over the door announced her arrival, but the clerk didn't even spare her a glance. In the pale fluorescent light, Jane's skin felt reflective. She was used to bending light around her, turning herself invisible, but this was true invisibility: being a white girl shopping while there was a Black girl to "keep an eye on" instead.

"Are you planning to pay for that?" the clerk said, his voice carrying as Jane headed straight for the back corner of the store. No one stopped her as she let herself into the office.

The room was dark, nothing but the glow of an ancient computer hooked up to a huge tangle of wires and what looked like five VCRs stacked together. Though, Jane realized, it probably wasn't an ancient computer yet—possibly, this was state-of-the-art surveillance technology.

Despite the faint glow from the monitor, it wasn't enough. Jane turned on the desk lamp, the room coming into view with a *click*. A crowded desk, a recycling bin stuffed with old newspapers. A huge bookcase towered over the desk, jammed full of VHS tapes.

Jane crouched down, running her fingers along the Sharpied labels. Each date in a row, perfectly ordered, not so much as a label out of place. They filled the bookcase top to bottom, except for one, a gap that stood out immediately. Her finger slid along the row, darting into the empty space as if she didn't know exactly what she'd find. Or rather, what she wouldn't find.

The tape she wanted was missing.

JANIE DID NOT MOVE, COULD BARELY BREATHE. IT WAS

impossible that anyone could see Janie—she stole a fast glance at her hand, steadying herself against the tree, and yes, she was still invisible—but it was also impossible to ignore the cold press of the gun against her spine.

"Don't act surprised," the voice said. "Did you think I wouldn't expect you? All I had to do was listen for a heartbeat that didn't belong to anyone I could see."

Lester. Janie should have known.

He stepped closer. Janie's traitorous, scared heart kicked up even faster. Lester trailed his finger up the length of Janie's arm, coming to rest on her shoulder. He leaned in, whispering, his voice muffled slightly behind a rubber dog mask. "Nice to know I can get you so excited." His grip tightened on her shoulder, and Janie barely bit back her cry of alarm. "Now call off the rest of your team."

Oh. So he thought she was not only Captain Lumen, but here on an official mission.

Janie supposed that made sense, but why did the *one* person validating her role in the team have to be a bad guy? Lester pressed the gun deeper into her spine, causing her to arch forward, and she had to come up with something. But if she faked calling the team on her comms, would he be able to tell? Would something in her voice give her away, or was his hearing so good that he'd know there were no comms whispering Janie's words into their ears? But if she did nothing—

She couldn't even begin to think about what would happen if she did nothing.

In the end, though, it wasn't Janie that spoke next. It was Clair.

"I wouldn't do that, if I were you."

Tears of relief pricked Janie's eyes, even as Lester turned, drawing Janie along with him as an invisible shield.

Clair, in full Mindsight mode, had her gun trained squarely at Lester's head. At least Janie hoped it was Lester's head—it was so close to hers it was impossible to really tell, except that Mindsight couldn't see Janie and there was no way Mindsight would actually threaten her directly. Right? Janie didn't understand how Clair had even known to follow her to park, but at the moment, it didn't matter.

Lester ran his thumb along Janie's shoulder. "Right on time."

Mindsight did not allow this remark to throw her. "You can't expect me to believe that you honestly wanted to be surrounded by a bunch of superheroes."

"Yeah, I get where you'd think that," Lester said. "But really, the more you all surround me . . . the more vulnerable the senator and my bitcoin become."

Lester let go of Janie's shoulder long enough to reach up and snap his fingers. A fierce cry broke the air, the same *SKREE* those Shadow Raptor things had kept making when they'd attacked the plaza where this whole mess had started.

Mindsight spared only the briefest glance over Janie and Lester's shoulders, back down the slope of the park, toward where Senator Maxwell was waiting. Whatever she saw couldn't have been great—the screams of the other parkgoers alone was enough to tell Janie that—but all it did was harden the face behind Mindsight's mask. She returned her attention to Lester immediately, tightening the grip on her gun.

"Hang on!" Lester said. "Think it through, Mindsight. Do you really want to fire that without being able to see your captain? After all, there's no telling what part of her you might accidentally hit."

Mindsight did not even appear to break a sweat. Just stared down Lester. Janie wanted to meet Clair's eyes, but of course that was impossible; all Janie could do was study her, Mindsight's dead-set expression utterly unreadable, and guess at what she wanted Janie to do next. Should Janie release her hold on the light, let Mindsight see where she was? But she was still wearing the outfit Clair had picked out for her that morning, not Jane's

Captain Lumen uniform, so if she did, wouldn't she be revealing her identity the same as she had in the video clip?

Mindsight did not seem concerned. Not about Lester, not about the senator. Not even about Janie's invisibility, because rather than standing down, she raised her gun higher, taking aim directly at Lester. A soft smile drew back a corner of Mindsight's maroon lips.

"I don't need to see her," Mindsight said. "I'll always know where my captain is."

A *CRACK!* split the air.

Janie screamed. Fleetingly, she couldn't help but wonder whose life was going to flash before her eyes—hers or Jane's— but no bullets tore through her, and nothing seemed to hit Lester either. Instead, a colorful whirl bloomed to full size beside Janie, tackling her sideways as a strong gust of wind swept up and yanked Lester backward, off his feet—away from Janie.

Janie and Pixie Beats tumbled to the grass, Janie's invisibility slipping from her like a cloak ripped away. "Stay down," Pixie Beats told her, even as she launched herself back to her feet and ran off. There was no way Janie was arguing. Down there, in the dirt, Janie was safe for the first time in what felt like her entire life.

"Janie!" Clair's voice, Mindsight's voice, one and the same, crashed over Janie as her best friend-turned-superhero swept over her. A firm, professional grip on Janie's arm as Mindsight asked quickly, "Are you okay?"

It was supposed to be comforting—but suddenly, looking up at Clair, all Janie could see was Mindsight's cold gaze, and the gun she'd pointed in Janie's direction.

Janie scrambled backward over the grass. "You shot him!"

"No, Janie—Janie, listen to me." Mindsight stretched across the gap between them, cupped Janie's cheek. The leather of her glove was warm against Janie's skin, a trickle of calm seeping in from the tips of Clair's fingers as they twisted through Janie's hair. "Janie. He's fine. It was a blank. There was no way I would risk hitting you, okay? All we really needed was the distraction while Windforce and Pixie Beats did their thing."

"A blank," Janie repeated.

"That's right. You're okay. You were always going to be okay. But we've got to get you out of here, all right?"

Janie squeezed her eyes shut for a second, fighting back a well of hot tears. "It was *so loud*."

"I know." Mindsight stood up, easing Janie to her feet. She gave Janie just a moment to catch her balance before she started guiding her forward. "That's right, here we go."

They'd just begun to move when the shriek of metal scraping against stone broke the air. Janie yelped, scrambling back, as a chunk of concrete flew by.

Mindsight seized her wrist, yanking her hard to the side. "This way!"

They raced for cover, ducking behind a statue of a man on a horse. Mindsight tipped her head as if listening to the comm in her ear, the furrow of her brow deepening.

"What's wrong?" Janie couldn't see the rest of the park, but the sounds were enough to paint a horrible picture. Roars and shrieks, thumps and wet squelches.

Mindsight set her jaw. "Nothing." She held her fingers to her lips, and Janie remembered what Keisha had said when they'd first been discussing Dog Squad: that he could listen in to the team's plans, and Janie knew their concerns had been right. How were they supposed to coordinate their attack if they couldn't discuss strategy with each other? Suddenly his superpower didn't seem as silly as it once did.

Mindsight craned her neck to see around the statue. Janie followed suit.

It wasn't a pretty sight. The Heroes were doing their best, but there were just *so many* Shadow Raptors swarming the park, it was almost impossible to track the team. While a lot of the parkgoers had scattered, a few were pinned down in clusters, a Hero or two holding the Shadow Raptors at bay as best they could. Blood painted giant brushstrokes across the grass, and Janie swallowed down the churn in her stomach, forcing herself not to wonder where it had come from.

In the center of it all was the senator. Gripped firmly between two Shadow Raptors, his feet swinging wildly as they carried him down one of the winding paths.

When a hand landed on Janie's shoulder, she nearly screamed; but it was only Mindsight, gripping her upper arm, trying to guide Janie to her feet. "We have to go," she whispered, or at least that's what Janie thought she was trying to whisper, with what little breath she was putting into it.

Janie shook her head. She pointed furiously around the base of the horse statue, but even after glancing over, Mindsight's brow only wrinkled in confusion. Mindsight tried to tug Janie to her feet again, but Janie wrenched her arm free, stubbornly planting her butt on the cold ground.

"What?" Mindsight mouthed, and Janie groaned in frustration. How was she supposed to explain if she couldn't actually *explain*? The senator was being swept away, and there was nothing the other Heroes were doing to stop it. And if Janie just ran, just let that happen . . . She'd never be able to forgive herself. No matter how different he was, this was still her *dad*. She had to get Clair to see that, but Lester would hear anything she said.

Unless she didn't speak.

Janie did not let herself question the idea. Mindsight was reaching out for her again, and this time Janie grabbed the extended hand, making sure to pinch down hard over the exposed tips of Mindsight's fingers.

She didn't know how this worked. If Mindsight could hear specific thoughts, how long it took, if Janie needed to be thinking about the idea she wanted to communicate or if Mindsight would just grab the entire contents of Janie's head in one scoop and sort it out herself. She hoped her confusion wouldn't muddy the point she was trying to get across, but that was the risk she had to take. If, somehow, she could get Mindsight to see, then it would be worth it.

The touch lasted barely an instant before Mindsight ripped her hand away. A surge of anger, not her own, prickled at Janie's fingers like a burn. Mindsight's face twisted up. It was clear there were things she wanted to say, a dozen emotions washing over her face at once. When it had finally settled, Janie wasn't sure what had won: Mindsight's sense of heroism, or Janie's silent plea.

In the end, it was a simple gesture. Mindsight raised a finger, wait, then pointed firmly at the ground between them. Janie did not need empathic powers to read it: *stay here*.

Janie crossed her heart, though she hoped not to die.

Mindsight's mouth slashed to the side in disbelief. But she got to her feet just the same, racing into the chaos. In her wake, Janie scrambled into a crouch. She steeled herself, then peered around the base of the statue.

Now *this* was a Hero at work. Forget the flash of some of the others' powers: Janie watched, breathless, as Mindsight charged straight into the heart of the battle. No plan that Janie knew of, no particular combat powers or excessive weaponry. She did not even draw her revolver. Instead, she cut through the teeming Shadow Raptors with a seemingly divine purpose, dodging and veering, ducking and rearing back, but never stopping for even an instant. When she got close she passed by Windforce, and with nothing more than a glance she'd gotten him to turn, throw a gust near her feet. It launched her up, vaulting her across a protective ring of Shadow Raptors that surrounded Senator Maxwell, his escorts, and Lester.

Mindsight's coat flared as she landed directly in the senator's path, settling as noble as any cape.

Janie's heart stirred. In the distance, Mindsight was saying something to Lester and the Shadow Raptors, her hands raised in a way to encourage them to stand down. If Janie had Lester's hearing she could have listened in, but she didn't really need to. She trusted Clair to do what she'd set out to do. She always had.

So maybe it was love, or maybe it was teenage naïveté that did not let Janie see what was clearly coming. But when the strike finally came, Janie gasped as sharply as if she herself had been hit.

A Shadow Raptor, launching in from behind. Mindsight whirled, trying to deflect, but they were not attempting to attack her—they were *grabbing* her. Scaly hands, the whole swarm closing in. The last thing Janie could see, before they closed ranks around Mindsight, was their cold fingers pressing down on any exposed patch of skin on Mindsight's face, her fingers, pushing up the sleeves of her coat.

Janie was running before she realized she was running, but she did not get far. In the instant it took her to process what she was doing but before she could panic, a colorful burst bloomed in front of her—Pixie Beats, appearing like some sort of punk goddess of the forest.

"Sorry in advance," she said and then hugged Janie around the waist.

What happened next was nothing short of an *Alice in Wonderland* mind trip. In an instant, the world began to balloon around Janie, everything growing and growing and growing, so quickly she was sure she was going to be sick, until they were living in a world of giants. Pixie Beats leaped, carrying Janie, the two of them little more than a grasshopper soaring over the expanse of the park in wide bounds.

She didn't let Janie go until they were safely across the street. And if Janie thought the process of unshrinking would be any less nauseating than shrinking had been, she was quickly disabused of that notion. The world warped again, this time it shrinking and Janie growing, so quickly and so much that when it was done, she was sure Pixie Beats had taken the process too far—surely Janie's head, her hands, hadn't always been this enormous? Her whole body still felt like it was spinning through the air, but Pixie Beats was ready for her. She pitched Janie over a trash can just before Janie retched.

"We have to . . . go back," Janie gasped between heaves of her stomach, but Pixie Beats just patted her between the shoulder blades.

"It's okay. They've got it. Look."

She pointed across the way. Janie wiped her mouth, peering over the lip of the trash can.

She'd expected the worst, but with the Shadow Raptors singularly descending on Mindsight, they'd made themselves vulnerable, and now the Heroes were sweeping them aside with something not quite bordering on ease.

Janie didn't see what happened next. Her stomach gave another heave and she pitched herself over the trash can again, Pixie Beats pulling back her hair and gathering it into a ponytail for her. By the time Janie looked up again, the remaining Shadow

Raptors were scattering, and the Heroes were hurrying off the scene. Clair lay limp and unconscious in Rip-Shift's arms as he carried her through one of the shimmering tears.

Only Deltaman ran over to the two of them. "Gotta run," he told Pixie Beats. "Lester escaped with the crypto, but we got Mindsight and the senator. You get back to HQ—she can ride with me."

Pixie Beats did not argue, and, after the amount of vomit she'd just witnessed, Janie did not begrudge her. She flashed a peace sign and took off, shrinking as she launched herself down the street.

Deltaman took Janie's shoulder. "You okay to get in a car?"

Janie threw him off. "No! What's going on? What did they *do* to her?"

"It's a flare—an overload of her powers," Deltaman said. "They're not human, and that much exposure to their minds . . . it's more than she can take."

"But she'll be okay, right?" Janie asked. She grabbed the edge of Deltaman's cape. "Cal. Tell me she'll be okay."

Cal straightened up. His hand wrapped tightly around hers. "It's going to be okay," he said. "I promise."

Which wasn't exactly the answer to Janie's question, and they both knew it. But for now, it was the best Janie was likely to get.

THE NEXT FEW DAYS IN THE MAXWELL HOUSE WERE stilted, to say the least.

It didn't help that Jane was still sulking over her failure at the convenience store. She'd been quiet as she drove Keisha back to school. She was so convinced the security footage would be the big breakthrough she was looking for—without it, she felt aimless, detached. Helpless.

It would be different if she still had her powers, the whole team together. They could stake out the convenience store. Or confront the owner, Mindsight skimming his memory to see if he knew where the tape had gone and, perhaps more importantly, why it was missing. Or Granite Girl could hack into their computer. Pixie Beats could keep an eye on the back room, chilling in an empty coffee cup to see how the owner reacted when he took stock of his security tapes. Bottom line, they would have options. *Jane* would have options.

Instead, Jane spun her wheels for the rest of the week. Kept her head down, only talking to people when she absolutely had to, tossing every spare minute into keeping up with the onslaught of homework and quizzes and essays. She saw more of Cal than her own "parents," which was just as well considering she and Paul still weren't on speaking terms.

In some ways, having a wall of cold between them was nice—or, if not nice, at least familiar. Jane knew what to do with a Paul Maxwell she refused to talk to. Though sometimes even now, sitting at the dining room table, eyes focused on her plate as she curtly offered up her one thing to share about her day, this version of Paul would make some offhand joke and Jane would find her traitorous lips curling into a smirk.

But all respites end eventually, and on Friday, Jane walked into the living room to find Paul waiting for her.

It was already early evening. Jane had just gotten home from studying with Cal. She kicked off her shoes as Paul's voice reached out from the living room, snaring her. "Jane! Can I see you for a moment?"

Jane hesitated, her foot still in the air. Her grip tightened around her backpack strap. She stared at the tollgate of the speech bubble in front of her, Paul's words blocking access. They existed only in her imagination—she could bat them away and they'd disappear in a puff of nothing—yet they stilled her just the same.

It was too late to pretend she hadn't heard him, and now Jane felt her resolve crumble, just a little. Was it even this version of Paul she was angry with? Or had she just fallen back into familiar patterns, the emotional distance she didn't know how to live outside of?

So she turned. Set her backpack on the floor in the open archway between the living room and the hall.

Paul got to his feet. He held out a small package, wrapped in Mickey Mouse wrapping paper that used to sit in the Maxwells' basement, unused in the years since Jane had outgrown it. Jane stared at it, just the hand and the present filling the frame, trapping it in paint and ink as she tried to wrap her mind around the gesture.

"A peace offering," Paul said. "I'm sorry we fought."

"That's not exactly the same thing as an apology." She took the package anyway, though. She knew better than to expect more, even from this softer version of Paul Maxwell.

Paul shrugged. "I don't think either of us are flexible enough to acknowledge our faults in this one. The downside of you taking after me so much, I guess. Let's settle for moving on amicably."

Jane's mouth soured. He was wrong, of course—Jane didn't take after him at all, not any version of him—but she didn't feel like arguing the point just to stir up shit. As much as she'd enjoyed having a few days away from him, she needed his help if she was going to get back to her own Earth, her own body. She could put up with him for that long, at least.

She ripped off the paper. Inside was a small department store gift box, worn around the edges from years of the Maxwells reusing it every Christmas and birthday. Jane lifted the lid, her eyebrows raising along with it.

"You got me . . . a Tamagotchi?"

"Technically, it's the one you—Janie—had when she was younger," Paul said. "But that's not the point. Simon and I modified it, so now it scans for the signature of your attacker. The range isn't very big, but it should help us narrow it down once Simon gets a hit off his scans. Push the left button."

Jane did as he asked. Immediately, the blobby pixel creature was replaced by a small compass arrow, and some sort of progress bar beneath it, currently empty. She had to admit, it certainly *looked* like a clever modification, but . . .

"Why a Tamagotchi?"

"We needed something you could carry around without looking suspicious."

"Sure, and maybe if I were still in middle school that would be a good idea." Jane held it up by the chain. "No one's played with these in years."

"Then you can be retro."

"It doesn't count as retro until it's a lot older."

"Yeah, well, you're older," he said. "Pretend it's retro for you."

"That's not how it . . . Never mind." Jane set the box down

and undid the snap of the chain, threading it to hang off her belt loop and tucking it into the top of her pocket to keep it out of sight like she used to when she was a kid.

Paul nodded in approval. "Looks good. God, that's a familiar sight. Do you remember when you first got that thing? You were *inseparable*. One time—" He cut himself off. "Sorry."

"It's okay," Jane said. She was trying to be patient with him, to remember that his daughter was missing somewhere in the multiverse, hopefully in the safe hands of the Heroes but with no way to prove that.

"Want to take it out for a spin? Simon's picked up a signal coming from out past the mall. We could go track it down."

How was Jane supposed to say no? Paul looked so pitiful, suddenly, standing there with his hand stuffed into the pocket of his jeans. Goddammit, he was *trying*, and the trying was almost more than Jane could take.

"Sure," Jane said finally. She bumped past him, toward the hall. "Let's just go and get it over with."

FORTY MINUTES LATER, JANE WAS WALKING ALONE DOWN a broken road on the outskirts of town. Ghosts of the last time she and Paul had gone out on a superhero mission hung in the air as they set out, so they split up "to cover more ground." Paul had his own localized scanner, disguised in a Palm Pilot. Jane tried not to be insulted when he'd shown it to her—she knew he would only argue that it wouldn't look "normal" for Jane to be carrying around something that a businessman would have used, and she didn't feel like explaining the finer points of the intersection of sexism and ageism with a middle-class white man who'd built his life in the suburban bubble of the nineties.

"You're *sure* the reading came from here?" Jane asked now.

The walkie-talkie in her hand crackled to life. Paul's muffled voice came out of the tinny speaker. "That's what it said on Simon's computer."

"It makes no sense," Jane whispered to herself as she slunk from shadow to shadow. "What would someone with her powers be doing *here*?"

It was a question she would have loved to ask the team over comms, if she'd been properly equipped. If she wasn't using bulky plastic walkie-talkies Paul had dug out of a box of Janie and Allison's old toys, knocking the corroded batteries out and cleaning the compartment carefully with Q-Tips and rubbing alcohol. To Jane, it was a wonder they still worked at all, though Paul had only laughed and told her it was a "dad skill."

Jane had taken hers without comment.

The walkies were a poor substitute for the comms Jane was used to. Limited range, prone to fading into a hiss of static, too loud to be used for a stealth mission. So she kept the question to herself. She stuffed the walkie-talkie into the oversized center pocket of her hoodie, the same one she'd worn when she'd gone out to bust the drug deal with Paul. Thankfully, he hadn't commented when she'd put it on, just grabbed his car keys and motioned for Jane to go ahead.

An electronic trill cooed in Jane's jeans pocket. She took the Tamagotchi out, pressing the button to switch it from the looping sequence of digital pet animations to the interface Simon had programmed into it. It agreed: the readings were definitely coming from somewhere in this area. She turned around, following the slow spin of the digital compass needle before setting off again.

This was an old part of town, one that had been rezoned so many times it barely knew what it was anymore. A plumbing supply store next to an X-rated video rental store next to an empty dirt parking lot that housed a rotating fleet of semi-truck trailers. Then four little one-bedroom houses from the 1950s, identical in both construction and the amount of paint peeling off the clapboard siding.

And at the end of the street, an old double-wide converted into a diner.

Jane stopped as it came into view.

Her mind reeled back. An overhead shot of two girls on opposite sides of a table, books and binders spread among white plates sticky with pools of maple syrup. One girl—flannel shirt, glasses, brown hair up in a messy ponytail bun—has a cheap ballpoint pen caught in her hand as she doodles a caricature of a teacher with a bushy mustache. The other—neat babydoll tee, cropped denim vest—is slid so far down in the booth she's almost under the table, her hand pressed over her laughing mouth, cheeks as red as the crusted bottle of ketchup sitting beside the napkin holder. The line work of the girls is crisp and detailed, every nuance captured, while the rest of the diner fades into watercolors, unbound.

A shiver passed through Jane, dragging her back to the present. Past. Whichever she was in right now. She bit the inside of her cheek to ground herself. The Tamagotchi in her hand was blinking rapidly, the compass needle pointing straight to Raina's Diner.

Jane quickened her pace. Her feet remembered the path better than she did, but she supposed that was only fair. She'd spent so much time here, after she and Clair had gotten together, before they dared tell anyone. It was the perfect respite: unpopular, out of the way enough that none of their friends would find them, the waitresses too busy gossiping about lousy, no-good, cheating boyfriends to bother paying attention to two girls doing their homework.

Clair's familiar laugh drifted through the evening air.

Jane's head snapped up. She adjusted her glasses as her vision tried to shift in the darkness, then she cursed under her breath when of course it didn't work. It didn't matter. She didn't need night vision to see what was happening beneath the spill of lamplight in front of the diner, though suddenly Jane wished she did. That the sight in front of her was still hidden, that she didn't need to witness this at all.

Her mind split the world apart, dividing it neatly into boxes. Clair and Hailey, unlocking their bikes from the rack just at the corner of the building. The setting sun catches the leaves of the trees lining the parking lot, casting a soft golden glow across the panels. Clair's shoulders from behind, her face caught in profile as she turns to laugh at something Hailey says. A close-up of youthful fingers not *quite* brushing against each other as Hailey hands Clair her backpack. Mirrored, down-turned eyelashes as two girls turn away from each other to grab their bikes. The spread was a basic grid, no inspiration or originality. Just one square after another, the most Jane could process.

Her breath came back to her in a silent hiccup, like the beginning of a sob. Jane caught it in her chest, holding it there until it burned. She wondered whose idea it had been to come here. She wasn't sure she wanted to know—in fact, she was pretty sure the answer would kill her, but the question floated through her mind just the same, the fluffy, cloudlike thought bubble knocking any other concerns from her mind.

The girls set off down the narrow road, pedals clicking in the growing darkness.

Jane never questioned that she would follow.

If she'd been in her own, grown-up body, this would be a lot easier. Jane would simply bend the light of the evening around her, reflecting and refracting the world until she was, in effect, invisible. Still, Jane was a superhero. She'd be damned if she couldn't manage to tail someone without them noticing, powers or no powers. So she gave them a head start, and then she set off after them. She shut the walkie-talkie off—there was no way she wanted to risk Paul's commentary, or his disapproval. This was something Jane had to do.

Each of Jane's footfalls matched the pounding of her heart. She tried not to watch them, but it was impossible not to. The languid turn of the pedals, just fast enough to keep from toppling over. The way the fading sunlight turned them into half-developed Polaroids, muddy shapes barely visible in the fog.

They were following the same path that Clair and Jane used to, in another life, so long ago and yet somehow still waiting in the future. A quiet little road, then a cut across an empty field. Eventually, they would meet up with the river that ran behind Jane's house, tucked just far enough out of sight to offer a slice of privacy. Especially beneath the old oak tree.

The tang of vomit hit the back of Jane's throat. She swallowed it down. It was fine, she told herself. There was no way they'd follow the path that far—Hailey didn't live on Jane and Clair's street, after all, so surely they'd have to part ways long before then. Even on the off chance they didn't, it was fine. It meant nothing. Just two girls, doing homework after school and hanging out. Gals being pals.

She had followed them nearly to the field when a furious beeping erupted from Jane's pocket. Jagged sound bubbles shooting toward the sky, the white of their backgrounds creating stark arrows pointing straight down to Jane. Jane leaped into the weeds beside the road, jabbing the buttons of the traitorous Tamagotchi until it shut up.

It was too late.

"Hello?"

Jane froze, hunched over the Tamagotchi like Gollum with his ring. An inked outline pinned her to the page.

"Is someone there?"

Clair's voice was drawing nearer, rapid footfalls approaching, and there was no hiding, no escape—Jane tripped backward, deeper toward the woods, but it was no use, and she didn't have her powers to hide her, and they were almost here, they would find her in just a second, and there was no time, and no other option.

Jane yanked her hood back, exposing her face as she stumbled out of the dark. "Oh, hey. Hi! How's it going?"

Clair yelped, the sound bubble bursting across the page. Only glimpses of her limbs could be seen around the jagged edges—an elbow here, an arched eyebrow there. In the lower corner, her sneaker catching on a stone in the dirt road, and then on the next page a set of two arms reaching out and catching her.

She hurried to right herself. Hailey brushed aside a stray leaf that had somehow tumbled into Clair's hair.

"Janie?" Clair asked, when she finally composed herself. She was nearly breathless from the effort.

"Yeah." Jane shifted from foot to foot, kicking the dirt. "Sorry, I . . . didn't mean to startle you."

"What are you *doing* out here?"

"Walking. Home. I was out."

Eyes as narrow as the panel that boxed them in landed on Jane. "Is that a Tamagotchi?" Clair asked.

Jane looked down. The screen was full of numbers, garbage output screaming at her. She closed her fingers over it, hoping

Clair hadn't noticed. "Yup. My dad got it working again—he thought I would want it, but, like, what am I, twelve?" Jane let out a laugh, trying not to sound strained. "He meant well, I guess. Anyway. Um. What brings you out here? The two of you. What's . . . you know, up?"

Clair sidestepped. Just enough to wedge open the space between her and Hailey a little more. It was a seamless move, one so carefully orchestrated it could have easily been mistaken for her shifting her weight or scratching an itch. Jane would have been forgiven for not noticing it, except that she'd felt the cold sliding between her and Clair often enough, in those early years before they were out to anyone in their lives. Her throat tightened, seeing it now from the outside.

Hailey, of course, barely even seemed to register Jane's presence. It certainly didn't phase her. She flicked her bangs to the side, as cool-girl perfect as if Jane had drawn her specifically for audiences to hate. "Just out studying. You ever been to Raina's? It's actually hella cute. Very retro." She smiled at Jane, her voice dipping toward a purr as she added, "Pretty private, too."

Jane stretched her mouth into a smile, so wide her cheeks hurt. "Great! I'll have to—I'll have to try it sometime. Anyway, I should, uh . . . I should get home. I've . . . got to meet Cal. You know, for tutoring."

"Of course," Clair said, her speech bubble frosted over with dark shading. "Another tutoring emergency."

Dammit, Jane was never going to escape that stupid lie. "Right. That's the one."

She snapped her fingers, turning them into a set of finger guns that completely failed to strike the casual tone Jane had been going for. She balled them into fists instead, tucking her hands deep into the front pocket of her hoodie.

"Okay. I'm going now."

"Nice to see you, Jane!" Hailey singsonged, but it was Clair's icy "Bye" that hit Jane hardest. Jane clutched it tight to her chest, the crosshatched speech bubble dripping cold rain down her hoodie as she hurried home.

JANIE WAS LOSING TRACK OF THE DAYS. SHE HADN'T slept since the park—not properly, at any rate.

She tried to tell herself that Clair would be fine. That's what the team kept promising her, anyway, and Janie had to believe them. Besides, Janie could see the rejuve pod doing its job, every time she slipped in to check on Clair—more often than she let on. Clair was being held unconscious for medical reasons Janie wasn't even going to try to understand, but her color had gotten steadily better, her breathing smoother, her face softer and more relaxed.

So she made herself believe it, folding that reassurance into her heart every morning as she got dressed. And she made herself believe it as she idled away the hours, trying to keep useful.

The Heroes kept giving her small things to do. Meaningless tasks, really, but it helped keep her mind off things. Which was sweet of the team, if a little odd. Yes, okay, Janie was deep-down terrified for Clair, sure; that didn't explain why the others were tiptoeing around her, as if they were expecting her to flip out at any moment. Clair was Janie's best friend, yes—but *their* teammate. Someone they'd worked side by side with for years, fighting crime and holding back the freakish side of the universe.

Still, if they were willing to keep Janie busy, she wasn't going to complain. Senator Maxwell hadn't texted since the incident in the park, and since there was nothing left to plan for, Janie would otherwise be adrift.

Which is what made the nights so impossible. With nothing to occupy her thoughts, they swirled around the drain of worry and regret, all her failures impossible to ignore. Plus, there was a downside to this particular superpower that Janie hadn't considered until now: being able to see in the dark made it almost impossible to go to sleep. Especially when you were stressed.

And so, after a few hours of tossing and turning, after however many nights of tossing and turning, Janie threw off the covers. Slid from the bed. It took her no time at all to change her clothes, find some sneakers. She had only intended to wander around headquarters, snooping here and there, but after the third *Access Denied*, she gave up. She made her way to the elevator. She didn't know where she was going, not really—she just knew she couldn't spend another sleepless night staring at the same blank ceiling.

The night air was just a little too cold for the blouse she was wearing, but if Janie turned around to get something warmer, she knew she'd chicken out. She was already breaking about a hundred rules just being out by herself in the first place, much less at night. Not that it was *that* late, but she could still hear the voices of everyone who'd lecture her for this behavior. *It's too dangerous after dark, you're not old enough, what if something happened to you, don't be stupid, Janie.* They swam through her mind in a long line: her parents, Allison, her teachers, the Heroes . . . Clair. Everyone would have something to say about it, but that was the point, wasn't it? Clair *couldn't* say anything to her, not right now—and Janie was to blame.

Already the outside air felt less restrictive. And so Janie walked. Through unfamiliar streets, keeping track of her turns. They say Grand City never sleeps, and it was true. Not even night, not even the drizzle that started up twenty minutes into her walk, could deter the churn of people filling either side of the sidewalk. She was grateful for the crowd, as well as her night vision—it made this rebellion way less scary.

In fact, as she strolled, a smile began to tug at her face. Janie lifted her gaze, taking in the shop signs, her eyes open for a Beef-Up Burgers. One of their shakes sounded *amazing* right about now.

But it wasn't a burger joint that caught her attention.

Neon lights in the window, casting a pink glow over the sidewalk. Cartoonized women—not even women, really, just the basest silhouette, flowing hair and curves. Janie was only vaguely familiar with the term "objectified," so she didn't think it, but she knew it. Like mudflaps on a truck, like Lara Croft video games, like the doodles Cal sometimes showed her just to get a rise out of her. She was supposed to be disgusted by it, and she was, and her eyes averted like she was supposed to, and she hurried past the window like she was supposed to.

Except.

Unlike the mudflaps and the bursting-out flesh that splashed the pages of the comics Janie read, lingering occasionally when no one was paying attention, this wasn't just some idolized fantasy drawing, created for no reason other than to titillate. This was a *sign*.

And not one of those "pay attention, life is trying to tell you something" signs. This was a literal sign, stuck out front to advertise the contents. Like a coffee shop with a cup on its door, or a gas station with a pump on the roof, or a fancy restaurant with a bunch of grapes and a bottle of wine in its logo. Symbols going back long before the average person could read. Come in, they said, come in, this is what you'll find.

Women. Or, in the language of the business: *girls, girls, girls!*

The drizzle kicked up into a light rain. It was a ridiculous idea, one that burned her cheeks just thinking about it. There was no way she could, no way she should. She ducked beneath the overhang of the next business down, stamping her feet to work out some of her nervous energy. Her stomach was jumping all over, and a vaguely sour taste stained the back of her mouth. She'd been on her way to buy a *milkshake*, of all things. The duality of the moment was giving her vertigo: the safe draw of childhood, the spiked thrill of adulthood. Plus, she needed something to eat. That explained the feeling, right? The weird little lurch, like someone had hooked her navel?

Only she didn't know where the nearest Beef-Up was, and . . . these kinds of places (it was safer to think of it that way, "these kinds of places," like Janie didn't know exactly what it was, like it was the *word* that was sharp and interesting) served food, too, didn't they? Hadn't Janie heard that somewhere? In a movie or something?

Her feet were carrying her back the direction she'd come from. She hadn't told herself to move, but as soon as she was, she knew there had never really been a decision at all. That weird little lurch wasn't hunger, but the feeling of certainty, where you knew you were going to do something even if you told yourself you weren't. It was the same feeling she'd gotten when she was eleven and she'd steal a lightning-fast look in Clair's direction when they'd peel their sandy bathing suits off before leaving the beach, two in a stall to save time. The same feeling when Cal had dared Marie to steal a dirty magazine from the collection hidden in Devin's older brother's room, and the group had been so terrified once they actually had it that a fast game of Hot Potato had landed it, unexpectedly, in Janie's possession, and she knew she would keep it even though she swore she stuffed it into the trash can behind the gym. The same feeling when, last year, she'd faked a stomachache to stay home all by herself, and locked the bathroom door, and filled the tub, and masturbated for the first time ever, and then spent the rest of the day wondering what an orgasm was supposed to feel like for a woman, and had she done it, was that it, that must have been it, right? She couldn't ask anyone, and wouldn't even if she'd had the chance.

She stepped toward the entrance and her stomach flipped again. Rebellion (surely it counted as rebellion, even if her parents had never explicitly told her, "Janie, don't go into strip clubs when you're still fifteen") turned her head into a balloon, ready to float from her shoulders. Could this actually work? But why wouldn't it? Janie caught a glimpse of her own borrowed body in the window of a parked car, startling herself. There was no doubt from the outside that she was old enough to march in without question, and suddenly her mind was filled with all the things she'd be allowed to do, out from under the scrutiny of the Heroes: buy cigarettes, drink beer, rent a car. Have sex. She wasn't planning to actually *do* any of them, she wasn't stupid, but the mere possibility was enough to fill her already overfilled head, to the point where she was now legitimately worried she'd pass out before she made it inside.

Still. There was only one way to find out, and Janie's feet were once again carrying her forward. Toward the door, toward the chance, toward the only way she'd ever actually know if she could do it.

Janie made it inside.

That was about as far as she *had* made it. Not because she'd been caught, not because someone managed to see through the magic of maturity her body projected, not because they'd peeled back her disguise and shouted, "Look! A child in our midst! Someone stop her!" These things all filled her mind as she held her breath and stepped over the threshold. But they didn't *actually* happen, and instead Janie stumbled through, the bouncer nodding at her in a bored sort of way. She hurried past, into a room held in the throes of darkness.

Janie blinked, her eyes adjusting. Adjusting really, *really* quickly, in fact—too quickly. In an instant, a gray-green haze settled over the room. The crowd and the . . . dancers . . . popped to vivid life with a halo of orange. It was a weird mix of the way they showed night vision goggles on TV, and how her family had all shown up when they'd played around in the infrared room of the local science museum when Janie and Allison were little. Though Janie tried not to think about that, because the mix of such an innocent memory with the actual scene before her was enough to cause a wave of vertigo to wash over her.

She reached out, snaring the elbow of a passing waitress. At least, god, Janie hoped she was a waitress, though in her experience they did tend to wear more clothes. Janie steadfastly kept her eyes fixed on the waitress's face as she asked, "Excuse me, where's the bathroom?"

The waitress looked Janie up and down, as if sensing the child beneath her skin, and for a second Janie was *sure* she was about to kick her out. But then the waitress pointed toward the deeper shadows.

"Down the hall, hon. First door on the left."

"Thank you." Janie tripped as she hurried away from her, already drunk with the power of what she was doing.

Wait, what *was* she doing? Janie shoved her way through the ladies' room door and crashed against the nearest sink. Her fingers gripped the basin so hard her knuckles matched the porcelain. Janie took several deep breaths, gulping down the cool air of the bathroom.

At least it was a little brighter in here. Her night vision receded, her powers clicking off. Janie turned on the faucet. She ran her hands beneath the tap, cool water cascading over her fingers. This was silly, she told herself. She was panicking, and for what? Because she'd walked into a strip club? What difference did that make, really? It was just *skin*. It's not like she didn't know what it all looked like, and besides, surely she'd seen just as much at the beach, right?

Right. This wasn't anything Janie couldn't handle. In fact, if anything, being here proved her own maturity—that she could step through that door and it was no big deal. Never mind that she was currently hiding out in a bathroom. That was . . . a fluke. It wouldn't happen again.

Hands washed and dried, Janie took a breath and headed back out.

Now that she was marginally calmer, she realized she didn't even need to shift her vision. Most of the room was dark, yes, but there was still enough light to move around in. Besides, the points of the room you *were* supposed to see were lit up in dazzling, glittery, pink-hazed glory.

Okay, so maybe it was a *bit* more than you'd see at the beach. Janie stood for a moment, gawping. She knew she shouldn't. Knew that, even though no one could tell she was really a teenager, everyone could tell she was a woman.

It took longer than it should to wrench her attention away. Longer still to get herself to move. Janie surveyed the rest of the room.

She wandered up to the bar.

Did she actually have any intention of getting drunk? She wasn't sure. She knew it wasn't smart to drink too much on an empty stomach, even if she didn't entirely understand why. Something about alcohol poisoning, probably. She knew the phrase, even if she didn't really know what it was. And she knew that getting completely drunk her first time out, all alone in a city that was still unfamiliar to her, wasn't exactly smart. This knowledge was strong in her mind, even as she edged up to the bar, even as she toyed with the corner of a twenty dollar bill in her pocket. Janie had found it in the closet, in a pair of pants. She didn't even need to finish a drink—she just wanted to *order* one. Just wanted to know she could.

"Hi," Janie said when the bartender finally turned to her. "Yes, can I get a beer, please?"

The bartender raised an eyebrow. For a second a jolt of panic seized Janie, wondering what she'd done wrong, but then the bartender said, "Sure," and relief flooded her. Until: "What kind?"

Janie bit her lip. Crap, there were multiple *kinds*? Her mind flailed, dredging up random beer commercials and clips from movies. What was she supposed to say? Budweiser? Miller Lite? Wait, wasn't a lager a beer? Or was that a pint? What *was* a pint, anyway, when it wasn't talking about a carton of heavy cream? No, focus! She was taking too long, and now the bartender really *was* looking at her funny, squinting as if he was considering asking for her ID.

"I meant wine!" Janie blurted. "Red wine. House . . . red?"

"Look, miss—"

"Well, well!" burst a cheerful—and familiar—voice at her elbow. "Fancy meeting you here."

Cal sidled up beside her. He planted one elbow on the bar, a drink held loosely in his hand. His amused grin was a beacon in the dim light of the club.

Janie leaped back, practically colliding with another patron. "Cal! What are you—I mean, I didn't—I just—"

Cal laughed. He clamped a hand on Janie's shoulder. Pressure squeezed down, reassuring even as he turned her away from the bar. "Janie, Janie, Janie," he said, leading her off. "Relax. You're not in trouble. I'm not here to bust your balls."

Janie's eyes widened. Hopeful, stunned, disbelieving. "You're not?"

"Nah." And then, to Janie's shock, he stopped by a small, circular booth and slid into place. He glanced up, patting the seat next to him. "Come on, kid. I promise, your secret's safe with me."

Heat tore through Janie's cheeks. "I really wasn't . . . *looking*," she fumbled. "I'm not . . . I don't care about—I mean, why would I?"

"Sure," Cal said, a knowing tease in his voice. "I go to strip clubs for the food, too."

"Oh my god." Humiliation doused her. Janie curled beneath the weight of the downpour, her stomach seizing worse than cramps. The motion seated her without conscious thought, and she ducked her head into her folded arms on the table, her glasses bonking the surface.

Cal gave her a minute. Janie thought she heard him speaking to someone, maybe one of the underdressed waitresses, and then he was silent again.

"Jesus, Janie," he said finally. "I get that you're embarrassed, but it's really not a big deal. I had the internet when I was your age. You think I didn't spend hours waiting for shitty, pixilated porn to download?"

Tentatively, Janie peeped up at him. Through a tangle of fingers and the curtain of hair that had fallen over her face. He was just sitting there, one arm sprawled over the back of the booth, sipping his drink as if this was all totally normal. It was the surprise of it, the *calm*, more than anything else that got Janie to sit up. Did he really not *care* that she was looking at women? It felt impossible for this moment to pass as a complete nonissue, swept aside like it was nothing, and yet . . . He was just sitting there, sipping his drink as he watched the women on stage. Of course, it's possible that he hadn't thought the situation through yet, but . . . somehow, she didn't think that explained it. Janie brushed her hair off her heated face, trying to collect herself.

Cal raised his glass at her, approving.

The waitress returned, setting a red plastic tray of fries on the table between them, along with a glass full of dark liquid. She straightened up slowly, which Janie furiously did not watch, and then the waitress trailed her finger along Cal's shoulder as she walked away.

Cal stole a limp fry from the basket. He nudged the glass toward Janie. "It's Coke," he said. "And not the kind spiked with rum. Sorry."

That was fine with Janie. More than fine, in fact—after everything, she was glad to have something safe and familiar in front of her. She took the Coke, sipping the level down before pressing the cold glass against her cheeks.

"How did you find me?" Janie asked after a moment.

"Maybe I didn't." Cal jerked his chin toward the stage, somewhere fastidiously behind Janie's field of view. "Maybe I was just here for the show."

Fresh heat threatened Janie's face. She forced herself to sit there, to look across the table at Cal and wait for him to continue.

He laughed. "I mean, it's a great show, you're honestly missing out. How do you think she manages to twist herself around like that, though?" He glanced at Janie, but she wasn't about to rise to his bait. Cal spun his glass idly on the table. "I tracked your phone."

Janie blinked. "My phone?"

To Janie's amazement, they still hadn't taken the emergency flip phone away from her. Janie had stuffed it into her pocket before leaving headquarters, not even giving it any thought.

She was already adjusting to having it on her. She found something grounding and familiar about its presence. Now she felt the lump of it in her jeans, wedged in the fold of her lap beneath the table.

"Yeah, you'll find the downside of these things is they spy on literally everything you do. You get used to it," he added with a vague shrug as Janie stared in horror across the table at him. "Anyway, when I didn't find you in your rooms, I figured it couldn't hurt to check."

"Wait, why were you in my room?"

"Ah," Cal said. He straightened up, smoothing out his shirt. "Yeah, I guess I probably should have led with that. I thought you'd want to know . . . Clair's awake."

19

"IS IT REALLY A GOOD IDEA TO WORK ON THIS IN THE *garage*?" Jane asked.

Paul chuckled under his breath as he flicked on the light over his workbench. "Did *you* ever pay attention to what I was doing out here? Or, well . . . your dad, I guess. In his garage. When he was still alive." His mouth screwed up. "Shit. That was stupid of me. I'm sorry."

"It's fine." Jane ducked her face as she regarded the spread of parts and tools scattered over the workspace. The table here was cluttered but clean, the surface wiped down after projects, the little drawers of screws and brackets neatly labeled, but Jane wasn't really seeing it. Instead, overlaid across her vision was another garage, another workbench. The lights off, a single musty shaft of sunlight cutting over ancient packages of screws, glue, bolts of twine. All unopened, all coated with a thick layer of fuzzy dust. The scene is sketched lightly, thin pencil strokes and vaguely shaped blobs of color. It's a muted background shot, not meant to be seen in any great detail.

Jane blinked, and the image disappeared. Paul was looking over at her, already seated on a green vinyl bar stool that was once Jane's stepping stone between a highchair and a regular seat at the kitchen table. Stickers littered the backrest, faded and peeling: a frolicking cat with a ball of yarn, the girl inventor mouse from *Chip 'n Dale: Rescue Rangers*, a cutout of the starship *Enterprise*.

Paul picked up two plastic bags from beside his feet, supplies he'd bought at Radio Shack that morning. A second stool, just plain wood, had been dragged in from a far corner of the garage, and he patted the seat in invitation.

Jane had a project at school, Paul had told Olivia over breakfast. The two of them would probably be at it for several hours. Olivia had barely reacted to this, nodding as she continued to fold a mountain of towels. Like it was nothing. Like it was *ordinary*.

It certainly looked ordinary.

The stool wobbled as Jane sat down.

"So what's the game plan?"

Paul was already unpacking supplies. Spools of wire, tiny brackets, spare tweezers. "You said the scanner wasn't working right. We're going to crack it open, test it out. Fix it if we need to."

So straightforward. Take something apart, replace the busted component. Reassemble. Easy-peasy.

Jane hated to admit it, but she could use a project like that. She picked up a screwdriver and began to remove the back of the Tamagotchi. She may not be a tech wizard like Marie, but she could, at least, handle some of the basics.

Jane narrowed her focus. Tight shots. Just her mouth, in profile, as she takes a deep breath in, as she lets a deep breath out. The curling *whoosh* of wind in front of her lips. Then an inked sketch of the workbench blooms out before her, looking down on her hands as she works. No outlines, just washes of colors and shapes to represent the work, the surrounding clutter.

For a page or two, she found peace. Nothing but varying angles as she removes a tiny circuit board, as she disconnects a wire. It would make a terrible issue, but it's a soothing montage for the moment. Paul hovers in the background of some of the panels, shuffling around, doing something Jane isn't paying attention to. For a moment, it's almost nice. In the frames, there's no indication of an outside world, not anymore. No school, no stress. No villains running around body-swapping people. No investigations.

No Clair and Hailey, and therefore, no narrow space growing tighter between them.

Electricity snapped at Jane's fingers as she touched one wire against another. "Shit!" Jane said, yanking her hand back and sucking at the faint burn to her fingertips.

"Whoa, careful there." Paul reached over, glancing at the Tamagotchi as he switched off the soldering iron she'd been working with. "You didn't take the battery out first? Your head's not in the game, sweetie."

"I'm fine," Jane said quickly. She picked the wire back up and nodded toward the iron's base. "You mind?"

Instead of turning it back on, Paul lifted the iron from her grip. Gently, the way a father would. And although the gesture should have annoyed Jane—although the gesture *did* annoy a part of Jane—another, smaller part felt the weight of it leave her hands like a burden being lifted. She shut her eyes, heat building behind her lids.

"Girl troubles?"

Jane's eyes snapped open. Not just open, but *wide*. The force of it shifted her balance, and she actually had to splay her hands and catch herself against the workbench, a handful of parts skittering as she found her grip.

Paul picked up a pair of pliers, then started working on the next piece as if he'd said nothing out of the ordinary. "Clair called while you were out the other day," he said, more to the circuit board in his hands than to Jane. "She sounded really disappointed when I told her you couldn't come to the phone."

"Oh."

It was the only thing Jane could manage to say. *Oh.* Jane's mind was blank, even her comics abandoning her. She stood in the middle of an empty sheet of paper, utterly devoid of a script for this situation.

"How much do you . . . ?" Jane shut her mouth, took a breath. Tried again. "That is, did Janie ever—?"

"She hasn't come out to me, no." Paul shrugged. "I'm giving her space. She'll tell me when she's ready." He paused, the pliers hovering over his work. A sidelong glance at Jane, held in fatherly concern. "I assume *you've* been out for a while, though. At least, I hope so."

A narrow panel of Jane's fist snapping shut. "What's that supposed to mean?"

Paul just blinked, the lines of his face softened by confusion. "Twenty *years*, Jane. That's too long to deny who you are. I don't want that for my girl."

Jane looked away. At the fist in her lap. At anything but Paul. Her fingers uncurl across the next five panels, until her hand lays flat against her thigh.

"I caught Clair out. On a *date*." She spat the words out quickly, before she could change her mind.

A clatter made Jane look up. Paul had dropped what he was working on, a horrified expression on his face as he twisted to look at Jane.

For one freezing, terrible second Jane thought she'd misunderstood this whole conversation—that Paul hadn't realized what was going on, what he was *really* asking. She looked right at him, but all she could see was an older version of her father's face, the expression she'd never dared to draw. The way he looked at her, but didn't look at her, his lawyer face a perfect mask of his emotion. The fold of his hands on the table, as if he was listening to a client. The grip of those same hands around a suitcase handle the next morning, when he couldn't maintain the eye contact any longer.

But instead of grabbing his belongings, this Paul grabbed Jane's shoulder. "Clair's cheating on Janie?"

"What? No!" Jane shook her head, clearing the memories. "No, they're not . . . they're not together. Not yet."

Paul's eyebrow ticked up. He looked almost *hopeful*, which was nuts, because surely Paul didn't care, surely he wasn't . . . *rooting* for them. Right?

"Yet?"

Jane looked down. At her left hand, bare as it rested on her thigh.

How much to tell him? It wasn't really the future, exactly, and perhaps by now they'd already crossed the line. The better part of Jane's judgment was telling her to play it safe, play it close to the chest. This was still *Paul Maxwell*, after all. Still Jane's dad. Still the man who'd walked out the day after Jane had finally come out of the closet, though the few attempts Jane had ever made at drawing a firm connection between the two events were swiftly and sharply denied.

Except . . . as much as Jane had been trying to deny it, he wasn't, not really. This Paul hadn't gotten there yet.

And moreover, Jane was getting the distinct sensation, crawling up her spine, that maybe—just *maybe*—he might make different choices than her own Paul had.

Jane took a breath, drawing in her words before she could think better of it. She watched them drop between them, as if laying out a speech bubble. Not really hers.

"You know how you asked me if I ever got married?"

She risked a glance up. There it was, then: the moment of truth. The deepest truth, the only one that mattered. Coming out was never just one moment, over and done forever. It was small choices every day. It was a scale constantly shifting in your heart, weighing the dangers and merits. The last time Jane had done it to this face, it had shut down, his expression wiping itself clean. His eyes had stayed fixed on her only because he didn't want her to see them slide away in discomfort—a situation somehow worse. His gaze had unlocked, a lawyer trick that allowed him to look without seeing.

Jane got her eyes from her father, which made it even worse.

This time, those mirrored eyes didn't unlock. And they didn't slide away, but neither did they force themselves to stay put. Instead, they widened, entirely without shame or carefully modulated control.

"For real?" Paul asked. His voice was breaking, and he tried to clear his throat, but it didn't help. "You and Clair? Like, for *real* real, legal and everything?"

"Eventually," Jane said, trying to keep the bitterness out of her voice. "Though that's not a very articulate way for a lawyer to ask."

"Oh, Jane, who cares about articulate?" He was already on his feet, already drawing Jane into a tight hug against his chest. Jane squeaked, the surprise escaping as his arms enveloped her.

When was the last time Jane had hugged her father? It must have happened at some point—he'd been present in her life when she was little, after all, when all she needed from him were Band-Aids for a skinned knee and someone to carry her over mud puddles.

This was different. Those early actions, the simple act of scooping Jane into his arms, of soothing away childhood hurts, had been an easy, perfunctory act of parenthood. It didn't take a loving dad, merely one who hadn't turned into a complete monster yet.

The arms around her now were not obligatory. These were warm and kind, locked unselfconsciously around her, gripping her as if she was something . . . precious.

"I'm sorry," he said as he let her go. Before Jane could wrap her mind around it, before she could dare consider hugging him back. He sat back on the old bar stool, the metal creaking underneath him. He dabbed at his eyes with his knuckles. "I'm sorry, it's just . . . I've been so worried about her. Janie, I mean. I know it's not easy being gay. I just want her to be happy, and to know that she *will* be, that it gets better . . ."

Jane didn't argue as she stepped away from him and fixed her glasses. Better, yes—but it wasn't like the future was some magical time when tolerance reigned supreme and hate speech had faded like bad gas.

Still. Looking at Paul now, the *hope* that expanded his chest like a sail caught by the wind . . . Jane wasn't about to ruin that.

"So what's the problem, then?" Paul asked finally. "I mean, you know this thing with the other girl won't last."

Jane's mouth twisted up. But she's already come this far. She took a deep breath. "Yeah . . . see, that's the thing: I *don't* know. There was no 'other' girl in my world. We're supposed to share our first kiss in a week, and I don't know how to fix this. I've never had to fight for Clair's affections before. She's always just been . . . mine."

Jane swallowed down the fear that this admission stirred up. She hadn't said it out loud before, but it was true. For all the years Jane and Clair had spent together, she had no idea how to actually fight for her. How to prove that Jane was a better choice than someone else. It had never been an issue before, never *really* a question as to whether or not the two of them would ever end up together.

But what if Jane couldn't figure it out in time? There was only so much Jane, this Jane, was able to do, only so many things she could bring herself to say to this teenage version of Clair. She was sure, in the deepest reaches of her heart, that the Janie who used to inhabit this skin would have admitted her feelings on schedule, the two of them set off on the same trajectory Jane knew so well.

And if not . . .

Jane couldn't even imagine an "if not." UltraViolet, the version of herself she'd replaced back on the world she was living on now, had missed her chance, and look what had happened to her: bitter and alone, turning full-on supervillain when the opportunity arose. Jane liked to think she was generally a good person at her core, that she would never make the same decisions that particular doppelgänger had. And sure, there were obviously a lot of factors that went into UltraViolet's corruption, it wasn't *just* the fact that she and Clair had never gotten together like they were supposed to. They hadn't been as close as they should have been, even before they missed the opportunity of their first kiss. And yet. It felt impossible to untangle that mistake from everything that had unfolded afterward.

"Go to her."

"What?"

"Go to her." Paul slid the opened Tamagotchi away from Jane's workstation and physically turned her toward the door, his rough hands on her shoulders. "Right now. Make it better between you."

"I . . . No, wait, I can't." Jane's foot caught on the floor, the sole of her shoe dragging against concrete.

"Yes, you can. You *have* to."

"No, I . . . We have work to do, I can't just—"

"Jane, listen to me. It doesn't matter what's going on, or what kind of obligation you think you have to solve it. I'm telling you right now, as a father: this superhero life, it will consume you if you let it. It *always* feels more urgent than anything else, and sometimes that's fair. But if I've learned one thing, it's that you *can't* put it before the things that truly matter in your own life. Otherwise . . . what's even the point?"

JANIE WASN'T ALLOWED TO SEE CLAIR UNTIL THE NEXT day. She didn't know if the decision belonged to the Heroes, or Clair herself. Janie tried to tell herself it didn't matter, that it wouldn't hurt either way.

In the end, it was Keisha who came to get her. A swift knock on the door, and two snaps of her fingers once Janie had opened it. Janie followed without hesitation.

She thought she'd be taken to the rejuve pod where Clair had been recovering. Or perhaps a suite like Jane's, identical in layout but decorated to Clair's refined taste. Even, perhaps, the lounge or the kitchen, if Clair had wanted to get out and stretch her legs. Instead, Keisha took Janie to the command room, entering her credentials and then stepping back as the door slid open. "Good luck."

Janie crossed the threshold. *Welcome, Jane.* They still hadn't updated the computer system to recognize her as herself. Janie fought hard not to be too offended by this as the door whispered closed.

Clair was at the main bank of screens, directly across from the doorway. She did not turn to look at Janie—did not, at first, acknowledge her presence at all. She was dressed in her Heroes uniform: a slim-fitting pair of slacks, a crisp white button-down, suspenders and a leather holster catching her curves. Maroon fingerless gloves danced across a projected keyboard in front of her. Closer to Janie, Clair's vintage trench coat lay over the back of the only chair at the conference table, claiming it. Janie wasn't sure where she was supposed to sit. *If* she was supposed to sit. A wiggle in her stomach gave her the distinct feeling of being called down to the principal's office, not that she'd actually experienced that before.

"I've been catching up on recent events," Clair said suddenly, and Janie jumped. Clair had not raised her voice, had not turned around, but somehow her words carried as clearly as if she was standing right in front of Janie.

Janie fiddled with the cuff of Clair's abandoned coat. She didn't know what to say, but apparently this wasn't the sort of conversation where she had to say anything.

"We need to be prepared for Lester's next demand to come in," Clair continued. "I'm relieved he's been quiet lately, but it won't stay that way. Now that he knows the senator can be bought, he'll milk that for all it's worth."

So this is where it started. Janie was hoping she'd have time to warm up, to ease into it. To be able to ask Clair how she was doing, to hear Clair's own reassurance that she was fine. Though of course Janie could see for herself that Clair was fine. It wasn't Clair that Janie had to worry about, she realized now, but rather the friendship that had always stretched out between them, tying them together in an easy, unspoken bond.

"I'm sorry," Janie said. There was so much more to add, so many layers of regret and fear and relief and guilt to unpack, but it had to start there.

Clair flicked a hand. "It's done."

Janie's breath constricted in her chest. "Clair—" she started, a desperate plea that cut off when she realized she had absolutely no idea where to take it next.

For a dizzying second, Janie considered just telling her everything. The whole of Janie's heart, laid bare before her. How hard was it to say? *I love you. I've always loved you.* Did it really matter that this version of Clair wasn't technically the same one she knew? That she was so much older, that she still looked at Janie like she was a child? Maybe nothing would ever come of it, but it's possible nothing ever would have come of it if the body-swap hadn't happened. At least Janie would have finally unlocked the words in her chest and *said* it. At least Clair would finally understand.

But then Clair turned. Her face in profile, just enough to glance over her shoulder like Janie was something half-forgotten. And how could Janie tell her then? She didn't even have Clair's full attention. A faint scowl marred Clair's otherwise perfect face. Impatient, expectant.

"I think we should tell people I'm Captain Lumen," Janie said instead.

Well. *Now*, at least, she'd gotten Clair's attention.

Clair spun on her heel. The glow of the screen caught the back of her head, haloing her like the portrait of some Catholic saint. "You're joking."

Was she? The words had surprised Janie as much as they had Clair, but maybe there was something to them. She remembered Cal the night before: the way he'd just shrugged and bought soggy fries for her, teasing her as he watched the strippers.

Janie straightened her spine. "I'm not."

Clair's face set. She crossed the room, yanking her chair away from Janie. She sat down, crossing first one leg over the other, then her arms over her chest. "Okay, not that it's going to make a difference because that is the single stupidest idea I've ever heard . . . but *why?*"

"Dog Squad can't blackmail us with a video proving I'm Captain Lumen if people already know."

Clair pinched the bridge of her nose. "Janie . . . the whole point of blackmail is they threaten to do something you *don't want* to happen. Letting it happen may gut their leverage, yes, but at what cost?"

That's what it always came down to, wasn't it? The cost of living your truth. Janie had spent her whole life feeling like people would hate and shun her if they saw who she really was, and obviously some would. But now she knew the feeling of being seen. Of having someone know her secret and it *didn't matter*, like maybe it didn't even need to be a secret in the first place.

She sat down on the edge of the conference table, right by Clair. Close enough to swing her foot out, nudge Clair's shin.

"Would it really be so terrible? I mean . . . I get the danger, I've seen enough movies, but my family seems more than capable of keeping themselves safe from supervillains. If anyone would even target them to begin with—which, like, we don't *know* they would."

"It's not just about protecting your family," Clair said, shaking her head. "Janie, telling everyone you have superpowers . . . Do you even understand what that would mean? Grand City is fairly accepting, but not everyone is thrilled to have a team of superheroes running around essentially above the law. And with the powers we have? It scares a lot of them. There are plenty of people who'd like to outright *ban* who we are."

"Okay . . ." Janie hadn't realized the situation was quite that bad, but honestly, it wasn't any scarier than crushing on girls at the turn of the millennium. "Okay, I get that it's scary, but it's got to be better than lying to everyone all the time. I'm *tired* of hiding who I am. Isn't it better to be yourself, even if . . . even if not everyone wants to accept it?"

"It's not about *hiding*," Clair said, a sneer in her voice. "It's about being *smart*. It's about keeping yourself safe. Besides, it's not your choice to make. Once we find your world—"

"Yeah, but what if we can't? What if we *never* find it? Or even if we do, what if there *is* no way to undo this swap? What if I'm stuck like this for the rest of my life, and there's nothing we can do to fix it?"

"That's not going to happen." Clair's words were clipped, abrasive like a teacher having a bad day.

Janie pushed through them. "You can't promise me that. Even Marie says she can't promise me that."

"Well, then Marie's full of shit!" Clair said, then caught herself, paused. Shut her eyes. Took a deep breath. Started again. "Look, I get that it's scary. And I know it's tempting to run through all the different 'what if's, but that's only going to drive you crazy. Trust me. We're *going* to find your world. We're *going* to fix this. Okay? So just . . . just stop with whatever doomsday scenario you have running around your head, because it's *not* going to happen."

"But if we can't—"

"We *will*. I'm sorry, but it's settled. We're not revealing your identity. Ever."

Heat rushed to Janie's cheeks. As if she was just some dumb kid, being dressed down by their mother. But Janie wasn't a child—and Clair sure as shit wasn't a mom.

"No," Janie said. "You don't get to make that decision. I want—"

Clair slammed her palm against the conference table. "I don't *care* what you want! This is not up for debate. I will not let you waltz in here and ruin my life just because you *feel* like it."

Janie rocked back. "Ruin *your* life?"

Clair glanced away for a second, chastised. Not because of her behavior, exactly—her embarrassment was more like she'd said too much, let slip her true feelings.

"Oh my god," Janie said, the weight of Clair's discomfort hitting her in full. "This was never about what's best for me—or Jane. This whole time, it's been about protecting *you*. Because *you* don't want to be seen with me if people know who I really am. What I really am."

Clair turned back, her face slack with resignation. "Janie, you literally do not know what you're talking about. There is so much more to this situation than you understand—"

"Then tell me!"

"No. No, we're done with this conversation." Clair spun out of her chair, retrieving her coat and sliding her arms through in one fluid motion. The hem swept across Janie's vision like a cape, as if Clair was a magician and she could make Janie's argument disappear with a snap of her fingers.

And, really, that's exactly what she was doing. Clair held all the cards, and if she didn't want to share them with Janie, there was nothing Janie could do about it. In a second Clair would walk out that door, again, and Janie's protests would be shut down, again, and no one was going to stop it. Janie's fists snapped shut. Her vision flared bright. Light seemed to vibrate around her, responding to her rage.

She didn't care what anyone else said: these powers were hers now, had been from the moment she'd been dumped into this body. So was this life. And maybe, one day, the Heroes would figure out how to send her back to her own world, but until that happened, Janie was done being treated like she didn't get a say. She was Captain Lumen. No matter what kind of history the rest of them had, she's the only one who would really know what that meant.

"Fine." Janie drew the light in as she jumped to her feet, letting it envelop her, wrapping up as a protective layer. She shoved past Clair, bumping shoulders. Janie was already a ghost, fading from sight as she passed through the door. She turned back as the last of the light smudged her from view. "Then I'll just have to find the answers myself."

IT TOOK A FEW HOURS FOR JANE TO TRACK CLAIR DOWN
to the mall. She'd forgotten how much *work* everything took,
in the days before phones were everywhere. In her own life, it
would have been so easy. A swipe of the screen, a tap on Clair's
name. *Where are you?* Send. Three bouncing dots, and within
seconds, she'd have her answer.

But this was the year 2000, the dawn of the new millennium,
and the age of convenience was still a few years off. Funny how
it had felt so expansive at the time—the digital era just dawning,
technology new enough to dazzle at every turn. Jane didn't even
know how to function in it, anymore. She tried going down the
street to Clair's house, ringing the bell, but of course there was
no answer. Why would there be? Clair was out, Simon was out.
In Jane's reality, Clair had a string of younger brothers, but they
didn't appear to exist here—which she supposed made sense,
given what had happened to Donna.

Even once she'd arrived at the mall, how was she supposed to begin? The food court was packed with so many bodies it would be impossible to spot Clair. Jane racked her brain, trying to remember: where did they used to go, when they were kids? What stores did they like to haunt, at what ages? This was long past the days when Climo Toys would have held appeal, unless of course they were visiting for laughs. They were far too young for practical concerns like dorm room sheets or their first dish sets. So what did that leave? Jane walked to a directory near the base of an escalator, her eyes scanning the long list of shops and restaurants. Most of them she didn't even recognize, their names meaningless.

She was getting too old for this. Being a teenager again was *exhausting*, all this angst and hormones running around in her veins, all this drama. Standing there, in the middle of the mall, suddenly all Jane wanted was to go *home*. Her own home, with her own wife waiting for her. Safe and secure, no need to make sure that she wasn't out flirting with someone else.

Jane's stomach twisted. She had that to look forward to, sure—but *Janie* wasn't going to get that, not if Jane gave up now.

She plunged forward, through the mingling crowds. And there she was: spotted through the window, perfectly framed in an *O* of Brosgol Records. Clair was listening to music samples, her hands cupped around giant, puffy headphones, eyes closed as she bobbed and swayed to the notes only she could hear.

But then a hand touched Clair's shoulder and she turned, her face lighting up. Clair slid her headphones up just enough to say something, static raising strands of her hair to wave in the air like sea anemones. Hailey ran a casual hand over Clair's head, settling them back in place as Clair held a CD out for her to read the track listing.

Jane took a sharp breath. She was a woman on a mission, she reminded herself firmly. If she could face up to Bionic Slingshot and his plasma bolts, if she could take down her own evil doppelgänger, if she could handle being a widow for a year and a half, then surely she could face an unfriendly fifteen-year-old girl.

In truth, Jane wasn't sure she believed that, but she squared her shoulders and made herself put one foot in front of the other as she approached the music store.

They were laughing as Jane approached, the two of them lost in their own world. Their heads dipped toward each other, Clair twisting the ear of the headphones so that Hailey could lean in close enough to hear a thin thread of music escaping the confines.

"—literally the worst," Hailey said, giggling. She covered her mouth with her hand, and the motion turned her just enough to spot Jane hovering nearby. The mirth and her hand dropped in sync. "Oh. Jane. Hi."

Clair's sharp eyes snapped up. She pulled the headphones off slowly as Jane plastered a bright smile across her face.

"Hi guys!" She tossed out a cheery wave. "God, it's so funny running into you."

"What are you doing here?" Clair asked. No preamble, no bullshit—and no warmth. The headphones hung around her neck, raised like bristled shoulders.

Jane waved her hand in dismissal, as if it didn't even matter. "Oh, my dad dropped me off. He was heading for the hardware store, and offered to let me hang out here while he was shopping."

"You mean the hardware store on the opposite end of town?" Clair said.

"Right. No, but we were . . . at his office before this. Which makes it on the way."

Clair's mouth pressed into a hard, disbelieving line. So, *that* was a great start.

But Jane didn't need a great start, because she wasn't going anywhere. She'd find whatever excuse she'd need to stay by Clair's side for the rest of the day. She'd make this right, whatever it took.

Surely the situation could only improve from here.

JANIE STOOD ON THE FRONT WALK, STARING UP AT THE darkened windows before her. It had taken the rest of the day to track down the address, tucked away in an upscale residential corner of the city. Riding buses, doubling back, walking blocks and blocks at a time. A couple of times she thought about hailing a taxi, but the truth is she didn't really know how that worked, and anyway there weren't nearly as many of them driving by as she expected.

In the end she'd found it, though, and now she stood in front of a bright blue door in a row of turn-of-the-century townhouses leaning shoulder to shoulder. An interlocking brick walkway led to the front porch. Flower boxes lined the windows, what looked like mini purple daisies lending brightness to the house's exterior. The number was made of wrought iron, bolted one digit on top of the other on the crisp white doorframe. It matched the one listed on the driver's license pinched between Janie's fingers. Her own driver's license, one she'd earn sometime in the future. Janie had gone snooping a few days ago, in what she'd assumed was Clair's purse, only to open the wallet and find her own crappy DMV picture staring back at her. At the time, she wasn't sure if she'd have the nerve to actually *come* here. Stand on this front stoop. Walk through this door. She still didn't know if she had it in her. This was her house, but she had absolutely no idea what she'd find inside.

The yap of a neighbor's dog broke Janie out of her reverie. She jumped, scrambling for the keys that she'd swiped along with the license. She looked over her shoulder, wondering if someone would poke their head out to see what was going on, but the dog moved deeper into its house, the barks receding, and the street was quiet once more.

It didn't take long for her to figure out which key fit the lock. She took a deep breath, pushing the door open. A faint *beep* greeted her as she crossed the threshold, and a soft, buttery-smooth computer voice trilled, *"Welcome home, Jane."*

Home.

Janie had lived in the same house her whole childhood. Though she looked forward to the day she'd move out on her own, the idea that this was already *her* house didn't seem quite real. Janie reached out, running her fingers along the wall. She found a light switch, and the front hall snapped to life.

For a moment she could only stand there. Both she and the townhouse seemed to be holding their breath. Now that she was actually *here*, she found herself suddenly shy, as if on a first date. The whole hall echoed as she took a tentative step forward. It reminded her of when she used to pet sit for the Jackson family next door; even though she'd been welcome in the house, even though they were paying her to turn the key and let herself in, Janie had felt like she was trespassing every time she set foot on the plush, ordered carpets, every time she opened a can in their spotless kitchen. She used to wonder if they'd set up nanny cams in the collection of Mrs. Jackson's display of vintage teddy bears, or the Furby that sat on their coffee table, if they scrutinized the footage upon arriving home from Florida, their skin still smelling of suntan lotion as they watched blurry shots of Janie coming in to feed their cat. Janie had never lingered, never dared to touch a thing beyond the stack of bowls in the cabinet, the bottle of dish soap on the sink, the scoop for the litter box in the basement.

But there were no nanny cams then, of course, and there were no nanny cams now, Janie told herself firmly. And even if there were, what would they see? She lived here.

She *lived* here. A giddy bubble rose up in Janie's chest, and she had to bite down to keep from laughing as she moved deeper into the house. Her nerves melted as she let herself into the kitchen. Her kitchen. She lived here, she cooked here. Janie ran her hand across a granite countertop, trying to picture the life this other Jane lived—older, mature, sophisticated. Would she host dinner parties? Janie stood in front of the stove at the center island, miming this wiser self sautéing, one hand held out as if cradling a wine glass. She laughed at a sea of invisible guests. In the cabinets she found rows of canned tomato products, carefully organized spice jars, boxes of tea bags that smelled like cinnamon and fruits and something leafy she couldn't identify. She found bran flakes and oatmeal, all suitably adult, and then, in the next one, a half-empty box of Twinkies and one last foil packet of Pop Tarts.

In the living room, still more delights. A whole wall was nothing but bookshelves packed to the brim. Comic books, novels, oversized art books stuffed along the bottom where they wouldn't bow the shelves. A variety of plastic figures sat in front of the books, overlarge eyes painted onto overlarge heads that looked like they were supposed to bobble, but didn't. Janie recognized a few of the characters—here a collection of Yodas, there a Wonder Woman—but most of them were unknown. Art prints and paintings lined the remaining walls, and Janie turned in place to take them in. In the corner, a flat-screen TV sat on a low bench, a variety of what were probably gaming systems on the shelf below it. Janie scooped up a soft blanket from the couch, wrapping it around her shoulders as she leaned in to examine a row of pictures framed on the windowsill. She smiled at Clair's presence in them—it was comforting to know they were still close, even all these years later. Janie ran her fingers across the glass, tracing the line of Clair's jaw.

Across the hall was a home office/art studio. A tidy desk with a gigantic, flat-screen monitor displayed the time in one half of the room, and a wide open drawing table faced it along the opposite wall. A cozy chair in the corner, a stack of books beside it. Janie lingered in the doorway, afraid to go in. Even from here, she could see how talented her older self had gotten. Sketches were pinned up above the drawing table, half-finished concepts. Clair's smiling face, rendered in pencil and paint and ink.

Bedrooms felt safer. Janie turned away and climbed the stairs, the blanket trailing behind her.

There were other rooms, but an open door led her straight into what had to be the master suite. She grinned at the size of the bed, so inviting that she almost stopped there. Amazingly, somehow, the older Jane had learned to actually make her bed in the mornings—her mother would be so proud. Janie smoothed her hand across the blanket, the perfect corners that Clair must have finally taught her. A stack of books sat on either nightstand: one a pile of comics bound into glossy trade paperbacks, the other a biography stacked on top of what looked like a historical novel. Hand cream sat next to those, the same kind Clair used, and Janie wondered if the bottle had been a gift to Jane.

The closet took Janie's breath away.

She had *so many* clothes. Far more than Janie could ever imagine using. Folded stacks of T-shirts and jeans, a row of blazers in gray and pink and floral patterns. Vintage dresses, some in plastic dry-cleaning bags. In racks and neat rows along the floor, velvet pumps and leather Mary Janes lay next to Converse sneakers and flip-flops.

It was here the first inkling of understanding began to creep up Janie's spine. Too vague to make sense of at this point, but enough to get her moving. She hastily set down the wide yellow belt she'd picked up, and slipped through to the gleaming bathroom. Two electric toothbrushes on the counter. Two razors in the shower—one pink, one purple. Janie's mouth went dry, as if she'd swallowed cotton. She raced out of the bathroom, searching frantically, and there, finally, she was rewarded: another cluster of framed photographs, sitting on top of a dresser.

She found what she was looking for immediately. It was just *sitting* there, front and center, on display for anyone to see. A simple silver frame. Two familiar faces, bent forward as they leaned their foreheads together. Eyes locked in adoration. There were other photos of them on the dresser, too—Jane and Clair, always together, kissing or spinning each other on a beach, their arms thrown around each other as they posed with family, with friends—but it was this one Janie couldn't pull away from. It was this one she lifted from the dresser, her hands shaking as she traced her fingers across the glass. Jane and Clair. Foreheads pressed together. Eyes locked. Soft smiles. Between them, two bouquets of flowers blended together so closely they almost became one. It was taken in what looked like an art gallery, the display lights catching the white of their dresses so intensely they nearly glowed.

Jane Maxwell wedding. She'd just assumed it had to be with a man.

"I thought I'd find you here."

Janie yelped at the sound of Clair's voice. She leaped back, the frame falling from her hands.

Clair swept forward, catching it as gently as if it were a baby. She glanced down, smiling at the picture. No sense of surprise marked her face, no embarrassment at being caught out. When she straightened up, she and Janie were almost exactly the same height. Clair looked at Janie, her beautiful face turned warm with pity, and Janie looked at Clair, and a wave of vertigo swept up and dragged Janie down.

"Oh my god," Janie whispered as she stumbled back. Her legs bumped into the bed, and she let it catch her fall. The whole room spun around her, all those smiles in all those pictures turned mocking as they seemed to leap out and pummel against Janie. The one in Clair's hands worst of all. The gleam of white dresses, searingly bright in the dim light of the bedroom. Janie drew her feet onto the bed with her, wrapping her arms around her knees as if she was still a child.

Clair crouched down in front of Janie, but Janie couldn't look at her, didn't dare. Janie's cheeks burned as she realized it didn't matter how careful she'd been around Clair. Clair knew. The deepest desires of Janie's heart, the one secret held tightest against her. She'd known from the beginning.

Tentatively, Clair reached out. Laid a hand across the top of Janie's foot. "Janie," she said. "It's okay. Don't be scared."

A strangled laugh escaped Janie's chest. What she asked was, "How long have you known?" but what she meant was, *Does my Clair know?* and, perhaps more importantly, the question Janie didn't even dare to form, not even to herself: *Does she feel the same way?* Clearly one did, but as everyone kept telling her, there were no guarantees from this would-be future she'd found herself in. Not even that.

Clair rubbed her thumb along Janie's foot as she considered this. Her face had gone still, a look Janie recognized from her own Clair. She was weighing her options. She didn't want to say something she didn't mean.

"I think I've been at least half in love with Jane from the moment I met her," Clair said finally, and there was such surety in her voice that the sound of it squeezed Janie's eyes shut.

The moment they met. Maybe it had been different for them, but for Janie, that had been kindergarten orientation. Twenty screaming kids packed into a classroom together, the ones who'd been prepared for it already racing around and playing with the piles of blocks or the sandbox in the corner or the stacks of crayons. Janie had hung back, clinging to her mother's leg, wide eyes drinking in the chaos, when the teacher clapped her hands and asked them to form a circle, and a little girl with long brown pigtails had raced straight up to Janie and taken her hand like it was nothing. Like they'd already been friends forever.

Now that same hand, or a version of it anyway, was resting gently on the top of Janie's foot. A platinum ring gleamed on her finger, tree branches bound together in unity. Janie had seen it plenty of times, of course, studying every inch of this grown-up version of Clair. She'd never imagined what it had meant—wouldn't have guessed the truth, even if she'd dared.

"I didn't think it was fair to tell you," Clair said. "I didn't want to put that kind of pressure on you, to think you had to recreate the same thing once you got home. It's something that, if it's gonna happen, it should happen naturally, you know?" She laughed softly under her breath. "No, but how could you know?"

"I know," Janie said.

She didn't say that she'd already been looking for the right moment for more than a year now. That she'd been studying Clair, every long look, every pause, every time their fingers inched toward each other in the backseat of Allison's car. There were times Janie was sure Clair felt the same way, that she was just an inch from saying it, but then something would always come up, time slipping forward again, and they'd break apart and Janie would convince herself she'd just imagined it. It had felt so impossible.

She didn't say that she'd have given anything to have someone hold her hand and tell her that it wasn't. That, even if there were no guarantees, no promises, the *possibility* existed in more than just her daydreams.

Clair let go of Janie's foot. She sat back, crossing her legs on the carpet. As if this was a sleepover, and Janie was up on her bed and Clair was settled onto her sleeping bag on the floor, and they were up late swapping secrets.

"So you can see why I'm so vested in protecting my wife's identity," Clair said, and Janie couldn't prove it but she swore Clair had dropped the *W* word like a dare. She studied Janie for just a second before continuing. "I would never ask you to hide who you are. But this is different from coming out. Jane and I put ourselves in danger in this work—worse, even, than what you've seen. The personas we've crafted keep that life from ruining *this*."

A simple sweep of Clair's arm. Janie's eyes took in the bedroom before she knew she was doing it. Now that she knew what to look for, it seemed impossible that she'd ever missed the truth. It was Jane's bedroom, yes, but signs of Clair were *everywhere*, blended so seamlessly it felt inevitable. Janie had suggested telling people the truth about Captain Lumen because she'd wanted freedom, but here was true freedom. Her and Clair. Living the way Janie had always secretly wished, and apparently without serious consequence.

And now she knew Clair was right: there was no way Janie was risking all *this*.

JANE HAD NEVER BEEN SO GRATEFUL TO GO TO SCHOOL BEFORE.

The trip to the mall was nothing short of a disaster. Jane had dutifully stuck with Clair and Hailey, wedging herself between them, making jokes, suggesting activities. Under normal circumstances, she knew, Clair would have been more than happy to go along with it, laughing and piling on; as it was, her face had gotten more and more stony, a silent, pissed-off wall that Jane couldn't break through no matter how hard she tried.

The rest of the weekend, then, had passed in sluggish agony. Jane alternated between trying to call and visit Clair (getting repeatedly turned away), lamenting her situation to Keisha, and gorging herself on a freezer full of pizza rolls and ice cream sandwiches. Paul kept trying to talk to her, every time she'd emerge from her room to heat up another tray of greasy, pepperoni carbs to smother her feelings in, but she ardently refused to talk about it and eventually he stopped asking.

But *now*! Now it was Monday, and there was nowhere for Clair to hide. Jane had, at least, managed to get through to Simon on one of her many, many botched attempts at calling Clair's house, and he assured her that he was not about to let Clair skip school just because of teenage drama.

So now Jane scanned the halls, her heart a constant drumbeat, *Clair Clair Clair Clair*. This wasn't how it was supposed to go. None of this was how it was supposed to go, and it was all Jane's fault, and what if she couldn't fix it, what if she *failed*, what if nothing unfolded like it was supposed to, what if the entire future of this parallel life was fucked over, all because of her?

And then she spotted her. A cascade of brown hair just brushing her shoulders, standing out in intricately penned detail against a sea of otherwise muddied background figures. Even from the back, Jane would recognize her. In a thousand lifetimes, Jane would recognize her.

"Clair! Hold up!"

Jane's voice ballooned, a giant white bubble rising over the hall, pressing all the other conversation down into the crowd of students. A narrow panel: Clair's form, stilled in more than just a captured moment, her shoulders raised just enough for Jane to notice. It's barely there, a sliver of time, and the next second overlaps it like a jock elbowing a nerd out of the way. Clair's face resumes her animated conversation, turned away from Jane now, as if she didn't even notice the shout that got everyone else's attention. As if she didn't notice the heads turning to measure the distance between Jane and Clair.

But fuck it, who cared about gossip? Jane raced up the hall, jockeying for position until she slid into place by Clair's elbow.

"What was going on yesterday?" Jane asked by way of hello. "I was trying to reach you all day."

Clair turned, setting off down the hall. "Really."

"Yeah, I mean . . . Simon said you were out, but I *know* you were home. And now . . . it's like you're avoiding me?"

"That's funny, because I didn't think you noticed what I was up to these days."

"Don't be ridiculous," Jane said. "I'm always here for you, you know that. If something's bothering you—"

"You know what, just stop. I know what's really going on here."

Jane's pace slowed, her feet dragging against the linoleum. "You do?"

Clair rolled her eyes. "Of *course* I do. You're not exactly subtle, Janie. Especially not when you have a crush on somebody."

Jane rocked back. No—no, this wasn't how it was supposed to go, not yet, not here. Not like this.

It's true that Clair had always been the astute one, long before she'd ever gained her empathic superpowers—but her own crush on Jane had mercifully blinded her to Jane's early affections. At least in Jane's reality.

"What ... That is ... Why didn't—why didn't you say anything?"

Clair's bitter laugh broke through the hallway. "When did you give me the *chance* to? You and Cal have been so busy making moon-eyes at each other, there hasn't been *time* for the rest of us—"

"*What?*"

"—but I didn't say anything because it's none of my business, and it's fine. It's fine. I get it, you're busy with your new boyfriend. You do whatever you need to do, Janie, but don't come at me like I'm somehow a villain when I branch out and start making a new friend in the meantime. It's not fair."

A rush of breath escaped Jane's chest. Not quite a laugh but not quite *not* a laugh, either. "Oh my god. You think . . . you think I'm in love with *Cal*?"

Clair gave Jane a sidelong glance. "I mean, I wouldn't go *that* far, but, like, you have been spending an awful lot of time together."

"We're helping each other *study*!"

"Sure," Clair said with a snort. "Whatever you want to tell yourself."

"It's the truth! I don't even *like* Cal!"

"Yowch," came a voice from behind them. "Harsh."

Jane spun around. "Cal! Perfect, come here." She lunged, dragging him closer. Jane gestured roughly toward Clair. "Will you please tell her there is nothing going on between us?"

Cal's mouth glubbed open. When his voice followed, it was weirdly pinched, like he was squeezing the words out with a vice. "I mean . . . yeah. Totally not."

Clair raised an eyebrow. She glanced down, drawing Jane's own eyes along. A fake rose was gripped tightly in Cal's sweaty hand, the cloth petals already fraying around the edges.

"Shit," Jane whispered. She looked back up, at Cal's pale, sweat-pricked face. "Cal, no. Don't tell me you actually thought—"

"Of course not," Cal said, his voice rushed and cracking. He ripped something off the stem, a paper he was now trying to hide. Cal thrust the rose forward. "It's for Clair. From—from an admirer. Only, uh, he told me to keep his identity secret. Sorry."

Clair took the rose, twirling it beneath her face with such a convincing imitation of flattery that even Jane could almost believe it. She gave Cal a kind smile—always so kind—as she said, "Thank you."

Cal forced a nod. Once, and so stiff it was a wonder he didn't break in half from the effort.

Jane sighed. "Guys, no, listen, you don't understand. I don't—"

The bell cut her off, drowning out whatever excuse she was going to dredge up. Cal was already darting away. Jane grabbed for him, but he veered, slipping free.

"No, wait, Cal! Clair!" She spun back, but both of them were gone, swallowed up by the crowd. Jane let out a strangled cry of frustration. "Ugh! I hate high school!"

The speakers crackled overhead, a jagged, jarring speech bubble breaking over the top of the hallway. *"Jane Maxwell, please report to the office. Jane Maxwell to the office."*

WITH THE SECRET OUT, CLAIR HAD FINALLY DECIDED there was no reason why Janie *couldn't* stay in Jane's house instead of the headquarters.

Not just Jane's house, though: Jane and *Clair's* house. The one they had bought together, the one they lived in together. Because they were married. Because Jane had a *wife*.

The thought still sent Janie's head spinning. Even now, after a whole weekend tucked away in this marvel of a place, she couldn't bring herself to believe it. It didn't matter that the evidence was all around her—photos of the two of them together, Clair's stuff mixed up with Jane's in every cabinet and closet and dresser, rainbow flags and orange-white-pink flags hanging in the most random places around the house. Clair had told her the design was the lesbian pride colors, and Janie's cheeks had burned hearing the word "lesbian" spoken out loud with such casual *normalcy*. She'd stared at the flag after Clair had walked off, her fingers running over the silky bands of fabric. She tried to picture this older Jane, brimming with confidence, living loud and proud and damn the consequences. Janie tried to make herself say it, there in the hallway by herself, but the most she could manage was a whisper.

The rest of the weekend passed like a dream. Janie spent her time watching movies and stealing books from the shelves, sneaking sequels to series that weren't yet finished in her time. In the evenings, she and Clair made dinner together, Janie telling Clair about memories that were still fresh, and watching as Clair's eyes either snapped to life in recognition, or as she laughed to learn how things had unfolded differently between their two lives. In these moments, in her own kitchen, Clair was softer than she'd been with Janie since her arrival—though she still wouldn't answer any of Janie's questions about the details of their relationship.

On Monday, Clair left Janie home for the day. Clair had a huge pile of things to take care of. Jane's lawyers, which Clair had been in touch with over the weekend, had thankfully found the loophole they'd needed, and now Clair was trying to smooth things over in Jane's absence. Janie did offer to go back to the office, promising to behave this time, but a sharp look from Clair stilled her tongue. Plus there was the usual business of Clair's own job, which she'd been calling out of long enough that even her incredibly lenient boss was getting fed up. Not to mention checking in with Marie and Devin's progress at the Heroes' HQ, and the looming threat of their blackmailer popping back up—he'd been quiet since the park, but neither Janie nor Clair let themselves believe the matter was simply *over*.

"Don't get in trouble while I'm gone," Clair admonished as she stood in the doorway, keys in hand. "I mean it, Janie. I've got the security system programmed to zap you unconscious if you dare even think of walking out the door."

"Can it do that?" Janie asked.

Clair smirked. "Do you really want to find out?"

A part of her kind of did, but she planned to stay put anyway. She had finally found a way around the TV's parental controls and was currently working her way through the last few seasons of *Voyager*. Plus there were still plenty of snacks in the pantry from a quick grocery run the day before.

She was helping herself to some of them, a few hours later, when the doorbell rang. Janie crept through the foyer, her socked feet sliding silently across the polished wood floorboards. Tentatively, she stole a glance through the peephole.

A movie-star version of her mother stood on the front stoop.

She'd lost weight, first of all, her body toned and tanned in a way she hadn't been even as a young woman. Gone was the perm Janie's mom maintained; instead, her hair had been straightened past the point of her natural state, falling just below her shoulders, and bleached a shockingly convincing blond. Unless it was natural here? Janie supposed it was possible. But it was the face that rocked Janie most: every line smoothed out, every imperfection erased. Instead, her cheeks bore a bright sort of sheen, flawless and entirely manufactured.

Mrs. Maxwell's face twitched—what may have been the beginning of a frown, if she allowed such things.

"Honestly, Janie, you'll need to answer the door eventually. I know you're in there."

Janie bit her lip. She didn't think Clair would approve of her letting people in, but . . . wouldn't Jane's mom have a key? Surely she could let herself in if she really wanted to.

Tentatively, Janie opened the door.

"Finally," Mrs. Maxwell said, pushing it the rest of the way open and striding in as if she owned the place. "Now, I don't care when you ignore the senator's texts, but I thought we had a better understanding between us by now."

"Oh . . . you think I'm . . . ," Janie trailed off. When Mrs. Maxwell had called her *Janie,* so effortless, as natural as breathing, she'd just assumed someone had told her what was going on.

Janie's stomach twisted up. Crap. What was she supposed to do now? Should she *tell* her? It didn't seem her place, especially since she didn't even know if Mrs. Maxwell was in the loop about things like parallel worlds. Heck, did she even know her daughter was a superhero? Clair had certainly been careful to keep her and Jane's identity a secret, but this was her *mom,* so . . . did that change things?

"Jane? Are you even listening to me? I need to know if you're going to . . . Oh." Mrs. Maxwell narrowed her eyes, leaning in to peer into Janie's face. Then she stepped back, pinching the bridge of her nose. "Not again."

"I'm sorry?"

"Fuck it, I need a drink." Mrs. Maxwell turned abruptly, letting herself through to the kitchen.

Janie scrambled to keep up. "Wait, what did you mean by—?"

"Nope." Mrs. Maxwell raised a finger, pausing Janie's question. She pulled a couple of glasses down from a high shelf, then drew out a bottle of wine from a rack above the fridge. Next, a corkscrew from a drawer. She stabbed the top of the bottle with perhaps more force than was necessary. "Don't even try to deny it—they've already passed off one Jane as my daughter, I'm not going to fall for it again."

A wave of relief passed over Janie. "Okay, cool, you know about that. I mean, you're right," Janie said. She sat down on one of the bar stools at the kitchen island. "But, like, I wasn't trying to fool you, I . . . I thought you already knew."

Mrs. Maxwell raised an eyebrow. She popped the cork. "Well," she said as she poured a glass. "That's a refreshing bit of honesty. I might like this version of you."

She slid the glass across the counter between them.

"Oh! No, uh—thank you, though. I'm fifteen."

"I beg your pardon?"

Janie raised her hands in an apologetic shrug.

Mrs. Maxwell yanked the glass back, looking at Janie now as if she was a cockroach that had scuttled up onto the island. "How is that possible?"

"Body-swap?" She didn't know why she'd phrased it as a question. She motioned at herself. "This is still the Jane that lives here, but . . . with my mind."

"Good god." Mrs. Maxwell tossed her head back, downing the glass of wine she'd poured for Janie in one go. "What's next? Clones? I swear, if a whole army of you turn up, I'm going to fucking lose it."

She poured herself another drink.

Janie giggled. She kind of liked this version of her mom—loose, no-nonsense. It reminded her a bit of the mother she knew, though with more swearing.

"It's not funny. You try keeping up with this shit," Mrs. Maxwell said. She glanced at the counter, the open boxes of Rice Krispies Treats and Fruit Loops and the brownie mix Janie was thinking of making. "Shit, I probably shouldn't swear in front of you, should I?"

"It's okay," Janie said. Then, because she could, and who would really know any better, she added, "My mom lets me swear."

"Nice try. There's no version of me that would let that fly in my household."

Oh well, she'd tried.

Mrs. Maxwell took another sip of her drink, studying Janie. "Wait, so if you've actually body-swapped"—she shook her head, as if she couldn't quite believe she was even saying this—"then does that mean the Jane I knew is stuck in your childhood body?"

"We think so."

A single bark of laughter broke through the kitchen. "Sorry," Mrs. Maxwell said quickly. She waved her hand in front of her face, as if she could brush the laughter away like a stink cloud. "I'm just trying to picture that. She must be absolutely miserable."

Janie squirmed in her seat. The idea that her life was somehow the lesser version, the one Jane would hate to be stuck in . . .

Sure, she would have to go back to being "in the closet," Janie supposed, and Allison could be a pain in the butt sometimes, but the rest of it wasn't so bad. She couldn't complain about her mom, and her dad . . . well, her dad was amazing. Certainly nicer than the one Jane was used to.

"Can I ask you something?"

Mrs. Maxwell spun her glass by the stem. "Why not?"

"Why is this version of my dad so . . . cold?"

"What do you mean?"

Janie considered her words for a second, unwrapping a Rice Krispies Treat from the box. She'd thought the question was obvious. This Paul Maxwell went against everything Janie had ever known her dad to stand for, and the fact that no one else seemed to know that was . . . unsettling.

"It's just . . . he's not himself," Janie said finally. "He's distant, and calculating, and it's almost like he doesn't even care about his family sometimes. I barely even recognize him, and I guess I was just wondering what happened to him. To make him like this."

Mrs. Maxwell looked down at the glass in her hand. "Well. I suppose it's nice to know there's at least one version of my husband out there who's still something of the man I married." She sighed. "I wish I had an easy answer for you. The truth is that sometimes people get so fixated on what they think they want, they lose sight of what they already have."

What they think they want. Janie froze. She glanced up at Mrs. Maxwell, who had turned back to her glass to drain the last of the wine. A sour expression that probably had nothing to do with the drink crossed her face. When she was done, she looked back across at Janie, still staring at her.

"What?" Mrs. Maxwell said, raising her fingers to her face. "Did I smear my lipstick?"

"No," Janie said, because of course Mrs. Maxwell looked flawless. A slow grin broke across Janie's face. "But you've just given me an idea. I think I know how we're going to deal with our blackmailer."

"I HOPE EVERYTHING WORKS OUT OKAY," THE SECRETARY
said as Paul ushered Jane from the office.

He waved over his shoulder. "Thanks, Georgia. I'll keep you
posted."

"Georgia?" Jane asked.

Paul rested his hand on the back of Jane's shoulders, just
above the slouch of her backpack. "Yeah? What about her?"

"Nothing, just . . . since when do you know the name of the
school secretary?"

A low chuckle broke through the empty hallway. "It's called
being a parent, Jane. You've gotta know the names of your kid's
teachers, nurses, school secretaries . . . It helps."

"All the more reason not to become one," Jane muttered.

"What's that?"

"Nothing."

Paul glanced at her for a moment as he pushed open the
door and the two of them spilled out into the bright autumn

morning. They set off down the school's front walk. Paul's car was parked along the curb where the buses had so recently been lined up to drop off their charges. Jane hadn't known what to expect when she'd been called down to the office, but whatever scenarios she'd imagined, being picked up early by her "dad" wasn't one of them.

"Anyway," Paul said as he drew out his car keys, "I'm sorry to just pull you out of school like that, but—"

"No, don't worry about it. This is fine. It's good, actually. There's nothing for me there."

Paul laughed under his breath. "You, maybe. My daughter has a grade point average to maintain."

"Right. Sorry."

"It's okay," Paul said, brushing it off. His voice was light, forced in a way Jane was used to hearing from her own mouth.

They settled into the car, distracted by the usual preamble of seatbelts and ignition, turn signals and navigating their way out of the parking lot.

When they were finally on the main road, Jane asked, "So what's really going on?"

Paul reached out, turning the radio volume down. "There's been some developments on the Whisper front," he said. "The name we got? Turns out he's a middleman, but we've been working our way up the chain. It looks like the drug may be being designed by an actual doctor—or at least someone who really knows their shit. We still don't know, exactly, but we did get a hit on the supplier. Tracked him down to the old butchers shop by Route 17."

Jane tried not to think about what Paul had gotten up to in the last few days on his own, to find all this out. Instinctively, she checked his knuckles for signs of a fight, but they appeared smooth, unbruised.

"And . . . you want me to come with you?"

"It's not ideal," Paul said, his grip tightening on the steering wheel. "But it's been suggested your experience could be useful."

"Active voice, please."

Paul tossed Jane a reproachful look, just enough time with his eyes away from the road to make Jane's heart skip. "Simon, okay?

Simon pushed this. Since the drug makes people susceptible to suggestion, it's obviously more than simple narcotics, and he thinks we shouldn't ignore your experience just because you look like a child. I'll go in first and clear the guards. After that, it should be safe enough for us to snoop around."

Jane sat back, absorbing this. She couldn't imagine what Simon had said to make Paul go along with that. She supposed it must have been some sort of father-to-father heart talk . . . or maybe they'd just gone to a bar and gotten drunk and punched each other until one of them agreed. Jane wasn't exactly versed in the language of men—fathers, less so.

Still, she wasn't about to look a gift horse in the mouth. Jane turned to the window, the best way she could think to give Paul space in such a confined area.

"Please just promise me you'll be more careful this time," Paul said. The words had the potential to be scolding, but they weren't. Instead, his voice was soft, almost pleading. "I know it's got to be frustrating. But I don't think I could handle if anything truly bad happened to you."

Jane rolled her eyes, turning back to him. "You mean to Janie's body."

"That, too."

A squirm settled in the pit of Jane's stomach. She looked out the window again, fingers running idly along the seam between glass and frame. It meant nothing, she told herself. He wasn't her dad, and even her own dad didn't exactly have a great track record of caring about what happened to her.

If Paul noticed her discomfort, though, he didn't show it. He reached out, adjusting the radio so that it hopped from the commercial break on the current station, to a song on another. The sound was still low, more background noise than active music. Still, his fingers found the beat of it against his steering wheel.

"Anyway," Paul said after a minute, "I was thinking, after we wrap this up, maybe . . . maybe later, you can tell me how to do some of those other tricks. That you've figured out for our powers."

Jane's fingers stilled against the window. She shut her eyes.

And no, he wasn't her father, but dammit he was *trying*—for once in Paul Maxwell's miserable life, he was trying. What sort of person would Jane be if she spat that kindness back? Maybe it would amount to nothing, maybe this Paul would eventually turn into just as much of an asshole as the ones she knew, but if there was even a chance he'd be better for his own daughter . . .

She wouldn't be the one to ruin that for Janie. Jane took a breath, shoved a smile upon both her face and her voice.

"Sure," she said. "I can do that."

"I CAN'T DO THAT!" JANIE SAID, INCREDULOUS.

Mrs. Maxwell laughed. She set her water glass down on the spread of papers laid out on the kitchen island. "Okay, maybe we don't need to go quite *that* far."

Janie sat up straighter, stretching her back. They'd been gathered around the kitchen island for a few hours now, snacks and papers between them as they ironed out the idea Janie had earlier: a way to lure Lester in, dangling the hope that Jane Maxwell was ready to strike a bigger bargain in exchange for the video clip. She cleaned her glasses on her shirt as she shifted through the latest notes Mrs. Maxwell had been taking. It was all coming together pretty well, Janie thought. Definitely better than the plan she'd cooked up with Senator Maxwell.

Janie had just picked up a pen when the click of the front door unlocking echoed down the entry hall. *Welcome, Clair,* the computer voice purred, its greeting cut off by a call of, "Janie? I'm home!"

Janie's heart skipped. Clair came into the kitchen, a tote bag of groceries looped over each shoulder. Her attention swept the room, a tiny stitch growing deeper between her eyebrows. "What's all this?"

Before Janie could answer, Mrs. Maxwell had slid from her barstool. "Clair, darling, welcome back." Mrs. Maxwell padded across the kitchen, sweeping a kiss just beyond the touch of each of Clair's cheeks. In her stocking feet, Mrs. Maxwell had to raise to her toes to do it, but she still made it look effortless. She took a step back. "Let me help you with those."

"Thank you," Clair said, sliding one bag from her shoulder. Her voice was as stiff as her arm, though, as she passed the groceries over. "I didn't realize you'd be stopping by today."

"You mean you hoped I wouldn't," Mrs. Maxwell said as she turned away. "Otherwise, you'd have told me about Janie."

"Yes."

Mrs. Maxwell snapped her fingers, pointing at Janie. "See, I told you Clair was the honest one in this relationship." She set the bag on the counter and started to unload it. "I love my honorary daughter, but Jane really needs to learn how to open up with the people she's supposedly close to."

Clair's eyes drifted across the kitchen, finding Janie as if on instinct and then snapping away again. "She has her reasons."

"Everyone has their reasons," Mrs. Maxwell said. She glanced over her shoulder. "Janie, why don't you bring Clair up to speed on our progress today?"

Janie blinked, thrown by the sudden shift. She hopped down from her own barstool. "Um, yeah, sure."

"What progress?" Clair's question wasn't even directed at Janie, thrown instead to the only other "adult" in the room— at least as far as Clair saw it. Clair had joined Mrs. Maxwell at the counter by now, the two of them opening cabinets and the fridge and passing groceries across as a seamless mechanism of domesticity, grown women who knew exactly what they were doing in a kitchen.

"I can help with that," Janie said, rushing forward, even as Mrs. Maxwell said over her, "Oh, I think it's better if Janie explains."

The collision was inevitable. Clair turned to see what Janie was going to say. Janie reached forward to grab something from the grocery bags. The jar of pasta sauce was knocked from Clair's fingers, hitting first the lower cabinets and then the floor. A gasp, a yelp, a crash. Sauce sprayed out in a starburst, throwing streaks up their legs like bloody gashes.

"God*dammit*," Clair said, and Janie's cheeks flushed as red as the mess at her feet.

"I—I'm sorry." Janie started to crouch down to clean it up, but a single sharp glance from Clair stilled her.

"No." Clair waved Janie back, snapping a rag she'd grabbed off the counter in Janie's direction. "Not you. You go and rinse that shit off before it stains—those are Jane's favorite pair of jeans, and I won't have you ruining them on top of everything else."

Mrs. Maxwell gasped. "Clair!"

"Save it, Olivia," Clair said. She was already picking bits of glass from the red smear, tossing them into the sink with a series of *clunks*. "I'm tired of tiptoeing around in my own house, worrying I'm going to hurt her feelings. She wants to playact at being a grownup? She can deal with the consequences of her own fucking actions for once."

"She doesn't mean that, Janie," Mrs. Maxwell said, but that's where she was wrong. Clair had always been a beautiful person, a kind person—but when she snapped, she snapped. And maybe by most people's standards, this blowup wasn't even enough to warrant notice—certainly, a lot of Janie's friends had been nastier when they got into fights. But this was *Clair*, and the heat of her aggression burned Janie's cheeks.

Perhaps Mrs. Maxwell saw that, because she took a step toward Janie now. Arm outstretched, ready to offer some sort of maternal comfort, but suddenly that was the last thing Janie wanted. Clair glanced up, eyes narrowing into a glare. The question of why Janie hadn't left yet was written all over her face, at least for anyone versed enough to read it.

"Janie . . . ," Mrs. Maxwell started, her voice soft and reassuring, and that was more than Janie could take. She spun on her heel, hating how immature it looked—running off to her bedroom like an angry teenager—but there was nothing to be done about it. Janie was gone, clomping up the stairs before she could stop herself.

THE STOREFRONT WAS GRAY-BROWN AND PEELING, A page that had been sitting out in the sun too long. It sat in a three-business strip mall between a cigar store (still open), and a nail salon (shut down), just off the exit from the highway. At one point they'd probably done well for themselves, but the arrival of a Super Walmart on the opposite end of town in the mid-nineties had drained most of the suburb's commercial traffic eastward, tipping the economic balance just enough to dry up this whole side of the tracks. By Jane's era the gentrification process had begun, organic boutiques and refurbished houses with midcentury architecture springing up in neat rows all up and down the streets, but that was still a long way off for this world. Right now, even the grass poking up from the cracks in the pavement was brittle and sad.

They parked at a safe distance, blending in with a row of cars in front of a nearby bank that was still hanging on. Paul had most of his hero suit on already, awkwardly hidden beneath a too-big pair of slacks and a button-up closed all the way to his neck. He and Jane ducked behind the bank, where he slithered from the outer layers and replaced them with the glittery cape crammed into the bottom of his gym bag. To Jane's surprise, he'd also brought her oversized hoodie.

"Okay, so what's the plan?" Jane asked once they were dressed.

Paul took a second to adjust his mask before answering, as if he wasn't entirely sure he wanted to. "It's like I said: I go in first to secure the area. Do *not* follow until I tell you it's safe. You got that, Jane? I don't care what happens or what you think you can handle. I don't care if you think I'm *dying*, you stay here unless I tell you otherwise or I swear to god I will never let you out on another superhero mission until you're forty, you hear me? This is your one chance to prove I can still trust you."

"Technically, if you're dead you can't stop me from doing whatever I want. I'm kidding!" Jane added hurriedly. "Learn to take a joke, old man. Also, for the record, I'll be forty in a few years anyway, so that's not really the threat you think it is."

One last warning glare as Paul handed over the walkie. Jane snatched it from him, twisting the knob to turn it on and clicking the test button a few times just to make the one at his hip shriek. She really needed to stop needling him like this. The part of her that was still approaching forty knew this, even as the teenage sass kicking through her egged her on.

He turned down the volume on his own walkie until it was nearly silent and set off without another word. Jane clung to the shadow of the bank as she watched him sprint carefully across the parking lot. Well, as carefully as a glittery disco ball of a superhero could.

At least he ducked below the frame of the butcher shop windows. Not that it was strictly necessary, given the number of handmade posters still advertising sales long since expired. The front was papered in them, corners curling, paint faded in the sun as they stubbornly clung to their offers: 2-for-1 on lamb chops, American cheese at $2.49/pound, all seafood 30% off. Unless the guards stationed inside spend their days peering out between the cracks, it was highly unlikely anyone would see Paul's approach.

Still in a crouch, Paul inched the shop door open. Jane sucked in a breath, bracing for a jaunty bell to announce his arrival; she wouldn't hear such a small noise from all the way across the parking lot, but he didn't flinch as if his stealth had been compromised, so she had to believe he made it inside without alerting anyone to his presence.

For a while, the front of the butcher shop was still. Nothing to see, no indication that anyone was there. The lack of gunfire was a good sign, though her stomach twisted up just the same. What if there continued to be nothing but silence and stillness—how long, exactly, was Jane supposed to wait before she decided something had gone horribly wrong? She gripped her walkie-talkie tightly in her hands, but she did not dare press the button to ask him how it was going, for fear that innocuous act would give away Paul's position to the enemy.

God, but Jane missed the comms her own team used. Her heart ached, a sharp tear in her chest as she thought about the Heroes, but she stanched the feeling down fast.

Finally, after what felt like an eternity, the jagged edge of a speech bubble crackled from the walkie's speaker. "All clear."

Jane didn't hesitate. She stuffed the walkie deep into the front pocket of her hoodie and set off across the broken pavement. Unlike Paul, she had no reason to slink—a teenager in a hoodie may have meant mischief or vandalism, but it was hardly a sight worth any real alarm. Still, she kept her pace up, feeling oddly exposed beneath the blazing sun. Jane took a breath, slotting her situation into familiar boxes. It was fine, nothing to worry about. Look: a distance shot of the building, the parking lot empty save for one brown beater car from the seventies, and a dumpster covered in flies. Jane's figure is little more than a shadow climbing up the storefront. Below, a string of images show her own point of view: dirty sneakers kicking across the pavement, a quick glance up at the quiet road. The panels are rounded, the outer edges shaded with the red of her hood.

Finally, her hand gripping the door, the faded "CLOSED" sign half visible behind her knuckles.

Inside, it was as if the owners had locked up for the night and simply forgotten to come back the next morning. The main room of the shop was wide and shallow, a single glass case running the length. Handwritten price signs were still stuck in front of upended styrofoam trays, and dried, bloodstained papers littered the places where meat used to be. To Jane's back, along the windows, metal racks with a handful of rusted cans and dusty bags of petrified potato chips sat between a spread of bistro tables and chairs. Ghosts filled the shop of Jane's mind: a pair of old men seated at the table closest to her, half-eaten Rubens on wrappers between them as they gesture to the butcher behind the glass counter; a string of customers milling in front of the meat selection, a mother with her head dipped to choose chops of steak while a toddler drags at her hand, his greedy eyes on a nearby shelf of candy.

Jane blinked, and the store restored itself to the dusty reality. She didn't know if she'd stirred up some ancient memory, or if it was just her imagination running loose. She didn't *think* her parents had ever visited this place when she was a child, but she couldn't be sure.

"This way," Paul whispered, despite the fact that they were alone. He was already at the back of the shop, standing by the ticket-number sign as if he was about to take a new customer. He didn't wait for her, just pushed through the door to the back room.

Jane followed. Two guards lay unconscious on the floor behind the counter, piled together like puppies taking a nap. She stepped over them gingerly. Let herself through.

Finally, they found what they'd come here for. Instead of

whatever the room used to be, now it had turned into a drug lab. Counters lined the walls, each littered with beakers and Bunsen burners, while wrapped stacks of supplies spread across the heavy butcher blocks still bolted down in the middle of the room. Jane inched her way through, keeping an eye out, while Paul reached behind himself and drew an instant camera from beneath his cape.

"Paul. Do you have a *fanny pack* under that thing?"

"You got a better way for me to carry all this?" He lifted the camera in one hand, the walkie in the other. A plastic evidence bag was caught between his fingers. Paul shook his head, as if Jane was the one being silly. He tucked the walkie away, then twisted the film in the camera to the next shot. *Snap.*

Later, Jane would not remember the exact moment when the attack came. All she had to go on were Paul's photos, and a narrative pieced together from what she was told. The dark smudge of her own small figure standing near the doorway. Paul, leaning over, camera to his eye as he focused on the materials scattered across the counter. He'd blame himself for not paying attention, but who could say if he was really at fault?

Supposedly, the first sign of trouble was a yelp from Jane. Paul's camera hit the floor, the shutter button clicking and capturing a blur of his legs racing to help.

There was probably a scuffle, as Jane tried to fight off the person who'd snuck up on her. Jane couldn't imagine a world in which she didn't fight back, no matter the odds. But the fight, if it existed, was a blank space in her mind, overridden by the first clear image she could provide for herself: an inset panel in a sea of disordered chaos, a close-up of a needle piercing her neck. It had stuck her to the page, a pushpin to tack up the moment of her defeat for all to see.

Reality slipped from Jane's grip, a page fluttering to the ground.

A woman's face fills the frame, eyes locked on the reader. A basic black mask rings her eyes, hair drawn back into a French braid. There is something deeply maternal about her—like a soccer mom dressed for a day of crime, her costume earnest and just slightly off. Not Jane's mother, but someone's. The part of

Jane that is still fifteen leans into her, curling against the woman's shoulder until the outlines separating them overlap with only a single thin pencil mark. A hand cradles the back of Jane's head. Jane's closed eyes, cheek to collarbone in a slim moment of peace.

Then a cold blade is pressed into Jane's palm. She sees it without looking, passed from hand to hand like a tradition, like a burden, caught between them in the moment of transfer.

In the next frame, a curled finger raises Jane's chin. Faces in profile, one wide-eyed and innocent, the other darkened with sinister purpose. A speech bubble fills the frame behind them, blocking out the background, spiky red letters spelling out a single command. "Kill him."

A wide, knife-shaped panel captures the uptick of Jane's lips. Who was she to argue with such a clear and simple directive? Her pliant mind did not even consider it.

Jane turned as the woman slid from both view and consideration.

Kill.

Him.

The stacked words form the panel borders as Jane scans the back room: cluttered counters and darkened corners caught in glimpses within the outline of the letters. All is empty and dim on the top half of the page, *Kill* full of nothing but shadowy shapes. Until there, second row down, the *i* of *Him* is lit up like a candle. Narrow borders capture a slim figure, horror spotlighting his face. Kill.

Jane burst off the page, her rage unchained. The light of *Him* leaped to the side, a spark hopping from the fire. Her blade led the way, though she didn't need it—in the moment, she was feral, ready to tear *Him* apart with her bare hands.

"Jane, stop!"

She heard the desperation, but it did not register, did not sway her. All her attention was fixed on the sight of *Him* as he leaped back, a glint of light dancing as a sunbeam for Jane to pounce on.

A flash of light hit Jane like a face full of acid. She snarled and staggered back, swinging her blade wildly while she wiped at her eyes as if she could mop the exposure shadows from her vision.

"Jane, listen to me! You don't want to do this!"

Oh, but that was where he was wrong. Jane wrenched her eyes open, narrowing them into a cold glower. By the time she spotted *Him* again, he'd picked up a metal tray and was holding it in front of him like a shield.

He raised his free hand, like taming a tiger. "Please, stop. It's me—it's your *father*."

A flicker of hesitation stilled Jane's hand. Her father?

That didn't feel like it could be true. The man in front of her, *Him*, shimmered with light and sunshine; Jane's father was a tower of darkness. But he was saying it, and Jane's mind was absorbing it, primed and ready to listen to what she was told. But he *couldn't* be—but he *had* to be.

Pain flared across Jane's forehead. She pressed the heel of her palm against her brow. "No," she said.

"That's right," he said. *Him*, her father. Her target. His voice was soft now, comforting. His words slipped in like a knife, cutting out her heart. "That's right, it's me. It's Dad."

"No!" Jane shouted, but the damage was done. When she looked up she no longer saw *Him*—all that was left was her father.

On the page, he's only vaguely human shaped. A furious scribble, pen digging deep into the paper. Slitted red eyes glow from the depths, molten heat trails streaming out of him. He looms over the room, the bulk of him filling the spread.

Jane blinked, and the frame skipped forward: a massive, monstrous black arm reaching toward her. Even his voice is wrong, block letters dripping with darkness. *Jane? What's wrong?*

A howl burst out of Jane as she charged. The command that had compelled her to *kill him* was gone, replaced by a much deeper hurt.

The massive form of her father leaped back, trails of smoky darkness lingering in his wake. *Jane!* Her name boomed out, shaking the room. Dust littered the floor as Jane veered, lunging at him from the side.

Her father raised a shield. Metal clashed against metal. Jane leaped back. She whirled, kicking out, building up speed. Her knife led the way.

He was faster than a beast of that size should be. His hand bound her wrist like a shackle as he wrenched her arm back and slammed it across his knee. Jane's knife clattered to the floor as pain seared from palm to elbow.

The raging sea of scribbles enveloped her. Jane roared. She twisted and squirmed, kicked and snarled. In the moment she wanted to rip him to pieces, tear flesh from limb, sink her teeth in and chew him to bits if she had to. But he'd wrapped his arms around her from behind, lifted her from her feet like she was nothing. He was shouting at her through the black storm, a firm and steady tone like she was being scolded, and all Jane could do was writhe and tantrum, even as the voice behind her calmed, switching tone.

Shhhh, Jane, it's okay, it's okay. Go to sleep. Just go to sleep. I've got you.

Anger surged, molten-rich, through her. Sleep was the last thing she wanted to do, but already she could feel her mind accepting the command, the dull whir of her flailing limbs powering down. *Go to sleep. I've got you.* And that was the problem, and the curse—her one chance, slipping from her fingers. She tried to tell herself not to, but the scribbles were already closing over her vision, already folding her into her father's arms, and Jane fell, useless as a baby, into the embrace.

TIGHT SHOTS, JUMBLED TOGETHER. THE PANELS FALL IN shards across the page, jagged pieces that don't fit into any form or narrative order.

A cool hand on her sweat-pricked forehead. The same hand pinning her down as her chest bucks up in a convulsion. Her head cradled against a bedazzled white torso as she's carried like a child being put to bed. Jane's face, open in a banshee scream. Drool slipping down her cheek and pooling on a plaid green pillow beneath her. An oxygen mask slid over her face. Jane asleep on the backseat of a car, her body reduced, a child curled up on a long drive. Her hand slamming against someone's side, a faceless body cracking against the wall. Looking up at a pint of blood hanging from a metal pole. Needles sliding in and out of her veins.

Speech floats untethered between the panels. *We don't have time for that!* or *Hold her steady,* or *No, no, please, god, Jane, hang on,* or *What happened?* or *—nearly reached her heart,* or *Now!*

A page of white, tinged red around the edges. The faintest impression of veins seem to crawl across the page, but then you pick it up for a closer look and maybe you just imagined it.

Jane?

The question feels like it comes from Clair, though of course that's impossible. She's not in this issue, and her absence stings like constant paper cuts. Her face returns on the next page, faded against the white background as if in a dream: lying sideways on a pillow, smiling softly at the viewer. Her fingers curl in front of her, palm up and outstretched in your direction. But her features are slipping, clear in one shot, blurred and patchy in the next—a missing eye, then lips, her face rearranging like a Picasso.

It's not working!

Hang on, Jane. Hang on.

THE WORLD CAME BACK TO JANE SLOWLY. THOUGHT first, disconnected and floating. God, but she *ached*. Why did she ache? She tried to dredge up a scrap of memory, something that would explain things, but the issues of her life were jumbled in a pile on the floor and it would take far too long to sort them out. She should open her eyes, but that was a monumental task.

Sound next, as she took a deep breath. The whoosh of air, and soft footsteps rushing over as if drawn along by the gust.

"I think she's coming around."

Her father's voice, sour in Jane's ears. Or . . . was it? Something, some trail of memory, clung to the words like cobwebs. A hand took Jane's, calloused palms warm and rough beneath her own, and her fingers squeezed his in reply without the need for conscious will.

"Jane? Honey, are you okay? Can you hear me?"

Paul. The name, and the distinction from her own father, rushed back to her.

Jane pulled her hand away. She slid her arms beneath her, pushing up as she opened her eyes to the yellow-green buzzing of fluorescent lights.

"Easy, easy," Paul said. He was hovering beside her, a steadying hand on either side, ready to catch her if she fell.

Jane shoved him away. "What happened?"

"You were dosed with a hit of Whisper," Paul said as he handed Jane her glasses. "Overdosed with it, more accurately. We were attacked at the butchers—she went straight for you. I don't . . . I'm sorry, I should have—"

Jane raised a hand, cutting off the apology. She didn't have the stomach for his guilt right now. She didn't have the stomach for anything, in fact—nausea raced up her throat. Jane leaned over the side of the couch, and someone shoved a prepped trash can beneath her as she heaved up a thin stream of bile.

"Easy there," a gentle voice said. A woman's, one Jane didn't recognize. Someone's hand, not Paul's, rubbed her back. "Just breathe through it. You'll be okay."

The question of this new person's identity could wait a few seconds until Jane was done. Whoever she was, she was already here, had already seen . . . something. Paul clearly trusted her, if he'd brought her in while Jane was in such a state.

Jane spat, then sat up and wiped her mouth with a tissue offered by the mystery woman. She was younger than Jane expected, maybe thirty at most, with a kind face and a wide, open smile. She was also wearing a pair of scrubs covered in cartoon hamsters.

"Feeling better?"

Jane nodded. She was still far from fully healed, but that wasn't the question.

"This is Dr. Rothenberg," Paul said. "She's the pediatrician who owns the medical practice below me. We've, um . . . come to certain arrangements, regarding injuries I've sustained in the field."

"I don't file paperwork or report his extracurricular activities," Dr. Rothenberg said. "And he helps me out whenever an ambulance chaser tries to throw a malpractice suit my way. Plus"—she grinned, drawing something out of her pocket—"all my patients get free lollipops if they're good."

"I told you not to do that," Paul said, but Dr. Rothenberg pressed the cellophaned candy into Jane's hand just the same. Paul shook his head. "She's kidding. She doesn't give me lollipops."

"That's because you're a terrible patient."

A weak smile passed over Jane's lips. Carefully, she unwrapped the lollipop and popped the end of it into her mouth. Sour apple hit her tongue, punching out the taste of vomit.

"So what's the prognosis, doc? Am I going to live?"

Paul winced, but Dr. Rothenberg gave Jane another grin. "Yeah. If you were going to die from it, you'd have done it by now. Though it'll be a while before you're back to fighting form. I'd recommend you stay here tonight to rest up and recover— moving you at this point is asking for trouble. I'll be back tomorrow afternoon, but I expect you'll be on your feet by then. Kids are so resilient. You're lucky you're so young."

Jane tossed Paul a quick glance, catching him in an uncomfortable squirm. So apparently he hadn't filled the good doctor in on *everything*, then. That was just as well—how were they supposed to explain something like this to a medical professional?

"Thanks," Jane said finally.

The doctor smiled at her. She patted Jane's knee. "It's what I'm here for."

She left a few minutes later, after murmuring some additional instructions to Paul and pressing a prescription into his hand. He stared at the slip of paper for a moment in the wake of her absence, then folded and tucked it neatly into his back pocket.

"I'll tell Olivia you're sleeping over at Clair's," Paul said.

"No—not Clair."

Paul raised an eyebrow, surprised and concerned by the force of Jane's reaction.

Jane licked her dry lips, pausing for time. "Tell her I'm at Keisha's."

Keisha at least knew about the whole swapped-bodies-and-superheroes thing thanks to her own stubborn curiosity. Jane would call her later, explain enough of the situation so they could keep their stories straight.

It was clear Paul wanted to ask—but, thankfully, he also knew enough to keep his questions to himself. Jane really didn't think she had it in her to explain, not right now. Exhaustion was catching up with her rapidly, even though she hadn't been awake for long. She laid back down, the scratchy cushions delightfully soft beneath her.

"All right," he said, "Keisha it is. In the meantime, I'm going to let you rest. I bought some Gatorade and chicken soup, they're in the mini fridge under my desk, and I assume you remember where the bathroom is? It'll look suspicious if I stay here with you, but I left my cellphone number taped to the phone, and I want you to promise you'll call if you need anything, okay?"

"Okay." Jane tried to ignore the pinch in her chest as she thought about him leaving her here, alone in his law office. It was just a side effect of the drug, she told herself, even though she knew full well the ache of loneliness. Why would Paul want to sit with her, anyway? Even if he didn't have good reason for leaving, he'd surely want to. Jane had attacked him, after all—she remembered that, if nothing else. And yeah, you could blame the influence of the drug, the order she'd been too addled to ignore. But surely Paul could see that for the convenient excuse it was. He had to know that part of her had meant it.

Jane slid down into the couch, squeezing her eyes shut to ignore the sting of tears building up. The fuzz of sleep was already creeping up her shoulders, dragging her deeper into the cushions.

So it had to have been her imagination that gave her the feeling of a hand brushing back the hair on her forehead, a set of dry lips kissing the space they'd cleared. By the time the words *Love you, kiddo* drifted across the page, she was already asleep.

THE KNOCK ON JANIE'S DOOR DIDN'T COME UNTIL HOURS later. Long after Janie had rinsed off her tomato-stained clothes and tossed them onto the laundry pile building in the corner of her bedroom; long after she'd taken a soothing shower. She'd stayed in there for well over an hour. The hot water cut tracks through the grime of her annoyance, tracing its fingers down the inside of her elbow and along hidden curves past her waist. Janie had tipped her head back, her face engulfed in the water flow. She wanted to be pissed off—she was pissed off—but she was also hurt, lonely, confused, and the water was activating recently discovered nerve clusters. Her body may be old but her mind was still obsessed with the delights of self-exploration. Janie had discovered, two days earlier, that this body was responsive in a practiced way her own was not; and that, if Janie stopped thinking about what she was doing, her hands had muscle memory she'd later teach them.

She was in pajamas and feeling better, then, by the time Clair came to check on her.

"Hey," Clair said, poking her head in through the bedroom door. "Can I come in?"

Janie's stomach squirmed. She scooted farther up the bed, crossing her legs and stuffing her guilty hands beneath her thighs. "Yeah, of course." How weird it must have been for Clair to even ask. It was normally her bedroom, too, but she'd kindly let Janie stay there the last few days.

Clair slipped into the room and shut the door behind her. She sat on the foot of the bed. Facing away from Janie, as if the things she wanted to say were better said to the wall.

"I just wanted to tell you I'm sorry for earlier. You're a good kid—you don't deserve that."

Kid. The word punched Janie, caving in her chest. Her hands bunched into fists around the sheets. She wanted to protest, but knew by now that doing so would only reinforce Clair's view of her.

"You're under a lot of stress right now," Janie said instead. Trying to be reasonable, mature. Grown up. "I get it."

Clair sighed. And then, to Janie's shock, she fell back across the bed. Her head landed by Janie's knee, her hair fanned beneath her. Clair reached across her chest, patting the knee. "I *am*, but that's no excuse for flipping out on you. You didn't ask to be put in this situation, but you're making the best of it. In some ways, that's more mature than I've been."

All Janie could do was sit there, frozen. Clair had tipped her head by now, her cheek leaning against Janie's knee, still held loosely beneath her gloved hand. It was such a casual pose, more like the teenage girl Janie remembered, rather than the oddly stiff grownup who'd replaced her. Clair's eyes were unfixed, staring idly at the ceiling, lost in her own pain.

Tentatively, Janie drew her own hand out. She made no sudden movements, terrified of spooking the doe that had settled against her. Piece by piece, she lifted the bangs from Clair's forehead, smoothing them to the side. Clair shut her eyes.

Would it really be so terrible if Janie had to stay here? Sure, Clair would miss the Jane she'd known, at least for a while. But a part of her was still here, in Janie. They were the same person, after all, two ever-so-slightly different shades of the same color. The difference couldn't matter *that* much—and Janie could learn. What kind of person she'd grown up into. What she'd done to make Clair fall in love with her. How to be her wife.

She was lost in thought when Clair's hand snared Janie's wrist like a vice. Janie startled. Clair was glaring up at her now, her coldness returned in force. Too late, Janie realized that her bare finger was still hovering, forcibly stilled, above Clair's forehead. That Janie had absently started to stroke the space above Clair's eyebrow, skin to skin, every one of Janie's thoughts exposed like an open circuit.

Janie's mouth gaped open, her voice creaking in her tight throat. "I . . . I'm sorry, I didn't—"

"I know." And of course Clair did know—the truth and the unspoken excuses, both.

Clair sat up, moving Janie's hand out of the way and passing it back to her as if it was a rotting fish Clair had found on the sheets.

"Janie . . . you understand that's *not* going to happen between us, right?"

"Yeah, I *get* that," Janie snapped. She curled her knees up to her chest. "I'm sorry, okay? But you can't just . . . just take that from my head and blame me for it, when I didn't even *say* anything."

Clair flinched. "You're right," she said, her shoulders sagging. "For what it's worth, I didn't mean to read it off you."

Janie's mouth soured. As apologies go, it wasn't great: the unspoken blame on Janie herself, *You shouldn't have touched my forehead*, echoed louder in Janie's mind than the half-hearted excuse. And Clair hadn't, technically, even said she was sorry.

Instead, Clair was already moving on, as if they'd put the

matter to rest. She sat up a little straighter, her face smoothed out, all business. "Mrs. Maxwell brought me up to speed on your plan."

For a second, Janie's mind flailed. Everything before the fight felt distant, until she finally remembered that Mrs. Maxwell had been helping her come up with a way to deal with Lester and the blackmail threat. But of course Clair would remember. It was probably why she had come up here in the first place.

"And?" Janie dragged the words through the block in her throat. "What do you think?"

She wasn't actually sure if she cared, not right now.

"I think the idea behind it comes from a good place," Clair said, which of course meant she hated it. "It's just a little . . . inexperienced."

Janie's face soured. Because of course a *kid* couldn't possibly have a good idea, right? She sat up a little straighter, hoping the extra length in her spine might make her look more serious. "That's not fair. You can't dislike it just because I came up with it—Mrs. Maxwell helped."

"Mrs. Maxwell isn't a superhero," Clair said, her voice gentle and painfully patronizing. "And I'm sure your intentions were great, but . . . I'm sorry, it's not going to cut it. He'll see through your lure immediately."

Just like that, all the time and effort Janie and Mrs. Maxwell had put in was swept aside. Never mind that Janie might have an answer to whatever Clair's objections were—or, at the very least, might be able to brainstorm one, perhaps even with Clair's oh-so-*experienced* help. No, the almighty Mindsight had made up her mind, and now the verdict was set and Janie's plan was crap.

Janie took a breath, steadying herself. She was tired of just rolling over and letting Clair make all the decisions.

Before Janie could *actually* gather her courage to push forward, though, Clair's cellphone buzzed.

Clair drew it from her pocket. She frowned at the screen. "That's weird." She tapped something, and a projection leaped from the display like some kind of evil jack-in-the-box. Clair gasped, dropping the cellphone onto the bedspread. She grabbed Janie and backed them both away from it.

An image of Lester hovered in the air above the screen, as if he was a ghost they had summoned by talking about him too much. The projection flickered slightly as Lester grinned, unmasked and unconcerned, at whatever camera he was broadcasting from. "Hello, Heroes. You didn't think you'd heard the last of me, did you?"

"Phone," Clair said quickly.

Janie blinked. "What?"

"Your emergency phone," Clair said, snapping her fingers. "Give it to me. Now."

"I . . . I don't have—" Janie started, but the recording of Lester cut her off.

"Listen, I'm a patient man, but I don't forgive. You fucked up my plans, now you've got to pay—literally. First up, let my idiot brother out of jail; we've got important business to complete. Second, send the senator back to our meeting place, only this time with twice the previous amount. You have twenty-four hours." Lester leaned in, and the projection pressed forward, crowding the bedroom. "Piece of advice: don't try anything stupid this time, or the city will find out exactly how vicious these dog bites can get."

THE NEXT TIME JANE WOKE UP, IT WAS WITH A STIFF NECK and a head stuffed with wet rags. At first, she just laid there, her thoughts blissfully blank. She stared up at the faint, 5H-pencil outlines of ceiling tiles; industrial, like you'd find in a school or an office building. The room was dark, the only light coming from a power strip in the corner. Without windows, it was impossible to tell what time it was, but as Jane sat up she spotted a clock on the wall: quarter after seven. A.M.? P.M.? She supposed she'd figure it out eventually. The couch cushions creaked underneath her as she rose, and finally a sense of place returned to her.

She helped herself to some of the Gatorade that Paul had left in the office mini fridge. Her hand lingered over the light switch, but a headache was already blooming at the mere idea of nineties-era fluorescent lights.

Paul's law office was the same as Jane remembered it from her own childhood. A reception area when you walked in, the bathroom off to the left. Generic, abstract paintings hung over the couch, while a sailboat calendar and motivational poster filled the space behind the receptionist's desk. Jane's own dad felt that allowing his receptionist to keep "useless tchotchkes" cluttering her desk would give a less-than-professional first impression, and Jane was pleased to see that Paul was less restrictive.

Beyond that first room was his own office. Jane made her way to the window behind his desk and twisted open the blinds, letting in just enough morning sunshine to see what she was doing.

Paul's desk took up most of the space. It was the same heavy oak desk that Jane's dad had inherited from Grandpa Maxwell, a gift for opening his first law office, but somehow it looked less stuffy and imposing than Jane remembered. It was also a *lot* more cluttered. Picture frames scattered all around the edges, practically crowding out the heavy computer monitor.

Jane tried not to look at the photographs, but it was impossible. There was one of the whole family together at Disneyland, Paul in a pair of Mickey ears and a young Janie in a yellow Belle dress, her gap-toothed grin pointed at the camera. Another featured Allison holding up a driver's license and a pair of keys as she leaned against the hood of her hand-me-down car. One of a cluster of small girls at what was clearly a birthday party, Janie's face caught in profile as she licked a bit of blue frosting off Clair's nose like a pair of tiny brides. Allison and Janie in bathing suits at some random beach. Janie's eighth-grade graduation, an arm thrown around each of her parents' shoulders, all three of them sticking their tongues out at the camera. One, framed in silver and sitting beside the phone, didn't feature the girls at all: instead, it showed Paul and Olivia in their best eighties finery, seated at a fancy restaurant somewhere. Glasses were raised between them, their eyes soaking in every detail of each other as if drunk off the affection pouring out of them.

Jane slammed the picture frame facedown on the desk. Maybe she should have tried to leave things the way she found them, but in the mess of papers he might not even notice.

She was about to turn away when something beneath the papers caught her eye. Jane moved a file folder, and found herself staring down at a VHS tape.

A very familiar VHS tape. One with a handwritten label, the blocky letters spelling out the date Jane had arrived on this parallel world. One that matched the bookcase full of security tapes in the back office of the convenience store she'd snuck into. One that had been missing from that collection.

Jane's skin prickled. She didn't know how or why Paul had gotten his hands on it, but she wasn't about to waste this opportunity. Jane whirled around, heading for a TV in the corner of the office.

It took her a second to remember how to work a VCR again, but thankfully both the TV and VCR were exactly like the ones that used to be in the Maxwells' living room when Jane was younger. Hell, they may have been the same ones, brought here when the family bought newer, better models.

A few moments later, the screen flickered to life and the video started playing. An overhead view of a convenience store parking lot, a single beat-up car parked out front. According to the timestamp, it was five-thirty in the morning—way too early to be useful to Jane. Jane jabbed the fast-forward button, watching the numbers tick up. On the screen, people and traffic whipped by, flitting like flies. Finally, there it was: two people in costume, running behind the building. They were almost out of the frame, just cutting across the corner briefly, but it was enough. Jane hit play again, watching, waiting. A few minutes of nothing but the normal passage of traffic. Until it wasn't. Jane sucked in a breath.

She didn't know how long she sat there, rewinding the footage to watch the same ten-second clip over and over again. Long enough that she probably should have started to worry about wearing out the tape. It's impossible to know how much longer she would have continued, transfixed, a single repeating frame of her face awash in the blue glow of the screen. The only thing that finally interrupted her loop was the click of a door, Paul's voice calling out from beyond view, "Jane?"

"In here."

Jane listened as Paul stepped through. He drew to a cautious stop in the doorway. "Is . . . everything okay?"

Jane shot to her feet, her youthful muscles propelling her from her cross-legged spot on the floor. She motioned at the TV, paused behind her, jabbing at the screen with the remote in her hand. "When were you going to tell me about this? Do you know how hard I tried to get my hands on this tape?"

Paul's mouth twisted, confused. "I . . . didn't think it was important."

"How did you even *get* this?"

"From the convenience store next to Braddock's," Paul said. "I spoke to the owner shortly after you told me how you'd arrived. Said it was for a case I was building. I figured it couldn't hurt to check, but there's nothing useful on it."

"That's because you didn't know what you were looking for!" Jane threw the remote into the butt of a nearby chair. It was a childish outburst. Jane knew it, still couldn't stop it. Teenage rage filled her like fire. She wanted to trash the room— knock the TV down, rip the photos from the wall over Paul's desk, overturn the trash can. In the mess of emotions, it was impossible to tell how much of her anger was at Paul, for keeping this from her, and how much of it was in response to what she'd found.

"I don't understand," Paul said. He was looking at the screen now, the image jumping slightly as the tape struggled to hold its place. "What difference does she make? She's just a pedestrian."

"The difference is *I know her*. As an adult. From my world. She doesn't belong here—and she's walking out from behind the store just after I was attacked. It has to be her."

It had to be—but it couldn't be. Even now, hours after Jane first spotted the glimpse of her in the corner of the security footage, she couldn't wrap her head around it. Yet there she was on the screen, her face turned up toward the camera clear as day, pink hair turned orange by the streetlight. She'd changed out of the outfit she'd worn during the attack, though a spray of stars up her sleeve remained, almost as if she was taunting Jane.

Paul ran his hands through his hair. "Okay," he said. "Okay, I'm sorry I screwed up, but . . . if you know her, then isn't that a good thing? At least we have something to start from now, right?"

A sour laugh escaped Jane. "I wish." She pointed at the screen again. Maybe, if she finally said it, even to herself, it would somehow make more sense. "That's Blue Hamilton. My best friend. And I have absolutely no idea why she'd be this pissed at me."

THERE WERE ONLY A FEW HOURS LEFT ON DOG SQUAD'S
deadline, and already Janie was facing an obstacle she wasn't
sure she could overcome: her uniform.

The team had dropped it off first thing that morning, in a
slick metal case like something out of a spy movie. It arrived during breakfast. Tony set the case on the kitchen island, knocking
against their bowls of cereal. Clair's mouth had pinched. She'd
gotten up to refill her coffee, though Janie was sure it was just
a convenient excuse to turn her back on both the delivery and
Janie.

They had Senator Maxwell to either thank or blame for Janie's
involvement. The Heroes had gathered for an emergency planning session the night before, Senator Maxwell joining via video
chat as if this was some far-flung science-fiction future. He'd
been more than ready to capitulate again, but it turns out he
and his wife do still talk sometimes, because he'd already heard

about the plan Mrs. Maxwell and Janie had cooked up—and it was the only version of events he'd agree to hold back for.

Clair had argued, of course, and so the plan had changed shape from Janie and Mrs. Maxwell's initial vision. The discussion had dragged on for hours, well into the night, ironing out everyone's issues. Clair still had her doubts, but at least in the morning she hadn't turned away the delivery of Janie's uniform.

Now all that was left was for Janie to, you know, put it *on*.

She stared down at the case lying innocently on her bed. Tony had unlocked it before leaving, and Clair had told Janie to take it upstairs to her bedroom. They couldn't actually enact the plan until this evening, though, so Janie spent the next few hours ignoring the case. It was almost lunchtime when she crept back to it. She had, at least, gone so far as to open the case, but now she stood back, hands on her hips, gnawing her lip raw as she assessed the folded layers of red.

She didn't understand. This was everything she'd wanted since arriving here, and now they were finally letting her *wear* it, they were finally (sort of) treating her like one of the team, and now—*now*—Janie's nerves were failing her? How was she supposed to be taken seriously as a superhero if she let a stupid piece of clothing hold her back?

It was almost a blessing, then, when the doorbell rang. Janie slammed the case shut and ran down the stairs.

She found Keisha on the front stoop, cellphone in her hand and a frazzled look on her face. "Hey," she said, pushing a curtain of braids back over her head. "We're trying to get through to Clair—can you get her?"

Immediately, Janie's stomach cinched. She gripped the doorknob tighter. "She's not here."

"What do you mean she's not here? Her tracker's here."

Janie tossed out an unaffected shrug, trying not to get too weirded out by the future's casual disregard for privacy. "She got a text and told me she had to go to headquarters for a bit. I thought she was with you guys."

"Shit." Keisha tapped her cellphone and raised it to her ear. The faint trill of it ringing on the other end of the line drifted from the speaker as Keisha said, "You're sure she was going to HQ?"

"That's what she told me."

Keisha nodded, acknowledging this. "Hey," she said into the cellphone. She pressed her finger to her free ear, blocking out the street noise. "Janie says she went back to—Wait, hold up, slow down . . . *What's* missing?"

Janie tugged at Keisha's arm. "What's going on?"

Keisha sidestepped. She shook her head, still listening to the call. "Yeah . . . yeah, okay . . . No, I got it. Thanks."

Keisha tapped the cellphone, hanging up. She stuffed it into the pocket of her jean jacket, then took a second to breathe deeply before turning back to Janie.

"The good news—what I came here to tell Clair—is that Marie's scans finally came back with a result. We found your world."

Janie rocked back.

This shouldn't have hit her so hard. It was, after all, what she was supposed to have been waiting for with bated breath. A chance to go home, to resume her normal life. To put all this behind her and grow up at her own painfully slow pace.

To go back into the closet.

"And . . . the bad news?"

"We'll have to clean up this Dog Squad mess without Clair," Keisha said. "One of the world hoppers is missing. It looks like she's gone to find Jane on her own."

JANE SPENT THE REST OF THE DAY IN A FOG. SETTING aside the question of when and how Blue had gotten super-powers—and it's not like Jane had any room to judge Blue for keeping that information private—there still was no reasonable explanation for *why* she'd attacked Jane and Clair to begin with, *why* she'd brought them here, trapped Jane in this body, in this version of her life.

No matter how much Jane tried to understand it, she couldn't. They'd been getting along great when Blue left for vacation. Jane had done nothing to her at work to raise her ire. And while they hadn't hung out socially in quite some time, that was more the result of conflicting schedules, busy lives, obligations with other people. They saw each other all day at the office, it was only natural they'd hang out less in their off hours. What else could it have been, then? Nothing made sense.

"Jane?"

"Hmm?"

"Would you care to share?"

Jane blinked, and the world snapped into focus. The Maxwells were gathered around the kitchen table, plates of spaghetti laid out between them. For a second Jane was off balance, like she'd jumped from one issue to the next in her favorite comic with none of the real world in-betweens that filled a normal day. But then she took a breath, remembering the long afternoon spent rewatching the same tiny moment of the security tape over and over, the way she'd chewed out Paul for neglecting to give her this information earlier, the tense ride home, helping Olivia set the table. It's just that she'd been so lost in the sea of her own thoughts, sketches of Blue and Jane and their friendship scattered around her as she dug through memories, that she'd forgotten everything else unfolding in the real world.

Now the real world was back, front and center. And it was waiting for her to say something.

"Oh, right." Jane went silent for a moment, casting around for anything to offer up about her day. The one she'd lived out in their minds, if not in actuality. Going to school like everything was normal. Wait, had Allison noticed Jane wasn't at school? Or had Paul offered up an excuse for why Jane didn't need a ride home after the final bell?

She shook her head, chasing those concerns away. Her "family" was still waiting for her, patient and expectant. "Um . . ."

All she could think about was the security tape. Blue's face, glancing briefly toward the camera, open and defiant as if she knew one day Jane would see it.

"I, um . . . I've got a math test coming up on Friday," Jane said finally, digging her fork into the spaghetti. "Cal wants me to help him study."

Allison smirked. "Really? *That's* your one thing?"

"Sorry my life isn't interesting enough for you."

"Oh, I think it's more interesting than you're letting on."

Panic raised Jane's head. It . . . wasn't possible for Allison to have worked out any of the superhero shit unfolding around her, right? Carefully, Jane picked through her dinner as well as her words. "I mean, I think math tests are pretty important, but maybe that's just me."

"Yes, I'd hate to disparage *math*." Allison rolled her eyes. "Only I heard you got into a big fight by the lockers yesterday. Rumor is, Clair was *really* upset about it afterward."

Jane's chest loosened in relief. Was that all? In the burst of everything that had happened after, Jane had almost forgotten about her pseudo-fight with Clair, the misguided assumption that Jane had hooked up with Cal. It was a mess Jane would have to mop up, sure, and quickly, but it hardly seemed worth Allison giving her shit about.

Apparently, this sounded more concerning to Olivia, though. She looked up sharply. "What's this? Janie, is everything all right with your friends?"

"Yeah, of course," Jane said. Too quickly, too defensively. "It's fine. It's nothing. It wasn't even a fight—more a miscommunication. We're fine."

"That's not what I heard."

"Then you heard wrong."

"Oh, come *on*," Allison said, drawing the word out. "Casey saw Clair go running into the bathroom before first period, and word is she didn't come out until lunch. Apparently, she looked *awful*—like she'd been crying."

"Since when do your friends care what goes on with a bunch of sophomores?"

Allison put her hand to her chest in mock-offense. "I care about my little sister, Janie. I pay attention. You'd be surprised how much I know, if you ever bothered to ask."

Jane looked over sharply. Her world settled and stilled, familiar lines and colors crawling over the surface of her reality until it had been boxed, reduced, sliced up into manageable pieces. Each moment separated by the comfort of a white gutter, each threat cushioned by the pillowy confines of a speech bubble.

"Shut up," the cartoon version of Jane says. She's safe in a wide shot of the kitchen. Warm yellow lighting and cluttered counters lend an air of domestic normalcy. Her family, gathered with her around the table: her parents' heads are ducked, ignoring this minor squabble between sisters. The picture is framed like something out of a sitcom, safe and boring. The next panel tightens, Jane in profile as she angrily brings a forkful of twirled pasta toward her mouth. Her speech bubble curls like a dog by her feet, almost an afterthought. "You don't know what you're talking about."

"Don't I?"

In one shot, Jane's eyes are on the pasta held in front of her lips. In the next, they've snapped up, just a bit wider as they stare across the table. The double panels are nearly identical, bridged only by the one line of Allison's dialogue. Two words, a single question. *Don't I?*

But oh, it was so much more than that.

Olivia cleared her throat, flipping the page. "Okay, Janie, Allison's just trying to be a good sister," she says. She's captured in Mom Mode, her shoulders as straight as the frame line above her, her fork held aloft as if wielding a mighty point. "One day, you're going to be grateful for her attention. And she's right— if something's going on between you and Clair, you should talk about it."

"Oh, something's *going on*, all right."

A swift kick to Allison's shin. Hidden from parental view, boxed and enlarged in the darkness beneath the table, the angry point of contact rendered with red and orange spikes. Above it all, Paul glowers at his daughters. *"Allison."* The text is as dark with warning as his voice.

It makes no difference. In the next frame, Allison's face is zoomed in, something wild dancing in her eyes. *"Please,"* she says, her words slipping out like a serpent. "You think no one's noticed you're a dy—"

"ENOUGH!" Abruptly, the slur is cut off, pierced by a spike rising from the frame below it. Paul's letters: bold, enlarged, slanted with fatherly sternness. Beneath them, his fist is slammed against the table, a spray of tick marks noting the collision with the woodgrain. The shot frames the fist, perspective forcing it

so large it looks as if it's coming for you; but once you finish wincing, your eyes naturally trail the length of his arm, where the dark shading of his open mouth, and the cut of shadows across his cheeks and eyes, turns him into an angry god looking down from on high.

Jane had never seen her father so pissed off, and for a moment it rocked her clear of the safety of her comics. She blinked, her eyes sliding across to the now fully animate Allison as Paul added, "Your room. Now."

"What?" Allison said. "I'm just saying what we already know!"

Except this wasn't *quite* the common knowledge Allison assumed, and maybe a part of Allison realized that—too late. She and Jane and Paul exchanged a quick glance and then, as if drawn by an invisible force, each of their heads turned toward the last seat at the table.

The three of them, arranged around the curve of the table as an arc at the top of the page. Each looking at the reader: Allison, uncertain; Paul, steady; Jane, vaguely nauseous. The space for the table itself is a cutaway, another pane coming through beneath. Olivia, framed by the faces of her family.

For once, her expression is unguarded, her lips gaped open just a fraction. Her unfocused gaze is turned inward, spilling memories across the bottom of the page in sepia tones and messy sketches. Janie at five, in a princess dress and a plastic sword that she waves in her mother's face; at nine, in a tie-dye T-shirt and overall shorts, gripping hands with Clair as the two of them race barefoot across the lawn; at fourteen, cloaked in baggy flannels, ducking her face behind her overgrown bangs. A smattering of drawings from her bedroom walls separate the moments— Belle and Deanna Troi and Xena and Trinity and original characters, all women, most bearing guns and lasers and whips and daggers.

Jane's throat clogged with everything she wasn't saying. Everything she hadn't said to her mother when she was a teenager, everything Janie hadn't said to the mother's face staring at Jane now. It didn't matter how many times Jane had come out, it never really got easier. Not when it was someone that mattered.

There was always that moment, when the balance finally tips, the truth laid bare, and you know the person you're talking to finally *understands* what you're telling them, and there's no going back, not anymore.

Olivia blinked, long enough for her to break eye contact, long enough for her to refix her gaze on her hand, splayed flat on the table beside her napkin. A fixed point to steady herself on, each of her fingers pressed firmly against the surface. This was the only secret Jane was ever able to keep from her mother, and it wasn't until now, decades after the first time she'd admitted the truth to that face, that Jane began to wonder if the reason her mom never figured it out is because she hadn't *wanted* to see it.

"Janie?" Olivia asked, her voice as small and fragile as a baby bird. "Honey, is . . . is that true?"

The only answer was the scrape of Jane's chair.

Jane was on her feet and racing for the door before she even registered what she was doing. Narrow slices of panels: her shoes pounding the floor of the hallway, her silhouette at the front door as the porch light spilled in around her. She thought someone called out after her, but her blood was rushing in her ears, and the only thing she heard as the door slammed behind her was the shrill sound of her mother shouting, "You *knew*?"

The night air kissed her skin as she ran around the house, raising goosebumps on her flesh. Jane cut across the back lawn and met up with the old footpath, the ground sloping toward the riverbank. She didn't know where she was running to, but as soon as she saw the oak tree she knew it wouldn't have been anywhere else.

Jane stopped just shy of crashing into the tree, her breath racing in her chest. She gulped down the cold night air, eyes burning with unshed tears.

It doesn't matter. They're not your real family.

Jane felt the narrative text boxing her in, the first sentence in the upper left, the second in the lower right. Between them, caught in a frozen moment, she leans her head against the oak tree. Mentally kicking herself. Trying not to.

If she told herself this enough, splashing these words over

the rest of the story, would she start to believe them? Would the heat in her cheeks, the ache in her heart, the twist in her stomach, all just go away?

Unfortunately for Jane, this wasn't actually one of her comics, and she couldn't control how she felt, any more than she could control what happened from one moment to the next. Nothing would really make her feel better. The only thing that ever did was . . .

"Janie?"

Jane shut her eyes. Under any other circumstances, the sound of Clair's voice would have been the one thing she'd welcome most in all the world.

Clair's footsteps edged closer. "I saw you from my window."

Of course she had. Of course Clair would have been looking out at that exact moment, would have cared enough to throw on her shoes and race after Jane, despite the weirdness between them. Despite everything Jane had done to mess things up. Jane felt the presence of a hand hovering just behind her shoulder, hesitate, then drop.

"Are you okay?"

A manic laugh escaped Jane. She turned around.

Clair just stood there, an angel in the moonlight. God, she was perfect in any era. Was it any wonder all those young Janes, scattered all across the multiverse, had fallen in love with her?

Clair stepped forward. Tentative at first, then slightly more confident. An extra sweater was folded neatly over her arms. She held it out to Jane.

Jane reached out, her fingers brushing the knit. Her chest burned with everything she wanted to say. Clair's youthful face had grown familiar again, like the clock had turned back for both of them. They had never needed a second chance, but here it was all the same. Jane had been so obsessed with getting herself swapped back, with lining everything up exactly like it was before, last time, the way she remembered.

But it was never going to happen the way she remembered. Not again. Not for Janie, whose life was already so different, long before Jane had stepped into her skin.

She took the sweater from Clair's hands. Gingerly, as if the whole thing were made of glass.

"I'm really sorry for how I've been acting lately," Jane said before she could question herself. "You're right, I've been . . . jealous, of your friendship with Hailey. I'm just—I'm used to things always being the two of us, you know?"

Clair nodded. That much, at least, was nothing revelatory. Even among the rest of their friends, there had always been a tighter duo, Jane-and-Clair, friends with everyone else. Their names had been used in a single breath long before the nature of their relationship had changed into something more.

"And I meant it, earlier: there is *nothing* going on between me and Cal. We've been studying together lately, that's all, I swear."

"It's fine, Janie," Clair said. "Really. I believe you, but even if you were going out, it's none of my business. You don't owe me an explanation."

"*Yes*, I do."

Clair took a sharp breath. Jane glanced down; in the moment she'd been so insistent, she'd also taken a step forward without realizing it, had taken Clair's hand out of instinct. Jane stilled her thumb, which had already begun to trace small tracks across Clair's knuckles. She was close enough now to smell Clair's body spray, peachy and summer bright. Exactly the way it had been the last time, beneath this same tree.

Clair had always been the brave one in their relationship. It was Clair who mustered up the strength to admit the way she felt first, Clair who finally managed to convince Jane to come out to their respective families, Clair who suggested they move in together and damn what anyone else thought. The only thing Jane had ever done first was propose, but that was more than a decade later, when the state's ruling finally passed, long after they'd considered themselves spouses in their hearts. There was no risk to the question by then, no doubt of Clair's answer. But the moments when they hovered, teetering on the edge? The ones that really mattered? The thing that finally propelled them forward to the next step, time after time after time?

Those were all Clair.

So Jane recognized it happening now. The familiar way Clair

was studying her with sparkling eyes, sizing up the situation, weighing the risks. The steely glint that locked in place when she'd made up her mind to go for it. Her gaze slid to Jane's lips.

"Stop," Jane said, just as Clair started to lean forward. She let go of Clair's hand. Took a step back, a rush of cold air sweeping in between them. As familiar as all this was, it wasn't *her* Clair standing in front of Jane, being brave. This was another version of her, a *fifteen year old*, a *child*. Jane's stomach turned. "I can't do this," Jane said. "I'm sorry, it's just—it's not right."

Jane saw her mistake as soon as the words were out of her mouth. To her ears, of course, every bit entirely rational—Jane was an adult, being an adult. Body-swapped into a teenager or not, there was no way she would ever consider kissing this version of Clair. But without those facts on hand, to a nervous, closeted, brave young lesbian taking her first step forward . . .

Clair was already retreating. Making herself smaller. Her voice was tinged with a kind of hysteria as she did her best to backpedal away from danger. "Yeah, no, of course, I'm sorry, I wasn't—I would never—"

"No, Clair," Jane said. "I didn't mean *that*, it's not about—"

Whatever else they were trying to say, their words stumbling between them, was cut off by a flashlight beam bouncing toward them. Jane turned, squinting, raising her hand to see the silhouette rushing down the lawn. She supposed, on some level, she should have been concerned about being caught out here, with Clair, but by now the space between them ranged several feet, and there was nothing to see.

"Jane," Paul's voice boomed. His footsteps drew to an unsteady halt, and though Jane couldn't see his face in the dark behind the flashlight, she could imagine it well enough. Mouth parted in surprise, the smallest pinch between his brows that was half embarrassment, half curiosity as to what he'd just interrupted.

Jane shook her head, just slightly. *It's not what it looks like.* It would never be what it looked like, not so long as it was thirties Jane, rather than teenage Janie stuck in this gangly body.

Paul lowered his flashlight. "Sorry, but . . . you have a phone call," he said finally.

"I should go," Clair said.

"No, wait!"

But she was already turning away, already retracing her steps up the hill. "I'll see you tomorrow," she said, her voice carrying through the darkness.

Jane whirled. "What, Paul? What the fuck was *so important* you had to interrupt me?"

"You have a phone call," Paul repeated.

"So? You couldn't have taken a message for me?"

"No. Trust me," he said. "You're going to want to take this one."

THE PARKING LOT LOOKED EXACTLY THE WAY JANE remembered it. The same stretch of decaying asphalt, the same overgrown grass, the same pale moon rendering everything ghostly. An aging factory loomed over her, the whispered trace of letters spelling out the name Jane had drawn into dozens of panels: *ChemWerks Industries*. In her own timeline, it would only be a matter of weeks before Jane and her friends piled onto their bikes and went looking for places to hang out, landing them here. Locked doors and a lack of windows would make their trip a bust, until a single command would carry across the open parking lot: *Look!*

"Jane."

A different word, but the same voice. Jane whirled as a figure slipped from the shadows. Vintage trench coat, the sharp lines of a Roaring-Twenties bob beneath the jaunty angle of a downward fedora.

When Jane had answered the phone earlier, she couldn't believe it. Clair, her own Clair, had found her way back.

Jane ran forward, kicking up loose stone. She threw her arms around Clair, hopping slightly to make up for the sudden difference in height. Clair scooped Jane into her arms, turning the momentum of their collision into a single spin around. They rocked in a hug for a moment, relief and rightness crashing over them as the cloud of low-grade terror Jane had been living under finally broke.

Until reality crept back in.

"Sorry," Jane said, suddenly self-conscious. She pulled back, tucking her hair behind her ears. "I . . . I would kiss you, but—"

"Yeah, no," Clair said. "Don't even worry about it. That would just be weird."

"Okay. Good. I mean, not good, but—"

"Yeah." Clair bit her lip. "Are you okay?" she asked, tentative.

"I'm fine," Jane said. "Fifteen, but . . . fine. All things considered."

"Good. I've been so fucking worried about you."

"I've been so fucking worried about *you*," Jane said, laughing slightly over her words.

A pair of awkward smiles, profiles on opposite sides of the panel.

Broken pavement crunched behind Jane, footsteps gently approaching. Clair glanced over, wariness on her face. "Jane . . . ?"

"It's okay," Jane said as Paul came to stand beside her. "He knows."

Paul held out his hand. "Clair. It's such an honor to finally meet you."

Clair didn't take his hand—not yet. She paused a moment, sizing him up. She had to be able to tell he wasn't exactly the same as the Paul Maxwells she was familiar with, but Jane couldn't blame her for being cautious.

"If it helps, you're welcome to take off your glove." Paul turned his hand, palm up toward the moonlight. An open offering. Jane had given him a basic rundown of Clair's powers on the drive over, nervously chatting to fill the space.

Clair tipped her head, acknowledging the gesture. "That won't be necessary." She reached out, accepting the handshake, keeping the exposed tips of her fingers away.

Jane shivered, flipping up the collar of her jacket. "So where's the rest of the team?"

"They'll be along later," Clair said. Was that the tiniest flinch, just before she answered? In the moonlight, it was hard to tell. "They had to finish something first."

Jane let this explanation stand. It had the air of a lie, but she was willing to give Clair enough leeway to ignore it for now. Jane adjusted her glasses, hoping to appear casual. "And . . . everything else all right at home? Everyone's well? Things at Dream Sequence going okay?"

Clair pulled back, just a smidge. She studied Jane for a second as she said, "I mean, there's been some drama, but . . . I think everything is more or less on track at this point. Definitely nothing you need to worry about now."

"Yeah, of course," Jane said. "Besides, I'm sure Blue is on top of it."

"Jane, you know Blue's been on vacation."

Jane's stomach twisted. It wasn't exactly the news she'd been hoping for, but . . . it didn't definitively *prove* anything, either. There were still other explanations—hell, how did they know the Blue who appeared on the security tape was even the same one Jane knew?

Okay, so this line of thinking was probably a stretch. Still, Jane clung to it, at least for now.

"So," Clair said brightly. Too brightly, clearly searching for a safe topic to settle on, but Jane wasn't going to complain. Clair jerked her chin toward Paul, who'd stepped away to give them space. "He's . . . different."

"He's all right," Jane said with a shrug.

"High praise." Clair laughed a little under her breath. "I guess that explains why Janie is such a daddy's girl."

Jane flinched. "She's safe, then? The . . . other me."

"Yeah. The team's been looking out for her. Not that she's making it easy—she's too much like you for her own good. Still, I suppose that means she'll make a great superhero some day."

"I wouldn't be so sure about that."

"What do you mean?"

Jane glanced over her shoulder. Paul was idly studying the empty parking lot at a polite distance. Still, Jane turned away, drawing Clair along with her. Jane lowered her voice as she said, "Paul got the powers."

Clair jerked back. "*What?* How?"

"Same way we did, only it happened back when he was in law school. It's a long story," Jane said. "I don't fully understand it yet, but yeah. It doesn't look like Janie or the rest of us will get their chance this time."

"Huh." Clair went silent for a moment, considering this. "Okay, but wait. Does this mean that, like, all our parents are secretly superheroes, or just Paul?" Clair gasped, grabbing Jane's wrist in excitement. "Wait, does Donna have powers? Oh, please tell me it's flight—she's always wanted to be able to fly."

Jane's face soured, wishing Clair had asked about anything else. She didn't want to tell Clair what had happened to this version of Donna, at least not here, not like this, but there was no getting around it. Clair assumed Donna getting superpowers would be a happy outcome, not the nightmare it actually was, a twisted version of the mother she knew.

A mother. In an instant, something about the attack in the butcher shop snagged Jane's awareness. A memory, half-forgotten in the haze of everything that happened afterward, but now: there had been a face, after she was first injected, hovering warm and maternal over her as the drug hit Jane's system.

A mother, but not Jane's mother. She'd thought there was something so familiar about her, but even if she'd been in her right mind, why would Jane have ever thought of Donna in that context? It made no sense.

It still made no sense, but now certainty had hardened the memory and Jane was sure of what she'd seen.

"Oh my god," Jane whispered. "It was Donna."

"What was Donna?" Clair asked, but Jane was already pushing past her, running off.

"Paul! The woman who attacked me—did you get a good look at her?"

Paul turned, obviously startled. "The . . . what? No. I'm sorry, but I didn't. She was in costume, and if you haven't noticed, I kind of had my hands full."

"It was Donna."

Paul's eyebrow ticked up. A controlled look, meant to project his clear disbelief without outright denying his opposition's statement. "That seems . . . unlikely."

"What attack?" Clair said from behind her. "Jane, are you okay?"

Jane waved her off, still fixed on Paul. "Unlikely," Jane said, "but not impossible."

"Just about impossible," Paul said. "Donna's been under constant supervised care since she was admitted to Cedarcreek."

Clair grabbed Jane's elbow. "She was *what*?"

"More impossible than you developing superpowers?" Jane asked, still ignoring Clair's confusion—she'd bring her up to speed soon enough. "More impossible than me getting body-swapped with your daughter? For fuck's sake, Paul, we deal with impossible literally every day."

"That's not the same. And even if she could have," he added, talking louder to barrel past Jane's intake of breath, "why would she? Donna's a good person—there's no reason she'd be skulking around drug manufacturing sites, attacking innocent children."

"I get that it sounds crazy, but I swear to you, I know what I saw."

"And I'm sure you believe that, but Jane . . . you were drugged. Are you sure you weren't hallucinating?"

"Not about this," Jane said, and there must have been something in her voice that made impact, because Paul actually stepped back, considering.

It was not, by itself, enough to convince him. One person's recollection, however trustworthy, would never be enough to convince Paul Maxwell of the facts of a case. So Jane stepped back, resting her hand on Clair's shoulder, and pressed on.

"Look, we think the drug's being made by a doctor, right? So maybe it's one of hers. But if you really want proof," Jane said quickly, turning to look at a befuddled Clair, "there's one way to find out."

* * *

THE HEROES DIDN'T HAVE THE LUXURY OF WAITING FOR Clair to get back.

Janie stood in a little sitting room, pacing tight circles and trying not to freak out too badly. Not that her efforts were working. She'd applied probably fifteen coats of deodorant under her pits before she'd suited up, but even now a suspicious amount of warmth dampened her beneath the shirt of her uniform. She could only hope it was made of some fancy-pants futuristic fabric that magically took away armpit stink.

Ugh, this wasn't helping. Janie turned around, taking a shaky breath in. She waved her hands around, trying to shake out her nerves through her fingers. "You've got this," she whispered to herself. "It's just a speech."

And really, it could have been a whole lot worse. It's not like Janie was being asked to step up and fight some megapowered supervillain on her own. Or at all. No, instead they'd ironed out her plan so that, if all went well, Janie would completely avoid any kind of confrontation. All she had to do was stand in front of a group of people and talk. Like giving a presentation at school. No big deal.

Never mind that Janie usually puked before presentations. She wasn't going to do that here. She was a grownup now, and grownups didn't get nervous before speaking in public. Or at least, superheroes didn't. Yes. And if she wanted to prove herself, she couldn't be acting like a child, getting stressed enough to—

Nope. Janie's stomach roiled, and she raced over to a potted plant in the corner, one she hoped was big enough that maybe no one would notice the expelled contents of her stomach soaking into the dirt.

A knock sounded at the door. "Captain?" An unfamiliar voice, probably someone from the event. "We're almost ready for you."

"Great!" Janie called, forced cheer tasting even more sour on her tongue than the trace of vomit. She wiped her mouth and considered trying to find something to bury the evidence of her nerves in the potting soil, but there wasn't time.

It felt wrong to be doing this without Clair. Janie couldn't believe she'd just *left* like that. Not a word to anyone, no time to prepare or consider what she was doing. Just an alert on her cellphone, and she'd left without a second thought. On some level, Janie supposed it should be flattering—Jane was, after all, also sort of her. But in the end, all it really did was hurt; an ache Janie couldn't will away.

But now they were here, and the aide from the event knocked again and let herself in, and it was time for Janie to stand in front of a crowd and tell them who she was.

No pressure or anything.

It was a last-minute booking. Clair had found it—a contact from her job at the museum, she'd said, someone throwing a big fundraiser for a youth charity. A few quick calls, and they'd added Captain Lumen to the lineup.

Now Janie tried to unlock her knees, following the aide out into the lobby where the fundraiser was being held. The whole room was glass, the glamour inside reflecting just as brightly in the windows as the nighttime glitter of the city outside. Janie cut through the crowd, all these high-society grownups and their high-society, grown-up money on full display through their tailored tuxedos and thousand-dollar dresses and jewelry fat and ripe as fruit.

A soft crackle whispered from Janie's earpiece. "You got this, kid."

It didn't matter which member of the team it was. They were spread around the perimeter of the building, covering all the exits and sightlines. Waiting and watching for Lester to turn up. Safely hidden in the dark. Only Janie had to go in front of this crowd, stand up under the bright lights with all eyes on her.

The aide led her to a narrow glass podium, where some woman in sequins had just finished introducing her. And then there was polite applause, and a brief stumble as Janie stepped up, and sweaty index cards laid down in front of her, and her palms gripping the edge of the podium like it was the only thing holding her upright.

Janie blinked a few times, trying to adjust to the contact lenses that came with the uniform. She leaned in toward the microphone. She did not look directly at the crowd, instead finding a point just behind the farthest person—a suggestion from Clair, before she'd gone rogue and abandoned Janie to her fate.

No, don't think about that. There was no time for that.

She cleared her throat.

"Good evening, I'm Captain Lumen. But . . . you already know that. You're here tonight to find out something you don't know."

Okay, okay, good start, minimal shakiness in her voice. One short breath in, one short breath out. Keep going.

"Of course everyone wonders about the identity of super-heroes. Why wouldn't they? We put on masks, we go out there and risk our lives for the protection of others. It's only natural that you'd want to know what sort of person you're putting your trust in. So I'm here tonight to tell you."

Janie paused. She didn't mean for it to be for dramatic effect, but it had that impact just the same. Despite her vantage point, she could see a few people leaning in, eager to hear what she had to say.

She still wasn't sure she wanted to say what she had to say. But it was too late for second guessing now. Bite the bullet. Suck in a breath. Let it out.

Here goes.

"I'm a lesbian."

JANIE STOOD THERE FOR A MOMENT, LETTING THE blood rush in her ears. All she could do at first was grip the little podium and breathe. Had she really just said that? Out loud? To a room full of people, many of them holding cellphones aloft in a way Janie had learned to recognize as recording a video? She thought for sure she'd chicken out at some point, but now in the pause she knew she hadn't. For the first time in Janie's life, she'd *come out*.

And so had Captain Lumen.

That part still felt a little weird, but Clair had sworn up and down that Jane would be okay with it, had even been talking about doing something similar for a while now. Something about visibility and representation and giving bigots the middle finger. Janie had liked the sound of that, even if the plan itself made her nervous as hell.

Now Janie took a breath. Glanced back down at the index cards in her hands. The rest of the speech—about community and the importance of being seen—swam in front of her as she hurried to find her place.

The truth was, it didn't actually matter what she said at this point. Not in terms of the plan, anyway. The Heroes had circulated rumors that Captain Lumen would be giving a speech about her identity, in the hope Lester would hear it and think they were getting out ahead of his blackmail. Clair had felt confident that, if they threatened his cash cow, he'd show up. *"Luring people in with what they want is hit or miss,"* she'd said at the team meeting. *"You want them to show up? You threaten them with something they fear."* She pointedly had not looked at either Janie or the video box with Senator Maxwell's glowering face—even then, he'd refused to apologize for setting up the meeting to hand over Lester's demands.

For her part, Janie had bitten her tongue and tried not to say *I told you so*, since, technically, this was a variation on her original idea to just admit who she was and be done with it. Apparently, some things just have a way of going full circle. Even though she had to admit she liked Clair's coming-out variation better.

So now here she was, fumbling to find her place again after dropping the biggest truth-bomb of her life, when a voice broke through the crowd—one she never thought she'd be so happy to hear again.

"Oh, I'm afraid that's not the only thing we'll be revealing here tonight."

Bingo. Janie fought to keep her mouth from twitching up in a smile as she raised her head again.

The crowd parted around a figure in a pit-bull mask, several shrieks and gasps escaping as the social elite hurried to get out of his way. Lester stalked forward, his cellphone raised in his fist like a grenade—which, in some ways, it was, for the explosion that would erupt in Janie's life if he was allowed to send that video.

"Would you like to know what she's *really* hiding?" He pushed his mask up, the dog snout smushed over his hair, an open scowl on his face. "It's not her taste for pussy, believe me."

Janie's cheeks heated. Of course he would assume she had *actually*—

No. Janie wasn't letting her mind go there, not in the middle of a crisis.

Her mouth flubbed open. This was where Captain Lumen was supposed to have some sort of witty retort. But she wasn't Captain Lumen, not really, and she wasn't even supposed to be confronting him. Already over the comms she could hear the team scrambling to regroup, hissed accusations about who should or shouldn't have seen him as they raced to catch up. Janie ripped the earpiece out, dropping it and stamping it under her boot to keep Lester from listening in. The team would be here any moment now, but how many moments were too many? How long before Lester hit the button on his cellphone screen, the big red one just under his thumb?

Lester smirked. He'd seen that she'd seen, and he knew that Janie was—however temporarily—in this alone.

"Well, Captain? What's it going to be? You know what it'll cost to keep my silence."

Janie's eyes darted to the gathered crowd. They'd backed up enough to give Lester his space, and several tuxedoed members of security had joined them, holding steady until, what, Captain Lumen gave them some signal to move in? They were all waiting to see what Janie would do, and it didn't take superhearing for them to know she was being threatened. She couldn't capitulate to his demands, not even temporarily to fake him out, not with that kind of audience.

"Cat got your tongue, huh?" Lester said. "Let's see what you have to say once people have a taste of the truth."

"No!" Janie shouted, already reaching forward as Lester's thumb slammed the button on his screen.

Janie's body must have already known what to do, because she sure didn't. In an instant, before she could process what was happening, her powers stretched out. By the time she caught up with herself her hands were cupped in front of her, palms facing each other as if cradling a glass soccer ball between them. Lester's phone, meanwhile, was lit up with a wash of not-light, like the wifi frequencies Marie had tested in her lab—but the not-light was caught in a bubble only Janie could see, a bubble mirroring the size and shape of what she wasn't actually holding in her hands.

She let out a startled breath. Was it possible she'd actually caught the signal, before it had fully escaped his phone? The very possibility felt absurd, but then, she was living in the absurd every day she was in this skin.

Lester glanced up at his phone, then the crowd surrounding him, then back to his phone. "What the . . . ?" he muttered. He pulled it down, jabbing angrily at the screen—Janie quickly followed with the line of her arms, the bubble slipping slightly before she caught it again. Each new jab of the button sent a fresh wave of wifi bubble outward, slamming against Janie's palms in a way that wasn't technically physical, but somehow felt it.

Sweat pricked Janie's forehead. Whatever she had done, she wasn't going to be able to hold it forever. Especially not if Lester kept adding more and more waves of pressure to the sphere building in Janie's hands.

Gritting her teeth, Janie started to squeeze her hands together. She didn't know if it would work. It was either a wildly unfounded guess, or instinct—but instinct, or something like it, had brought her this far. She might as well follow it through.

"What are you doing?" Lester asked, more annoyed than concerned.

"Stopping you," Janie said. She hoped.

At the very least, she finally sounded badass. Janie would take that win, if nothing else.

The wifi bubble resisted. Lester—maybe guessing Janie's plan, or maybe hoping to leak the footage before she pulled off whatever she was doing—began slamming the button even more forcefully than before, his finger hitting faster and faster, the bubble pushing back against Janie's efforts to compress it.

Janie tried not to think about that, gripping the ball as tightly as she could. Her hands were shaking. She just kept squeezing down, tighter and tighter, until her palms burned and her arms ached, until the sight of the not-light bubble had seared itself across Janie's vision and it was the only thing she could see, the only object in her world, until she was so frustrated and so tired and so scared that all she could do was let out a feral sort of scream as she dug one last surge of energy from her muscles.

Her hands clapped together with an enormous *POP!* like the burst of a bubble as a shockwave crashed over her. An explosion of both light and not-light, throwing her off her feet, ripping fiercely through the lobby. The crowd tumbled like bowling pins and Janie landed hard, sliding across the lobby floor, coming to rest only when she crashed into a pair of sturdy legs surrounded by the swish of a Matrix trench coat.

"Captain . . . ," Rip-Shift said, his voice tinged with awe. "That was . . ."

"Lester!" Janie gasped. "Where's—? Don't let him get—!"

"It's fine, relax." Rip-Shift helped Janie up, and pointed across the ruined lobby. The rest of the team must have swarmed in during the explosion, though they probably didn't need to hurry. Lester lay sprawled on his back, his clothes and the tips of his hair singed with smoking black. A cracked cellphone lay smoldering on the floor beside him, just out of reach of his reddened fingers.

Janie's throat went dry as she swallowed. "Is . . . is he going to be okay?"

"Oh, for sure," Rip-Shift said as the team began to gather Lester up. "Got his ass handed to him, but trust me, we've seen much worse." He cut Janie a careful glance. "Are *you* okay?"

"Yeah," Janie said, automatically at first, and then, looking down at herself, she laughed. "Yeah, I'm . . . I'm fine. I'm good. I . . . Wait, does this mean I actually did it? We . . . we stopped him?"

Rip-Shift raised one eyebrow. Janie's own startled, stunned expression reflected back in his mirrored sunglasses. "Yes, Captain. *You* did."

He held his hand out for her. Janie glanced at it, uncertain for a second, before accepting the handshake. Rip-Shift grinned at her.

"Congratulations, kid. You're a Hero now."

JANE AND PAUL SAT ON THE HOOD OF HIS CAR, PARKED just down the street from the empty butcher shop, as Clair crossed the moon-soaked parking lot. Jane had been wary to let Clair go in alone, but Clair was worried Jane and Paul's current emotional states would "stain" the impressions she was trying to read off the place. It had already been trampled by the police, who had swept in and cordoned off the area with yellow tape after Paul had notified them anonymously and turned over his evidence. The police were disinterested parties, though, so Clair was confident that, if Donna was truly Jane's attacker, there would still be some trace left for her to find. But not if it got any additional emotions splashed all over the building.

So they hung back, waiting, as Clair ducked around the police tape and let herself inside to see what she could learn. A bag from Beef-Up Burgers rested on the hood between them, a purchase Paul had insisted on since Jane hadn't really gotten dinner.

"So that was the famous Clair," Paul said, finally breaking the silence that sat between them as Jane licked the salt from her fingers. He gave a single, curt nod. "I like her."

Jane blushed. Such a simple thing, *I like her*. It shouldn't have meant anything—it's not like Jane cared what any version of Paul thought about her life—and yet . . . neither Jane's real dad nor Senator Maxwell had ever expressed a direct opinion on Clair either way. Oh, they were never anything but *polite*. There was no overt disapproval, no nasty comments whispered behind Clair's back, no passive-aggressive texts. But a lack of disapproval wasn't the same thing as *approval*. And now, sitting in the glow of Paul's enthusiasm, Jane couldn't help but realize how parched she'd been for it all these years. How was it even possible to wait for something without knowing you wanted it?

"Won't Olivia wonder why we're out so late?" Jane asked, changing the subject.

Paul brushed off Jane's concern as easily as the crumb that had landed on his slacks. "Don't worry about it. Your mom went to bed with a migraine, and Allison's been grounded for probably the next century for what she did tonight."

The fry in Jane's mouth turned tasteless. This news wasn't as reassuring as it should have been. One of Jane's parents had retreated to their bedroom after Jane had come out, too. Only he'd gone to pack his bags, setting off without a word the following morning.

Olivia's not Paul, Jane told herself firmly, but it didn't help. If, somehow, for some reason, the truth of Jane's sexuality was too much for this version of Olivia—and if Jane, however inadvertently, caused this Janie to lose her relationship with her mother . . .

"Hey," Paul said, cutting through her thoughts. He reached out and gave Jane's knee a quick squeeze. "It's gonna be okay, Jane. Your mom loves you—loves Janie. What Allison said won't change anything."

A strangled laugh escaped Jane. "It always changes things. Trust me."

Paul lifted his paper cup and caught the top of the straw with his tongue, taking a quick sip before he answered. "Okay, I won't claim to know better on that front. But I promise, she's going to be okay with this. She's not going to make the same mistakes her family did."

"What are you talking about?"

"Jerry," Paul said, like it was obvious. He stole a quick glance in Jane's direction. "Her cousin? Oh come on, you must know this."

"I honestly have no idea what you're talking about."

"Seriously?" Paul sucked in a breath, then let it out slowly. "Okay, well. I guess it's possible things didn't happen the same for your own mom. But here, well . . . Jerry was her aunt Trudy's kid."

"Yeah, I mean, I know who Jerry was. I just don't see what he has to do with anything. He died when he was a kid. A boating accident or something."

It wasn't a story Jane's mom told often, or in any great detail, so it's not like Jane remembered much. But she knew about The Dead Cousin. Jerry was a cautionary tale, one her dad brought up when he wanted Jane to wear her life vest even when she felt too old for one.

Paul was silent for a moment as he set down his drink and wiped his fingers carefully with a paper napkin. Then, without warning, he said, "It wasn't an accident—Jerry drowned himself when he was sixteen. He was gay."

The darkness of the parking lot loomed around them suddenly, reducing them to tiny figures sketched in the center of a black void. They float across the page, the only stars in a sea of nothing.

Jane's voice, written so small you'd need a magnifying glass to read it. "What?"

Paul pressed his hands against the hood of the car, talking more to his shoes than to Jane. "Your mom doesn't like to talk about it, so I'm not sure how his parents found out about him. But her aunt and uncle weren't too keen on having a gay kid under their roof. All I know is they made things hell for him, and he couldn't take it anymore."

"Oh my god."

"Yeah," Paul said, his voice tinged with sympathetic pain. He turned back to her. "So if you think for even an instant Olivia is going to give you, or Janie, any crap about who you are, you can stop worrying about it right now. In fact"—he paused, gave a slight chuckle—"before she went upstairs, the last thing she said to Allison and me is that if either of us had a problem with you, we were welcome to pack a bag."

A single panel: her father's suitcase, resting on the floor by his feet. The image made Jane's head spin, so hard she had to catch herself against the metal of the hood.

"Hang on, she . . . she actually *said* that? She actually used the phrase 'pack a bag'?"

"Oh yeah, word for word. Like I said, you've got nothing to worry about from her."

But it wasn't Olivia that Jane was thinking about anymore, not really. It was Paul. Or rather, a version of Paul—the one who'd done just that, coming down the stairs the next morning, suitcase in hand. All these years, Jane had assumed it was his idea, but now . . . what if it wasn't? What if, like this Olivia, Jane's mom had given him an ultimatum: be a good dad, an accepting dad, or . . .

It still didn't excuse her dad's choice. Because it *was* a choice, even if he'd been forced to make it. But it did *change* things, even if Jane wasn't sure exactly how yet.

Thankfully, Jane didn't need to sit in these feelings for long. Before she could even begin to sort through the tangle of her emotions, the door to the butcher shop cracked open, a figure slipping out into the night.

As Clair drew closer, Jane didn't need to ask to know what she'd found.

"It's true," Clair said once she was next to the car. She was talking in her professional voice, the one she used when presenting bad news at meetings, even and controlled. "Donna was here, but . . . it's like part of her mind was shut down. Most of the impressions I got felt like daydreams, like she was lost in memory and not really conscious of the world around her. I don't think she knew what she was doing."

A breath whooshed from Jane's chest. It was no less than she'd been expecting, considering how Whisper worked, but it still landed harder than she'd thought it would. Jane didn't want to ask, but . . . "Do you think someone was controlling her?"

"Probably," Clair said with a wince.

Jane reached out, giving the gloved portion of Clair's hand a reassuring squeeze. Clair couldn't return the gesture without touching Jane with her naked fingertips, but she did press a smile onto her face.

Of course, the question now was who was using Donna like this.

Jane's first horrified thought was to wonder if somehow Blue had something to do with it, but she soothed herself with the knowledge that Paul had been investigating this drug ring long before Jane—and therefore Blue—had turned up. While Blue was probably capable of taking advantage of the situation, it seemed unlikely she'd have gotten that deeply involved so quickly.

Which meant they'd just have to crack through to the center of the drug ring—hopefully sooner rather than later. And while they hadn't had much luck with their attempts so far, two things were now in their favor: they had Clair on their side this time . . .

And now they knew where to start looking.

DONNA'S CARE FACILITY WAS A LOW-SLUNG BRICK BUILDING
on the edge of town. There were no windows along the front,
just a single door with *Cedarcreek Mental Health* etched on the
glass. One sidewalk led the way in, surrounded by hedges so
high they created a natural hallway.

The three of them stood in the parking lot for a while, just
taking it in. They leaned against the sides of Paul's car like they
were on the cover of a nineties alt-rock album.

"So I guess we're doing this." Jane stuffed her hands deep
into the front pocket of her oversized hoodie. The first hard frost
of the season had hit overnight, their breaths pooling in front of
them.

Paul's hand settled on her shoulder. "You don't need to come
with us."

Jane shook him off, with more force than was strictly necessary. "I'm not a *kid*."

"No," he said, his voice coming out as a heavy sigh. "I don't suppose you are."

She looked like one, though, and that was the problem. Paul and Clair could have easily gone in posing as doctors, lunchroom workers, or even government oversight goons—any number of excuses would have gotten them in the door. In some ways, it would be smarter to hang back and let them do it, but Jane couldn't imagine sending Clair in to deal with this situation on her own. So now here they were, and there was only one reason a teenage girl would be getting past the visitor's lounge in a place like this: if her dad checked her in as a patient.

Not exactly ideal, no, but time and resources were limited. They'd kicked around a few other ideas—what if Clair and Paul snuck in first and tried to let Jane in a side door, what if they tried to pass her off as an adult, what if they smuggled her inside in some sort of box or bin or something ("I'm not going to jump out of a cake like a stripper," Jane had said). In the end, simple seemed smartest. Clair had done a fantastic job with Janie's makeup kit, applying dark circles under Jane's eyes, a handful of bruises to her arms and legs in various stages of healing. Jane shook down the extra-long sleeves of her hoodie, and pulled her hair to fall across her face and tangle with the edge of her glasses. She kept her head down, sullen, as they crossed the parking lot.

Inside, staff offices branched off the foyer, while a wide set of steps led down to the reception area. Rust-orange carpet, worn thin, and textured cream wallpaper lined their route.

Jane and Paul went down to the check-in desk while Clair peeled off, making her way for the staff door. A lab coat and a fake badge would take care of half the lie, and Clair's powers could convince anyone of the rest. She would get inside first, snoop through patient records until she found Donna's file, then meet Jane and Paul in Jane's own room once they completed their paperwork. From there, the three of them could find Donna and figure out exactly what the hell was going on with her.

As plans went, it was pretty straightforward, if a little open-ended. She looked back at the stairs as Paul spoke to the receptionist, and then she was following Paul as he carried a clipboard to a small waiting area across from the receptionist's counter.

"So there's a forty-eight-hour window where I can change my mind," Paul said as he settled into one of the chairs, "unless they decide you're an immediate danger to yourself. So don't ham up your performance, got it?" A boxy TV hung, muted, over his head; two people on a soap opera were talking dramatically in someone's hospital room.

"Wait," Jane said, "I'm not just breaking out of here once we're done with Donna?"

"I have to hand over real insurance information to get you into this place, Janie—Jane," Paul corrected. "They know who I am. You think they're going to be okay if you just disappear from their care?"

"No, but . . ." Jane fell silent. She was so used to the way the Heroes operated, with falsified identities and hacks into whatever database they needed. What did she expect a lawyer and his computer-programmer sidekick to do, and on less than a day's notice? Of course Paul was going to have to check in his real daughter to this facility's tender care.

A ribbon of guilt twisted up Jane's insides. Every doubt about the plan wrote itself out, the words traipsing in a merry, circuitous parade around a cross section of Jane's guts. In her mind, she reaches out. A close-up sketch of her hand, falling over the back of Paul's, stilling him as he writes. His cautious face as he looks up, uncertain. Jane's dialogue, already scripted: *Maybe we should find another way.* The subtle relief that would untense his shoulders. A single nod, and then he's returning the clipboard to the reception desk, the silhouette of his back beneath the giant CHECK IN sign.

Instead, Paul's pen scratched across the clipboard. The bottom of the panels fell open, characters tumbling in a heap to the waste bin of Jane's mind. Paul rose, but this time, the real time, he handed the clipboard back with all of Jane's information filled out, his insurance card pinched in the clip.

A nurse showed them to Jane's room. Plain walls, plain sheets. An empty desk. Nothing for Jane to hurt herself on.

"Your dad can bring your stuff to you anytime before the end of the day," the nurse said, eyeing Jane's lack of suitcase.

Jane tossed an accusing look at Paul, who at least had the

decency to flinch at his oversight. He cleared his throat, trying to cover it up with a dry laugh. "Yeah, I uh . . . I wasn't really thinking. Guess I was so focused on getting her here. I'd forget my own head if it wasn't attached."

The nurse offered up a soft smile. "Well, at least you remembered the most important piece."

She left them alone, to settle in and say goodbye. A single awkward beat passed, Jane and Paul trying not to look at each other, and then the door opened up again. Clair breezed through, an extra lab coat over her arm.

"Donna's not in her room," she said as soon as the door was closed. "According to her daily schedule, she's supposed to be in something called 'sensory therapy,' whatever that means. There's no room number for it."

"Guess we'll just need to search," Jane said, glad of something concrete to focus on. "I'll check the patient rooms, you two nose around in the offices and filing rooms."

"Sounds good." Clair handed the extra coat to Paul, who shrugged into it and slid a pair of thick-framed glasses onto his face.

Jane raised an eyebrow. "Really, Clark Kent?"

"What?" Paul said. "They just saw me check you in, they're going to notice if I'm suddenly walking around like a doctor."

"And you think *that's* going to help you?"

"Okay," Clair cut in. "Jane, it's fine. Come on, Paul. I think we should start with the counselors' offices."

"Hey." Jane reached out, giving Clair's gloved hand a tight squeeze in lieu of a kiss. "Love you to pieces."

Clair smiled. "Love you back together."

Jane glanced over. Paul was standing like an anime schoolboy, his hands clasped in front of his chest, eyes replaced by giant hearts as he watched their exchange. Jane jerked her chin. "Please get him out of here."

"Can do," Clair said with a laugh.

Outside, the hallway was clear. They split up, Paul and Clair heading off to the left, Jane peeling off to the right.

She ignored all the bright and easy hallways. The ones with encouraging posters and patient-created artwork taped to the walls. Instead, Jane dove deeper, as far into the underbelly of the operation as she could get. It took some time—without her invisibility, she had to time her sojourn to avoid patients, orderlies, and the occasional doctor. Twice, she was nearly spotted: once near a group therapy room, its session just letting out. And once when a nurse abruptly turned around as if forgetting something.

It was this last one that did it. Jane veered hard to one side, letting herself through the first door she came to. A darkened room in a darkened hallway, guided as if by fate. At first, Jane didn't even pay attention to what she'd found, instead peering back out into the hallway to make sure the nurse continued by. It was only once Jane had sighed a breath of relief and turned around that she realized her fortune.

They'd been looking for a corrupt doctor—now it looks like they'd found him, or at least his handiwork. Donna, stretched out on a metal slab that could not possibly be called a bed, hooked up to a series of IVs and monitors. The situation unfolded as neatly as if it came out of a comic book: an overworked physician looking to line his pockets, using patients not expected to recover as lab rats or muscle. If Jane had written the issue, her character would find a video log on a series of VHS tapes that she could play in the background of the frames as she flipped through paper files, the story unfolding in recapped narrative.

But this was the real world, and even if there was convenient evidence lying around, she wasn't about to take the time to snoop through it. Paul could return later to dig up the details if he wanted—all Jane was concerned about was Donna.

She tapped her earpiece as she hurried to Donna's side. "Guys, I've found her. Take the service elevator to the basement—end of the hall, on your right."

"Thank god." Clair's voice, warm and reassuring in her ear. "We'll be right there."

Jane tapped the earpiece off again. She hovered over Donna, assessing the array of straps lashing her down, the drugs feeding into her system.

It didn't take Jane long to get Donna unhooked from the IV drips. All the Heroes had extremely basic medical training, a week-long course that made Jane continually queasy but that she couldn't complain about now. Jane nudged Donna, testing, though it was still way too early for her to wake up from whatever sedation they'd had her under. That was fine—they didn't exactly have a lot of time, but Jane still had to free Donna from her restraints. Jane's fingers had just undone the first buckle when the door creaked open beside her.

A single line of a speech bubble threaded between the equipment to tap Jane on the shoulder: "I should have known you'd be behind this."

Jane whirled. For a second, she'd been so sure it was Blue's voice that her mind had already slotted her into the open doorway, light from the hall twinkling the stars on her sleeve even in shadow. But then in the next frame the woman steps forward, and an unfamiliar face glowers at Jane. A lab coat over a white blouse and blue pencil skirt. Brown hair in a chignon. And a pair of thick-framed, Clark Kent-style glasses, exactly like Paul's.

It was the glasses that got her. There was something deeply *wrong* with them, like they were mocking her. She couldn't explain it. But she watched them as the woman approached, and she watched her own reflection in them as she raised her hands defensively. Never mind that Jane was currently holding no weapons, that she couldn't conjure up a flash of distracting light or a laser bolt from her palm. There was comfort in the gesture. And maybe, if Jane was really lucky, it would be enough to throw the woman off balance, to make her question if attacking was really the smart move. Because she *was* going to attack—Jane felt this to her core, her superhero's instinct still sharp.

"The thing I can't figure out is *why*," the woman said. She circled the perimeter of the room as Jane turned to keep her in view. The woman jerked her chin toward Donna, stretched out between them. "Is it because there's *one* version of Clair you can't have? Are you really so petty that you need to make her life miserable? Or do you just enjoy fucking over innocent people?"

"Wait, you think I did this?" Jane motioned at the room, at the drip leaching into Donna. "I'm trying to stop this!"

"Don't insult me," the woman said. "Fool the world all you like, Jane Maxwell, but I see through your lies."

"What *lies*?" Jane said. "How do you even know me?"

It seemed an obvious question, and yet it drew the woman up short. "You really don't know?"

"Should I?"

Even as Jane asked it, sketch lines began to superimpose themselves over the woman's face. Unfamiliar shapes at first, just an outline of what was already in front of her; but then, bit by bit, pieces erased and new markings took their place. A color filled in here. A shadow lent shape there. And before Jane knew it, the illusion had broken, and a wholly new image filled the frame in front of her. Spiky pink hair, shorn close to the head. Sharp lines defining the nose, forehead, jaw.

Jane blinked a few times, as if clearing her vision. "So it is you."

A smirk cut across Blue's harsh face. "Took you long enough. You know, for a liar, you're not very good at seeing through other people's projections." She tipped her head. "But I can help with that. Now: stand down, Jane. No one needs to get hurt today."

Jane sidestepped, moving toward the foot of Donna's bench. If she needed to defend Donna, she didn't want any obstructions between them. As if in response, Donna's breathing deepened, a subtle stirring. "You're one to talk about people getting hurt," Jane said, hurrying to cover the shift in Donna's breath. "After you started this whole thing. Chasing me down, body-swapping me into a parallel self."

"A necessary step," Blue said, entirely unapologetic. "Sometimes the truth can only be found when we get a different perspective."

"What *truth*?"

Blue smiled. Cold, calculated, devoid of any true joy. "If you have to ask, you clearly haven't learned your lesson yet."

The door banged open before Jane could dig deeper into Blue's nonsense. Clair and Paul, stumbling to a halt at the unexpected sight in front of them.

It was all the distraction Blue needed. She lunged toward Donna. Jane threw herself forward, but an inset panel rose up: her foot, snagging some sort of cable, a spark kicking off from the toe of her shoe.

The jolt raced up the cord to Donna's table. Donna bucked,

her chest rising, and Jane leaped back, colliding unexpectedly with Blue. The two of them stumbled, a mad scramble, until they slammed into a shelf by the wall.

"Paul, don't just stand there!" Jane shouted. "Get over here and grab her!"

"Are you nuts? I'm not going to attack a *child*!"

"What? She's not—!" Jane blinked, thinking maybe Blue had used her powers to put another disguise back on. But no, there she was, plain as day, and every bit the adult Jane knew.

Blue grinned. "What can I say? People see what they expect to see. With a little encouragement, of course."

"No, but . . . I don't . . ."

"Oh please," Blue said. A surge of strength threw Jane off. "Try to keep up, Jane!"

A groan from the table drew everyone's attention; Donna, beginning to stir.

"Donna!" Clair raced forward, only to be cut off by Blue, who snatched an instrument off the table and slashed it in Clair's direction like a knife.

"Stay back," Blue said, "I won't let you hurt her."

"*Hurt* her? That's my mom!"

Donna roared, as if triggered by something in Clair's voice. Jane turned, the world slowing and stilling for an endless second: Clair, reaching for her mother; Blue, raising the instrument to block Clair's efforts; Donna, eyes wide and wild, muscles flexing hard enough to burst through the fabric of the jumpsuit she'd been wearing.

When time snapped back, it rushed forward all at once, like the back of a rubber band catching up with itself. Donna ripped free of her restraints and barreled toward the door in a heartbeat —Paul just had time to leap forward, knocking Clair off-course so that the instruments Donna sent flying wouldn't collide with her. Blue landed a fast punch at Jane, sending her crashing to the ground, then vaulted across Paul and Clair, hot on Donna's heels, and the instant Paul verified that Clair was all right, he took off as well. For a second, Jane could only lay in a jumble, her head spinning, assorted panels of legs and fists scattered around her.

"Jane!" Clair clambered around the overturned mess of medical equipment to get to her. "Jane, are you all right? What's going on—who *was* that kid?"

Jane shook her head, trying to clear the fuzz. "I . . . it was . . ."

She didn't get a chance to explain. Before she could, the door burst open again, a breathless Paul racing in. He grabbed Jane and Clair by the arms, hauling them up.

"Security's on its way," Paul said, not bothering with pleasantries. "We have to go. Now."

IT WAS EASY ENOUGH TO DODGE SECURITY, BUT unfortunately that didn't get them out of the building. Paul insisted that he still had to check Jane back out, regardless of the hurry.

So they split up: Clair heading back to Paul's office to see if she and Simon could figure out a way to track Donna; Jane and Paul wrapping up the paperwork as quickly as possible and then racing to Central Oak High to find and protect the teenage version of Clair. The emotional residue Donna had left behind was filled with what Clair had called "mama bear rage," and while there was no chance that Donna would ever purposefully hurt the younger Clair, there was no telling what kind of things would happen accidentally in Donna's current mental state. It was better to be proactive and bring Clair somewhere safe until this was over.

At the school, Jane powered through halls that had become familiar again. Her eyes scanned the crowd of students, snapping everyone into individual portraits—the laughing jock, the nervous girl leaning against the lockers, the nerd twirling her hair around her finger, the cheerleader snapping gum. None of them the face she needed. None of them Clair.

But there was one who could help. Leaning over to get a drink from the water fountain, brown hand holding back her box braids.

"Keisha!"

Keisha looked up, wiping her lips with the back of her wrist. "Hey, Jane . . . I thought you were out sick?"

"Bit more complicated than that," Jane said, nearly out of breath. "Listen, where's Clair?"

"I don't know," Keisha said. "She took off with Hailey during lunch."

"Hailey?"

"Yeah." Keisha paused, frowning. "It was really weird. She was out this morning, too, and when she came in, she pulled Clair aside and they had this *really* intense-looking conversation. I don't know what it was about, but they left immediately after."

"But that doesn't make any sense," Jane said, until suddenly, in a horrible instant, it did. Blue's twisted smile flashed through Jane's mind. *People see what they expect to see,* Blue had said. *I'm not going to attack a child!* Paul had said.

"Oh shit. Oh my *fuck*," Jane said. She bent down, tucking her head between her knees at the rush of vertigo that had swept up behind her. Would she have seen through it earlier, if she'd known sooner that Blue was the woman who started this whole mess? "Hailey" had arrived at the same time Jane had, and had been doing her level best to drive a wedge between Jane and Clair from the beginning.

"Jane?" Keisha asked. She rested her hand on Jane's back, patting it as if Jane was choking. "Jane, you okay? What's happening?"

Jane took Keisha's arm, using it to pull herself up. "I have to find Clair." Instinctively, she reached up to tap the comm in her ear, ready to signal the other, adult Clair—only, without the satellites they normally connected to, their earpieces were limited to near-range communication. Jane gritted her teeth.

"Jane!" Paul's voice boomed down the school's hall, sending waves of underclassmen scattering. He was supposed to be waiting in the car, but suddenly Jane didn't care about him breaking their agreement. Jane needed to find Clair, and Paul had his emergency cellphone gripped in his hand.

"Paul, perfect, let me—" Jane started, while Paul said, "It's Simon."

He held the phone out to her, already flipped open.

Jane's mouth went dry. She took the phone, turning away from Paul. "Hello?"

"Jane, turn on the news."

Jane looked up. There was an empty classroom right across the hall, and Jane let herself through, making a beeline for the rickety TV stand in the corner. Jane's high school was pretty underfunded, but one thing they had sprung for were TVs in every classroom—part of some civic engagement initiative, so the students could watch the news during homeroom and learn how to Engage in Discourse and be Well-Adjusted Individuals.

Unfortunately, Jane could not remember whatever convoluted button sequence was required to bring up the right input. She swore, hitting the boxy TV with her remote.

"Give me that," Keisha said. She snatched the remote from Jane before Jane could do any real damage. "GCN?"

Jane nodded, and in an instant the screen was warping to life, a reporter's voice overlaid above shaky footage from outside the mall. Shoppers clustered in the parking lot, a crowd of faces both panicked and curious as they craned to get a better look. The camera was set up on the rooftop level, pointed toward the giant skylight that looked down into the mall.

"—still no indication of the attacker's motive, but authorities have warned the public to keep their distance. So far, only minor injuries have been reported."

Jane raised the phone back to her ear. "I guess we found Donna."

"Guess again," Simon said as the camera crew zoomed in. Down through the skylight, to the central court of the mall, a figure with a trail of stars up her arm darted across view.

Jane's fist tightened around the phone. "Blue? What's she doing attacking a mall?"

"I don't know, but it gets worse," Simon said, his voice tinny over the speaker. "Jane . . . she's got my Clair."

THE MALL PARKING LOT WAS A TANGLED MESS OF reporters, police, and cranky interrupted shoppers. The whole area had been cordoned off, no one in or out until they got a handle on the situation. Paul parked in the corner lot of a local video rental store, which was farther than he wanted to be, but as close as he could manage without someone spotting them getting out of the car. Simon and Clair would meet them at the mall when they could. Meanwhile, Jane and Paul ran down the block, Paul in his proper uniform, Jane in her oversized hoodie— they'd changed with lightning speed in Central Oak's gym locker rooms before leaving.

Surprisingly, the crowd parted with ease for Paul, or rather for Mr. Lightshow. A few people smirked or raised their eyebrows at him, but most actually seemed excited to be in his presence, wishing him well or darting out to shake his hand on the way by.

Jane slid through in his wake, an accompaniment people didn't entirely understand but weren't going to question.

They met up with the person in charge on the upper level of the parking lot, on the mall's roof. A police lieutenant, probably the highest rank available without calling in backup from Grand City itself. As they approached, she visibly sagged with relief. "I take it you heard." She eyed Jane warily, but made no comment.

"Only what's already on the news," Mr. Lightshow said. "What's the real status?"

"Hard to get a clear picture of how it started," the lieutenant said. "But our attacker arrived just after one o'clock. White female, maybe thirties or forties, the damn costume makes it tricky to pin down. We managed to clear the mall pretty quickly, but . . . she's got a hostage. A teenage girl."

Jane's stomach clenched. It wasn't news, but it still landed harder than she expected.

Mr. Lightshow pointedly did not steal a look in Jane's direction as he asked, "Any idea where they are now?"

"Last eyewitness put them in the food court, but we can't get a visual through the skylights. Looks like they moved on, but as to where? That's anyone's guess. We're confident they haven't left the mall, though—we've had all the exits covered."

Mr. Lightshow nodded. "All right. Thanks, Barb, you're doing great. Keep your people at a distance. We'll handle it from here."

"You got it," the lieutenant, Barb apparently, said. She turned away, already speaking into a radio at her shoulder.

They didn't waste time forming a proper plan. For once, they were both operating under a single, shared goal. Jane and Mr. Lightshow cut a line down from the upper parking lot, making a fast track for the entrance between Cloonan's department store and the cinema. It was the door Jane and Clair used the most when they were kids, and Jane tried not to read too much into that as she worked her way past the cops guarding it. She thought they might have a little trouble getting by, but apparently Barb was on top of it, and they were waved through.

The two of them stepped into the empty mall.

There was something *wrong* about a mall with no people in

it. Jane couldn't help feeling like she had walked onto the set of an old cowboy movie, right before a shootout. Her legs caught in profile midstride: one step in her slouchy teenage jeans, the next step in the Old West, cowboy boots kicking up dust.

On the next page, an overhead view, posed so the pathway of the mall shot straight to the horizon. Leaves from a potted plant crowd the left edge of the foreground, enormous this close to the viewer, bits of dead brown chewing a hole near the veins. Jane and Mr. Lightshow, midway down the scene, are caught in a shaft of sun from the skylights.

The image ripped from Jane's mind as the PA system cleared its throat with a crackle and squeal. For a moment everything was quiet, as Jane, Mr. Lightshow, and the mall held their breath. Waiting to see if they'd been caught.

But then, soft as a whisper, a sound began to drift through the empty passages. A voice, rising and falling in a familiar rhythm. It echoed out from PA speakers, but it was also being amplified from somewhere deeper in the bowels of the mall. Jane was too far away to make out more than snatches, but even at this distance, she would recognize that song. A childhood movie classic, Clair had to perform it for a school concert one spring, and Jane had helped her practice for hours and hours and hours.

She and Mr. Lightshow exchanged a glance. A profile shot of her turning her head, and then a streak of motion as someone crashed into her. The force of it tumbled them back, a tangle of limbs spilling through the window of the mall's arcade.

Training curled Jane's body into a protective roll, her mind forcing her unpracticed muscles into position. If she'd wrenched herself like this in her mid-thirties body there would be hell to pay, but this one was light, buoyant, her bones practically rubber as she rolled across the floor. A shower of glass stung at the thick fabric of Jane's hoodie as she bounced right back to her feet.

Blue drew herself up. Neon lights from the arcade splashed colorful shadows across her hardened face as she stalked through the broken glass toward Jane. Now that Jane knew who she was, it was impossible to imagine she'd ever missed it before. Goddammit, Blue had that same star pattern tattooed beneath her ear—it was like she wasn't even trying to hide who she was.

"Not so fast." Mr. Lightshow stepped between them, a pocket-sized mace spray in his hands.

Blue threw her head back, a bark of laughter bursting from her chest. "Oh, please."

She flicked her hand lazily in his direction, fingers spread as if tossing confetti. The same gesture Blue had made the first time she and Jane had gone up against each other, in the moment just before Jane started hallucinating.

"No!" Jane shouted—too late. The mace clattered to the floor, Mr. Lightshow following in its wake. Jane caught him awkwardly, easing him the last few inches to his knees.

Mr. Lightshow's eyes were wide, but he clearly wasn't taking in anything that was happening around him. Not Jane, waving her hand in front of his face. Not their attacker, chuckling smugly to herself. Jane snapped her fingers, just to make sure, and he didn't even flinch. Instead, he was whimpering, whispering to himself, and Jane had no interest in leaning in to hear what he was being tormented with. The hallucination reflected the ugliest part of your soul, Clair had described it when it had happened to them. Jane supposed Paul had plenty of ugly parts of his soul to work with. Even this nicer version of him.

"Come on, fight it," Jane said, jostling his shoulders.

"Oh, he'll be battling that existential crisis for a while," Blue said. "Some people really don't like admitting the truth to themselves."

Jane twisted around to sneer up at Blue. "You're one to talk. Pretending to be my friend and then trapping me here? How about the truth of *that*?"

"You're not my friend!" Blue shouted. She surged forward, a rage-filled attack sending Jane crashing into a nickel-fed prize machine. Released, Mr. Lightshow collapsed to the floor and curled up like a beetle, still blubbering.

Jane scrambled to the side, narrowly avoiding the crash as Blue toppled the prize machine. She stumbled, trying to get back to her feet, but the prize capsules kept slipping beneath her, and she collapsed back onto the grotty carpet.

The pointed tip of a boot caught Jane's shoulder, flipping her like a fish. Her throat closed up as Blue's heeled boot bridged across it. Jane grabbed at the boot, her fingers clawing the leather, but Blue just pressed down harder as she towered over Jane. Tight panel borders boxed in Jane's face, as restrictive as the clamp on her neck.

Blue leaned in. Jane's cheek was turning cold as Blue ran one finger down its length.

"Goodbye, Jane."

Jane opened her mouth to gasp, a plea already knotting up her tongue.

A feedback squeal pierced the air of the arcade, fierce and terrible. Like an air horn blasted too close into a microphone, the volume cranked to maximum. Blue staggered back, clutching her head, and Jane rolled aside, gulping down air.

Before either of them could regain their composure, a figure swept in between them. For a single heartbeat, Jane rejoiced at the sight of a glittery pink-and-green masquerade mask, until she realized the face hidden behind it was far too young to be her teammate—even the mask itself was cheap, feathers and sequins hastily glued to plastic that would crack before the day was done.

"Come on, quick," Keisha said, her teenage voice muffled in Jane's ringing ears. She tugged at Jane's arm, drawing her up to her feet.

"Keisha? What are you *doing* here?"

"Isn't it obvious?" Keisha asked as she and Jane ducked around the seat of a racing game. "We've come to help!"

"We?" Jane started, but the answer came before the question was even fully out of her mouth. Across from her, Tony, Marie, and Cal were crouched behind the prize counter. They were armed with Nerf guns and water soakers, an open bag of knitted Hacky Sacks on the ground between them. They grinned at Jane, and Cal waved, as if this was all some sort of grand version of paintball.

"Well, yeah," Keisha said. "Come on, I saw the news, too. I told the team everything, and we agreed: you shouldn't have to face this alone."

Jane pinched the bridge of her nose, her glasses riding up. "Keisha . . . that is so sweet, but you guys are *kids*. This is serious."

As if to illustrate the point, a scream broke through the arcade.

The scene slowed, ink pinning the vision in place: Blue, her arm raised like a warrior in the middle of a battlefield. Devin's neck is clutched in her grip, his whole body lifted from the floor. A single snap would be enough to wipe him from the issue, his life smudged out as easily as Blue brushing eraser scraps from the page.

Jane leaped up. "No!"

Blue did not seem to hear her. She threw Devin across the arcade.

He hit a bank of game machines. Yellow block letters, running down the edge of the page, bend beneath him: C-R-U-N-C-H, half-obscured, matching the sharp forward fold of his body. Devin collapsed in a heap on the floor.

Blue was advancing before he even finished falling.

"Blue, *STOP!*"

Jane couldn't be sure if Blue actually paused or not. If it happened, it was so small—the frame barely more than a sliver, too narrow to see what was happening inside the lines. In a blink it was over, Blue lifted from her own feet, caught in a whirlwind that sent her tumbling head over heels over head back out into the rest of the mall.

The gust settled, a pair of blue boots touching down.

Joy and relief burst out of Jane as the Heroes of Hope swept in. The real ones this time—a gleam of light split the skin of the world as Granite Girl, Deltaman, and Pixie Beats tumbled through. They landed in artful crouches, a spread of competence and maturity as they instantly surveyed the area.

"Oh my god, I am so glad to see you guys!" Jane ran up, throwing her arms around Granite Girl, the first one of her friends she came to. Even as a teenager, Jane was already taller than her, but the mass of Granite Girl's solid form didn't even rock beneath the tackle.

Granite Girl peeled Jane off. "Yeah, no, we're not hugging."

"Glad you're okay, Captain," Windforce said.

Jane smiled. She would have ruffled his hair if he wasn't wearing his full-faced spandex mask. "You, too."

"Whoa," an awed voice said behind her. The younger Devin edged around Jane. His eyes were wide as he drank in the vibrant blue and crisp white of Windforce's wingsuit, all reaction to crashing into the game machines forgotten in the face of his future.

Windforce tossed an awkward wave, wiggling his spandex-gloved fingers in Devin's direction. "Hi, kid," he said, his voice thrown low into a scratchy growl.

"It's okay," Jane said. "They know."

Windforce looked over sharply. "Is that wise?"

"It happened." Jane was going to explain more, but before she could, Devin launched forward. Instantly, his fingers were on the loose fabric that made up the flaps running like flying-squirrel skin between Windforce's wrists and ankles.

"So, do you *create* the gusts, or just ride on existing wind currents?"

"Erm." Windforce raised his arm, spreading the wing fabric to its fullest extent. "Create it, of a sort. It's more a matter of using the elements already around me, though."

"Weather," Devin said, breathless with reverence. He nodded. "I always did like meteorology."

"I mean, there's a lot of physics that went into this, too," Windforce said. He stretched his arm, the fabric running taut. "The suit's aerodynamics need to be on point, or the whole thing just drags. The fabric alone took ages to design."

"So cool," Devin whispered.

"Okay, okay," Jane cut in, knowing exactly how distracted either version of Devin could get over science talk. She glanced around. The rest of the kids were gathered nearby but not as bold as Devin, while Windforce, Granite Girl, and Pixie Beats waited next to the shimmering tear that still split the world. "What's taking the others so long?"

"Oh, come on, Main Jane," Deltaman said, his voice pouring through the shimmering tear as it parted for him. He paused, hands on hips in a hero pose, as he added, "A guy's gotta know how to make an entrance."

Rip-Shift's laugh followed Deltaman. "Is *that* what you call getting caught up in the zipper on your suit?" he asked as he stepped through.

Deltaman's cheeks flushed. "That was *one time*! One!"

"Sure, man," Rip-Shift said as he turned back to the tear. He held his hand out, as if helping someone from a limo, and an arm covered in a red leather sleeve reached through to accept it.

Captain Lumen had arrived.

It's funny—this wasn't the first time Jane had met a parallel self, nor was it the first time she'd seen someone wear her uniform as their own. And parallel bodies were more or less identical, save for the occasional bit of toning or wear and tear. So it shouldn't have been so strange. But seeing her from outside like this, Janie standing tall in not just the red leather Jane clad herself in, but the very muscles and bones she normally inhabited . . . a lurch squeezed Jane's stomach, some desperate need to reclaim what stood before her. She *knew* that body. She *belonged* in that body, in a way she wasn't prepared for.

It was hard to tell if Janie felt it too. Her body—Jane's body—leaned back in parallel to Jane's helpless step forward.

The younger versions of the Heroes were edging closer now, drawn by the presence of one of their own. "Dude," the younger Tony said as he approached. "Janie, is that you?"

Despite the ingrained reserve in the body she was wearing, a tiny smile broke across Janie's face. "Pretty cool, huh?"

"Hell yeah," Tony breathed.

"Yeah, whatever, don't get used to it," Jane said. She turned back to Granite Girl. "Clair told me you were working on a way to swap us back. *Please* tell me you brought it with you."

"Of course."

"Good." She grabbed Janie's elbow, leading her toward the rest of the mall. "Because we're dealing with a hostage situation, and at the moment all I've got for backup is *Paul*"—she motioned at the dazed huddle that was Mr. Lightshow, just barely starting to come back to himself—"and he's not half the superhero I am."

"Wait, Dad?" Janie scribbled confusion across Jane's real face. "He . . . he has superpowers, too?"

"More like instead, but yeah," Jane said. "There's been some developments while you've been gone."

✱　✱　✱

INSTEAD?

The word, and its implications, tumbled around Janie's head in an endless spin cycle. *Instead.* Such a hollow concept, a vacuum where Janie's powers were supposed to be. All she could think of were the times the Heroes kept telling her they weren't *actually* a picture of her future—that there were no guarantees *Janie's* life would shape itself even remotely like *Jane's* had. At the time, Janie thought she'd understood that, but now in the face of it, the idea of losing her powers gutted her. Instinctively, a tiny flare of light escaped Janie's borrowed fingertips, a flash of panic before she could stop it.

All Janie could do was stand there, stunned by the realizations. But to Jane, apparently, none of this was a concern. She went over to a man curled up by the door and was talking to him softly, helping him to his feet.

Janie sucked in a breath. His eyes were hidden behind a glittering white mask, but there was no hiding his identity from Janie. Mr. Lightshow, their suburb's very own superhero, really *was* her dad, the real Paul Maxwell. Sure, his costume was the most ridiculous thing ever, but that didn't matter right now.

She ran up to him without hesitation. Her dad caught her in a hug, grunting under the weight of her adult body.

"Oh thank god," he whispered into her hair. "I've missed you, munchkin."

"Missed you too, Dad."

The older Jane turned away sharply. She started walking, and the rest of them—Janie's friends, here in costume like mini Heroes themselves; the actual Heroes; and even Janie and her dad, grabbing hands—all fell into line behind Jane by some unspoken magnetic pull that the younger Janie tried not to be jealous of.

"Okay, but I don't understand," Janie said, hurrying to keep up as Jane led the group of them down the length of the mall. Faint music, like someone singing, played in the background as Janie stole an uncomfortable glance at her dad. "I mean . . . just because my dad's somehow a superhero, like, that doesn't mean I *won't* be. One day. When I'm supposed to get these powers or whatever."

Jane turned around, striding backward as she assessed Janie with a look that was clearly not impressed.

Truth is, facing her for real, *Janie* wasn't sure she was impressed by Jane, either. She thought she would be. The grown-up version of herself, the woman whose shadow she'd been living under for the last two weeks. The superhero, the self-made businesswoman, the out-and-proud lesbian who'd managed to steal Clair's heart. How could she *not* impress?

Yet looking at Jane now, she seemed . . . small. And not just because she was currently in the body of a teenager. As she filled in the other Heroes on the situation—apparently, her missing business partner had somehow turned villain and landed on this Earth as well, which, okay, Janie supposed that made sense in a comic book sort of way—there was something petty and bitter in the way Jane was describing it. It didn't sound at all like Janie, even a future Janie.

"But why would Blue have turned against you in the first place?" Windforce asked. "I thought you two were BFFs."

"I wish I knew." Jane stuffed her hands deep into the pockets of her jeans (Janie's least favorite pair), shoulders curling forward as if wanting to hide herself. "It doesn't make sense, okay? She was posing as a teenager, trying to make sure Clair and I don't get together, I guess—"

"*What?*"

"—but before I could get Clair somewhere safe, they were already gone, and now Blue's got her singing by the escalators where they usually set up the Santa display."

A wash of vertigo swallowed Janie as she tripped to a halt. Heat flooded her cheeks, turning them as red as her Captain Lumen uniform. It was one thing for Janie to have claimed her identity in front of people who didn't know her—the anonymity of the mask had helped, like posting secrets under a screen name. But to have Jane drop the news of it in front of her childhood friends like that, so casual, like it was *nothing* . . .

It was not nothing. And while this wasn't news to the Heroes themselves, it certainly would be to their younger counterparts. Not to mention Janie's *dad*. Janie stood rooted in her spot, ready to die. She fixedly did *not* meet her dad's eyes, did *not* turn to look at her friends, gathered around the periphery of the adults, though she did not kid herself into thinking they weren't all staring at her. How could they not be?

A heavy hand settled on Janie's shoulder, and she did not need to see the white of his glove to know it was her father. He squeezed, just enough pressure to be reassuring. "I love you," her dad whispered to her. "I'm proud of you. Always."

Janie gave a shaky nod. There was more they'd need to discuss, of course, but at least for now this was one person Janie didn't need to worry about in the immediate aftermath.

In the meantime, the Heroes kept turning the situation over between them. Janie forced her knees to unlock as she hurried to catch up.

"Singing?" one of the adult Heroes was asking, their voice muffled and ballooned as if Janie's ears were full of water. "Why's she got Clair singing?"

"Hell if I know," Jane said. "Maybe Blue thought it would be funny."

"There's got to be more to it than that."

Jane's response, prickly and sharp, cut through the haze and snapped Janie's world back into focus.

"Yeah, well, if there is it's beyond me, but we don't exactly see eye to eye these days. Your guess is probably better than mine."

Janie's eyes jumped up as her fingers curled into fists. Here Clair was, in some kind of unknown danger, and what, Jane didn't even *care*? What kind of Jane *was* this?

But just as Janie took a breath to yell at her older self about it, the younger version of Cal jogged forward, breaking into the circle of adults.

"Hold up, can we backtrack a second? You said this Blue person was trying to make sure Janie and Clair don't get *together*?" A waggle crossed his eyebrows, sending Janie's cheeks an even deeper crimson. "You mean, like—"

Keisha swatted his shoulder from behind, shutting down his question. "Not now."

Devin, meanwhile, punched Tony on the arm. "I told you!"

"Ow," Tony muttered, rubbing the spot Devin had hit.

Cal grinned. "So hot."

"No, shut up, I'm confused," Tony said, "I thought you were upset that Jane dumped you."

Janie blinked. Her blotchy cheeks suddenly turned cold. "She what?"

"I didn't dump—" the older Jane started, but Cal was already waving her off.

"Nah, man," Cal said, "that was before I knew she was into chicks. Now it all makes sense."

Marie snorted. "Yeah, because *that's* the only reason a girl wouldn't like you."

Cal ran his hands back through his hair. "It's not my fault I'm the real deal, baby."

"Oh my god," Deltaman cut in, a pained expression on his grown-up face. "I don't really sound like that, do I?"

"Yes," Jane said in an instant, a sentiment that was quickly chorused by the rest of the adults.

"Yeah, dude."

"Pretty much exactly, yes."

Windforce laid a hand on Deltaman's shoulder. "Sorry, bro."

All Janie could do was stare. What had she missed while she'd been away? And more importantly: what else had Jane managed to screw up? Janie couldn't even imagine.

And yet, this distraction with Cal seemed to be all anyone needed for their attention to move on from Janie and whatever personal revelations her friends had just learned about her. Janie took a shaky breath, trying to calm her racing heart. It was . . . fine. Somehow, impossibly, they were fine.

"All right, let's fix this," Jane said, and Janie's attention snapped back. The older Jane rolled out her borrowed teenage shoulders. "God, I can't wait to be back in my own body."

"I can only imagine the horror," Granite Girl said, shooting a fast look at her counterpart, who tipped her head back and rolled her eyes. Granite Girl ignored it, fishing the finished device from a deep pocket of her cargo pants.

Janie had seen it, of course, before leaving headquarters— Granite Girl had stayed up all night after they'd apprehended Lester, making the final adjustments. A pair of straps that had probably been repurposed from headlamps, metal plates and wires worked into the fabric in a variety of vaguely terrifying, mad-scientist sorts of ways. Strung between them was the weird crystal from Marie's lab, rigged up and pulsating like an exposed heart.

Granite Girl handed one of the head straps to the older Jane, who wrinkled her nose as she accepted it. "Not one of your more elegant designs."

"You want pretty, or you want functional?" Granite Girl snapped.

"I'm not complaining," Jane said. She slid the fabric harness onto her head, unquestioning, so ready to take back everything Janie had been learning to live in.

Janie's chest seized. Granite Girl held out the matching harness. Janie knew she was supposed to take it. That's what they always expected of her: follow their orders, be the good girl, respect her elders. It didn't matter what she wanted. She was always just a placeholder to them.

The same could not be said for Jane. Jane, who'd gone crashing through Janie's life, spilling her secrets, turning her friends into tiny superheroes, ruining her chances with Clair—god, what must Clair think of Janie now, after two weeks of this imposter wrecking havoc on their friendship?

"Janie?" Jane said now. Snippish, impatient. In charge, without anyone ever having said so. Jane grabbed the harness from Granite Girl's hands and shoved it at Janie. "Put the damn thing on and let's get this over with."

Janie stepped back. She looked down at the harness, caught in her hands despite herself. A tether of cables strung her to Jane, this self that was both older and younger at the same time. This self she didn't even recognize. What made her somehow magically the leader? Who said she even had to be?

Before she could question it, Janie tossed the harness back. Jane scrambled, catching it before it fell. "What the hell—?"

"No."

JANE SHOOK HER HEAD AS IF TRYING TO CLEAR WATER
from her ears. Surely she had misheard. "No? What do you mean
'no'?"

Janie squared her shoulders, planting her hands on her hips
in a perfect mimic of Captain Lumen. "I mean no. I won't switch
back with you."

Okay, that time there was no room for misunderstanding.

Jane took a threatening step forward. "Listen, you little
brat—"

"Whoa, whoa, Jane," Rip-Shift said. He grabbed Jane by the
shoulders, stilling her.

Jane stepped back, raising her free hand to show she wasn't a
threat. And at the moment, it was true. *Janie* held the powers of
Jane's body. That was the problem. Rage coursed through Jane,
raw and unchanneled, what felt like enough to fuel an entire city.

Paul tossed Jane a quick look, then stepped up to his other daughter—his real daughter. He lowered his voice, not enough that the others couldn't hear him but soft enough to soothe a temper tantrum.

"Janie, it's okay," Paul said. "There's nothing to be afraid of. I'm sure Jane's people tested it, or they wouldn't have brought it with her."

Granite Girl scratched the back of her neck. "I mean . . . it's powered by a single-use Adephyte crystal, so I wouldn't go so far as to say *tested*—"

"Not helping," Jane snarled, and Granite Girl actually shut up for once.

Janie shook her head. "Guys, that's not it. I'm not *afraid*. Well—like, yeah, sure, I guess I am, a little, but that's not why I won't do it."

"I'm not listening to this." Jane thrust the other harness forward. "Granite Girl, put this on her."

"Don't you dare," Janie said, and to Jane's infinite frustration, Granite Girl actually hesitated. Janie threw her arms wide, the red Captain Lumen suit gleaming in the light of the mall. "Look at this mess! My dad running around with superpowers? My best friend kidnapped? I didn't leave things like this. You've ruined *everything*, and now you expect me to just step in and clean up your mess? No offense," she added quickly to Paul, who waved it off.

The smallest flinch of guilt struck Jane, but she barreled past it. "You'll manage," she said. In fact, Janie seemed like the best person to clean up Jane's "messes," as she'd put it, but Jane wasn't even going to get into that argument.

It seemed Janie wasn't, either. She crossed her arms over her chest, unmoved. "Why should I? No one ever asked me if I wanted it back. And even if I did . . . I'm starting to build a *life* for myself, where I am now."

"*My* life," Jane snapped. "You have no fucking right to steal it."

"I didn't steal anything. I was there, trying my best to hold things together for you, while you just crashed through mine with no regards for how it would affect anyone else.

And you're calling me selfish?" Janie scoffed. "I'm not the one acting like a child here."

Jane flapped her hand, dismissing Janie's arguments rather than countering them. She turned to Granite Girl and the other adults, the only *reasonable* people here at the moment. "Look, why are we even arguing this? I don't give a shit what she wants. Someone slap this on her, and let's just get this done."

"I'm not sure forcing it without her consent is wise," Granite Girl said.

"Are you fucking kidding me right now? What about *my* consent? I don't consent to stay in this pathetic teenage body!"

"Not the point, Captain."

"Isn't it?" Jane said. "What part of 'it's my life, and I want it back' is so hard to understand?"

"I'm not saying you're not in the right," Granite Girl said, cutting a nasty look in Janie's direction. "I just don't know that it would be safe to perform the procedure on an unwilling mind."

"Bullshit," Jane said. "I wasn't willing when it was done to me in the first place."

"Yes, but you didn't know it was even a possibility, so your brain wasn't actively against it, either. And besides," Granite Girl said, talking over Jane's objections, "Blue was using superpowers —this is a different science. We're essentially just going to blank the brain, and allow it to come back to itself. You'll be mentally linked, so your 'essence,' or whatever you want to call it, should flow back where it belongs. But not if it doesn't want to go."

"Oh, it'll go, all right. If I have to reach in there and—"

The crackle of the comm in Jane's ear cut her off. Clair's staticky voice, breaking in and out as she hovered on the edge of range. "Jane, can you hear me?"

Jane swallowed down her annoyance. She tapped her earpiece. "I'm here. And so is the rest of the team."

A rush of air, like a grunt, passed over the comm link. "Thank god. Tell them to get ready—we're going to need all the help we can get."

"What do you—?"

"We found Donna," Clair said. "She's drugged out of her

mind and rampaging through town. But Jane, listen: she saw the news footage in a shop window. She's coming for Clair."

THERE WASN'T TIME TO ARGUE. THE REST OF THE Heroes immediately huddled around Jane, folding her into their midst until Janie and her younger friends found themselves on the outskirts. Janie's pride bristled, but she supposed she'd done this to herself.

In truth, even Janie was surprised by her refusal to switch back. It hadn't been planned. She'd come here fully intending to return to her old life, but suddenly, seeing the mess Jane had made in just a few short weeks . . . and then to look around, and know what she could have instead?

It was a cowardly reaction. Janie knew this, just like she knew deep down that she'd probably, eventually, need to cave on the issue. That didn't mean she was prepared to do it yet.

"Okay, good," Jane said finally, glancing up at Janie and the other teenage Heroes. "Let's go."

For a second, Janie had the irrational fear that Jane was reacting to Janie's thoughts, but when she looked up, she found the adult team was already moving on—Janie's team, ready to leave her—and suddenly that rage surged back again.

"Wait!" Janie called, and to her relief, they did. "What about the rest of us?"

Jane's eyes narrowed, already dismissive. "What about you?"

"You're not leaving us." Janie motioned around them. Keisha and Devin, already standing tall by Janie's side, Tony and Cal and Marie waiting nearby.

"Janie," Jane sighed. "You're *kids*—"

"Don't even start," Janie snapped. "I've been dealing with that crap from the rest of the Heroes for ages now, and I did not come all this way to listen to you demean me again. I already proved myself to your team. They can prove themselves, too."

Jane's eyebrows went up. A twisted, skeptical look splashed over the face Janie knew from her own reflections. The older Jane turned, glancing at the rest of her team—no doubt expecting them to back her up on this, to make the same tired arguments they would have made a few days ago. Moment of truth, then. Now they'd all find out how far Janie had managed to convince them of her status as a true and proper Hero.

"I mean . . . surprisingly, she was pretty solid in the field," Rip-Shift said finally. "Not perfect, but . . . I don't know, I'm inclined to let them help. So long as we can keep them out of the worst of it."

Janie and Jane sucked in twinned breaths. Well. That wasn't exactly the ringing endorsement Janie had hoped for, but she'd take it.

"You can't be serious," Jane said.

"At the very least," Pixie Beats said, "they can work on clearing the crowds from the parking lot. I don't like how many gawkers we're attracting. They make a pretty tempting target, if Blue decides to attack."

There. Surely that had to convince them. Janie tossed Pixie Beats a grateful smile, but Jane was already shaking her head.

"No. I don't care. Maybe my powers are making her slightly useful, but the rest of them have got nothing. I won't have that on my conscience. You," she said, turning back to Janie. The older Jane straightened her spine, rising as tall as her borrowed teenage body would allow. No doubt she was trying to look intimidating, though it wasn't as effective as she'd hoped. "You want to prove yourself? Stop being childish and take your friends to safety while the rest of us sort this shit out."

"But—!"

"The discussion is over. Go. We'll deal with the rest after I've contained this."

Janie looked to the other Heroes, plaintive. But even she could see she wasn't going to win this one. For all the effort she'd put in, all the respect she'd managed to scrape together for herself handling Lester, at the end of the day it was clear *Jane* would always be their one true leader.

They were already turning away, already following her into battle. Even in her smaller, borrowed bones, the older Jane was still somehow more of a Hero in their eyes than Janie would ever be.

So Janie hung back. Fists balled, heart raging, but . . . waiting.

She let the Heroes run off without her, chasing the smaller, weaker version of herself. Then she turned back to the others, still gathered around her.

"So . . . we're not *really* going to just run away and hide, right?" Marie asked.

Janie grinned. A surge of warmth coursed through her as she took in the sight of them. Her real friends, not the older, grizzled versions they might one day become. She didn't care what those adults thought—she knew they were capable.

"Oh heck no," Janie said. "Let's do this."

"ALL RIGHT, HERE'S THE PLAN," JANE SAID. **"LIGHTSHOW,** Deltaman, and Pixie, secure the perimeter of the central court— we don't know when Blue will turn up again, but you can be sure she's not done with Clair yet. Rip, Granite, and Windforce, head outside and meet up with Mindsight and Simon."

Jane did not wait for her team to acknowledge this. She turned away, stepping up to the edge of the balcony that oversaw the central court. She didn't think she could look at her team right now—especially Granite Girl.

Unfortunately, Granite Girl did not seem to feel the same way. She reached out. "Captain—"

"There's no time to waste," Jane said, twisting away.

Jane took a steadying breath. One thing at a time. It helped to have something concrete to focus on: defensive strategies, assignments to the team. These were patterns Jane had become intimately familiar with over the last few years, and they soothed her now the way comics once did. Dealing with an enraged, superpowered Donna wasn't exactly going to be fun without her powers, but it was what Jane had at the moment. Later, after they'd won, she could take both Granite Girl and Janie aside and give them the talking-to they rightly deserved.

"Okay, so that's the rest of us," Deltaman said. "What about you?"

Jane pushed the hood of her sweatshirt down and pulled out her scrunchie, shaking her hair free of its ponytail. Below, the younger version of Clair sang on, oblivious. The song had already looped a few times now, and her voice was starting to shake from exhaustion, but she clung to both her task and her microphone with a desperation Jane couldn't read. So far, no sign of either Blue or Donna, and so that left only one thing to do.

"I'm going to rescue her," Jane said. She turned away, stalking toward the escalators before anyone could object.

It was a slow, exposed ride to the ground floor. Jane kept her attention on Clair, trusting her team to provide cover from an attack. Clair's back was to Jane as she approached, but somehow she must have known what was coming, because when Jane finally did reach her, touching the back of her shoulder, Clair didn't even startle as she turned around.

She brought the microphone with her, the song drawing out of her with hardly a falter. Her eyes widened at the sight of Jane, confusion at odds with the big dreams and longing of the lyrics.

Jane reached for the microphone. "Come on, we've got to go."

Clair reared back, shaking her head furiously. She still would not stop singing—even as Jane made a second attempt for the microphone, even as Clair dodged Jane's grip.

"Clair, come on, this isn't funny."

Clair's face twisted up in frustration. And then, without breaking stride, the lyrics shifted. The same tune that had been ingrained in Jane since childhood, unfamiliar words slapped in.

"Ja-nie you shouuuuld-n't be in the maall riiight noooow. / It isn't saafe for you, trust meee."

"What the . . . ?" Jane started as, message over, Clair switched back to the regular lyrics. "Are you serious right now? Clair, you're in danger."

Another quick shake of Clair's head. *"No you do not . . . un-der-stand . . . / I have to save my mom."*

"Wait, you know about that?"

"Of course / I know / But how do you know?"

"Oh, for fuck's sake!" Jane ripped the microphone from Clair's grip. "We're not in a musical. This is serious, Clair."

"No duh—" Clair started in song, then paused and cleared her creaky throat. "Yeah, no duh it's serious, why else would I have been standing there singing *Beauty and the Beast* for the last half hour? Now give me back the mic."

"No." Jane threw it across the open courtyard. It landed with a squeal and two soft *thumps* somewhere in a cluster of fake potted plants. She seized Clair's hand. "We have to go, now, before your kidnapper comes back."

"Kidnapper?" Clair said, incredulous. "Janie, I wasn't *kidnapped*! She's the only woman who's been honest with me about what's really going on with Donna. Like, I always knew 'rehab' was a load of crap, but I never would have guessed superpowers."

Jane supposed she shouldn't be surprised. Telling the truth about Donna was a pretty good way to get Clair to trust Blue, after all—and in a world that already contained superheroes, it probably wasn't as difficult for this Clair to accept as it would be otherwise.

Still, that didn't take away from the danger they were in—or the urgency.

"Listen, I'm glad you know about Donna, I really am, but this woman isn't who you think she is. She's a liar, and—"

"Funny," Clair said. She took a single step back, tugging free from Jane. Crossed her arms. "That's what she said about you."

Shit. The word sat in a narrative box, hovering in the upper-right corner of the frame.

"Where's my friend?" Clair asked, her dialogue heavily shaded. "Where's the *real* Janie Maxwell? What did you do with her?"

"I didn't do anyth—"

"Do you see it now, Jane?" Blue said, her voice echoing down from somewhere above. "The damage you create, in everything you touch?"

"What are you *talking* about?" Jane spun around, looking at the upper levels, the arched skylight far beyond them. She shouted at the ceiling, "Blue, this is absurd. I've done *nothing* to you!"

"Killing my best friend is *nothing*?" Blue asked, her voice cracking through the mall like thunder. "Stealing her whole identity is *nothing*?"

Jane rocked back. "That's . . . that's not what happened," she said. "I never killed anybody. Jane—your Jane—she's alive, it's just . . ."

"Save your speeches. I know the truth. Unlike you, there are some people out there willing to be honest."

Like who? Jane wanted to ask, but it wasn't the time. "I'm sorry," she said instead. "I wanted to tell you the truth."

"You would say that—now that you've been caught. Liars are often remorseful when they can't lie anymore."

Jane threw her hands up. "How am I supposed to argue with that? Blue, I'm trying to accept fault here, but no matter what I say, you spin it into further 'proof' that I'm manipulating you. Come on. You're better than this."

"Don't you dare try to dodge the blame!" Blue shouted. "I gave you *more* than enough chances to prove you could be honest with someone. Instead you ignored Clair for over a *week*."

"She's a child! I couldn't tell her!"

"It's always something."

"For fuck's sake," Jane muttered. She looked back up, trying to find where Blue was hidden. If they could just *talk*—properly talk—Jane knew she could resolve this.

They didn't get the chance. Before Jane could find Blue, a CRASH split the page gutters as, one floor above them, Granite Girl burst through a freshly made hole in the wall.

"Look out!" Granite Girl yelled, but there was no need. In an instant, a pair of fists were punching the hole wider, and in a cloud of plaster, the feral, tangled-haired outline of Donna burst in like the Kool-Aid Man. She blinked for a second in the bright light of the mall, the light from the sunroof casting angel-beams through the dust.

"She's here," Blue said. She turned back to Clair. "Quickly!"

"On it," Clair said. It took only two steps for her to return to her spot on the makeshift stage. She looked to the ceiling, bursting into song again at the top of her lungs, lack of microphone be damned.

Something about this whole situation was very, very wrong.

"Blue, what are you doing?" Jane asked.

"Like I'd tell you." Blue raced off, leaving Clair alone and exposed, pouring her heart into a solo rendition of an ensemble number.

A crash from above drew Jane's attention. Donna had Granite

Girl hefted under her arm like a sack of flour, and was ripping a bench out of the floor. The powers she'd gained from falling into an experimental vat all those years ago had given her increased strength and speed, pumping up her muscles, and Jane watched as she spun the loose bench like a discus. It launched over the top of the central court, narrowly avoiding Lightshow. The bench landed against a wide pillar with a harrowing *crash*, a spiderweb of cracks splitting the skin of the marble post.

"Time to go," Jane said. She raced back to Clair, scooping her gangly teenage body into a bridal carry in one fast sweep.

"Hey!" Clair shouted, her song abandoned as scattered notes fallen to the floor. "Put me down!"

"Not a chance." Jane started to run. If she was lucky, she'd be able to get across the central court and out the exit before anyone spotted them.

For whatever reason, though, Clair wasn't having it. She bucked and kicked at Jane, squirming in an attempt to get free. Jane stumbled, dropping Clair's legs, but managed to clamp her arms tighter around Clair's torso just as Clair shouted, "Donna!"

A child's cry for her mother. Even Jane could recognize the pitch of it, wailing through the mall. It threw her off for just a second, her grip tightening as she said, "What do you think you're *doing*?"

Clair ignored the question. She stomped at Jane's foot. "Donna! Help!"

Donna's roar broke through the mall, fierce and maternal. Jane clamped her hand over Clair's mouth. "Be *quiet*, you idiot!"

The admonishment came too late.

A splash page caught Donna's werewolf-like leap. Hungry eyes, claw-like fingers curled at the reader, teeth flashing as she set her sights. And on the opposite side of the spread, Jane and Clair, huddled as small as mice against the enormous empty backdrop of the mall's entrance hall. There was no way they were getting away in time.

But with the flick of a page, Blue stepped between them. Her back to Jane and Clair like a shield, her elbow raised in a way

Jane now recognized as the beginning of the gesture that would mentally "whammy" her opponent with hallucinations of their own inner ugliness.

Jane almost didn't see the thin lines snaking along the bottom of the frame, the first stirring of wind tangled up around Blue's feet.

"Stop!" Jane shouted, too late.

In the moment, she didn't really know who she was trying to stop: Donna, rampaging forward; Blue, ready to strike out; Windforce, doing his best to protect them against a threat they still didn't entirely understand. But Jane was starting to think maybe—just maybe—she was beginning to.

The thought did her no good. The gust caught Blue by the ankles, flipping her before she could finish tossing her power in Donna's direction.

Donna hit the ground with a crash to rumble the tile beneath Jane's feet. Jane spun, flinging Clair wildly in Windforce's direction and watching as he gusted her over to Lightshow, who lifted her as easily as putting a child to bed. Jane tapped her earpiece as she lunged to avoid the oncoming force of Donna's fists.

"Granite, Pixie, get over here! You've got to draw Donna out of the mall!"

A messy huff ruffled the miniature speaker. "What do you think we're trying to do?" Granite Girl said.

Jane ignored the reproach. Donna was coming for her again, and Jane barely ducked in time. A heavy *whoosh* cut the air above Jane's head as Donna's arm, strong as a baseball bat, struck out.

Blue, meanwhile, had also sprung back to her feet. "Don't listen to her, you fools!" she shouted at the rest of the Heroes. "That's not the real Captain Lumen!"

"Yes," Jane said sternly. "I am. Far more than your old Jane could have ever been. My team knows that, even if you don't."

Blue's nose wrinkled into a sneer. "So you've already corrupted them."

"No," Mindsight said, stepping forward, slightly out of breath from racing to join them. "She didn't. *Your* Jane's the corrupt one. She went rogue, rebranded herself as UltraViolet. My Jane only stepped in to fill the void yours left behind."

"Liar!" Blue shouted.

Mindsight laughed. "I thought Jane was the liar? What, you're going to accuse all of us now? How does that make sense?"

"Please, Blue," Jane cut in. "I promise, I haven't corrupted anybody. I'm not the bad—"

She didn't get the chance to finish. Blue had spotted her opening, and she wasn't wasting it. With one deft twist of her body she'd pulled back, arm raised and ready.

"No, don't!" Jane shouted, but it did no good. In an instant, Blue had thrown a hallucination in Donna's direction.

Donna stumbled back. A scream tore from her chest, enraged and unchained, more animal than human.

"You idiot!" Jane called, but Blue was ignoring her, already fleeing. And to think, for one wild second, Jane had actually toyed with the idea that Blue was trying to do some *good* here, in her own, twisted way. Jane never should have let her guard down. Jane grabbed Mindsight's hand, the two of them running to the side. "I'm so glad to see you," Jane said, once they'd reached cover.

Mindsight grinned. "Same. Simon's outside, trying to convince the police that we can handle Donna on our own, but I figured you could use some help in here."

"Could we ever."

When a speech bubble reached out from behind them, tapping Jane on the shoulder, she shouldn't have been surprised. Still, she gritted her teeth in annoyance, knowing who it was before she'd even finished speaking.

"Good thing we're here, then."

JANIE WATCHED IN SATISFACTION AS THE OLDER JANE whirled around in surprise, Mindsight following suit. Or possibly (more likely) as Jane whirled around in annoyance, but Janie would still take the fact that she'd managed to catch her off guard as a win. What used to be Janie's own eyes narrowed.

"I told you to get out of here."

"And I told *you* we could help."

Jane threw her head back in exasperation. "Janie . . ."

"We have a plan," Janie said. "I know you think we can't do this, but watch."

Janie pointed as her team rushed in. Strung between them were a series of jump ropes knotted end to end. A more juvenile sight than Janie wanted, but it was all they could find in a pinch—there was no hardware store in the mall, so they'd raided a sporting goods store, and it was either this or a whole crapload of shoelaces.

They hadn't seen what all the fuss was about, really. So Clair's mom was running loose, clearly not herself. The girls of the group had babysat enough toddlers to understand a temper tantrum when they saw it, and while hog-tying their charges was not typically an option, there was a certain satisfaction in being able to do that here.

"Janie, no," Mindsight said as she and Jane watched the group.

The older Jane clutched Janie's wrist. "This'll never work—call them off!"

Such adult overreactions. Janie rolled her eyes, already pulling her wrist free. In front of them, her team had nearly surrounded Donna and were doing *fine*—

Until they weren't. Donna swung her fist out just as they were beginning to close in, and the force of it sent Tony flying. The rope snapped taut, still clutched in each of their hands, dragging the whole crew to tumble in a scattered mess, like toys knocked from a highchair tray.

It was all the "proof" the older Jane needed. She swept her arm toward the scene. "You call *this* help?" she asked as Mindsight took off in the direction of their friends.

Janie gritted her teeth. "Okay, yeah, that wasn't great—but we can do better!"

"Do better by protecting your team," Jane said. "Janie, they're going to get crushed out here. You have to see that."

"Yeah, but—"

"No. You're their *captain*. Your first job is to keep them safe."

Janie's cheeks heated. She did not want to agree, but even as righteous indignation rose up within her, a cold thread of fear made her wonder if Jane was right.

It didn't matter if she agreed. With a roar to shake the mall, Donna leaped up, impossibly high, so high she was able to land on the upper level like it was nothing. She ripped up a pair of gumball machines from in front of a candy store, a rainbow of sweets flying out as she lifted them overhead, then tossed them back down to the central court.

Janie's team managed to dodge them, but only just, the metal posts barely missing their heads and cracking the floor tiles where they landed. With a painful grimace, Janie knew she'd lost this argument.

"Guys, fall back!" Janie shouted, but either her friends didn't hear, or they didn't care. Tony and Cal were already racing up the escalators, while Marie and Keisha and Devin gathered up the string of jump ropes between them. Mindsight was yelling at them, trying to get the ropes away, but not making much progress.

Tony was the first to reach the upper level. He raised his Nerf gun as Donna turned, her hungry eyes narrowing in.

Janie couldn't see the tear that appeared beneath him, not from this angle—but her light-sensitive eyes could see the glow emitting from it, splashing up his body. It appeared for only an instant before he yelped and fell through, tumbling out onto the stage near the others. "Not fair!" he yelled, though Janie may have been the only one to pay attention to his protest. Donna surged forward, perhaps intent on chasing him straight through the tear, but it sealed up before she got there, and she slid, belly-style, across the slick mall flooring.

Another tear opened up above her, Rip-Shift stomping down to land by her face. His black Matrix coat fluttered behind him as he prowled a wide perimeter around Donna, who snarled and drew herself into a crouch.

It was hard to say, with all this drama, exactly what made Janie look across the mall just then. A flutter of color, or some sound she couldn't remember hearing. Janie turned, looking from one side of the open gap above her to the other, in time to see a woman step out from a shoe store across from Donna and Rip-Shift. A suit of shimmering blue and pink, a spray of stars up her sleeve. She was staring across at the fight, a delighted smirk on her face.

"Jane?" Janie asked, something wary in her voice. She reached behind her, trying to get her older self's attention, as the woman in the shimmery suit reached up and snapped her fingers.

A yelp made Janie look back. Rip-Shift had staggered, clutching his head as if he was dizzy or sick. He stepped back, nearly tripping over his own feet, only for a colorful burst to bloom up beside him as Pixie Beats caught him by the shoulders. "Yo, you okay?" she asked.

"Yeah, I—" Rip-Shift cut himself off. He coughed, clearing his throat. Tried again. "I'm fi—what the heck?" He raised his hands, and a tear split the world just in front of him. Rip-Shift yelped again, leaping back from it.

Pixie Beats tapped her earpiece. "Guys, something's wrong with Rip, I don't . . . he's . . ." But then she, too, staggered forward and clutched her head.

"Oh, shit," the older Jane said, twisting up to look for the glittery woman. "She's swapping them."

Janie's eyes swept the mall, instinctively seeking out the younger Tony to confirm this. But what she spotted was Clair— the real Clair, her gorgeous, youthful face set as she raced up the escalator.

Janie took off like a shot. The older Jane shouted after her, but Janie ignored it. To heck with what that bossy know-it-all thought Janie should do. If she truly knew anything, understood anything, it's that Janie would never stand by while Clair was in trouble.

"Donna!" Clair shouted as soon as she reached the top.

At the sound of Clair's voice, Donna whirled. Too quickly— her arm flailed out from the momentum of her spin, colliding with Clair with enough force to lift her off her feet.

They say that time slows down in the moment just before an accident. Janie, tucked safe in her boring suburban upbringing, had never had cause to experience this before. Even the danger she'd seen since slipping into Captain Lumen's shoes had never felt quite like this, this absolute refusal to admit what she was seeing was real. Because it couldn't be real. Everything about this situation was as absurd as a comic book, and look: for just an instant, Janie could have sworn it was, the silhouette of Clair hovering above Janie like a five-point star, nothing but shading and outlines and flat colors. Nothing to fear.

It was, perhaps, this disconnect and the sense of calm it brought with it that gave Janie the final burst of speed she needed as the world snapped back to itself, time rushing to catch up with what it had missed.

"Gotcha!" Janie caught Clair and swept her aside in one graceful movement, a hero with a damsel tucked snugly into her arms. She set Clair down and Clair clutched at Janie's uniform out of preservation instinct. At this height difference, she fit perfectly. Clair's breath came rapid in her chest, pressed to Janie's side.

"Th-thank you," Clair whispered in awe. She stared up at Janie, at the eyes hidden behind the red Captain Lumen mask. "I . . . I owe you my life, Miss . . . ?"

Janie swallowed, her throat dry. She could do it. Slip the mask off, tell Clair the truth. And then?

It was hard to imagine a "then." Even now, their face inches apart. Even if it was the one daydream she'd had every day since she was eight years old.

But she had to say something, and so she dug deep, summoned her courage. Took a deep breath.

Clair convulsed before Janie could say anything, head thrown back. It happened so fast, faster than Janie could react, and as Clair brought her head forward again something in her face changed, muscles resettling in a new configuration. Something . . . older, and deeply annoyed, adding brow wrinkles to Clair's otherwise youthful face. It was a look Janie had gotten used to over the last two weeks, and she resigned herself to the inevitable scolding as Mindsight, in Clair's body, took in the situation. The lack of distance between them, the way their arms wrapped around each other.

"Janie . . . please tell me you were not just about to kiss me. Her. Young me."

"What? No!" Heat flooded Janie's cheeks. And it was true, she wasn't. Most likely. Probably not, anyway, even if the idea had crossed her mind. It was clear Mindsight didn't believe her, though, and so Janie dropped her hold on Clair/Mindsight's waist, stepping back to put plenty of space between them. "I *wasn't*."

Though really, was it fair for Clair to insist she didn't? It felt like a double standard: Janie wasn't allowed to kiss adult Clair back when they were both in adult bodies because Janie was still a teenager inside; now Janie wasn't allowed to kiss her own Clair, who was also a teenager, because what? Janie was still inhabiting an adult body?

"I just—" Janie started, but Clair convulsed again, something in her face flickering. This time her head snapped up to meet Janie's, eyes popping wide as she gasped.

"What the *heck*?" Clair shouted. The young Clair again, back to herself. She leaped back, whirling, patting down her body as she turned to assess her surroundings. "I was just . . . but then . . . I don't understand, what—?"

"Clair, it's okay, calm down." Janie clutched Clair's hands, stilling them. The motion brought them closer again, and once more Janie found herself staring down at Clair's breathless face. With her blinking, wide eyes, her glossy lips parted just a fraction. In a flash, Janie saw how it could finally happen. It would be so easy: a single brave move, a threshold of just a few inches to cross. She *could* do it. But she didn't.

Instead, she reached up and took the mask away from her eyes. And even though it was years too old to be properly herself yet, Clair must have spent as much time studying Janie's face as Janie had spent studying Clair's, because recognition immediately flickered in Clair's eyes. "Janie?"

Even as she asked the question, Clair's hand slid up to cup Janie's cheek, and Janie cupped Clair's hand. She traced the line of Clair's finger with her thumb, the skin soft and warm beneath her touch.

"Yeah. It's me," Janie said. "Listen, there's . . . a lot I should probably catch you up on."

"NO, NO! THAT'S WHAT I'M TELLING YOU, IT'S NOT—" JANE was saying, but then Mindsight convulsed again and this time, when she blinked back into herself, it was really her.

"Oh thank god," Mindsight said as she clutched her hands over her heart. "That was horrifying."

Jane snorted. "You think?"

"Sorry," Mindsight said with a wince that Jane tried to brush off.

"It doesn't matter. Right now, we need to focus on getting Blue to stop using the team as her own personal playthings. Which is not cool, by the way!" she shouted out at the mall, just in case Blue was within earshot somewhere.

"Captain!" Rip-Shift, in Tony's younger body, shouted across the mall. "Little help here?" He was racing back up the escalators, and suddenly Jane could see why: his younger self was freaking out, slicing open holes randomly in the surface of the world. A bench had already fallen through one, crashing into the escalators—Rip-Shift managed to leap over it, but if Tony wasn't swapped back soon, there's no telling how much damage he could cause. A slice in the wrong place could easily split apart a person. Lightshow was with Tony, trying to calm him down, but apparently not having much luck.

Jane and Mindsight started running toward the escalators, trying to catch up, when a sweeping black shape cut across their path. Deltaman, fully kitted out, was raising his arm toward Tony in Rip-Shift's body, the wrist-mounted dart gun Deltaman was so fond of aimed and ready.

"Call it, Captain," he said. "I've got the shot."

Jane gasped. "He's a *child*!"

"It's a *tranq*!" Deltaman said, as if that made all the difference.

Jane still hesitated. They'd reached the base of the escalator by now, Deltaman already about halfway up and rising. But before Jane could make the call, before Deltaman could decide to overrule her and fire anyway, he convulsed, clutching his head, and when he came back up, he laughed. "Oh man, so cool!" Cal, in Deltaman's body, shouted.

Granite Girl's voice came over the comms. "We can't keep operating like this."

"Says you," Cal said through Deltaman's earpiece. "This is *awesome*."

"Hey, punk!" Deltaman shouted from down below, teenage voice creaking. "Don't you dare touch that stuff, do you hear me?"

Cal rolled Deltaman's eyes. "Sure, old man."

"This is my point," Granite Girl said. "Madness!"

"Okay, everybody calm down," Jane said as she and Mindsight reached the upper level. "Look, no one knows better than me how much this sucks, but we have a way to undo it now."

"Yeah, *one* way to undo it," Granite Girl said. "Don't forget, Captain, I had to use our only Adephyte crystal to power it. We get the one shot, and then it's fried."

"Right, but can't we just get more of them once we get back?"

A messy huff came over the comms. "Sure—if you can find a way to travel to a pocket of interdimensional subspace."

Mindsight rested a hand on Jane's arm. "We only have it because an elemental creature crash-landed in our reality," she added, no doubt filling in blanks from Amy's stored memories. "They produce them as a waste byproduct."

"Are you telling me that returning me to my body depends on a *shit crystal*?"

A crash over the comms, as Granite Girl clambered up through one of the tears Tony had sliced open. "Don't be a baby. The world is a beautiful and complex place, and yes, sometimes we use other species' shit. What do you think fertilizes the crops you eat?"

Jane shook her head. "I am never eating salad again."

"You see?" the young Keisha called from Pixie Beats's body, her voice carrying too loudly over the comms. "Rabbit food!" She yelped, leaping to the side as Donna's fist swung past. For a kid, Keisha was doing pretty good at dodging the punches thrown her way, but that luck would not last long. Someone was going to need to help her, but neither Jane nor Mindsight would get there in time.

Luckily, they didn't need to. Keisha's own voice, cutting in as Pixie Beats, in her younger body, plunged straight into the fight. "Duck!" She leaped, pointed toe leading the way, a modified ballet move that struck Donna right in the throat.

Donna staggered, clutching her throat, gasping for air. Jane knew from experience that she'd be all right in the end, but the move packed quite the wallop, and Pixie Beats wasn't wasting it. She jumped over Donna's hunched form like it was a gymnast's vaulting platform and landed in a spin that knocked Donna's feet out from under her.

Even with the reduced stature of Keisha's teenage body, she was still toned from years and years of ballet—the swap was barely even slowing Pixie Beats down. She ran over, clutching

Keisha's hand, trapped in the body Pixie Beats normally controlled. "Deep breath in, hold and focus," Pixie Beats told her younger/older self. "On my mark, we leap like Mme Belmont taught us, got it?"

"Got it."

"Now!" Pixie Beats shouted, just as Donna was dragging herself back to her feet.

A perfect frozen moment, rendered in ink: Pixie Beats and Keisha, hands clasped and jumping in unison so that it was impossible to tell from a drawing who was who. They leaped with every ounce of grace you would expect from a classically trained dancer—toes pointed strong and proud, arm raised in a perfect arch despite the danger of the situation. On the opposite page of their spread, Donna charges at them like a bull, but neither of them even blinks. Around them, the faintest shimmer is sketched in loose scribbles, barely visible.

In the next instant they'd shrunk down, so small they may as well have been, well, pixies. A colorful flutter blowing past in the breeze kicked up from Windforce's outstretched arms. Donna, thrown by the sudden disappearance of her target, started to spin, lost her footing, and fell to the floor, sliding backward until she crashed into a stone planter.

A stone planter that was directly by Mindsight's feet as she stepped from the escalator. Mindsight swept down, but her fingers had barely brushed Donna's forehead when Mindsight clutched her head again. A second later, Clair blinked Mindsight's lashes as she looked down and saw the fallen form of her mother. Clair, in Mindsight's body, cupped Donna's face. "Donna? Oh my god, what did they do to you?"

"Exactly what I told you they would," Blue said, stepping out of the shadows.

Jane whirled. Rage exploded out of her as she ran up and shoved Blue in the chest. "Blue! Goddammit, swap them back! Can't you see we're trying to clean up your mess?"

Blue barked a laugh. "*My* mess? You're the ones who keep interfering!"

"Because *you* keep putting everyone in danger!" Jane stepped back, running her hands through her hair in frustration. "Look,

I don't know what your plan is, but if you're really trying to help Donna somehow, then so am I! I don't know how else to convince you, but we're on the *same side*. So can we please, for the love of god, stop stepping on each other's toes and cooperate for once?"

"It's a good story, Jane," Blue said. She moved to the side, and Jane matched her, keeping herself between Blue and Donna. "If it were true."

Jane threw her hands up. "Oh for—! I lied about *one* thing! Which you might not have even believed me about if I had told you, I might add. And yes, maybe that was wrong, but I was scared, and I'm *sorry*. I'm so sorry. If I could go back and tell you right from the beginning, I would. But please, we have to put that behind us, or a lot of innocent people are going to get hurt."

"I don't believe you."

"Why not? Because someone told you not to trust me? What makes you think *they* weren't lying to you?"

"I would know. My powers would tell me."

"And what do your powers tell you about what *I'm* saying?"

For a single frame, Blue hesitated. And maybe—*maybe*—if they'd had more time, Jane could have gotten through to her, but they didn't. Before Jane could press the issue, a tear appeared in the floor beneath her, Tony in Rip-Shift's body still ripping apart the world at random. Jane dropped, landing on the lower level of the mall again.

Jane scrambled back to her feet as Donna jolted back to herself. Even from below, Jane could see as Donna leaped up with enough force to throw Clair, in Mindsight's body, aside. Jane's heart skipped, until Mindsight called out, "I'm all right!" She waved as she drew herself back to her feet. She was apparently back in her own body and, as Jane did a quick scan of the upper level, the others were shaking their heads to clear them as well.

Unfortunately, that did not solve their problems. The other Heroes tried to close in around Donna, but Donna grabbed a directory sign, ripping it from the tile floor with a sickening crunch. Sparks danced from the cables as she waved it in the Heroes' directions, herding them back, and then, to Jane's horror, Donna reared back and hurled the directory sign up—straight through the glass of the skylight, up to where all those people were still huddled around trying to get a glimpse of the action.

Jane tapped her earpiece. "Windforce, Rip, check that everyone is okay—and for fuck's sake, get those gawkers away from the skylights!"

"On it." They took off, before any further disasters or meddling on Blue's part could stop them. Jane didn't blame them for being grateful for the excuse to step away and deal with something simpler. In truth, she wished she could do the same.

But wishing didn't make something happen—if it did, Jane would have swapped back with the others—and unfortunately they still had a crisis to deal with. Enraged by her shower of glass, Donna was lunging even more forcefully at the team members still trying to contain her.

"I'm open to suggestions, people," Jane said over the comms. "Mindsight, did you get any clues as to how we might get through to her?"

"Only that it's not looking good," Mindsight said, voice muffled as she ran for cover. "I only got a brief glimpse, but from what I can tell, her senses are so hyped up she can't even see straight. All she feels is this enraged need to find and protect, well, me—or at least, my younger self. She's lashing out at anything she perceives as a threat, but right now she's so out of it that *everything* feels like a threat."

"Great, so how long until she calms down?"

"I don't know if she can. She's been on these drugs for so long . . . Her sense of self is beyond scrambled, I don't know if it's even possible to reach her."

Not exactly the news Jane was hoping for, but if she was honest it was what she was expecting. So it was back to square one, then.

They had to find a way to contain Donna, but *where*? Sending her back to Cedarcreek wasn't an option even if they had the means to physically restrain her. Jane loathed the idea of turning her over to a military or police force, to be locked in a black site somewhere, entombed in thick, concrete walls. If they were home, they could rig something up back at headquarters, or possibly put together some tech to calm her, maybe even fix her, restore her back to herself, but—

Jane drew to a halt. Oh, but how she hated the idea that had just struck her.

It's possible it wouldn't work. She was not, after all, a scientist. But she knew someone who was.

Steeling herself, she tapped her earpiece. "Granite Girl, you said you'd have to blank our minds, right, in order to let my own consciousness return to my body?"

"Yes, but if Janie's not willing—"

"Forget Janie," Jane said. "What if there was no other body?"

"Then it would be a pretty shitty body-swapping device."

"But it would still reset a person, right?" Jane asked. "If they were under some other influence, and not being themselves?"

"Jane . . . ," Mindsight's voice cutting in, low in warning. "Don't make me remind you we've only got one charge out of that thing."

"Answer the question," Jane pressed. "Would it work?"

Granite Girl was silent for a moment. Just long enough for Jane to regret asking. "I'd have to modify it."

"So that's a yes?"

"It's not a no," Granite Girl said. "But like I said, this hasn't exactly been FDA approved. It's all experimental. I'm making no promises."

"I don't need promises," Jane said. "Just your best assessment."

"Then yes," Granite Girl said. "I can make it work."

"Do it, then."

"Jane." Mindsight's voice again, much closer than a comm link. Mindsight's hand found Jane's upper arm, and she spun Jane to face her.

Jane looked up, her gaze crossing the few inches of height that still separated them. Mindsight's face was set, stern in a distinctly grown-up expression, as if Jane was *actually* a foolish teenager. She'd taken off her mask, facing Jane not as a superhero, but a wife.

She did not ask for an explanation, for how could Jane explain it? Save herself, go back to the cozy life the two of them had built—or save a version of Clair's mother, giving her back to a teenage daughter who still needed her. It was possible they could contain Donna some other way, condemning her to a life of imprisonment and experimentation. But they *had* a solution, here, now. A real solution, one that would give Donna back not just the half-lived life she'd been stuck with since the accident, but a full one, home where she belonged.

What kind of Hero would Jane be if she chose herself instead? And how could Clair ever look at her the same way again?

Jane saw in Clair's eyes the moment when she processed this. The logic of it, run through to its conclusion. The knee-jerk denial, the desperate search for a hole in Jane's line of reasoning. The horror as she realized it was solid.

Clair didn't say anything. Instead, she shot forward, arms wrapping around Jane in a hug as fierce as their love.

"I won't tell you this changes nothing between us," Clair said, kissing the top of Jane's head. "But I promise, in a few years, when you've finished growing up again—"

"I know."

A few years. The idea of spending any time apart was a dagger to Jane's chest, but the truth is, they'd lived through worse. Or, at least, Jane had—Clair had been spared the agony, skipping from the moment of her death to the moment of her rebirth without the pain of the endless days between. It was a year and a half Jane tried not to resent her for.

Jane stole one last squeeze from the hug. Then she made herself peel Clair off her. Professionalism kicked in, a Band-Aid on Jane's heart, and in an instant they were Captain Lumen and Mindsight again. And they still had a job to do.

Mindsight did not say goodbye. Just set off into the fray, not needing orders to find ways to make herself useful.

Jane looked around for Granite Girl, and found her sitting on the floor a short distance away, the device splayed open on a mall bench as an impromptu workstation.

"Is it done?"

"Almost." Granite Girl stole a quick glance up. "Captain . . . are you sure about this?"

"Do you have a different way to help Donna?" Jane asked. "Because if you do, I'll take it."

Granite Girl's face set hard as stone.

"That's what I thought." Jane stepped away, leaning back to spot where Pixie Beats was still keeping Donna somewhat occupied on the upper level. "Just tell me when we're ready, got it?"

A stiff nod was all Jane got in response.

It was all she needed.

"Jane!"

Jane braced herself as she turned around. "Please, Paul, I can't justify myself to you, too."

"I'm not asking you to." Paul rushed up to her and opened his hands between them, a gentle pulse of light cupped in his open palm. How foolish: she'd assumed he'd come to her as a dad, but of course he wasn't Paul in this context, but rather Mr. Lightshow. "I thought you might like some help getting to her. I figure I'll distract, you attack?"

"Oh." Jane took a second, assessing. "Yeah, um. That'd be great, sure."

Granite Girl cleared her throat. "Um . . . not to interrupt, but it's done."

"Good." Jane made herself believe that as she shook out her nervous arms and legs.

Lightshow lined up beside her. "Ready?"

Jane set herself into a start position, knees bent and buoyant. "Ready."

She wasn't ready, but what did that matter? Jane had spent most of her life doing things she wasn't ready for.

Beside her, Lightshow settled into his own stance. He stole a quick glance at Jane. "Also . . . ," he started. He hesitated for a second, then took a steadying breath. "I just want you to know, I'm very proud of you."

Jane startled. He was *proud* of her? The very notion was so unheard of as to be absurd. Jane didn't even know how to process such a statement, let alone respond. She finally settled on "Thank you," which didn't feel quite right, but Lightshow gave a curt nod.

There should have been more. Jane's chest burned, unspoken words she couldn't quite identify pressing thickly against the base of her throat. Paul wasn't her dad, she kept reminding herself, but would she ever get another opportunity like this?

Maybe not, but the moment was gone before she could begin to untangle the knot clogging up her voice. Granite Girl cut over Jane's doubts.

"Now!"

THE MALL WAS A TWO PAGE, WHERE'S WALDO? SPREAD OF CHAOS.

In the upper corner, seen only through the glass of the sky-lights, a tear split the world from the sky to the parking lot. Gusts, painted in white, guide protesting onlookers through, cupping them like giant cartoon hands.

Dust trails ominously from the ceiling, scattering across the backs of Donna and Pixie Beats, Deltaman and Blue. They're paired off like dance partners, sparring on opposite sides of the page. Kid Heroes scatter the space between them, Nerf guns raised as they huddle behind potted plants or display signs. Only Mindsight cuts between the children, hand pressing against one of their foreheads, a small trail of their compatriots gathered like ducklings in her wake as she convinces them to follow her to safety.

And racing in from the bottom of the page, a tiny triad of Jane and Mr. Lightshow, Granite Girl in the lead.

In her hoodie, Jane could have been any teenager caught up in the mess. An innocent bystander, a stupid kid causing trouble, a brash young hero dead-set on doing what was right.

They cut a straight line for Donna and Pixie Beats. Jane did not even need to explain herself—by now, the team was seamless, a perfectly tuned unit that operated on instinct, and one Jane was going to miss so badly the thought nearly killed her.

But that was a problem for later. For now, this one shining moment, she was still their Captain Lumen, even without her powers. And so for now, as Granite Girl slapped the harness into her hands and gave Jane a boost, Jane took a literal leap of faith, knowing that Pixie Beats would catch her, that they'd shrink down together, that they'd land where they were supposed to.

Donna didn't even have time to react. A burst of light from Lightshow temporarily blinded her, and by the time Jane and Pixie Beats expanded to full size, Jane was grabbing hold of Donna's back like a child, while Keisha swung around front and secured the chin strap. Jane pressed the activator button and they jumped aside, scattering like water droplets shaken from a dog.

Jane had been bracing herself for the possibility that it wouldn't work. Probably, if she was willing to be brutally honest with herself, a part of her had been hoping it wouldn't. Failure would have been an absolution: she imagined the pages where she had to shrug it off, oh well, at least she'd tried, it wasn't her fault she now had to go back to the original plan of body-swapping back to her real life.

This vision was so strong that for a second, she did not even recognize the alternative—that it was *working*.

And maybe it was hard to see from the outside, but Jane could imagine it well enough. Donna, fallen to her knees, clutching the straps harnessed to her head, mouth opened in a silent scream. Billowing thought bubbles surrounded her, clear images of the past few hours packed tightly against her body—but outside that, a widespread haze of older memories pressed in like a thick fog. They snuck between the newer thoughts: a summer day in the park with baby Clair here, an anniversary dinner with Simon there.

"Get back!" Jane shouted as Donna curled farther forward, collapsing on herself until her forehead kissed the marble floor tile. The harness with the Adephyte crystal sparked and hissed, a pulsating glow casting Donna's face into brilliant relief as it passed from agony to confusion to fear and then, finally, something like peace as she lapsed into unconsciousness with a delicate sigh.

Jane crouched down beside her, easing the head strap off as the others rushed in around them. The crystal wasn't just used. In a pointed *fuck you* to Jane, it had turned black and was beginning to crumble to dust in her hands.

Her teenage hands, now her own again. Jane turned them over, stretching the muscles, studying the youthful skin. She'd considered them borrowed for the last two weeks, but now she'd have to start accepting them.

She pushed herself to her feet, letting Lightshow and Granite Girl tend to Donna. They gathered her up between them, carrying her to a nearby bench where Granite Girl could look her over.

Jane had just begun to move away when the mall seemed to shudder underfoot. A series of *cracks* split the air like fireworks, jagged letters racing lightning-tracks as they zigzagged across the ceiling. Plaster dust flurried over them, and Jane barely had time to blink and shade her eyes before it dusted her face. "What the . . . ?"

Her question was answered for her when she was finally able to look up. A network of cracks, all leading back to a single marble support pillar—a support pillar that had kinked under pressure in the middle like a crushed soda can, the surface littered with broken lines. A support pillar Donna had heaved a bench into earlier.

As soon as Jane processed this, the support pillar bowed a little more. Another series of snaps and pops echoed through the mall, louder even than the racing footsteps of most of the Heroes as they circled around Jane.

"Captain—"

"I see it," Jane said. Instantly, her attention snapped back to the skylight. Bits of glass sprinkled from the hole Donna had created by throwing the directory sign through it, and even the intact panes had started to break, the glass cracked but holding together. For now. But if the rest of that let loose it would, frankly, be the least of their concerns. The ceiling above them was the floor below the open parking lot, and she didn't need to comm Windforce and Rip-Shift to know they hadn't finished clearing away the crowd. "We've got to find a way to shore up the ceiling."

"Granite Girl could probably straighten that pillar back out," Pixie Beats said. "But that wouldn't fix the cracks that are already there. The weight of itself, even with the pillar back in place, is likely enough to collapse it."

"What about Paul?" Deltaman said, jerking his chin to where he was still helping tend to Donna. "Or Lightshow, or whatever you call him? Doesn't he have the same powers you do? Couldn't a laser beam seal up the cracks?"

Jane shook her head. "He does, but he doesn't have the energy he'll need for a job like that. If I still had my powers—!"

She bit off the end of that sentence. It hurt too much to think about.

"This is all my fault," the younger Janie said. She'd come over with the rest of the Heroes, blending in so well in her Captain Lumen uniform that Jane hadn't noticed. "If I had just agreed to switch back—"

"Then we wouldn't have had the charge necessary to calm Donna," Jane cut in. She steeled herself, a horrible realization seizing hold as she turned and grabbed her old body's shoulders. "Listen to me. I'm not saying you did the right thing, but you'll drive yourself crazy second guessing in this line of work. Now, I know this is scary, but I *need* you to dig deep right now, okay? Deltaman's plan was good, but . . . Lightshow isn't the one who can do this. We need you."

Janie's eyes widened. "I can't."

"You can," Jane said, more forcefully than she felt. "You can do this, I promise. You're *Captain Lumen*."

"I'm not."

"*Yes*, you are. I saw you out there. You were brave, and that's exactly what we need from you right now."

"You need my *powers*."

"That's right," Jane said quickly. "*Your* powers. They're in there, and this body knows what to do with them. You just need to get out of your own way and trust yourself."

"But I don't *want* them anymore!" Janie's voice caught, hiccuping slightly as she gulped down air. "I'm sorry. I was so stupid and so jealous, and if I'd just *listened* to you—"

"None of that matters right now!" Jane sucked in a breath, trying to bite back her anger. Dammit, this was hard enough without trying to give the younger version of herself a pep talk. "Janie. Captain. You wanted to prove yourself as a Hero. I'm telling you, right here, right now: this is how you do it. We need you to go out there and save those people."

Janie's face blanched. Jane couldn't blame her. It was an absurd ask, impossible. But Jane couldn't take the time to wait for Janie to gather her courage. Jane tapped her earpiece. "Windforce, we need you back here."

The comm crackled. "But the crowds—"

"Forget the crowds. If this works, it won't matter. Rip can keep working, but have him send you back inside."

There was only the slightest hesitation. "Aye, Captain."

An instant later a shimmer appeared, Windforce stepping through a gap in the world. Deltaman ran over to him, no doubt to fill him in, as Jane gave Janie a push and Janie deathmarched herself into position below the worst of the network of cracks.

All Jane could do was stand there. Hoping it worked. Bracing herself for the consequences.

She was so wrapped up she didn't even see Mindsight approach. She only realized when Mindsight's hand rested on Jane's shoulder, startling Jane back to her immediate surroundings.

Jane sidestepped from beneath Mindsight's touch. She cleared her throat. "How's Donna?"

"Unconscious," Mindsight said, "but I think it worked. Thanks to you."

Jane shifted uncomfortably. "Glad to hear it."

Mindsight nodded toward Janie, who was shaking her fingers out as she stepped into position. "Do you think she can do it?"

"No," Jane said. "But I've been wrong before, and she's the only chance we've got."

"Maybe not."

At the sound of Blue's voice, Mindsight stepped in front of Jane, but Jane put her hand on Mindsight's shoulder. "It's okay. Let her through." After all, what further harm could she do at this point?

Blue approached with caution. "You really think you could help those people?"

Jane squared her shoulders. "I know I could."

"I could switch you back," Blue said. "But . . ."

"You still don't trust me."

"No," Blue said. "Despite the grand gesture you just pulled, it doesn't prove anything."

"That's fair," Jane said.

Blue rocked back in surprise, but Jane was done being angry with her. Their whole problem right now was that they didn't want to listen to each other's point of view—and maybe Blue would never learn to, maybe what Jane had done would break them in a way that couldn't be repaired. That was definitely possible, and . . . that had to be okay.

Jane held out her hand. "Please, just let me help these people. After that, if you still don't believe I deserve to be Captain Lumen, you can swap us back again. I won't fight you."

Blue hesitated, her mouth gaping open. "Why would you do that?"

"Do you really have to ask?" Jane said. "Look, like it or not, *I've* been your friend and business partner these last few years—not that other Jane. You really think I wouldn't try to help if I could? That I'd put my own needs before everything else? Yes, you didn't realize it was me, but—come on, Blue. Part of you *had* to sense the difference."

"Okay, Captain," Windforce said from a distance. Jane snapped her attention, but he wasn't talking to her: Janie was in position, and with a single nod, Windforce raised his hands, gusts sweeping in to cradle the young, new version of Captain Lumen. A lump wedged itself into Jane's throat. She swallowed it down, returning her attention to Blue.

"Please, just let me help. Be the person I know you are. Janie's a good kid, but she shouldn't have to deal with this. I *promise* I'll switch back after, and your powers deal with truth somehow, don't they? So you know I'm not lying."

"But the person who told me—"

"Yeah, I can't explain that. Maybe they thought it was the truth, I don't know. Just please . . . give me this one chance to prove I'm not the liar you think I am."

The wind picked up around them. "Captain . . . ?" Windforce said, voice unsteady, and Janie shouted back, "I'm fine, I'm fine!" but she clearly wasn't, and Blue *had* to see that, she *had* to listen.

"Blue!"

Blue sighed. Janie started to scream—

—and Jane finished it, throat still raw as her consciousness took hold. It happened that quickly, a sudden jump from frame to frame. Under different circumstances, Jane would take a moment to revel in her hard-won victory. As it was, she could only react, her muscles jumping into action with a familiarity that nearly made Jane cry.

Light filled her up. The issue's hero shot: the outline of Captain Lumen from behind, held aloft by Windforce's steady breeze. Her hair billows around her as she shines as bright as a star. Lasers spring from her reach, one at the mercy of each of her raised fingers.

Her powers hummed through her, welcoming her back. Jane focused on her work, one tiny panel at a time. Each crack zoomed in and framed, lasers melting the lines closed again. It would never be as stable as it was before, but at least it would keep the rooftop parking lot from crashing in on them. Here in this body, it was easy, effortless, light snapping to attention like eager puppies wanting to show off their latest tricks. It wasn't just a light show, though—Jane *was* Captain Lumen, the true and proper one. But if this had to be her last hurrah before handing over the mantle, at least it was a good one.

The cracks closed up. One by one, the lasers snapped off. Windforce eased back, and Jane descended. The last of the gusts disappeared as her feet touched down, her hair settling around her. Jane took a breath, bracing herself. She turned around, ready to face judgment . . . but Blue was already gone.

So was this it, then? A rush of disbelief and joy raced to Jane's head, which she threw back in laughter. It was so sudden it felt like it must have been a trick, and yet Jane could not imagine what sort of other shoe might be waiting to drop.

Turns out, it wasn't a shoe at all.

One tiny corner panel, a ceiling fragment slipping loose. Jane didn't even see it, but Paul must have. One shot of Jane, oblivious, a self-satisfied grin on her face; another of Paul's horrified expression. Quick frames, rapid-fire: his feet pushing off, his hands shoving Jane aside, a spurt of red as the fragment pierced his side. Jane was sliding across the floor before she even realized what happened, put the sequence together only in agonized retrospective as she stared back at him, his scream splitting the mall as he collapsed backward.

Jane ran back to him. "You idiot! What were you thinking?"

He clearly hadn't been, if he was willing to throw himself in the path of the fragment to save Jane. Paul flinched. Both of his hands clutched around the fragment, but it wasn't doing any good—blood poured easily through his mess of fingers, no matter how hard he tried to hold himself together.

Jane ripped off part of her suit, the soft cuff of her base layer shirt. She tried to patch it around the tangle of his own efforts, though it didn't take a medical expert to know it wouldn't help. "Goddammit," she muttered, her breath sharp and panicked.

"It's okay," Paul managed to say. "It's okay. I knew what I was doing. I had to save my girl."

Grief caved Jane's chest in as she held the cloth against his wound, the one he thought he'd taken for his daughter. "Paul . . . I'm so sorry, but I'm not Janie. We switched back a few minutes ago."

A feeble smile stretched the edges of Paul's lips. He reached up, bloody fingers stamping Jane's face as he cupped her cheek. "I know."

"But . . . I don't understand . . ." Panic seized Jane as she reached up and gripped his fingers. He knew?

A fierce cough broke the moment. Paul doubled up, his hand slipping from Jane's. Blood splattered onto his crisp white uniform.

"Paul? It's gonna be okay, Paul, stay with me!"

But he wasn't listening. With a wince, his eyes fluttered shut, his breathing shaky. Jane cradled his head as it lolled back.

"No—no, please. Dad!"

Already she could hear the wail of sirens in the distance. But how far? And even if they arrived quickly, what use would they be? It didn't take a doctor to see this was a nasty wound. If they were back on Jane's world, she could probably still get him to a rejuve pod in time, but here . . .

There was only one thing to do. Jane did not hesitate. She scooped Paul into her arms, the ones she'd spent so many hours toning at the gym. With her proper adult strength and a boost of adrenaline coursing through her, he was as easy to lift as a child. The world hopper was already in place on her wrist, left from Janie's trip here.

It wasn't even a choice. Jane pressed the button, and with the rip of a sketchbook page, they were gone.

"DAD!" JANIE LURCHED FORWARD, TRYING TO REACH PAUL and Jane as they disappeared, when Mindsight grabbed her arm.

"It's okay," Mindsight said. "She's brought him back to our world. The rejuve pod will save him, I promise."

Janie whirled, desperation bleeding off her. "How do you know that's where she went?"

"She's my wife," Mindsight said, smiling down at Janie. "I know."

Janie's throat went dry. "Okay," she choked out. After everything they'd gone through, Janie owed the team, and Mindsight, enough faith to believe her. Plus, Janie knew for herself how well the rejuvenation pods worked. She made herself breathe, trusting everything would work out the way it was supposed to.

Speaking of . . .

"Janie?"

Janie turned, her breath caught in her chest.

Clair was standing in front of her, twisting her fingers nervously. Her Clair—the *real* Clair. Fresh and young, right at the beginning of everything. Janie's heart ached, her arms longing to reach out and tackle Clair in a fierce hug. But instead she held herself back, leaving a cold but familiar gap between them as Mindsight stepped away to give them space.

"Hey," Janie said, then fell silent.

Clair tucked her hair behind her ear, equally uncertain. "Hey. Is it really you this time?"

"Yeah," Janie laughed. "Yeah, it's really me."

A gentle smile. God, that smile killed Janie every time.

"Man, this is so weird," Clair said.

"Right? Like, parallel worlds and body-swapping are bad enough, but who would have thought our parents would have *superpowers*?"

Clair shook her head. "It's pretty nuts."

"Is Donna gonna be okay?"

"I think so," Clair said. "Marie—the grown-up Marie—thinks whatever they did put her mind back in order. She'll probably always have her superstrength, but . . . other than that, she should come back to herself again."

"That's good."

"Yeah," Clair said. "They say we might even be able to bring her home after she finishes recuperating, so . . . that's something to look forward to. I guess I should thank you."

Janie blushed. "I didn't do anything."

"It didn't look that way from where I was standing." She reached out, hooking Janie's fingers with hers.

Janie looked down. Her stomach squirmed, wrestling with all the emotions held fast inside her. She adjusted her glasses as she said, "Listen, I'm so sorry you thought I was doing . . . well, whatever that other Jane did while she was here. I know she didn't mean to hurt you, but—"

"It's okay," Clair said. She traced a line along the side of Janie's finger. "Now that I know what was going on . . . I mean, it was a pretty weird situation. Especially . . . well, with what she knew. About us. In the future."

Janie looked up, uncertain. "So you know?"

"Yeah." Clair took a breath. "And listen, I know they're not us. And, like, just because they felt like that—I mean, that doesn't mean we have to—And I don't even know if you want to, so it's not like I'm trying to pressure you or whatever, but—I mean, if you want to? It's totally okay if you don't feel that way. I'm not going to assume. I just—"

Janie laughed, cutting her off. "Oh my god, Clair, of *course* I love you. I've loved you since kindergarten."

Clair blushed, a rare and precious tint across her cheeks. "Really?"

"Really."

"Oh." She tucked a bit of her hair behind her ears again, the same steadying gesture Janie knew so well. But this time, Clair didn't look away. Instead, she met Janie's gaze exactly, her voice barely shaking as she said, "I've loved you, too," and Janie's chest exploded with warmth and nerves and joy.

Janie cleared her throat. "So I guess there's only one thing left to do, then."

She took a step forward, quickly before she could chicken out. Her heart slammed against her ribs, desperate and terrified all in one. It was the hardest thing she'd ever done, scarier than facing down supervillains, but Clair was already moving toward her, matching her courage point for point. And it was different from what that other Jane and Clair had once, all those years ago—it had to be—but that didn't mean it was lesser. Turns out, there was no wrong way for this story to play out, so long as it ended here. Their lips met, fierce and urgent between them, as the world seemed to slow and solidify, preserving the moment in a splash of ink and colors. Janie and Clair. Together.

The perfect note to end an issue on.

NOT *QUITE* THE END, THOUGH.

A panel of black, split by the faintest line of white running like a horizon across the middle. Back to black nothingness. Then, in the next one, the line has expanded into an almond-shaped bubble. Black again, then the bubble expands, but this time the white is broken up by the hazy outline of a person. Smudgy, the white still overwhelming, but the red of her shoulders is a telling sign she knows he'll recognize.

Jane forced a smile down at Paul, as comforting as she knew how to manage. "Easy there. It's okay, you're going to be all right. You're safe now."

She stepped back, giving him space as he came to. Paul took a few deep breaths, blinking in the light of the rejuve pod. He shifted up onto his elbows.

"Janie? Where—? What's going on?"

"It's okay," Jane repeated. "But it's me, it's . . . it's Jane. I brought you back to my own world, just temporarily. This is what we call a rejuvenation pod. It healed you."

Paul's eyes widened. "Medicine is that advanced in the future?"

Jane laughed. "No. Superhero tech. The team picked it up on one of their first missions—before I joined them. Honestly, I don't even know how it works, but . . . ," she trailed off. He didn't need a breakdown of the science that had saved his life.

He must have agreed, because he sat back, settling against his pillows. He shut his eyes, just for a moment. "Thank you."

"It was the least I could do, after you tried to sacrifice yourself for me."

Jane tried to keep her tone light, but a hint of reproach crept in around the edges. She was sure he felt, in the moment, like he was doing the right thing, and it wasn't that Jane wasn't grateful—obviously she was *here*, she had no choice but to be grateful. But what if there hadn't been the option of bringing him back here to be saved? What if he'd well and truly died in his foolhardy effort?

"I would do it again, you know," he said, as if reading her mind.

"You shouldn't," Jane snapped. "I'm not your daughter."

"Think that, if it makes you feel better. The way I see it, you didn't have a dad—someone has to make up for that."

Jane looked down. She picked at the edge of his blanket. "Yeah, but that's the thing," Jane said, her voice small. "I *do* have a dad. I lied to you, earlier, when I said my Paul was dead."

"Ah," Paul said. "I was wondering when you were going to admit that."

Jane's head snapped up. "You knew?"

He tossed her a soft smile. "You think I don't know when my girl is lying to me? Besides, you weren't acting like someone who was meeting an alternate version of her long-dead father for the first time. There was too much bitterness there, and not the kind you'd get from being angry that he wasn't around."

Jane sat back in disbelief. All this time, and he'd *known*?

"Why didn't you say anything?"

Paul shrugged. "I figure I had to be a real asshole to have caused *that* much bad blood between us. If you wanted to pretend he was dead, who was I to argue?"

Jane laughed. Softly at first, just a snicker, then a giggle—but soon it boiled up and tumbled out of her, filling the room.

"He *is* a huge asshole, yeah," Jane said when she finally calmed down. Her voice turned softer, shyer. "I'm glad you're not."

Paul smiled. "Me, too." He reached out, patting Jane's hand. "But since I'm here, you want me to go and punch myself for you? I've been told I've got a mean right hook."

Jane ducked her head, hoping he wouldn't see the blush warming her cheeks but knowing he probably would. "That won't be necessary."

"Your call," Paul said. "I'll leave the offer on the table until I go home. Speaking of which . . ."

"Right." Jane reached into one of the pockets of her suit, bringing a world hopper out. She hesitated, just a moment, before passing it over. "I had Marie lock the coordinates between our two worlds while you were recovering. This'll take you home whenever you're ready. And back here again if, you know . . . you ever decide you want to."

Paul glanced up. "You wouldn't mind?"

"No," she said, and a breath slid from her chest, tension she didn't even realize she was carrying suddenly loosened. "No, I think . . . I think I'd like to see you again."

"I'd *love* that." Paul's hand found Jane's again and he smiled, giving it a quick squeeze. "Thank you, Jane."

Jane took a deep breath. "You're welcome. And . . . you can call me Janie, if you want to."

Paul smiled. "Janie."

She didn't stay too much longer after that. Paul didn't say anything, but Jane could tell he was getting drowsy, so after a few minutes of idle chitchat, she found a convenient excuse and slipped from the room.

It was a weird feeling, knowing she'd actually made peace with a Paul Maxwell. But as she let herself out of the building, warm autumn sun shining down on her, it also felt somehow . . . normal.

Jane smiled to herself as her phone buzzed in her pocket. She took it out, glanced down. "Oh, you've got to be kidding me." She swiped to accept the call. "What do you want?"

"Hello, Jane, nice to hear your voice, too," Senator Maxwell said. "Is that any way to greet your father?"

"You're not my father."

This was always the truth Jane had maintained in her mind, and on the surface it couldn't be argued with. Senator Maxwell had lived on a completely different parallel world than the Earth Jane was from, after all. This version of him did not physically create her, nor did he raise her. But now Jane knew it ran far deeper than whatever the logistics of their past said about them. Senator Maxwell would never be Jane's father, had never truly been *any* proper father to *any* Jane Maxwell.

"Look, I know you think I'm angry," Jane said, "but honestly I am just too tired for this bullshit game of ours anymore. So here's the deal: I'll continue to show up where I'm supposed to, and smile for the press, but in private you have to drop the pretense that we're anything remotely resembling friends. Maybe some small part of you still cares for my well-being, but you don't actually like me. I don't like you. Can we be mature enough to be honest about that, at least?"

The phone was silent for a moment as Senator Maxwell mulled this over. Long enough for things to get awkward. Long enough for Jane to pull the phone away from her ear and check that the call hadn't been disconnected. Long enough that, for a second at least, Jane began to worry that maybe she'd actually hurt him. But then a deep breath.

"As you wish, Jane."

"Good," Jane said. "Then it's settled."

"I suppose it is."

"You know what the worst part is?" Jane added before she could stop herself. She shut her eyes for a second, letting out a sigh that stretched the distance between them. "You could have been so much better, if only you'd chosen to."

Senator Maxwell didn't say anything. But this time, Jane didn't wait for him. She hung up on the emptiness, feeling freer than she had in a long, long time.

PAUL SHIFTED THE CAR INTO PARK. HIS ATTENTION
landed on the rearview mirror, perfectly framing the two passengers in his backseat. Janie and Clair, glowing as they held each
other's hands.

"Okay. You girls sure you're ready for this?"

It was the sort of question he had to ask, as a dad, even though
he already knew the answer. Damn right they were ready for it.
Even without the growth both of them had shown during recent
events, these two girls were the strongest, bravest young women
he'd ever have the pleasure of knowing. Paul's heart ached, looking at them—pride and fear and anger at the world weighing in
equal measure in his chest. Because they could handle it, whatever came their way, but dammit: going to a school dance with
the person you loved shouldn't be an act of courage.

It'll get better, he told himself as Janie and Clair scrambled out
of the car. They stood tall at the curb, hands interlaced between

them, fingers gripped tight. They'd worn the same dress in different colors, their hair arranged by Allison into matching styles that tumbled over their shoulders. Preparations for this dance had been a party in and of itself, Simon and Donna and all the girls' friends gathered at the Maxwell house, laughter and soda flowing freely as the kids had all gotten changed and dolled up.

Paul grinned now as the rest of them tumbled from the minivan Simon had parked just behind him. Sure enough, the rest of the kids linked up just as they'd planned: Keisha and Marie, Tony and Cal, hands clasped in solidarity. The only mixed-sex pair was Devin, who'd finally worked up the nerve to ask out a long-standing crush—but even his date had apparently gotten in on the plan, dressing in a sequined suit and tie while Devin sported a knee-length skirt.

Across the parking lot, Jane and Clair, the adult versions of them, hovered near the door as volunteer chaperones. Clair at the folding table accepting tickets, Jane giving the line of kids last-minute rules and warnings, teasing them lightly for the things she knew they would spend the evening doing. She glanced up, catching Paul's eye, and tossed him a reassuring smile. The tension in his chest loosened a notch. They'd be okay, he told himself. Even without superhero protection, his girls would always be okay.

He watched until the kids spilled in through the open doorway, winking out in a flash of sequins and pride. Then he heaved a huge sigh and reached for the gearshift.

His cellphone rang in his pocket, breaking the silence of the car. Paul let the car idle as he took the phone out, flipping it open to answer. It was a number he didn't recognize.

"Hello?"

"Hi, honey, it's me." His wife's voice, a little softer than he was used to, but still unmistakable.

"Liv? I was just dropping the girls off—what's wrong?"

"No, nothing's wrong. I was just wondering if you could meet me? The old ChemWerks factory past the river? There's something we need to discuss."

Paul's skin prickled. It would be disingenuous at that point to say he knew something of what would unfold once he got there, but still some piece of him must have felt the wrongness of the call. It didn't matter; if his wife needed him, he'd be damned if he ignored that.

"I'll be right over."

He kept the radio on low as he drove across town. Simon followed in the minivan for a while, until Paul pulled over and called across the open gap between their windows that he had something to take care of, he'd meet them all back at the house later. And then he was alone, gliding along a path he'd retraced so many times over the years.

A car waited for him in the broken parking lot. He pulled close, but left a lane's gap between them. And then she stepped out of the darkness, pinned in the beam of his headlights.

It was Olivia Maxwell, all right, that much was instantly recognizable. But with a jolt, Paul realized it was not *his* Olivia. This one was sculpted, slimmed down, polished in a way that was almost artificial. Older, too, though it was hard to say exactly how much—she'd clearly had some work done around her face, her skin taut in a way that looked great but did not match the pull her cheeks had when she was truly younger.

Jane's mom. The idea slid into his mind as he shut the engine off and unhooked his seatbelt. But if she was here, what did that mean? Jane and Clair were supervising the dance. Had they brought her with them?

There was only one way to find out. Paul nodded a hello as he got out of the car. "Olivia. Or am I supposed to call you Mrs. Maxwell?" Her first name felt weird on his tongue, not right for a woman who wasn't actually his wife.

Mrs. Maxwell shrugged. "Call me what you like. I'm sorry for the subterfuge—I wasn't sure how you'd react if I explained over the phone who you were meeting."

"I'm well versed in parallel worlds these days."

"I'm sure you are," Mrs. Maxwell said with a smile. The one she usually reserved for dealing with small children who still needed things explained in neat, manageable bites. Paul tried not to be offended by it. She motioned for him to step up beside her own car. "We have a lot to talk about."

Later, he'd realize this was a stupid thing to do. That he should have been more suspicious, that he'd never have stepped forward if it was anyone's voice other than Olivia's asking him to. But it was, and he did, a lamb trotting merrily to the slaughter.

She struck before he could react. A rag jammed against his face, over his nose and mouth. A sweet, chemical smell stabbed at Paul, sucked in from the shock. Chloroform. She'd struck like a cobra, her other hand clamped behind his neck so Paul couldn't jerk away.

He collapsed easily enough. He never could hold his liquor either, Mrs. Maxwell thought as he hit the ground. She straightened up, tucking the rag back into her purse. Car doors were already slamming shut behind her, men in dark suits slipping from the town car she'd driven over here. They began to gather Paul up with brisk efficiency, as if they'd done this a hundred times over.

She tried not to think about the fact that they probably had.

"Promise me you won't hurt him?"

A deep voice clucked behind Mrs. Maxwell. "When have we ever hurt anyone? No, Olivia, quite the contrary—we'll have him tucked back into his bed before his family even realizes he's been gone."

Mrs. Maxwell turned around. "You'd better."

A patient smile. Her contact (she steadfastly refused to think of him as her handler, even though they both knew that was probably more accurate) never rose to Mrs. Maxwell's threats. That didn't mean she would stop making them.

Mrs. Maxwell turned away. She brushed her hands off on her skirt. They weren't dirty. They were never dirty, not physically anyway, but the compulsion remained, as if the mere pretense of these people, this deal she'd struck—so long ago now it was hard to even remember—sullied something in her. It was a foolish gesture, sentimental and weak. She'd have to do something about that, she supposed.

She could probably help with that. The thought struck fast, hitting the back of Mrs. Maxwell's mind so suddenly she wanted to swat it like a mosquito. *No,* she told herself. She would never stoop so far as that. She dug her keys out of her purse, settling into the black town car.

Behind her, Paul was being tucked neatly into the back of a van that had just arrived, flashes of light catching the corner of Mrs. Maxwell's rearview mirror. Mrs. Maxwell reached up, adjusting it until the van was no longer in sight.

He would be fine. Her contact had never given her reason to believe they weren't keeping their word, and besides . . . Mrs. Maxwell had her own family to protect. Really, given the choice between them, there was no contest.

She pushed the button for the ignition, and the car purred to life beneath her. Time to go home.

HOURS LATER, JANE AND CLAIR WERE WALKING BACK TO their house. The dance had been long and grueling for the adults so that it could be a delight for the kids. As expected, the stance the younger versions of the Heroes had taken caused a bit of a stir. Whispers flew between the other students, bristled outrage stirring among some of the teachers and staff. There were several points throughout the night where it looked like it was going to get ugly. But each time, just before someone could step in to take a bigoted stand, Jane would cause a minor distraction and Clair would clutch the offending person's hand, and by the time things settled back out, the impulse miraculously would be forgotten. It was tedious, this process. Changing hearts and minds, whether they wanted to be or not. Ordinarily, it wasn't something Clair would use her powers for, but neither she nor Jane complained about it.

Now they strolled up their moonlit street, hand in gloved hand, laughing and recounting the events of the night. It was so weird to see a version of their past that hadn't happened, like watching an alternate ending for a movie you'd loved for years. The whole time Jane had spent in Janie's life she'd been so obsessed with protecting her own memory of how things had unfolded, never once stopping to consider that something different might have been special, too. But there was no denying the joy that had just permeated the dance floor, the radiance glowing off the two stars of the show.

Jane settled her head against Clair's shoulder as they walked. "Could you imagine if we'd come out that young?"

"Not really," Clair admitted. "These girls are a lot bolder than we were."

"Does that mean we could have been, too?"

"Maybe." Clair nudged Jane's head with her shoulder. "But we got where we needed to be."

Jane smiled. She tightened her grip around Clair's arm. "I can't argue with that."

"It *was* pretty funny getting to see you as a child again," Clair said.

"She seems like a good kid," Jane admitted. "I still can't believe she wanted to tell the world I'm Captain Lumen, though."

Clair laughed. "Yeah, that was pretty ballsy. Oh, and don't worry about Lester." Clair raised her hand, wiggling her fingertips. "I paid him a visit in prison after we got you back. Poor man. He's convinced he knows the identity of Grand City's leading superhero, but for the life of him he can't remember who it is."

"Thank you."

"No problem," Clair said, easy as a breath.

They were almost back when they spotted a familiar figure sitting on their front steps. Pink hair caught in the light of their front lamp, sharp features turned to face them. Jane and Clair slowed as they approached.

Blue drew to her feet. "Can we talk?"

Clair touched Jane's wrist, an unspoken question. *Are you okay?*

Jane slipped her fingers to hook with Clair's, the confirmation passed without a word.

"I'll be inside," Clair said aloud, more for Blue's benefit than Jane's. A statement and a warning—she'd be *right* inside, should Jane need anything. Maybe Blue wouldn't pick up on that, but Jane took reassurance from it, which was probably the whole point.

They waited until Clair shut the door before either of them spoke.

"I got your resignation email," Jane said. "I didn't think I'd see you again."

"After this, you probably won't. I only came back to tell you something."

Jane stuffed her hands into her jacket pockets. "Okay."

"You need to be careful," Blue said. "There's a lot more going on in this city than I think you're aware of."

Jane waited for a second. The air blustered between them, kicking up leaves from the sidewalk.

When Blue added nothing to this statement, Jane barked out a bitter laugh. "That's it? Blue, I live in a world with literal supervillains. I'm sure there are a lot of things being plotted out there that would keep me up terrified if I stopped to think about it."

"I know, but . . ." Blue hesitated. She brushed a piece of her pink hair off her forehead, and it immediately snaked back in the breeze. "Look, I didn't just take things out on you at random, okay? Someone told me about you not being the Jane I knew, about your powers. At the time, I was just angry to learn the truth about a friend I thought I knew, and grateful that at least *someone* was being honest with me. But the longer I sit with it, the more deliberate I think her intentions were. She asked me to make sure you were off world for a while. You, Jane. Specifically."

"Why me?" There were plenty of other things Jane could ask about, after an admission like this, but it felt better, simpler, to start here. If this was personal, she'd need to figure out why. What she'd done to offend someone enough to set up an elaborate attack—and if it was even her, and not UltraViolet, that this new person wanted "off world."

At a certain point, you'll have to stop blaming her for all your problems. Jane shook Clair's old admonishment off.

Blue kicked at the sidewalk with the toe of her boot. "I don't know why she chose you. I didn't ask, and . . . I don't think she would have told me, anyway."

Jane let this sit between them for a while. Partly, she was waiting to see if Blue had anything more to add. When it became clear she didn't, Jane shook her head.

"Okay, great. What am I supposed to do with this? You come here and give me a story about some mystery woman, who you don't even actually know but apparently she wanted me 'off world'—which is supposed to mean what, exactly?—and you expect me to just . . . what, look into everything that happened in Grand City while I was gone, in case it *might* be a sign of something sinister?"

The whole idea was so absurd. As if the Heroes could keep track of everything that happened in such a large city. As far as Jane knew, the only thing out of the ordinary going on lately was the weird frequency from the wifi Janie had reported. Marie said she'd been able to isolate the range Janie had seen, but neither her scans nor Jane's own eyes had picked up anything new since she'd gotten back. If it had been anything, it was long gone by now.

Blue shrugged. "I just thought you should know."

"And I appreciate the sentiment behind that, but . . . Blue, this constant game of half secrets and only telling each other the truth when shit hits the fan isn't helpful to anyone. If you want to do good, and I mean really do some good . . . you should stay. Join the Heroes. We could use someone like you."

Blue rocked back, dumbfounded. "You're serious?"

"Yeah. Look, I may have been lying about being your Jane, but you know, part of that's because I didn't want to risk losing you as a friend. You're actually really great. I'm going to really miss you if you leave."

A blush tinted Blue's cheeks as she turned her face away. She kicked at the sidewalk. "I appreciate that," she said. "Really, I do. But I need to spend some time with myself for a while. Figure out what these powers mean for me."

Jane nodded. "Okay. I get it. Just promise me that if you need a friend, you'll remember where to find me."

Blue smiled. "I promise." She took one last deep breath. "Okay, well. See you around."

She turned, started up the sidewalk the way Jane and Clair had come.

"Hey, wait," Jane called. Blue stopped, turning back. Jane took a breath. "Do you think she pulled it off?"

"What?"

"Whatever this mystery woman wanted me off world for. Do you think it worked?"

Blue fell silent. Her gaze turned inward, as if she was really considering it. "Again, I don't know. I'm sorry, I wish I did. But I was a pawn in this, as much as you were. Just . . . listen, if she can convince *me*, with my powers, that something is true when it isn't . . . what could she do to the rest of you?"

It was a good point, and not one Jane had considered yet. The breeze kicked up, and Jane tightened her jacket around herself.

"Be careful, Jane," Blue said. She took another careful step, ready to leave. "Not everyone is as truthful as I am. I fear your enemies may already be closer than you think."

TO BE CONTINUED...

ABOUT THE AUTHOR

If JENN GOTT could have any power in the world, it would be superjumps. Lacking that, she fills her days writing stories about people with extraordinary abilities and tragic pasts. Her weaknesses are parallel worlds, time travel, and girl heroes. She lives in New England with her equally nerdy husband and their rambunctious orange cat.

🌐 jenngott.com
🐦 @gottwords
📷 @jenngottbooks
✉ jenn@jenngott.com

Sign up for the latest news and updates at:
jenngott.com/newsletter